MAGNO

 Happy Joe Control

www.happyjoe.net

Happy Joe Control books may be purchased for educational, business, or promotional use. For contact information visit Happy Joe Control at www.happyjoe.net.

Library of Congress Control Number: 2014913544
ISBN: 978-0-9906365-0-2

FOR JILL

ACKNOWLEDGMENTS

Thanks to everyone I've ever met. You've all been part of the experience.

1 — MAGNO IN MANHATTAN

Magno Girl stared across the windswept roof. Her lips shimmered in the moonlight like a couple of beer-soaked cherries. From the depths of Manhattan below came the clanging sound of a city that was never satisfied.

Was she thinking about me? I was desperate to know.

I took a deep breath. "Mags, when can I see you again?"

She stared at me with those vivid green eyes. Her black hair, streaked with savage shades of crimson, billowed in the hot summer breeze.

"I'll be around," she said. Then she looked away. "I have to warn you, Ron. I'm not very good at relationships."

I grinned. "That's just one more thing we have in common."

"Also, I don't want to do any commercials for soft drinks. That's definitely out."

"No problem—the soft drinks can slide. What else?"

"Well, since you asked, I'd like to fight some crime. I've discovered an evil plot, and my superpowers might not be enough to handle it. Things could get crazy and absurd."

"Hey, I want to help you with that. I'm totally on board!"

She smiled. "Okay, call me tomorrow. I've got a job for you."

"Count me in."

I puffed out my chest and stepped toward her, wanting to wrap my arms around her sleek body and kiss her long and hard—but she saw it coming, and she put out her hand and stopped me. She leaned forward and gave me a quick kiss on the lips.

It was something, and it was good. My whole body felt electric.

"Just tell me what you need, Mags. Anything."

There was a spark in her eye. "Sometimes I need to be left alone. We'll talk soon."

She leapt from the roof, her powerful body snapping like a switchblade as she dove into the death-black valley of bricks, glass, and steel. I briefly envied her ability to fly and then took the stairs to the street. I hopped on my chopper and rode to the liquor store.

I woke up alone the next day, with the morning sky vomiting its sunshine through the grimy window of my East Village apartment. I groped around for my phone and found it under a pile of empty beer cans. I fumbled a bit and finally made the call.

"Hi, Mags. It's me."

"Hi, Ron. Can you meet me somewhere?"

She sounded friendly, and for a second I felt like I was floating. But as usual, there wasn't much talk.

"Any place you want. Did you eat breakfast?"

"Yeah, but it's noon, so I guess we can eat lunch. I'm over on St. Mark's."

"I'll be right there."

2 — GREEN TEA CONVERSATION

I met Magnolia in Brooklyn a week ago. I'd been doing my job as a bouncer, trying to get a grip on my car crash kind of life, when she floated down from the sky. She could fly, she could fight, and the Gaze of the Guilt was her special superpower. Mags could reduce a hardened criminal to a state of blubbering confession. She was on my mind every minute.

I knew she'd be at the café when I arrived. She was always early.

I squeezed my chopper into an illegal parking spot on St. Mark's Place and walked fast down the street. The sidewalk was bulging with tourists and tattooed hipsters sucking on cigarettes, and the air was filled with honking horns and blinking lights— but I spotted Magnolia, sitting by a window inside a cafe, drinking green tea. She was talking to some guy.

I clenched my fist. The guy was standing next to her table, wearing a shirt and tie. He looked like a software engineer, and I figured he was trying to coax her into an enchanted evening on a virtual tropical island. I felt myself itching to crown him with a coconut, but there wasn't a palm tree in sight. She saw me and flashed a little smile.

"Hi, Ron."

I grinned. "Hi, Mags."

"What are you doing over there?"

"Nothing. I was looking for a coconut."

The guy glanced at me and then looked back at Magnolia. "Nice meeting you," he said.

I tried not to snarl too much as he walked away. Then I slid down into the wooden chair across from her, and I shrugged.

"Is something wrong, Mags?"

She cocked her head and gave me a cool stare. "Yeah. If you're going to be jealous every time a guy talks to me, that's a problem."

"No!" I said with wide eyes. "I wasn't jealous at all!"

She kept staring at me, and I swallowed hard.

"Okay, maybe I was a little jealous," I said. "Maybe I wanted to bust a tropical tree over his pointy skull. I promise I won't do it again." I took a deep breath. "I just think you're interesting."

"I think you're interesting, too. But I don't want any trouble."

"You think I'm interesting? That's great!"

"Yeah, but I don't want any trouble."

I was beaming. She thought I was interesting! Had she mentioned something about "trouble"? I was great at that, too.

She shook her head. "You totally scared that guy."

"What are you talking about?"

"Take a good look at yourself."

I shrugged again. I was wearing a black sleeveless T-shirt and black Levis, like I always did. I also had a couple of bulging biceps and a body inspired by a few thousand psychotic workouts. I'd forgotten to shave, and I hadn't cut my hair for a while, and I had a few edged weapons stashed in various places. And of course I had that one tattoo on my arm that said "Out Of Order," or something like that.

"Ron, you look dangerous."

I smiled. "Do you like it?"

She didn't smile—but she said, "Maybe." I was about to puff out my pectorals, but she hurried on to the next subject.

"Here's the situation... There's a butler named Jonathan who works for Thaddeus Stone III—you know, the guy who founded Americamart. Anyway, this butler got the job two years ago through my friend Martina's employment agency. Martina says this butler is looking for a new job because there's something evil going on in Thad's house, and he doesn't want to be involved. Apparently, Thaddeus has teamed up with another bad guy, and they're planning to launch some kind of plot. I'd like you to go undercover at his house and find out what's going on. You can go in as a cook. Martina can get you in there tonight."

I grinned. "Mags, you look really great this morning."

"Thanks," she said, putting down her tea. "Did you hear anything I just said?"

"Sure, I'm gonna be a cook. And you think I'm interesting. Do you want me to make you a burger later?"

She leaned forward a bit. "Ron, there's something you should know."

I braced myself. This sounded bad.

"What?"

"I'm a vegetarian."

My heart almost stopped. So there it was—an area of incompatibility. My brain quickly considered a life without barbecue. I took a deep breath and soldiered on.

"That's okay. I can deal with it."

"Deal with what?"

"The fact that you don't eat meat."

"There's nothing to deal with, Ron. Just don't give me any hamburgers."

"Oh—right. I can do that, Mags. I'll just…eat them myself."

"Great. Also, I'm not very good at relationships."

"You told me that yesterday."

"I'm telling you again," she said with a tight smile. "I don't want you to be disappointed."

"I get it. No burgers, and no relationships."

She studied me for a bit, and then glanced away. "Look, I'm not that fanatical. I still eat shrimp, and sometimes tuna."

I smiled big. "So maybe there's some hope."

"Maybe."

3 — THE BIG HOUSE

To most guys, the average girl is an emotional enigma. Of course, we're usually too fixated on getting them naked to really care. Mags had me thinking different thoughts. I was frantic to know how she felt about me, and I didn't want to screw up this chance to help her—and to get closer to her. But why did I have to be a cook? Why couldn't Thaddeus own a motorcycle factory?

He had a place on the Upper East Side, so I jumped on my Harley Softail chopper and headed over there. I was using a phony name, "Salvatore Siciliano," because I thought it sounded exotic—like a racecar driver. I was supposed to be a chef, but what the hell, I'd once opened a can of tuna with a tire iron.

As the founder and CEO of Americamart, Thaddeus Stone III lived on a street of whitewashed stone towers that overlooked Central Park, in a mansion that popped from the pavement like a gargoyle-encrusted cathedral. I rang the bell and was greeted by a smiling black guy named Terrence who escorted me into the house. The place was modern with a medieval flare, and featured Picassos in the parlor and satellite dishes strewn across the battlements. The kitchen included a Viking stove with ten burners, top-of-the-line Corning Ware, three ovens, and a center-island big enough to corral a cruise ship.

Terry grinned. "I'm the head of security around here. So, you're the new cook? What's your specialty?"

"Six-pack flambé. Don't touch the cans until they're cool."

A cute little Haitian woman walked into the room and started sweeping the floor. She had eyes like pinto beans and sugar cube teeth. "Hello, you're the new chef? My name is Leila. I'm the maid."

"Yeah, my name is Sal."

She giggled. "Oh, I don't remember the names. The cooks get fired so fast."

"Really?"

"Yeah. The boss likes things a special way. The last cook broiled the salmon too long and he was out. So watch your salmon, Sal."

"Salmon? That's a fish, right?"

She giggled again and scurried out of the kitchen. I decided to call Mags on my phone. What the hell, it was an excuse to hear her voice.

"Mags, it's me. What do you know about cooking salmon?"

"Hi, Ron. It's easy. Use fire."

"Thanks. I'll nominate you for a Nobel Prize. Mags, I'm probably not going to last too long on this job."

"Well, try to find out something first."

"What am I going to find out before dinner? Hey, I see they have a brand new flax seed grinder. I guess that's something."

I hung up the phone and swore at myself. Then another guy approached me. He was a crinkled old butler who spoke with an obligatory English accent, and he said, "Hello, you must be the latest culinary master. I am Jonathan."

"Hey, Johnny, nice to meet you," I said, shaking his hand. "So, I hear there are strange things going on here."

"Strange? Why, yes, it's always strange here." He narrowed his eyes and lowered his voice. "This place is haunted, and this weekend there will be a special dinner. Melvin Shrick, the food industry magnate, will grace us with his presence, and you will be expected to prepare something worthy of your gourmet expertise."

"Haunted, huh? You mean by a ghost?"

I guessed Jonathan was the disgruntled butler Mags had mentioned. Obviously, he knew a few things, and I'd have to come up with a clever way of getting more information from him. I figured I'd get him drunk. But first, I'd better come up with tonight's meal. I got on the phone and called my brother, Al, who owned a restaurant on Bleeker Street called Al's Big Pie.

"Al, you gotta get a couple of Sicilian pies ready, with peppers and onions. I'll pick them up in an hour. I'll pay you later."

"Pay me later? You always say that."

"Listen, Al, the whole world could be at stake."

"You always say that, too—when you're trying to get into some girl's pants. I'll get'em ready."

"Yeah, great, and throw in a couple of slices on the side, too."

I was hungry, and it was going to be a long night.

4 — THE ROUND MAN GOES DOWN

The night turned out to be short. Apparently, Thaddeus Stone III was away until the weekend and my services wouldn't be needed, so I was told to go home for a couple of days.

This was a good thing. I knew my position as a chef would be compromised if I actually had to cook. I called Magnolia from 5th Avenue, standing in front of my chopper while the cars, buses, and shoppers rumbled by. I kept my voice calm on the phone while giving her a few details—and then I made my move.

"So, Mags, I'd like to cook you dinner. How about coming over to my place? After all, I am a chef."

There was a moment of silence, and I held my breath.

"Sure, that sounds good," she said. "What time? And where do you live?"

She was coming to dinner! My head was swimming.

"My apartment's a mess," I blurted. "And I'm a lousy cook. Can you come at six?"

She gave a short laugh. "Wow, that's some invitation. I hope I can contain my enthusiasm."

"I can get pizza. We can eat it outside, on the balcony."

"You have a balcony? That's great."

"Well, it looks like a fire escape. But I don't have air conditioning, and it's probably too hot to eat in the kitchen."

She paused again. "I'll be there."

I gunned my bike through the snarling traffic, barely noticing the honking horns and raised middle fingers. I had to get home and give my place an overhaul.

I rushed up the squeaky steps to the third floor. I flung open the kitchen door and surveyed the scene.

The place was a disaster, with peeling paint, battered cabinets without knobs, piles of dishes, and a scattered collection of wrenches and power tools. The best form of overhaul would involve a match. I was doomed, but then I spied the three samurai swords hanging over the toaster. They shined! They really brightened up the dingy room and I was saved.

I decided to clean myself up, so I shaved and took a shower. There's something about a straight razor that makes me feel good, even when I'm only cutting myself. I didn't know why I was so nervous. Put me in the middle of a barroom brawl and I'm more comfortable than chrome on a wheel. And as far as women were concerned, they liked me and I liked them, at least for a couple of hours. But I'd known Mags for over a week, and it was different. She was well outside the painted lines, and that's where I lived.

There was a knock on the door and I jumped—and then there she was, looking beautiful in sleek black jeans and a pink T-shirt featuring the image of a fist wrapped in a flower.

She gave me that calm little Magno Girl smile and walked into my kitchen.

"Hi, Ron. Nice weaponry. Are you worried someone might try and steal your toast?"

"Hey, you have no idea how many people I've killed in this kitchen. Are you the kind of girl who appreciates a good samurai sword?"

"Most of the time. I can't say I haven't tried other things."

I was thrilled she was here. I offered her a bottle of beer and a glass. She examined the glass and politely decided to drink out of the bottle. Damn! I knew she was hygienic, and I cursed myself for not using more dish detergent.

We sat down at a beat-up wooden table. It was hot, and I felt the sweat running down my back. Mags seemed cool enough, though her shirt was a little clingy.

"So, what did you find out?" she said.

I grinned. "There's a fancy dinner on Saturday. Melvin Shrick will be there."

She took a small sip of her beer. "Melvin Shrick owns Pie Hole Pizza. Their headquarters are in Brooklyn, not far from my mom's house."

"Right. Is your mom still giving you a hard time?"

Mags sighed. "Yeah, she likes doing that. But she has issues, and I'm trying to be understanding."

"What kind of issues would make her hassle a sweet girl like you?"

"Lots of stuff," she said, looking away. "And what makes you think I'm so sweet?"

"I can just tell. You're like a flying bowl of sugar."

"Ha, this bowl has crashed a few times. There's a lot of spilled sugar out there."

I grinned. "Don't worry about it. Who doesn't love a good spill now and then? So what did your mom say?"

She gave a shake of her head. "She thinks I should get married and turn into a baby factory. Apparently, I need to find a man with 'real prospects.' "

"Do you think she'd like me? I can change a tire pretty fast."

"I don't know, Ron. She doesn't own a car."

She smiled at me. It wasn't a party smile or a flirtatious smile— it was a soft smile, like someone who wanted a friend. Man, I wanted to be that guy. I wanted to be so much more. I reached out and put my hand on top of hers.

She stared at my hand. Then her phone rang, and she looked at the display.

She leaped to her feet. "Hey, it's Skinny Man Jones. He's a cop I know. Sorry, but I should really take this." She put the phone next to her ear. "What? Okay, I'll be right there." She hung up and looked at me with wide eyes. "Someone just killed Joey the Round Man down at The People's Pizzeria. He's been burned and covered with pizza dough. They turned him into a man-sized stromboli!"

My jaw dropped. "Those dirty bastards." Most of my family was in the pizza business, and while Joey was not a relative, I hated to see a good tomato soldier go down.

Mags narrowed her eyes. "Ron, I need to get over there. I'm sorry. I'll see you soon."

She ran over to an open window and leaped out.

I was tempted to follow her, but of course I couldn't fly. I was still tempted to follow her, but I wanted to live long enough to have more sex. It was a basic thought that keeps most men from jumping out the window.

I raced downstairs and hopped on my Harley. I was only going a few blocks, but they were Manhattan blocks—dense walls of idiot-infested traffic, honking horns, and insanely expensive shoe boutiques. I exchanged a few rocket-propelled obscenities with a couple of overpriced pedestrians and finally arrived at The People's Pizzeria on Avenue A, right across the street from Tompkins Square Park.

There were three blinking police cars parked out front near a bunch of gawking onlookers. There were also a few cops standing there sucking down slices. I saw Magno Girl talking to a huge, bullet-headed police officer I recognized as Lieutenant Rod Saint Royd.

Saint Royd had less personality than a can of bug spray. He towered over Mags and said, "I told you, Magno Girl, keep out of official police business."

Mags laughed and stood her ground. "What are you doing here, Royd? Did you get thrown out of Brooklyn?"

"I got transferred."

"Why? You weren't committing enough police brutality?"

"I had my usual amount. It was all politics. And I should have you arrested. That T-shirt is not appropriate crime-fighting attire."

"Do you ever question SuperStan's right of access? Are fluorescent pantaloons acceptable to the NYPD?"

"SuperStan is the top dog of superheroes, honey. He's also a good friend, and all his stuff is tailored."

While Royd was distracted, I slipped inside the building and found a scrawny cop swigging a Coke and devouring a calzone. Instinctively, I guessed he was Skinny Man Jones.

"Hey, how are you, Skinny Man?" I said, holding out my hand. "I'm Ron, a friend of Magnolia's."

"Nice to meet you, Ron," he said with a mouth full of dough. "This is a real tragedy. Joey sure knew how to make a pizza."

"I know. We lost a good one. So let me see what's going on."

I walked behind the counter. A couple of guys were loading Joey's corpse onto a stretcher. They'd done the right thing and scraped most of the dough from his face.

I grimaced. "Any clues?"

"Just this…"

I recoiled a bit. It was a hideous note written in black ink, scrawled in spider web-like lines across the lid of a pizza box. It said: *The dough man is done. If you meddle, your worst fear will come true.*

Skinny Man cringed. "Hey, someone's threatening to send me home to watch the kids. I usually dump all that stuff on my wife."

While Skinny Man was busy detailing his fatherly neglect, I pulled myself together and noticed a half-assembled pizza on the counter. I also noticed something else—a jar filled with a dried herb labeled "FOOKI XXX." Huh? I knew this wasn't a normal pizza ingredient, so I scooped up a handful and stuffed it into a plastic baggy.

"Okay, anything else?"

"How many clues do you want? You've got a dead guy, a note from the killer, and lots of free pizza. A hot detective would've had the guy's jock size by now."

I walked back outside, knowing I didn't need to be that hot. And that's when I saw her.

She was a willowy blonde in a white dress, and she was staring at Magnolia. She could've been just another gawking onlooker—but my special *future sense* told me she wasn't. She smiled at me with teeth like smirking icicles. Then I turned my head for an instant and she was gone. I barely had time to drum up my sense of dread. Maybe it was nothing.

Meanwhile, Royd was still harassing Mags. He growled and said, "Magno Girl, why don't you take your menstrual cycle and go home?"

Mags laughed. "Royd, are you afraid I might destroy you with a tampon?"

Saint Royd thrust a finger muscle into her face. "You don't belong here. If you get killed, no one will help you."

"If I get killed, you'll still be ignorant."

Suddenly the screeching of car tires caused everyone to turn, and a red rocket-mobile came squealing to a stop in front of the restaurant. Out jumped Smashboy, superhero extraordinaire. He was dressed in a slick red bodysuit and a matching mask. The mask covered the top half of his face but did little to conceal his smugness. He ran to Saint Royd, who nodded in his direction. Smashboy said, "What's going on, Rod?"

"Hi, Smashboy," Saint Royd said. "It looks like someone put a hit on Joey. It doesn't seem like anything too important, but you can look around."

Mags cocked her head and gave the cop a cold stare. "Excuse me, Royd, but why is he getting in? Has he got a photo of you having intimate relations with a barbell?"

Smashboy turned toward Mags and laughed. "Who are you?" he said.

Royd said, "This is Magno Girl."

Smashboy smirked. "Great, just what we need—a magnetic female superhero. I'll call you when we have to fight the Tin Man."

"I'm not magnetic," Mags said. "My parents named me 'Magnolia.' And tin is a non-ferrous, nonmagnetic metal."

Smashboy gave a snort. "Oh, yeah? I'll remember that next time someone shoots me with a science exam. I hope you're not planning to throw flowers at the bad guys."

"I can take care of myself."

"Yeah, sure. I'll tell you what, you're very sexy. Come back to my place and I'll give your flower patch a good pruning."

"I doubt that your weed-wacker is up to it."

Smashboy laughed again. "If you'll excuse me, I have a crime to fight."

Mags looked at me, and I smiled. I also considered ripping off Smashboy's arms and legs, but decided to keep cool.

Magnolia glanced at the other guys. "Look, I'll take my little X chromosome and go home—for now." Then she launched herself into the night sky.

5 — STAR-SPANGLED PANTIES

I went back to my apartment, drank a beer, and considered my situation.

I was working as a bouncer and doing other more dubious things to make a living—but Magnolia was the main thing on my mind. I wondered about her past. She didn't have a boyfriend, but I knew she'd had her share of boys. She didn't have a girlfriend—and that was good because it's tough for a guy to compete with a girl. They just know too much about how to handle the hardware.

She also didn't know a lot about me, and I figured it was best to keep it that way.

I wanted to help her navigate the treacherous world of superheroes. If she could crack one high-profile case, she'd be set. So far she'd been involved in small-time stuff—dead dogs, backgammon scandals, and the theft of athletic tube socks. She needed a headline grabber, something that would shout to the world that Magno Girl could sell soft drinks. But of course, she didn't want to sell soft drinks.

She called me on the phone, and my heart once again jumped.

"Hi, Ron. Well, that was fun. Did you notice anything important?"

"Yeah, there was a note. It said don't meddle or your worst fear will come true."

"Okay, I better go check on my birth control pills. Anything else?"

I felt a jolt, like I'd just run over a pothole. Coming from a different girl, this news about contraception would be fabulous. But coming from her, it was like a spear through my heart—because who was she banging, and why wasn't that guy me?

"That was a joke," she said quickly. "I just meant that I don't want to end up riding around in a minivan full of kids and soccer balls."

"Yeah, that would be bad. You don't like kids?"

"No, I do. I just don't think I want any of my own. I have lots of things I want to do—and lots of things I *like* to do—and I know kids will take all that away. I don't want to end up like my mom. Anyway, come over to my dojo tomorrow morning and you can meet 'my kids.' It's kind of like a scholarship thing. They come from messed up family situations and they love martial arts, and I like to think I'm doing them some good."

"Wow. That's pretty nice of you. So you really are sweet."

"Yeah, sometimes."

She told me about her kids, and I could hear the enthusiasm in her voice. Apparently, she had three young apprentices. This was the first I'd heard of this, and it was obviously important to her—so I was thrilled she wanted me to meet them. She was bringing me into her world, and her world was crazier than I'd realized. Of course, I couldn't wait to get involved. I wanted to help.

I remembered something. "Hey, Mags, there was a jar full of 'fooki.' Do you know what that is?"

"I think it's an herb from the South Pacific. That could be a good clue. I'll look into it."

"Great." Then I tried to sound casual and said, "Maybe this case will make you the next Wonder Woman."

She gave a snort. "There are no star-spangled panties in my future."

"I know you don't want to do endorsements," I said with a little more urgency. "But maybe you should think about it. Patriotism is very popular. If you slap a flag on your ass, you could probably get into a car commercial."

There was an ominous moment of non-response. "Thanks for the thought, Ron, but I'm really not interested. Look, do you still want to come over tomorrow?"

Damn! She was annoyed, and I searched for a sharp object to shove into my eye.

"I'll be there!"

"Okay. I'll see you then."

I wanted to keep talking and smooth things over, but she hung up. I swore for about half an hour and then started drinking—or was it the other way around? It was all hazy until I fell asleep.

Early the next morning, I headed over to Magno Girl's place of business.

The Three Eyes See Martial Arts Academy was located in a dirt-colored brick building on a corner of East 6th Street, right above a Polish delicatessen. There was a nondescript wooden door right near a wide window that revealed a deli counter and a hundred hanging kielbasas. As I walked up the creaky steps to the top floor, I could smell sauerkraut, stuffed cabbage, and *pierogies*.

I knew Mags taught Bruce Lee's jeet kune do, *the way of no way*. To sum it up inadequately, Bruce said, "Don't get stuck on someone else's path—be yourself, and do what works for you," which seemed like Mags in a microcosm.

At the top of the stairs, I found a painted sign that said, "Look through eyes of iron, intelligence, imagination, and compassion." I studied the sign for a second and connected it to the place's name. Then I walked through a door and saw a cramped office and a large training room.

Mags was sitting on the floor of the big room, along with a girl I knew was Karina. Mags had said she was a tiny 15-year-old blonde with skull-cracking capability. She was one of three students Mags had met through a schoolteacher friend. Supposedly, they were bright kids from gloomy places.

Karina was dealing with an alcoholic mother, an absent father, and an evil curse. According to Mags, Karina's mom got involved with a lowlife magician, and the guy beat her up. Karina decided to clobber Mr. Magic with a top hat that happened to be filled with a brick. In retaliation, he afflicted Karina with the Curse of the Modern Blank Girl. He'd then disappeared into the polluted magic underworld of Staten Island, leaving Karina more "blank" all the time.

Karina spoke to Mags in a worried voice. "I'm getting blanker every day. I woke up this morning all worried about the thickness of my eyelashes. I was also watching a bunch of reality shows— especially *Hillbillies in Heels*."

Mags swore softly. "Did you visit any tabloid sites?"

"No."

"Did you buy the Augusto Expensile sunglasses?"

"No, but that's just because I'm broke. And then I wanted to quit the idea of becoming a research scientist and go to cosmetology school. I had a fantasy about giving full sets of French tips."

Mags shook her head. "This is a powerful curse. We've got to break it."

Karina gritted her teeth. "I'll try. I know you're right, but everything is getting worse. Last night my mom puked and passed out, and then Manny—the latest loser—stuffed a bunch of sausages into his fat face and fell down the stairs. He's probably still there, drooling pork and vodka."

Mags put her arm around Karina. "Don't blame yourself, honey. My dad ended up at the bottom of the stairs a few times, too. I think he broke his arm once and didn't notice until the next day, when he couldn't lift a six-pack. It's not your fault."

Karina frowned. "Manny isn't my dad; he's just the latest piece of shit to take my dad's place. I hate them all. I wish they would die. And I wish I had bigger lips—a girl needs big, full lips to be sexy."

"Your lips are fine," Mags said. "And eventually your parents will die. And believe it or not, you might feel bad about it."

"Did you feel bad when your dad died?"

Mags blinked a few times. "Yeah, I did. I was only eleven, and I hadn't seen him for about two years because of the divorce. He moved to San Diego to be with another woman and her kids—the asshole. But when he died I was upset."

"Why?"

"I don't know... I guess because he was my father." She looked away, her green eyes swollen with sadness. "I remembered the good times, and little things he did for me—like when he bought me an e-reader, because I liked to read, and then he showed me how to use it. In some ways, he was a cool guy and lots of fun. I remember thinking how I wanted to see him one last time, even though he made our lives hell."

"Did you ever use your superpowers to clobber him?"

"No. But I destroyed a lot of things around the house."

"What did your parents do?"

"They kept buying cheap tables and chairs, and occasionally a loveseat—hi, Ron. Karina, this is the guy I was telling you about."

"Hi, girls," I said with a grin. "All this talk about destroying furniture is making me hungry. I'm on my way to the fruit store. Anybody want anything?"

"I need bigger lips," Karina said. "How will I find a boyfriend without bigger lips?"

Mags smiled at me. "How do you like the place?"

"I love it! And Karina, your lips look great. Mags, your mom would be proud."

"My lips are too small," Karina said.

Mags sighed. "My mom would be thrilled to have a son."

I wanted to stay and talk and hear everything Mags had to say, but I got the vibe that Karina wanted to talk to Mags alone, and that maybe Mags would appreciate it if I gave them more time. So I told them I'd be right back and headed over to the fruit store. I was ready for some goon to try and kill me.

6 — PINEAPPLES AND OKRA

Sometimes a guy can just tell. Sometimes a guy can feel it in the wind or catch it in a malevolent whiff of Kung Pao chicken. I didn't see anyone following me as I headed down East 6th Street. As far as I knew, it was just another day in Manhattan filled with trendy trollops hauling around their over-priced handbags. I went into the grocery store looking for apples, and that's when I saw him.

He was a Chinese guy standing by the okra. Immediately, I was on guard; okra is a very slippery vegetable. Then he looked at me and grinned—and pulled a spike-covered mace from under a pile of chili peppers. With an angry shout he charged toward me with his weapon held high.

"*Hi-yah!*" he said.

He swung for my head but I swore and ducked beneath the blow. He swore back at me in Chinese as his medieval club smashed into a honeydew. I grimaced and fired a right reverse punch into his solar plexus. He gasped and doubled over as I followed with an uppercut that sent him tumbling backward into a heap of plantains.

I reached for my daggers. Where were my daggers? I snarled and seized a nearby carrot.

My opponent shrieked and attacked again. I sneered and stepped into his assault, executing a perfectly timed block of his bulky club with my left arm while my right hand stabbed him in the eye with my pointy vegetable of death. Meanwhile, the guy who owned the place started jumping up and down, yelling and screaming in the pinball machine language of his native tongue.

The assassin howled as the carrot gouged his retina. He also dropped his club as I knocked him into a pile of potatoes. I hit him with Idahos, Russets, and those little red ones that rich people on Long Island sometimes stuff with caviar. Then I walloped him repeatedly with my elbow until he slumped down into a pile of corn.

I grabbed him around his lapel and started my interrogation.

"Where are you from? Who sent you? And why are you trying to kill me?"

He shook his battered head and murmured, "I am from Taiwan. I was sent by Wong Tong Song. I am 'assassin-in-training.'"

In training? That explained how he'd struck out so easily when pitted against my crackerjack produce maneuvers. I had a long history of fighting with food, and it wasn't limited to vegetables. I recalled an unfortunate incident as a kid, and all those flashing police cars, and all those obliterated cans of Chef Boyardee SpaghettiOs.

My dad had been furious, but who'd taught me to behave so badly? The man had been an ape. If he hadn't been gunned down outside his bakery by a SWAT team, I'd have killed him long ago.

And then Wong Tong Song's man clobbered me with a pineapple, pulling me back into the fruit and vegetable struggle.

"Ho!" he shouted as I tumbled backward into a bin of summer squash. He raced toward the door while I looked up from the ground, shaking my head.

"Don't be so smug," I said. "I could catch you if I felt like it."

"Do you feel like it?"

"No."

"Ha-ha! I see you later."

I sat there as he vanished, reflecting upon childhood memories and the way they stroked my brutal indifference to everything. Then I picked up a couple of apples, threw the owner a twenty, and headed out.

7 — SMALL HARRY

I walked back to my apartment, picked up a pair of daggers, and then returned to the dojo. Karina was gone, and Mags had just finished giving a private lesson. She was sweating hard, practicing her punches and kicks in front of the mirrored wall. Her form was excellent, and her T-shirt was clingy. Her student was collecting his gear, and I realized I'd seen his picture on the internet.

Holy crap! Mags was training Biff Taylor.

Everyone knew Biff. He was a sparkling socialite who'd inherited a cabana full of cash when his daddy had turned up dead in a swimming pool. He was richer than a Belgian chocolate bar, and he also played bass in a local hard rock band. Biff was a known student of martial arts and had presumably come to Mags to increase his knowledge. But of course, I immediately suspected other motives—like, for instance, her vagina. I tried not to scowl too much.

Biff said, "I'm ready to fight, Sensei Magnolia. Lead me to the bad guys, and it'll be *my time to shine!*" He struck an exaggerated fighting pose and grinned through his glossy teeth. "When can I come with you on an adventure?"

"Maybe tomorrow," Mags said. "I'm going to Gristedes to buy fruit."

Biff grinned. "Tomorrow I'm playing golf in Connecticut." Then he looked at me. "Who are you? Do you want to play golf with me tomorrow?"

I showed no expression, other than some unbridled hatred. "My name is Ron. And at 5 a.m. tomorrow I'll be busy thinking about my hangover."

Mags gave me a sideways glance. "Biff, this is Ron. He's been helping me with a few things."

Biff combed his thick blond hair in the mirrored wall. "Great to meet you, Ron. If you change your mind about the golf, just give me a call. It's relaxing, you know."

"So is throwing up in the toilet."

Biff laughed. Then he winked at Mags and left.

I whirled and faced her. "You didn't tell me you knew Biff Taylor. Did he offer you a wild night inside his golf bag?"

She crossed her arms and gave me a hard stare. "Of course he did. But I told him I'd prefer a bed."

"You're not funny, Magnolia."

She threw up her hands. "What did I say about jealousy? Do you remember that conversation?"

I did seem to recall hearing something about it.

"Oh, right. I remember. You don't like it."

"No! I don't like it."

"Okay, I'm sorry," I said with a frown. "After all, why should I be jealous? I'm just 'helping you with a few things.' It's not like we're anything more than friends, right?"

She rolled her eyes. "Ron, I just met you! And I don't know what you want. I told you, I'm not really relationship material— especially if you're going to keep acting like a caveman."

I unclenched my teeth and leaned toward her. "I want to be more than a friend. And by the way, I'm not acting. *I was born in a fucking cave.*"

She hesitated—and then gave a short laugh. She shifted her weight a bit and twisted a finger through the ends of her black and red hair. Was she actually a little flustered?

"Okay, Ron. Maybe I'm interested."

"Good. Maybe I'll let you cook me dinner tonight."

She nodded. "Sure, I can do that. And by the way, Biff Taylor is nothing to me. I just want you to know."

I held out an apple. "Biff doesn't realize the adventure available at the grocery store. Some guy there just tried to kill me."

Now her eyes popped wide open.

"What? Who was it?"

"Some guy sent by Wong Tong Song. Don't worry. He only bruised me with a pineapple."

"Don't worry?" She stepped toward me. "We have a dinner date, remember? Who's going to eat all that linguini?"

I smiled and wrapped my arms around her waist. I was thrilled when she didn't pull away. In fact, I felt her warm body pressing against me.

"I handled it, Mags—and I guess I'll handle it again. The same guy is walking through the door."

It was true. Wong Tong Song's assassin was now walking into the training room. He was also struggling with an oversized cardboard box he'd apparently hauled up the stairs. He was breathing hard as he dropped the box and laughed.

He flashed me an oily grin. "So, we meet again."

I stepped away from Mags and pulled a pair of matching daggers from my jacket. I twisted my expression into face number twenty-six—*the smell of the stir fry*, which I'd learned as a student at The School of Thirty-Nine Faces. Sometimes, it would scare an opponent; other times, it would just make the room smell like shrimp fried rice.

Mags glared at the intruder. "Who are you?"

"I am Ton Lee," he replied. "I have special delivery." He sniffed the air, then shrugged and kicked open the cardboard box, unleashing an onslaught of smoke.

Mags staggered backward. "It's tobacco smoke!"

"What?" I said.

"It's a weakness of mine," she said while doubling over.

My lips snarled like a pair of angry snow peas. I didn't completely understand what was happening, but I understood enough. Apparently, this smoke was like poison to her—and that meant I had to come to her rescue.

Ton Lee laughed. Mags stumbled to a corner of the room, cursing and coughing. I watched through the haze, and then I saw him stepping out of the box—a depraved-looking midget with a magic cigar that puffed out smoke like a factory. His black sleeveless T-shirt and matching beret gave him no special dignity.

"You!" I said.

"Yeah, me—Small Harry."

Small Harry was an infamous criminal. Supposedly, he had acquired superpowers at a young age but had also experienced super-accelerated growth stunting from tobacco smoke. He denied the effect, and many of his fans claimed there was no conclusive evidence. Either way, it's not smart for superheroes to smoke before the age of fifteen.

But Harry was no hero. He could've been, should've been, but had chosen instead to follow the tar black road to super villainy.

Mags coughed again and said, "You've got no friends here, little man."

Ton Lee's eyebrows shot upward. "Hey, what you mean? I love the dwarf."

"I'm not a dwarf, you gook. I'm a *little person*."

"Who you calling *gook*, dwarf? I am proud non-smoker."

While the racist words were flying between the bad guys, Mags and I glanced at each other. We saw our chance. I grabbed the pole-mounted fan that was standing in the corner of the room. I switched it on and started blasting the smoke infested area.

Ton Lee was gagging. Obviously, he really was a non-smoker. Meanwhile, Harry saw the threat, and started puffing like a maniac on his evil cigar in an attempt to create more of the deadly haze. His face grew red and cross-eyed. His cheeks grew big as bullfrogs—but it was useless. The fan was stronger than the cigar's magic, and his mouth was too small.

"Your smoke is fading," I said.

"No!" Harry shouted between puffs. "Not yet!" He puffed some more and screamed at Ton Lee, *"Shut off the fan, gook!"*

"Do not call me 'gook,' dwarf!"

Ton Lee pulled a machete from his jacket. He gave a shout and swung it at Harry, chopping his cigar in half. Then he ran toward me like a bull with his ass on fire.

The guy with the machete usually comes for me. It's never the guy with the knife, the club, or the tiny sharpened screwdriver—no, it's always the damn machete. I remembered being a kid and strutting my knife-fighting stuff for my mother. She'd been unimpressed. I could've killed a hundred bloodthirsty bandits with a nail clipper, and she would've rolled her eyes and complained about how I hadn't put away my socks.

Ton Lee shouted again as he swung and missed. But he did strike a life-sized rubber practice dummy, and it swallowed the machete up to its hilt. "Damn!" he said as he tried to pull the weapon from the steel-sucking inner foam. It was jammed in there good and I wasn't surprised. I'd seen that type of dummy catch more than a few machete guys.

He said, "Ugh, uh, uh! I will kill you soon!"

I smiled and waited for him, but he couldn't free the weapon. He howled and heaved and yanked until his arms almost popped from their sockets, but it just wouldn't budge. I took a step forward with my daggers ready.

"Ah," he said as he eyed my drooling blades. "We will meet again, and next time—well, I will not stick machete into big foam dummy." Then he turned and dove out the window.

He'd forgotten we were on the second floor. Luckily, there was a fairly crowded street below, and he landed on a bunch of senior citizens who were out for their daily trip to the deli. Meanwhile, Mags and Harry had watched the fight, and now Harry had a little frown on his coconut-sized head.

Mags laughed. "Your delivery boy just abandoned you, little man. I guess he has bigger things to worry about."

Harry's face turned red with rage. "You're not funny, Magno Girl. But I have something for you right now!"

He hovered above the floor. Like many supervillains, he could fly.

I laughed. "Should I get the swatter, Mags?"

Harry scowled at me. Then in his hand there appeared a glowing blob of light. It looked like some kind of plasma-energy thing—a common supervillain shtick. Harry used a one-handed technique, leaving his other hand free for a cigarette.

He hurled it at Mags. She ducked, and it splattered against the wall like a big blob of—paint. Pink paint.

"Paint?" Mags said. "You're throwing paint at me? Do you have an off-white color? I'd like to redecorate this room."

"Shit!" Harry said. "I hate when that happens. Why can't I get my thunderbolts to work?"

"You're too small," Mags said.

"Too stupid," I chimed in.

"A loser," Mags continued.

In a state of blind fury, Harry started hurling more paint grenades. They kept splattering against the wall. The colors varied—turquoise, magenta, and forest green. He had a nice little palette, and it created an abstract effect across the white wall of the training room.

Magno Girl hovered above the floor and easily dodged his pigment bombs. The last one succeeded in knocking a potted plant from the windowsill to the floor. Then Harry sank down to the ground with his hands on his knees. He was breathing heavily, sucking up wind like a beached baloney. The little guy was all out of breath.

Mags gave a sarcastic laugh. "You're a wonderful supervillain. Maybe before you're done asphyxiating you can sign your artwork. It'll be worth more when you're dead, you know."

"Don't be so smug, Magno Girl," he said, panting. "I'm not through with you yet."

"Yeah," I said. "He wants to paint the bathroom, too."

Mags gave a little smile and looked at Harry. Her eyes went red as the Gaze of the Guilt came blasting from her retinas. Harry tried to block the beams with his baby-sized hands, but they were a special shade of flesh-piercing crimson. I knew it was over when Harry started to shake, stammer, and whine.

Harry said, "Ugh! I don't mean to be mean, but killing and destroying makes me feel so huge! I know I should stop stomping on the big people—with their big hands, and their big heads, and their full-sized footwear. I'm wearing boots the size of shot glasses!"

I saw a sympathetic glimmer in Magno Girl's eyes, but then she scowled and refocused her powerful glare. One of the problems with the Gaze is that she can't always control it, and it often spills out confessions of random shame.

"Why are you trying to kill me?" Mags said.

Harry grimaced and took a few deep breaths. "I took the money to do the job! I know I shouldn't kill for cash. I know I should've asked for more cash! I can't let you meddle with the fooki!"

Then Harry the half-sized hit man collapsed onto his back next to the fallen potted plant. He stared at the ceiling through glazed eyes.

Mags cocked her head. "Fooki? Did you hear that, Ron? That's the stuff you found at Joey's place. We need to revive him. He might be connected to the murder in some way."

"I'll get some ice water. By the way, what is fooki?"

"Fooki is a plant found in the South Pacific. I did some research and found that no major studies have been—"

"Ha!" Harry was back on his feet, holding two little fistfuls of dirt that he hurled into Magnolia's eyes.

"Damn!" She staggered backward, temporarily blinded. I reached for my daggers. But Harry only said, "See you later, honey! Sorry for the mess." He dove out the window. I started to follow him, but of course I couldn't fly. So I whirled back around and grabbed Mags by her shoulders.

"Are you all right?"

She cursed and continued to rub her watering eyes. "Yeah, it's only dirt from that stupid plant. Damn, we let him get away. I had more questions."

I smiled. "Don't worry about it, honey. Sometimes a guy's got more dirt in his hand than a girl can know."

She started to respond—but then put her hands on her temples and closed her eyes tight. She sank to her knees and started to stammer.

"I shouldn't have told my dad I hated him!" she wailed. "And I shouldn't have been such a bitch to Alonzo after that crazy night in the stairwell. Damn! Ugh!"

She took a deep breath and was silent. I'd seen this before.

The Gaze of the Guilt was a powerful weapon. It could force a person to feel tremendous guilt, and thus cause bloodcurdling confessions in an attempt to be rid of that guilt. But there was a catch. The Gaze didn't only force Magnolia's target to be overwhelmed with guilt—it also forced *her* to be overwhelmed, leading to embarrassing revelations. She'd learned to delay the effect, but she couldn't rid herself of it. This meant she needed to be careful about using her magic gaze.

I coughed a few times. "So, you don't like tobacco smoke?"

She stood up and took a deep breath. "Yeah. It disables me and takes away my superpowers. I don't know why. My dad was a heavy smoker, so maybe there's a connection."

"Okay, but we still kicked Small Harry's ass."

"Right," she said. "I guess we did." Then she blurted, "Alonzo was a guy I knew in High School. I made a few mistakes."

I shrugged, and then I laughed. "I feel sorry for anyone who hasn't made those kind of mistakes. They're some of my best memories."

"They're not my best memories," she said, shaking her head. "I need to create some better ones."

There was a moment of silence, followed by her tiny smile. "Do you still want dinner?"

"Of course," I said, inching closer to her. "Nothing makes me hungrier than a brawl with a nicotine-stained midget."

She reached out and touched the side of my neck, and then she kissed me hard. I hugged her like a python and shoved my tongue into her throat. She swallowed every inch.

My hands caressed her bottom, while her fingers squeezed my shoulders. We were groping and pawing for a few perfect minutes. I pushed her against the wall with more force than I'd intended. She hit it hard but it only seemed to excite her. And that excited me.

I undid my belt and let my pants fall to the floor. She reached down and stroked me as we continued to kiss, and then she shoved herself away. Her eyes were raging like a couple of whirlpools as she tore off her athletic wear.

Her gorgeous naked body was still sweaty from her workout, and her skin glistened like spilled Gatorade.

"Fuck me now," she said. "Fuck me on the floor."

I grabbed her in an embrace and we fell down to the mat.

8 — AL'S BIG PIE

Sex with Mags was even better than I'd expected. She was like a great rock and roll drummer—she kept it simple in a hard hitting way. She had the power and the passion, and she knew how to bang you good.

But it wasn't all about that driving beat. Her kisses were like a narcotic. When she kissed me, I wanted her to do it again—and she did do it again. She did it down on the mat, and while we were slamming against each other, and then afterward when we were just lying on the dirty floor in the sweaty summer heat.

I finally rolled off her and stared at the ceiling.

"That was wild," she said.

"Yeah, it was good. Do you want to do it again?"

She was quiet. She sat up and adjusted her hair. "Not now. I have a few things to do."

My heart skipped a beat as I sensed her shoving a little distance between us. I sat up and looked at her face.

"Mags, are you okay?"

"I'm fine. I was just wondering how Harry knew about my weakness for tobacco smoke."

"Oh," I said with some hesitation. "Is that what you were thinking? Maybe he saw it on the internet. I'm sure there's a blog out there that talks about your favorite kind of donut."

"I'm not that famous, Ron. As far as I know, my donut info is still confidential. So it's something to consider."

"Sure. We should consider it. I really like you, Mags."

"I like you, too."

"I'll be back later."

She gave me a little smile. "Okay. I'll be around."

She was still friendly, but the raging moment was over. I guessed she'd been burned before—but that was no excuse. Who doesn't get burned? Only the asshole who never takes a chance. She didn't say much while we got dressed, and I kissed her goodbye at the top of the stairs.

My heart should have been roaring, but I felt a little unsure. Then I recalled our glorious time on the floor, and my heart did start to roar. After all, I'd just planted my motor on top of a mountain, and like most guys I figured that would be enough to keep things going—unless it wasn't.

I couldn't wait to see her again. I also couldn't wait to help her solve the murder of Joey The Round Man, and I knew someone who might have information. I checked a few messages on my phone and headed over to my brother's place.

My brother, Al, owned Al's Big Pie on Bleeker Street, a gourmet pie-making place in the heart of Greenwich Village, where the world overflowed with food, drinks, music, members of the opposite sex, members of the same sex, and all the undulating good times a city can offer. Al did a good business, but he was always in debt. He could never roll enough dough to pay for all the cars, girls, parties, and wives.

I approached the counter where Al was making a calzone. He was massaging the dough with his fat fingers, but he looked up and said, "What's happening, brother?"

"Hey, Al, what's happening? Did you hear about Joey?"

He looked back down at his dough. "Yeah, I heard. Bad news."

"And what else? Any gossip coming down the old pizza pipe?"

He shifted his eyeballs around. "No, I haven't heard much. Joey might've been mixed up with the wrong guys, that's all."

"What guys? There are a lot of 'guys' in New York. Are we talking about anybody we know, or somebody we don't know, or a crew dedicated to low fat pizza—what?"

"No, No," Al said quickly. "Joey would never go low; he was always a good American. I really don't know much, Ron. I mind my own business." He narrowed his eyes. "Maybe you should, too."

I paused, and then returned his squinty stare. "Have you ever heard of 'fooki,' Al?"

His eyebrows jumped. "Fooki? Is that some kinda Japanese porno? You know I like the American stuff—bigger tits."

I grimaced. Something was out of kilter, a bit behind the bassinet. "I've been helping a superhero named Magno Girl solve this crime. We're gonna get the guys who whacked Joey."

"Magno Girl? You know her?"

"Yeah. Why? Do you?"

"No!" he blurted. "Not personally in a personal way. But you might want to keep away from her, that's all. I mean when you're done 'helping her' hide the salami."

"It's not like that!" I snapped. "She's a great girl."

"No kidding. Hey, I hear she's real good-looking."

"Yeah, she's beautiful. She's also smart and funny—and she can fly."

"Oh, yeah?" He crinkled his forehead. "That's great. Maybe she can do a little promo work for me. You know, wear a shirt with my logo and air deliver a couple of pizzas."

"Sure," I said. "I'll call you when she needs that job. Don't wait by the phone."

"It was just a thought. I'm trying to get a little use out of her before she dumps your dumb ass and runs off with SuperStan."

"She's not interested in SuperStan."

"How do you know? They could do it in the air. They could do it upside down under the Brooklyn Bridge."

I took a step toward him and started to shout about how I'd just 'done it' with her on the floor of her dojo—but I stopped.

For some reason, bragging felt wrong. Somehow, it would've cheapened my feelings for her. This was a new line of thinking for me, and it caused some reflection. But I kept my mouth shut and immediately felt good about it.

"Don't worry about Mags and me, okay?" I glanced around the room and changed the subject. "Hey, what's with the big crowd? It's only eleven. Are you doing something new?"

He shrugged. "I like to tinker. It's nothing, really—nothing." He stared at me for a few seconds. "Ron, about the Joey thing... I don't wanna see you get hurt, okay? You really should stay out of it. And maybe you should keep away from that girl."

"I don't think that's going to be possible, brother. So what do you know?"

"I told you, nothing."

"What do you know, Al?"

"Nothing!"

I clenched my fist. "What the hell do you know, pie man?"

"I know you should stay out of it! That's what I know!"

Dad had always liked him best, and I'd never understood why. Of course, my dad had been a baker, and Al was interested in dough, so maybe that was it. Also, my dad was a deranged lunatic who'd built an army out of bread men—so there was that, too. Really, I didn't care. Dad was gone and good riddance.

I lowered my voice. "Have you got anything else for me?"

Al glanced around before reaching under the counter and handing me an envelope. "Here's for the stuff last week, and I got some more in today. A couple of guys jacked a truck full of books—funny looking dictionaries. You know, the kind about dinosaurs."

"Dinosaurs? Are you talking about *thesauruses?* You guys hijacked a truck full of thesauruses?"

"Hey, it was a mix-up, and you know what they say—it don't cost nothin' to steal a bunch of books."

I laughed. "All right, I'll make a few calls to Jersey. I hear there's a university in Princeton."

He handed me a few thesauruses and said, "What about the teapots?"

Those damned silver teapots. Al had five thousand of them. It should've been a cinch, but I couldn't seem to unload them.

"Nothing yet," I said. "Not everyone likes tea." I turned and walked out.

I went back to my place and checked my messages. It didn't take long. Apparently, I'd been fired from my part-time job in Brooklyn as a bouncer. Come to think of it, I hadn't been there in a while. But I still had my gig helping Al's sorry crew unload a little swag. If I found a buyer, I'd get a cut. It was a temporary state of affairs intended to ease the desperation. Of course, I hadn't mentioned this to Mags.

I had mentioned the idea of her doing a few advertisements, and she'd reacted badly. Maybe I could get her to change her mind. Maybe the great sex would swing things my way. Then again, maybe I thought my penis had more power than it actually did—a common problem guys have. But it wouldn't hurt to keep trying.

I couldn't wait to get over to her apartment.

9 — MAGNOSAUCE

Magnolia lived in the East Village, in a grungy brick building a block from mine, in a post war walk-up on the third floor, in an old, converted grammar school where kids had learned the basics of bullying, name-calling, and alienation they'd eventually perfect as adults.

I brought her a huge bag of stuff. She opened the door, and I walked into her tiny kitchen, a room filled with cracked plaster, ancient plumbing, and floors older than France. There was also a noisy window fan puffing hard against the tide of tropical summer air. I dropped my cargo and looked at two kids crammed against the sink, eating apples.

I'd expected Mags to be alone, but I hid my disappointment with a quick grin. I knew these kids were important to her. She'd told me about them, and I was happy to make their acquaintance. I was also hoping they wouldn't hang around all night.

Mags was over by the stove, stirring a pot of tomato sauce. She looked heart-stopping in a pair of black shorts and a pink T-shirt. The kitchen was hot like a baked rain forest, and she was sweating, but she was one of those people who made sweat really shine.

"Hi, Ron," she said. "This is Pepe, and that's Jenni. They just stopped over. I hope you don't mind."

"Sure, that's great. What's up, everyone?"

I knew Pepe was a quiet 17-year-old guru of jeet kune do. He was a tall kid who supposedly had a big heart. He ran his fingers through a rattlesnake ponytail and smiled. Jenni looked at me with dark eyes that matched her coffee-colored skin and falling black hair. For a variety of good reasons, I knew she lived with her aunt. She was a lanky 16-year-old Dominican girl.

"Hi, Ron," Pepe said. "Magnolia told me you've got a motorcycle. I was just saying how I want to get a bike—a bad-ass chopper with lots of chrome."

I grinned. "Yeah, I'll never forget the thrill of my first bike. It was even better than my first beer. Of course, I never crashed a beer through the window of a Burger King."

The kids laughed. Pepe said, "So what happened to the bike?"

"Let's just say I moved on to my second bike."

Jenni frowned. "I hate beer. I'd rather smoke pot; it's got less calories. I know Magnolia doesn't want to hear it."

Mags gave her a sideways look. "I told you I've done it. I did a lot of crazy stuff, but then I decided a warrior should keep her body pure. Besides, I've seen too many people let drugs take over their lives."

"You mean like my mom? Don't worry. I'll never be like her."

Pepe said, "Your mother's pretty good-looking. I mean considering all the shit she does."

"She didn't look too good last time I saw her."

There was a moment of silence. Mags said, "Do you two want to stay for dinner? There's plenty."

"No, thanks," Pepe said. "We're going to the park. We'll see you tomorrow at the class. We'll be ready. We'll be pure, heh-heh... Hey, did you see Karina? She's wants to get injections in her lips."

Mags shook her head. "Yeah, I saw Karina. Don't worry, we'll find a way to save her. Stick fighting tomorrow." She raised a wooden spoon in a basic stick fighting pose as they left.

Okay, they were gone and I was alone with Magnolia. She gave me a little smile and pulled on her clingy shirt a few times, trying to circulate some of the sultry air. I noticed she was barefoot.

Then she handed me a beer and poured herself a small glass of wine. I knew she liked an occasional drink, but she wasn't a real drinker. Me, I was real.

I pointed to the bag of stuff on the floor. "I brought you some presents. Mostly groceries, and a new thesaurus."

She raised her eyebrows. "Do I look like I'm starving? And is there something wrong with my vocabulary?"

"No. I just thought I'd bring you something practical. I once gave a girl a set of screw drivers."

"Hm, how did that work out?"

"Pretty good. She fixed the blender."

"Well, thanks for the presents."

"Don't mention it," I said with a smile. "And I'm not even going to tell you about the money you could make from advertisements."

She turned back fast toward her tomato sauce. "I told you, I'm not interested in that stuff."

I glanced around the squashed little room. It was stupid to push the issue—but I just couldn't help myself.

"Sure, I know, and I respect you for that," I said. "But there's nothing wrong with thinking over the possibilities. You could have a house in the Hollywood hills. You could be the hip, modern chick on the cover of women's magazines. You could tell people about your lip gloss, and they would listen."

She gave a snort. "Creating shinier lips has never been one of my priorities—and I don't care about the latest miracle diet or the fifty 'new' sex tricks that will 'make his head spin.' "

"Yeah, but what about girls?" I said. "Young girls buy lots of stuff—dolls, T-shirts, nail polish... You could be a role model. With luck, you could be overexposed to a very profitable level."

"Ron, I don't care. It's not what I'm about, okay?"

I shrugged. "Okay," I said and swigged my beer. I also motioned at the beat-up walls, the battered cabinets, and the waiting roach patrols. "But what about Japan, Mags? Did you know SuperStan does commercials in Japan? He even dresses up like a chicken in one of them."

She put down her wooden spoon and gave me a cool stare. "Being in Japan doesn't make a chicken suit any less stupid."

I stopped swigging my beer. It was time to cease this conversation, mainly because I cared about her but also because an angry woman wasn't good for my sex life.

I grinned. "I'm sorry, Mags. I'm just trying to help. I'll keep my mouth shut."

"Good idea," she said with a tight smile. Then she served dinner, which happened to be a perfect plate of linguini in light red sauce with salad on the side. I immediately envisioned a commercial for *Honey Mustard Magno Dressing* but decided not to bring it up—at least for now. It was just as well since she changed the subject.

"It looks like Joey was mixed up in some kind of fooki plot," she said. "Whoever left that note on the pizza box is trying to scare away any investigation."

"Ha! What about our other investigation over at Thad's place?"

She opened her eyes wide. "Hey, did I tell you that Biff Taylor knows Thaddeus? He went to school with his son. They even wrote songs together and played in a band. So he might be able to get us some information."

I laughed. "Yeah, I'm sure Biff has a lot of information—mostly about being sneaky and self-absorbed."

"He doesn't seem sneaky."

"Girls never think good-looking guys are sneaky."

"Are you saying I'm a fool for a pretty face?"

"I keep hoping," I said with a grin.

She gave a short laugh. "Do you know what you're cooking tonight? You don't want to get fired before dessert."

"I don't have a dessert."

"These guys are big eaters. They'll want dessert."

"Don't worry. I'll think of something."

"Look, how about this? I'll make dinner. Call me when you're ready, and I'll fly over with it."

I didn't tell Mags my brother might know something about Joey the Round Man's death. I didn't want to connect her with the sleazier side of my family. It was bad enough that I was chained to the muck with all those mozzarella strands of DNA.

Magnolia's phone rang. She looked at the display and frowned.

"It's my mom. I'll call her back later."

"You can talk to her now. I don't mind."

"You should mind. She tends to aggravate me."

"Yeah, but it's better to be aggravated now than later. We might be busy later."

I raised my eyebrows a couple of times and flashed a suggestive smile. She gave it a quick thought—and then answered the call.

Ms. Mags sounded friendly enough, but I guessed that was the vodka talking. Her voice was pleasant with a tired edge. I pictured her as attractive, but worn around the edges, and maybe in the middle, too.

"Hi, Magnolia," she said. "I was just reading an article, and did you know a woman's fertility starts dropping at age twenty-seven?"

Mags cringed. "I wasn't aware of that, Mom—hello."

"Your eggs will be old before you know it, honey. You need to think."

"I've got time, Mom. My ovaries are shiny and new."

"Yeah, but time goes by fast and your eggs will expire. Do you want to wake up one day and have expired eggs?"

"Right now, I want to wake up and be glad I don't have to change a diaper. Did you get the money I sent you?"

"Money is no substitute for a phone call, Magnolia. Yeah, I got it. But I don't need it. I have my disability check."

"That check isn't enough to cover your rent and expenses."

"I don't care about my rent. Pretty soon I'll be lying dead in the gutter. Will I need to pay rent in the gutter? This is all your grandmother's fault, that bitch. I just want you to be happy, and all I see you doing is flying around and trying to do this super-hero thing. What about your future? What about a husband and a house and a family?"

Mags took a deep breath. "Grandma had good intentions. I'm happy the way I am."

"Your grandmother was only thinking about herself! She should have let you be normal. You think you're happy, but I thought the same thing when I was your age, and I was with an idiot—a crazy hell-raiser who I thought was cool. Time flies, honey. Stay away from those guys and find yourself a man with real prospects."

"I don't need prospects, Mom. I can take care of myself."

"Look at your brother. He's doing well."

"Oh, yeah? Is that what you think?"

"What's that supposed to mean?"

"Nothing, Mom. I'll let *you* bail him out of jail next time."

"Magnolia, you make me want to jump off a cliff."

"Mom, you live in Brooklyn. The cliffs are very limited."

"Okay, so I'll jump off a bridge. Are there any bridges in Brooklyn?"

"I don't think so. Go to sleep. You sound tired."

"I'll go to sleep when I'm done drinking. You go and find yourself a nice attorney."

"You're going to sue me for being single?"

"No. Marry a nice attorney. They make good money. And go back to school!"

Mags rolled her eyes, exasperated. "The stuff I want to learn isn't in a college, Mom. It just wasn't for me. Look, I'll talk to you later. Goodnight."

She disconnected the call, and then she was quiet. She was obviously upset, and that made me furious. I wanted to make her happy. I wanted to crush anyone who would hurt her. I wanted to rip off her clothes and bang her until she screamed.

I put my hand on top of hers. "Mags, don't worry about all that bullshit. I like you the way you are... Let's do it right now."

She looked at me like I had three heads. "Ron, are you kidding me? With my mother drunk and stupid, and my eggs on a death march?"

I shrugged, and I smiled.

She studied me for a long couple of seconds—and then she stood up, tossed back her hair, and pushed her chest out a bit.

"Give me a minute. I'll meet you in the bedroom."

A minute was too long. I leaped to me feet, knocking my chair to the floor. We crashed into an embrace and tumbled against the wall. I spun her around and she sat down hard on the table, scattering the plates and glasses. She was fumbling with her shorts. I knew we weren't going to make it to the bedroom, but the hot and steamy kitchen would be just fine.

10 — DINNER

I headed over to Thad's place early, determined not to let Mags down. I planned to poke around a bit and then pump the maid and butler for info.

As my bike idled in traffic, my mind flashed back to our kitchen encounter. There was a scorching hot movie playing in my head, the kind of picture most guys love—but I wanted more from her than sloppy kisses and wide open thighs. I wanted the girl inside. I clenched my teeth and tried to focus on my mission.

Jonathan was in the kitchen when I arrived, looking stiff and British. I flashed a big grin and got right into it.

"So, Johnny, is anything happening around here? Any evil plots I should know about?"

He eyed me like I was an imbecile. "Oh, there are many evil plots. This is an evil place. I'd love to quit this job and join my brother in the eyeglass business."

"Yeah, good idea. Most people have eyes."

"Yes, they need them to watch television."

Right away, I felt Johnny was opening up to me. Maybe he felt comfortable around the sort of stupidity my parents had always hated. I grabbed a bottle of Heineken from the fridge and watched another guy scurry into the kitchen. He looked like the offspring of a bookkeeper and a weasel.

He adjusted his glasses and glanced at me. "Hello there, hello," he said. "You must be the new cook. Do you mind if I make a sandwich?"

"Sure, help yourself. There's a bunch of dead stuff in the fridge."

"Why thank you, thank you. I like it dead. Dead is good—very good, heh-heh." He started poking around in the icebox.

"I didn't get your name," I said. "My name is Sal. There's bread in that cabinet, by the way."

"Oh, I'm Bob." He was piling on the roast beef. "Are there any pickles? I love a good pickle—a pickle, a pickle, my kingdom for a pickle." He slapped some dill chips on top of his sandwich along with a little mayo, and then he scrambled out of the kitchen.

I turned to Jonathan. "Who is he? What does he do here?"

"That was Subterranean Bob. He does mysterious work in his basement laboratory. He's been down there for over a year. We think he may be trying to do something about all the paranormal activity."

"You mean the ghost?"

"Yes, some sort of beatnik apparition. For some reason he's haunting Thaddeus."

Leila, the maid, came running in. "Sal, you're back," she said with a giggle. "The boss just got in so you better start dinner. He looks fat and hungry, like always."

I pulled out my phone and called Magnolia, who was busy cooking.

"Bring the food, Mags—the fat man is ready to rumble. Wear a disguise."

"A disguise? Nobody knows who I am."

"You could suddenly become popular. You could have a movie deal before dessert."

"Great. Save me an Oscar." She hung up and I noticed Jonathan staring at me.

"So, Johnny, what's the general procedure?"

He gave a dignified snort. "Normally, you prepare dinner and I serve it. Will there be a cocktail, master chef, sir? Or will we be plunging directly into your shockingly stupid entrée?"

I smiled at his insult, using face number twenty-two, *the thumb-screw of forgiveness*. "Fear not, Jonathan, for a fast grasshopper always jumps high." He winced and rubbed his right digit while I grabbed a bunch of grapes. Then he smirked.

He said, "When the grasshopper is done defecating into your future, you might want to prepare a cocktail and inspect the dining room."

"Right. Hand me that cleaver, huh?"

I started cutting the grapes from their vines while I considered the layout of the house. The dining room was adjacent to the kitchen. It looked like King Arthur's airplane hanger, complete with stone floors and a vaulted ceiling.

I peeked into the room and saw Leila dusting the various props. There were quite a few statues of plump, naked girls. Apparently, master sculptors liked their women on the thick side. Meanwhile, Jonathan was polishing the silverware. It looked like he was only setting two places. I turned back to the kitchen, and there he was—a long-haired guy with raggedy pants and a bong in his hand.

"Who are you?" I said. He just faded away into the air.

The clock struck six. Jonathan ran back into the kitchen and looked at the two wine glasses I'd filled with butchered grapes. He rolled his eyes and carried the fruit out to the table.

I peered around the doorway. Thaddeus was coming into the dining room, along with another round guy who I assumed was Melvin Shrick. I heard Melvin say, "So, this is an interesting cocktail. What is this stuff?"

Thaddeus gave a rumbling laugh. "It's called 'fruit.' I generally try to avoid it."

"I like a little fruit," Melvin said. "But it's cheaper to use an extract, and then maybe add some corn syrup and fry it in cottonseed oil, and then stuff it into little plastic bags and sell it to people who sit on sofas."

Thaddeus laughed. "I like the way you think. We're going to make a lot of money."

"God bless big, fat America."

They both laughed hard. Both guys had a musical, evil kind of laugh. I felt a tap on my shoulder. I whirled, and there was Magno Girl.

"Hi, Ron. I came in through the window."

I smiled. She looked great in a stylish black skirt and a tight red top. I noticed her shoes were flat with no heels, and I got very turned on. There's nothing sexier than a woman who keeps her feet ready for kung fu.

She glanced around at the impressive assortment of kitchen paraphernalia. "I made *Gamberi in Salsa*—shrimp with tomatoes and lemon. I've also got zucchini stuffed with porcini mushrooms."

"Mags, you look nice," I said. Jonathan came back into the kitchen and I grabbed his arm. "Jonathan, meet my awesome assistant, Magnolia."

"Pleased to meet you," he said, eyeing her black and red hair with suspicion. "Do you happen to know how to cook? And can you stay out of trouble?"

She flashed a tight little smile. "I know how to cook."

Jonathan sipped his wine and examined the food. "It appears you can cook somewhat, but doesn't this dish traditionally call for capers?"

"Capers look like bugs."

"A good caper can be very appealing."

"Maybe to another caper, but I don't want them fooling around in my food."

Jonathan sighed and took out some of the shrimp. As soon as Johnny went into the dining room, the raggedy-haired apparition appeared again. He was now holding a meat cleaver.

Mags eyes got wide. "Who are you?" she said.

I figured I should say something smart. "That's the ghost." It was the best I could do.

Obviously, this was the wrong thing to say. He let out a howl and attacked the vegetables. He said, "Get out of my house!" and plunged his blade right into a slab of squash.

Leila walked in and let out a yelp. The ghost snarled and lunged at her—but Mags dropped to the ground beneath his slashing blade and performed an elegant takedown with her feet. The ghost crashed to the floor.

"You're all gonna pay!" he said.

I was annoyed and grabbed a soup ladle. With a shout, I cracked the spirit over the head with it. Mags leaped forward and stomped on the ghost-hippie's chest. I dropped the ladle and picked up a crate of lettuce and smashed it down on his skull. Leila grabbed a broom and whacked him in the face. I looked around for a heavier box of vegetables, but then the ghost faded away without a sound.

Leila said, "Oh!"

I said, "I guess he's unhappy with the menu."

Mags grimaced. "Maybe next time I'll bring some asparagus timbales."

Then he reappeared. He still had his weapon, and he raised it high and charged. Quick as a blink, I snatched a cast iron frying pan from the counter and stepped to my left, avoiding his blow. Then I smashed that versatile piece of Southern cookware into his stomach. He said, "Oof!" and fell to the floor.

I was starting to notice something—this ghost wasn't too good at culinary combat. Mags leaped forward and kicked the knife from his hand. It flew through the air and clattered across the floor.

"Who are you?" she said. "And what do you want?"

Jonathan walked in and raised his eyebrows. "Ah, I see you're occupied with the apparition. I'd like you to know that your dinner has been well received. Subterranean Bob has joined the table, and he seems to be enjoying the food as much as the others."

Mags and I stopped fighting with the ghost. I looked at her and said, "Hey, this could be significant."

"You think Bob is part of the plot?"

"I think that a guy who eats a shrimp dinner after stuffing his face with roast beef is a real glutton."

It was all coming together now—the death of Joey the Round

Man, the zucchini and mushroom massacre, Miss Scarlet in the conservatory, the ghost with the butcher's knife in his hand—

"Look out!" Mags shouted. I ducked just as he swung the weapon. He missed and struck a bunch of pots that were hanging on the wall. They made a musical type of clanging. Then the ghost turned to face us.

I grabbed a cleaver from the counter and assumed a fighting stance. He glared at me with savage, red-rimmed eyes. But just as he was about to pounce, Magnolia's own eyes lit up like a burning pair of pilgrims, and the Gaze of the Guilt blasted forth. The ghost stumbled backward and groaned.

"Ooh!" he said. "That's strong stuff, baby."

He fell to his knees, then looked up at Mags and started wailing.

"I know I wasted my life! I know my dad was disappointed in me! And I know my mom is scarred forever!"

Then he faded away once again.

"What?" I said.

Mags shook her head. "It sounds like he had a dysfunctional relationship with his parents."

"I can relate to that."

"Me, too. But we should probably be listening to the dinner conversation."

"Have you heard anything?"

"No. I've been too busy fighting with a ghost and thinking about my unhappy childhood."

"I can relate to that, too. Do you think the ghost is important?"

"I don't know, but my parents were real bastards."

She gasped and dropped to her knees.

"Mags! Are you okay?"

She was not okay. She was breathing hard and holding her head—trying to fight the Gaze that was turning on its master.

"I made my parents miserable, and I enjoyed it! I was a traitor to my grandmother! And I should've treated DeShawn better the next day!"

I knelt down and grabbed her hand.

"Mags, hang on! You're going to be all right. Try and relax."

She was quiet. She rolled her head back and stared at the ceiling. Finally she groaned and rose to her feet.

She looked at me and sighed. "Can we just forget that ever happened?"

"Forget what happened?"

She gave me a little smile but looked away. I put my arm around her and gave her a hug. She seemed embarrassed, and I wanted to let her know it was okay. I didn't care about her rough and rowdy past; she was here now, and I was crazy about her.

Leila had been watching all this in the corner. She gave us a strange look and scurried off. From the other room, I heard Thaddeus talking to Jonathan. I motioned to Mags and we both listened.

Thad said, "Bring me a glass of ginger ale, old man—a clean glass would be a welcome sight. It seems that you're too old to see dirt. I hope you're not too old to see your next job application."

Jonathan shuffled back into the room. I'd seen happier heads down at the taxidermist's office. Mags glanced at me, and I had a feeling she was about to be impulsive. Sure enough, she said, "Jonathan, we have some confessing to do. I'm not a professional cook, and Ron is not a real chef."

Johnny looked at me and poured himself a shot of brandy. "Really? I thought you'd surely written a thesis on the art of opening a beer bottle."

I grinned. "Hey, I didn't think anybody read that one. You're not happy working here, huh?"

Jonathan gulped the shot and poured another one. He hesitated, and then said, "I'd like to go into the eyeglass business with my brother, but now I understand a new Americamart store is scheduled to open across the street from my brother's fine establishment—and of course, they sell discount eyewear—rendering his future uncertain. How ironic and depressing that I should work for the man who owns that beastly conglomerate of slave-wage produced lenses and frames."

He downed his drink and scowled. "How I hate him. I wish I could bring his entire empire crashing to the ground, but what can one old butler do?"

Mags and I glanced at each other. She said, "Jonathan, we're here to investigate Thaddeus. He might be mixed up in something sinister, and Americamart is probably involved. Maybe you'd like to help us?"

He gazed at us through brandy-soaked eyeballs. "If I understand the situation correctly, I might be willing to assist you. Assuming, of course, that I find a clean glass for that fat wanker's carbonated sugar-water."

I grabbed a glass from a nearby shelf and shoved it into his hand. "Here you go! If it's a little dirty, you can always spit on it. Or in it."

"Why, thank you." He proceeded to supply some ginger ale from the refrigerator and some saliva from his stomach.

"Okay, what do you know?" I said. "Has Thaddeus discussed an evil plot with Melvin?"

"I don't know the details of their plot," Jonathan mused. "But they often discuss fooki, and sometimes microwave ovens."

Mags was excited. "Ron, Thaddeus and Melvin are involved with fooki! That means they're probably the ones paying Small Harry—and they're behind the death of Joey! Do you see? I'm not sure where the microwave ovens fit in."

I was about to reply when Mags motioned for me to be quiet. The guys in the next room were starting to talk, so we crept closer to the doorway and listened.

Thaddeus said, "So the final formula is complete?"

Bob said, "Ooooh, yes, yes. Melvin's fashionable new facility on Mulberry Street is fully prepared. And our new man has already been doing some test distribution. We wanted to test everything at an unaffiliated location. The results are encouraging."

Melvin said, "Yeah, I was lucky to find him. He's a real dolt, but his information has been useful. In fact, I even used one of his 'flavor suggestions.' Pretty soon we'll control the whole world's economy. Take care of your microwave ovens, and I'll take care of the new fooki. I'm meeting our Chinese friend tomorrow night at the warehouse."

Bob said, "Ooooh, I can't wait. I love the smell of new fooki."

Thaddeus said, "Do you think you'll have any problem with the police?"

Melvin laughed. "The smartest kids in school don't become cops, Thad."

"What about the superheroes?"

"I'm not worried. SuperStan is busy filming a soy sauce commercial that's gonna be shown in Japan. Smashboy is doing an ad for 'the fattest foot-long wieners.' And Arachnid Man is tied up in a web of litigation over the legal rights to his new line of mosquito repellent."

"What about our other pest—the girl. I forget her name, but I suspect she's some kind of rebel."

"Magno Girl? Don't worry, our friends are keeping her occupied. Like I said, we have special information about her."

I scowled. "Arachnid Man has a bug spray deal? See, that's what I'm talking about. You could get something like that!"

Mags crinkled her forehead. "Did you hear what they said about me? They have 'special information.' "

"They think you're a rebel. What's more special than that?"

She ignored me and narrowed her eyes. "Something is wrong here. And when he says 'his friends,' he must mean Small Harry and his Chinese partner."

"Yeah, this is all starting to come together. We need to get into that basement. We need to investigate Bob's secret laboratory."

"How do you know he has a secret laboratory?"

"I can smell it in his aura. Then again, I once sniffed out the aura of a giant robot octopus."

"So you were wrong about that one, huh?"

"I was wrong that one particular time. Sometimes a cigar is just a cigar, and a cigarette just causes heart disease. But he has a lab—Jonathan told me."

"Ha, okay. Then we need to get down there and investigate. And we need to check out Song's warehouse tomorrow night."

Jonathan tapped my shoulder. "Excuse me, but do either of you have a dessert prepared?"

Damn. I knew I'd forgotten something. I grinned and said, "Not really. Can you throw a few oranges on the table, Johnny?"

"You served fruit for a cocktail. I tend to think they're expecting something a little better."

"Hey, we're all expecting something a little better."

I studied Mags, and as she considered my confectionery negligence, I flashed back to my childhood days and a dream of being an astronomer, or maybe a bounty hunter. Of course, my dad nixed the idea. He thought I should follow in his footsteps, join the Marines, and then go into the bread making business. He used to say, "A bread maker who can shoot straight will always be in demand." It's a shame the way it all had to end, with swarms of police encircling the bakery and my dad down to his last blob of dough.

Jonathan peered into the dining room. "It appears Bob is returning to his basement. It also appears that Mr. Shrick is leaving, and your mundane dessert will not be needed. How ironic that your makeshift fare was a smashing success."

I didn't want to strut too much—after all, Mags had done all the cooking, and I had an old injury that made strutting painful. I still regretted ever seeing that damned Zamboni machine.

I took care of the dishes and we headed out into the night.

11 — THE BEEF

We ended up going back to Magnolia's steamy apartment, where we did some ferocious fucking on a cracker-thin mattress in front of a few cheering mice. I kissed every inch of her hot sticky skin, and she moaned and clawed at me until the rodents ran for cover. Afterward, when we were lying together in our dark cubbyhole of the city, she was silent.

"Mags, are you still upset about your mother?"

"I suppose." She shifted around a bit. "But what if my mom is right? What if I'm just kidding myself with all this superhero stuff?"

I propped myself up on one elbow and stared in her shadowy direction. "Are you out of your mind? You've gotta be what you are, and she's gotta be what she is. And she happens to be a worn out old crank who doesn't understand you at all."

Mags gave a soft laugh, like she was covering some pain. "She's really not that old, but yeah, you're right. She's been through a lot, and she thinks that gives her the right to keep torturing me—but it doesn't. I have the Gaze, and I can fly, and she's going to have to deal with it."

"You love flying, don't you?"

"Flying is the best. I'm all alone up there. There's no one to hassle me or disappoint me—it's like being free."

"Yeah, that's how I feel when I'm on my bike."

"I can understand that, Ron. That kind of makes sense to me."

I grinned. I also wondered who had disappointed her, but I didn't ask. I just hoped it wasn't going to be me. I stared up at the dark ceiling, and in my mind, it morphed into a black storm cloud, hanging over my head like a raging splotch. I felt like it had been there my whole life.

I crossed my arms and flexed my muscles. "So, when did you realize you had superpowers?"

She hesitated, like she was debating what to tell me.

"I inherited them from my grandmother," she said.

"So your grandmother had superpowers."

"Not exactly. Let's just say she had some power, and she helped me develop my own, and my mom really resented it. My mom didn't want to be like her mom, and she sure didn't want *me* to be like her. But my grandmother was great."

"Okay, but how were you a traitor to her?"

She sighed. "I shouldn't have used the powers the way I did. I was supposed to keep them secret."

"Huh. How old were you when all this happened?"

"I was eight."

"What?" I couldn't keep from laughing. "Mags, an eight-year-old is going to use the superpowers. Hell, I would've kicked *everybody's* ass. So then what happened?"

"I did a lot of stupid things."

"Was your grandmother mad at you?"

"I don't know. She killed herself."

I stopped talking. It's hard to follow a line like that. Finally, I said, "I'm sure it wasn't your fault."

"No, it wasn't because of me, but who knows? My grandfather was a cop. He died from liver disease a few years before and she never recovered. But really, she wasn't happy before then. I think she gave me the powers as a last gift, and I wasn't ready for them, you know? I wasn't ready."

We fell asleep in each other's arms, and it was very romantic.

When I woke up the next morning she was still asleep. I decided to take a shower and then make breakfast. As the cold drops pounded against my skin, I heard Magnolia's phone ringing.

She yelled, "Ron, I have to go!"

I stumbled out of the shower, grabbed a towel, and ran into the bedroom.

"What? Where? What's wrong?"

She was yanking a pair of black pants and a pink T-shirt over her bra and panties. "Beef Man and his crew are robbing the Waffle Empire on 2nd Avenue! I've got to get over there."

"Beef Man! Mags, that guy is huge! Forget it!"

"I thought you wanted me to get famous."

"I do! But that guy is gigantic! And how are you going to use the Gaze in front of all those people? It'll come back at you, and who knows what you'll say? You should let someone else take care of it."

She grabbed a pair of sneakers and shoved them onto her feet. "Look, I know that's a potential problem, but I'll only use the Gaze if I need it, and I can delay the side effect."

I frowned and started to say something else—but then I stopped.

She was going to go no matter what I said, and why shouldn't she? It was her dream, and I'd be an ass to try and save her from it. In fact, I should be trying to help her, and Magno Girl could use some superstar publicity—and the media liked Beef. He wasn't the most successful crook, but he definitely had a following. So even if Mags didn't get much credit for kicking his ass, she'd still get her gorgeous face on the nightly news. And that always gets people wondering about a girl's brand of shampoo.

"Mags, wait a second, wait a second—hold on. You're going like that? You're not even going to brush your hair? There are going to be cameras there. If you're going to go, you need to look your superhero hottest."

She gave me a fierce look. "I thought you didn't want me to go! Now you want me to stop off at a salon? Ron, I'm a crime fighter. I don't have time to polish my head like some Hollywood princess."

I smiled. "Honey, I know you've got to get over there—but it's only a minute away, and believe me, SuperStan always takes a couple of seconds to gel his hair and squeeze himself into the right tights. Why not help your career a little? You'll get famous a lot faster, and just think what your mom will say."

She gave me a hard, silent stare—and then ran into the bathroom for a primping. She soon emerged with more superficial allure, then gave me a wave and jumped out the window. I yelled to her as she flew away.

"Smile honey! And be careful!"

I ran down the creaky stairs and jumped on my chopper.

The Waffle Empire was located at the intersection of East 4th Street and 2nd Avenue, and as I drove up I saw quite a scene. The restaurant is enormous; they're the mega mart of waffles. Of course, they serve other things as well, like bacon, eggs, burgers, fries, and a legendary sandwich of mishmash gluttony known as the Stomach Destroyer. Naturally, there were rollicking crowds of fat people clogging the street. They were standing, gawking, and eating. They looked worried, which was understandable; they were all at increased risk for diabetes.

The traffic was a clot of angry vehicles, and the air was spiked with horns and curses. There were police cars blocking off the whole area. There were lots of cameras and news crews. My biggest fear was that some other superhero might show up and try to muscle in on the action before the network folks could snap some killer shots of Mags.

And then I saw Bart the Beef Man. He was hovering ten meters above the ground, with his belly jiggling in the early coffee-hour breeze. He loved to put on a show, and he flashed a gluttonous smile, preparing to address the crowd below. The Beef wasn't too smart, and I expected little in the style of epic poetry.

The Beef said, "Ha-ha! So you think you've got enough ham in the Spam to roast my baloney? You think you can throw me like a whorehouse full of astronauts? You think I can be handled like a cowboy made of cheese?"

Like I said, he wasn't the sharpest sprinkle on the donut. The crowd laughed as they chomped on pretzels and chili dogs that guys were hawking in the street. Lt. Rod Saint Royd dusted off a few greasy pig parts and grabbed a megaphone. He said, "We've got you surrounded down here, Beef! Give back the cash and return the three Stomach Destroyers."

Beef said, "Ho! You are falling right across my pancakes, cop! You are barking up the wrong jug of soup! You are a small grape in the lagoon and I already ate forty-two sausages this morning."

He gazed down at the crowd and repeated himself, *"Forty-two sausages!"*

The crowd roared with approval and bought more snack food.

I started scanning the sky for Magnolia. Where the hell was she? She was perched on top of the apartment building across the street. She'd probably been there for a few minutes, but I didn't see her moving. I pulled out my phone and called her.

"Mags, what's going on?"

"I'm getting ready," she said. She was trying to sound tough, but I heard a hint of shakiness in her voice. "I've never fought in front of such a big crowd."

"It's nothing you can't handle, honey! This guy is a threat to the city. Look around—all these people are in danger."

She surveyed the bulging mob of hamburger-assed imbeciles.

"Yeah, I guess."

"Okay, look at it this way—that big slob is just the kind of tool these people love. His success represents mass market stupidity over brains and substance. And he *hates* vegetarians."

I was too far away to see her facial expression, but I saw her leap from the roof. She didn't say a word, but she was moving fast. Meanwhile, the Beef Man was preening for the crowd, still hovering and eating waffles.

He said, "Ha! Look out, cops, before your turkeys are cooked like a pile of old pontoons!"

He started flexing his biceps and gyrating his hips while continuing to stuff waffles into his gaping face-hole. Down below, his jolly crew of Beef Ball Men cranked up the music as the crowd roared. Beef Man snorted, crammed, and chewed. The crowd started chanting, "Beef! Beef! Beef forever!"

He motioned to his admirers to turn up the volume, and they did. His crowd was definitely here. I guessed they saw a bit of themselves in the Beef Man. Actually, they saw a lot of themselves; he was mostly fat. He was also a humongous target, and Magno Girl crashed right into him.

"Ooooooof!" Beef Man said, and went flying into the giant butter-colored sign that towered over the Waffle Empire. There was a loud smashing sound followed by a shower of plastic debris as he tumbled to the ground.

He shook his head and got up. He looked mean, like someone had just yanked a hunk of pastrami from the black hole of his throat. He said, "Arr!" and prepared to leap toward Mags. She grimaced, and her eyes scorched with magic pink light.

The Beef sucked in his breath and stopped dead in his tracks.

He tried to shield himself with his blubbery mitts but there was no escaping. He dropped to his knees and groaned.

"Oooh! I never wanted to be a man full of pork! My brothers all played sports. My sister was clever like a smart girl, but all I could do was read comic books and watch TV and eat! My life was bad until I became big and started pushing people around. Won't somebody, somewhere give me a sausage? I'll make it up to you all someday!"

The crowd was quiet. Mags looked at Beef and stopped her glare.

Beef shouted and charged right at her.

"Whoah!" she said, and leaped to her left while slamming her right foot into his skull. The Beef wailed and toppled over as a pile of waffles spilled from his foaming mouth. The crowd went crazy.

Everyone applauded and chugged their soft drinks. Camera

crews rushed to the fight scene—pushing, trampling, and making ample use of expletives as they shoved their way closer. A woman next to me said, "Who is that girl beating up the Beef?"

"It's Magno Girl," I said.

I could hear it all around me, "Magno Girl! It's Magno Girl." The crowd was speaking her name and singing her praises. The news people were interviewing and exaggerating. The lawyers were talking about psychological trauma caused by flying waffles as they handed out business cards. I made a mental note to print some flyers with Magnolia's picture and general publicity information.

The Beef was lying there like a tubby funeral mound. He groaned and pointed a finger at Mags. "I will finish you off *like a ham without a pickle!*" Then he gritted his teeth and got up.

Mags wasted no time in unleashing the Gaze of the Guilt a second time. As the scarlet rays flickered from her eyes, Beef stumbled backward and moaned once again.

"You know, I've never treated women with much respect! I just like the way they can sauté those fat chorizos! Ugh!"

Magno Girl stopped her attack and Beef Man just stood there, woozy from the Gaze and teetering like a half chopped tree. Mags leaped into the air and tapped him on the back of his shoulder with a roundhouse kick. The Beef groaned and crashed down onto his face. The crowd burst into applause. Mags turned around and viewed the scene.

She saw a stern ring of cops and a raucous horde of reporters. She saw a cheering crowd, eating and drinking. Everyone was slumming around like a sea of fat cockroaches, and everyone was shouting questions and writing down speculation. It was an historic moment made for American television, and I saw dollar signs inflating before my eyes like greedy balloons.

Royd stepped forward and gave a grunt. "Okay, Magno Girl, I suppose I should thank you for helping us do the impossible, but I won't. Stay out of official police business, you hear?"

Magno Girl crossed her arms and looked confident. "I'm tired of fooling around with you, Royd. Dump this crook into the city jail and go back to babysitting your pot of coffee." Then she leaped into the sky and flew away, leaving only tomorrow's headlines behind.

Royd turned six shades of red. Then seven of his men picked up the Beef and started to cart him off while the crowd hooted and hollered and threw general fast food refuse at the broken supervillain and his crew. No one likes a loser—from hero to zero in less time than it takes to eat a donut.

A guy shoved a microphone in Royd's face. "Would you say, Lt. Saint Royd, that Magno Girl did the job your incompetent police force couldn't handle?"

Royd grimaced. "Well, I suppose—no, wait, of course not. That's a ridiculous thing to say. My men are surrounding the scene and we are dusting for clues. We are always here, always ready, in the wind and rain, to, uh, what was the question?"

A female reporter with bouncy hair stepped forward. "Do you think Magno Girl is the sexiest superhero you've ever seen?"

Royd frowned. "Yeah, she's pretty hot—wait, I mean of course not, women don't belong in law enforcement—hold on, that's not what I meant."

While Royd was busy shoving a foot into the mouth of his career, I decided to hurry back to my place. And that's when I saw her again. It was the tall blonde I'd spotted at the scene of Joey's death. She was standing in the crowd, wearing a glare of cold menace and an aura that oozed no pity. She glanced at me for an instant and then she wasn't there. I shook my head and wondered if I'd even seen her at all.

12 — HOLLY HONEY

I called Mags, but she didn't answer. Then my phone rang, and I heard a woman with a voice so smooth and pretty.

"Hello, is this the management office for Magno Girl?"

"Yeah! Absolutely."

"This is Holly Honey with Channel Six News. Is Magno Girl available for an interview?"

"Sure! She'd love to talk to you. She loves your show. Come on over. Bring the big camera."

I knew it was the wrong thing to do, but sometimes the wrong thing is exactly right. Maybe not this time, of course, but sometimes. The phone rang again and it was my brother.

"What's happening, Al?"

"Hey, there's a bunch of people here. They're looking for that girlfriend of yours. They're all asking about her."

"Why would they be looking for her over there?"

"Ah, you know, I might've mentioned you knew a hot chick who was a superhero, and maybe she'd be doing some commercials for me."

I gripped the phone tighter. "Listen, Al, stop blabbing your bullshit all over town. And by the way, she doesn't do anything unless she gets paid for it—and she's gonna be expensive."

"All right, all right. You just make sure we get paid for those teapots."

"Don't worry. It's all under control."

Those damned teapots. I just hoped Al was being careful about covering his fat hoof prints. I decided to turn on the news and saw that it was one hundred percent Magno Girl. She was on the screen, kicking the Beef's pork-filled ass. I grinned. Then they cut to an interview with Smashboy, who was talking to Holly Honey. Holly had blond hair, a shimmering brand of lip gloss, and teeth that shined like a set of new spark plugs.

"Smashboy, were you impressed by Magno Girl's performance today?"

Smashboy smirked. "I suppose she did a nice job. I don't know about those red streaks in her hair, though. And where did she get that outfit? Yoga pants and a T-shirt? And by the way, some of that stuff she was doing looked a lot like witchcraft… Still, a respectable job against a weak opponent."

I ground my teeth—what a cretin, trying to tie Magnolia to witches and black magic. That lifestyle had become less underground lately, but the mainstream media and the public were still biased against it. I grinned; I could tell Batboy was nervous. There was a new girl in town, and she was looking good without trying too hard. If she ever sold out to the great gods of fashion, his career would be deader than the Green Lantern's first set of flashlight batteries.

Holly continued, "A lot of people think she looked pretty formidable, Smashboy. Do you think the days of a male-dominated superhero hierarchy could be numbered?"

I could feel the hairs on Smashboy's ass start to bristle, and I suddenly liked Holly Honey. Smashboy tried to smile as he forced out a laugh. "It's a little early to tell how she'll do against a serious villain, but hopefully she'll keep learning."

I laughed and cursed, and then Mags came flying through the window.

I grinned big. "Mags, that was amazing! You were incredible."

Her eyes were bright, and she gave me a quick smile. "Thanks. Yeah, it went pretty well."

She was trying to be modest—but I could tell she was thrilled. I wrapped my arms around her and gave her a kiss. "People are looking for you, honey. They want to give you money and fame. But you know what? I'm just glad you're safe… I like you, Mags."

"Yeah, well, I like you, too."

"Do you want a silver teapot?"

"You gave me a silver teapot the other day."

"That's right. What you really need is a better place to put it."

"Ron, I put it in the kitchen. That's where I make tea."

"Yeah." I glanced around the room. "I was just thinking about someday, when you'd be living in a nicer place. I mean, who knows? Maybe we'll move in together or whatever."

It just slipped out. What was I thinking?

She gave another short laugh and broke away from my embrace. She walked toward the window and stared at the city outside. "That's a lot to be thinking about—'or whatever.' I don't think I'm ready to share the teaware just yet."

"I don't mean right now," I sputtered. "It's just something to keep in mind—for someday."

She cocked her head and crossed her arms. "Don't take it personally, Ron. I keep telling you, I'm not too good at long commitments. I think you know what I mean."

I knew, and I changed the subject. "Mags, I think you might have a stalker."

"What?" She suddenly looked more comfortable.

I told her about the weird blond woman I'd now seen twice.

She crinkled her forehead. "Are you sure she was also at the scene of Joey's death? Maybe she just lives in the area."

"Yeah, maybe, but I'm picking up a bad vibe about this babe. Be on the lookout."

There was a knock at the door. A woman on the other side said, "Hello, this is Holly Honey from Channel Six. I was told you were expecting me. I'm here to interview Magno Girl."

Mags gave me a hard look, and I grinned. "Honey, this could be a good thing. You should've seen Smashboy making insults about your hair while his ass bristled."

"I like my hair, and I don't care about his bristling ass."

"Right, fuck his ass—I mean, you know what I mean. But you've still got to talk to the world."

"What am I going to say?" she said, throwing up her hands.

"Tell them about your soon-to-be-manufactured action figure."

"I don't want an action figure."

"Do you want to be a small time nobody forever?"

"I'm not a 'nobody.' I'm a 'somebody' who doesn't sell trashy merchandise."

"Okay—sorry. I didn't mean it like that. But what about your school? A little publicity can go a long way. Do you wanna be buried by Karate Mart?"

She stared at me for a long few seconds. "Okay, let her in."

I smiled and had explosive visions of Magno Girl T-shirts, mugs, and video games. Maybe even athletic wear and a line of contraceptive pills with a cartoon logo of a girl knocking out a sperm cell. *America, America, God shed his grace on TV.*

Holly came blustering in like a tornado in a teashop. She had two guys with her, and they both had cameras and lights. They started ramming equipment into every corner of my apartment. Holly lunged forward and surprised Mags with a hug.

"Great job!" Holly said. "I really love what you do."

"You do?"

"You are the best, honey. We're all rooting for you."

"Who is?"

"All of us, dear—all of us. Okay, now we can set up right here. This will be on the Eleven PM news. Put that light over there, Sean, and put that thing over there. Good, now roll the tape. The button—push the button, okay? Good."

Suddenly Holly's voice changed. She turned to Mags and said, "You looked great out there, Magno Girl. So why are you called 'Magno Girl'? Are you magnetic?"

"No. My real name is Magnolia."

"Oh, that's a pretty, feminine name. Are your parents surprised their little flower is out there slugging away at the bad guys?"

"Not really. My father is dead. My mother isn't too sober—I mean, surprised! She isn't too surprised."

"What about your magic gaze? You can paralyze people with feelings of guilt. Where does this power come from?"

"I inherited it from my grandmother. She's gone now."

"I'm sorry to hear that. Is your mom worried watching you fight? Beef Man has eaten plenty of superheroes for breakfast."

"Ha, I don't know what Beef eats for breakfast, but my mom is definitely worried about my eggs."

"Your eggs?"

"Yeah, the ones from my ovaries. I've got a pair of those."

"Right, that's what makes you unique among superheroes. Speaking of which, how do you feel about Smashboy calling Bart the Beef Man a weak opponent?"

"Is that what he thinks?" Mags gave a short laugh. "The Beef is certainly bigger than me. I'm sure he can bench press a few thousand cheeseburgers."

"Do the bad guys think they can push you around because you're a girl?"

"Yeah. But then, so do lots of the good guys. Either way, I'm here."

Holly smiled. "What's the story with SuperStan? Can you ever hope to equal his awesome power?"

"I'm not sure. I hear he can tape six commercials in a single day."

Holly laughed. "Did you know Smashboy made fun of your clothes? What's the story, Magno Girl, with the yoga pants and T-shirt? Certainly they're stylish, but have you considered something more sheer and shocking?"

"Not really. I like yoga, and I like these clothes. I'm a crime fighter, not a Barbie doll."

"What about your image?"

Mags narrowed her eyes. "I don't care about my image. I just want to kick ass and move on to the next guy."

Holly looked at the camera. "There you have it, folks: Magno Girl, the baddest chick in the city. I'm Holly Honey for CCB News."

The cameras and lights went off. Holly said, "Beautiful job, honey. Maybe I can do an in-depth piece on you soon. Who should I contact? I was told this is your management office." Holly turned to me. "Are you her manager?"

Mags gave me an amused look but said nothing.

I grinned. "No, I'm more like…a guardian angel. But I might be able to help."

Holly was a sly one. I could tell she was a smooth operator who was probably part of the plot to build that giant, robot octopus I'd never found. I was about to give her my number when I saw Mags write her own number down on a piece of paper.

"Thanks a lot, Holly," Mags said. "I appreciate it."

"Thank you, Magnolia. Call me any time! And be careful out there—watch out for Smashboy and his friends. Trust me, they really resent a woman showing them up."

"Oh really?" Mags deadpanned. "I didn't notice."

"Yeah, crime fighting is mostly a man's world—at least for now. Maybe we'll help change that."

Mags just responded with her little Magno Girl smile, and it looked like they were going to be pals. Holly smiled again and wished Mags luck before leaving with her crew in tow.

I grinned. "So I guess that went pretty well."

"Yeah, it wasn't so bad. In fact, it was good."

"Mags, it was great! And hey, you didn't have a reaction to the Gaze. I mean after using it on the Beef."

She gave a little laugh. "No, I did. It happened on my way home. I stopped off on a rooftop and confessed a few indiscretions to a couple of pigeons."

"Oh." This was good news; most pigeons totally flop on the talk show circuit. I wrapped my arms around her once again. "I'm sorry I put you through that interview, honey. I should've asked you first."

"It's okay. I forgive you—this time."

"Why do you like me?"

"Do you want the long answer or the short answer?"

"I want the answer that involves the most sex."

She gave it some thought. "I like you because you follow *the way of no way*—and I believe you care. So don't let me down."

My heart started racing. For some reason a picture of my parents flashed in my head, frowning about a trivial catastrophe. I blocked them out and gave Mags a squeeze.

"Was that the long answer?" I said. "I was expecting more about our wild adventures and the raging motorcycle."

"Your motorcycle has nothing to do with it."

I gave her a kiss. She kissed me back, but then pulled away.

"I have to go take care of a few things, Ron. Call me later."

"What things?"

She just gave me a wave and jumped out the window.

13 — THREE EYES SEE

The morning sun was like a fried egg hanging in the summer sky. I walked into the steamy office in Magnolia's dojo, where I found Mags sitting on top of the desk, dressed in a pair of black shorts and a tight pink T-shirt. She was talking to Karina, who was reclining in a chair that featured a punctured cushion and three yards of duct-tape.

I didn't want to interrupt them, so I went into the training room and watched Biff Taylor finish his workout on the heavy bag. But I could still see them and hear their conversation.

Karina said, "…then my mom starts screaming and cursing, and Uncle Anton says if Rinaldo comes around again he's going to kill him, and Rinaldo leaves and he hasn't called me back—and that's about it for my love life."

Mags said, "Whatever you do, make sure you use protection."

"Rinaldo used a condom. I like the guy, but I'm not stupid. Then my mom starts talking to me like she's some kind of saint. She's done it with a million guys, and that's what I told her, and she blew up—but I don't care. She's a drunken slut. Her boyfriends are all losers. And Rinaldo will never call me again, anyway, because I talked too much about a totalitarian government returning to Russia."

"What?"

"It's true. I spent too much time talking about the fucking news. Rinaldo is mostly into computer games and stupid comedy shows. I think I was boring him. Plus, I need breast implants."

There was a moment of silence, and then Mags said, *"Karina, are you out of your mind?* This curse is ridiculous. If Rinaldo is bored by your brain power, he's the wrong guy."

Karina shook her head. "Yeah, I know you're right. I can't believe the things I'm saying lately. I feel like I'm heading toward total blankness, and I want to kill myself. But I won't give up. So, how old were you the first time you had sex?"

Mags hesitated. "I was a little younger than you. I did it with a guy from school. It was a learning experience."

"And what happened?"

"He was pretty happy. I was kind of mystified."

"Mystified? About what?"

"About how ten seconds could make a guy so happy."

Karina laughed. "And then what happened?"

"I went through a few phases. Not all of them were good."

"What was bad?"

"Everything. My home situation sucked, and I felt bad about myself because of it. And I had these superpowers, but I didn't know how to use them, and they made me different from other people, and I guess I wanted those people to like me. So I did some stupid things, and some of those things involved sex. I had a lot to sort out—and I'm still sorting things out. Overall, I know things could've been worse. I was lucky. Just make sure you use protection, Karina. Always."

"Ha. So you use protection now?"

Mags just stared. "Of course I do," she said in a rush. "I'm very careful now."

At this point the two girls saw me, and I grinned.

"Hi, Ron," Karina said with a smile. "I was just leaving. I'm supposed to be in school."

"You're in a school."

"Yeah, but I should be in the other school—the one where I can't carry a sword."

"What? Are you kidding me? What if someone tries to steal your lunch?"

Karina laughed and muttered something about how she needed to lose another two pounds. She watched Biff hit the bag on her way out, but he ignored her.

Mags stared after Karina as she departed, apparently lost in thought. Then she said, "Let me look in on Biff." She walked into the other room while I sifted through a bunch of "final notices" on her desk that seemed to keep coming. Doesn't anyone know what "final" means? Actually, I knew what it meant. Mags was in trouble.

I heard her talking in the training room with Biff Taylor, and I peered around the corner.

He was grinning and toweling off his sweaty face. "Magnolia, my band is playing this weekend at High Society on MacDougal Street. You should come check us out."

"High Society? I was born in Staten Island, you know."

"I won't tell anyone. Hey, do you want a free guitar lesson?"

"Biff, I'm about as musical as a pound of dynamite."

"Yeah, well dynamite never looked so good."

Mags sort of smiled and looked away. "Is Thad's son coming to your show?"

"No. Why do you ask?"

"You told me you knew him. I was just wondering."

"Did I say that?" Biff shifted his weight a bit. "Henry doesn't come around anymore. Not for a long time." His voice trailed off. "So when can I come with you on an adventure? What have you got going on?"

"Nothing right now."

"Great, so maybe you've got time for a drink. We could go somewhere nice."

Biff leaned close and started talking to her in a low voice. She cocked her head to one side and listened. He was getting animated with his expressions, and she wasn't looking disgusted enough for my taste. So I walked into the room. It seemed less messy than removing Biff's brain.

"Biff, why don't you clean the bathroom?" I said. "That one urinal looks pretty dangerous."

"Hey, what's up?" he said with a smirk. "There's no urinal in there."

"What? Mags, how can I swing a samurai sword in that little stall?"

Biff smiled at Mags. "Don't forget about my band. We're loud and funky."

"Maybe we'll come."

"Yeah, try to make it. It'll be great." Then he glanced at me and smirked again. "Don't break anything until after our set, okay?"

I ground my teeth and wondered if that included his head.

Biff went home, and Mags and I sat down to discuss our strategy.

14 — LATER THAT EVENING

"Mags, what did Biff say to you? When he was talking low?"

"Ron—stop."

"Would you go out with him if you didn't know me?"

"What kind of question is that?"

"I want to know. If you didn't know me, and Biff asked you—"

"No! I wouldn't go out with him."

"Really?"

"Really."

"Okay."

"But I'd definitely have sex with him in the back of his Aston Martin. Those leather seats are amazing."

"*What? Are you kidding?*"

"Yes, I'm kidding!"

"You better be kidding!"

"You better stop being such an idiot!"

I grinned. "Tough goal."

"Work on it."

15 — HUBCAP HULLABALOO

The first step was to get the dirt on Wong Tong Song, and we hoped to find it down at Song's warehouse on the docks. We were both assuming it was Song. Melvin hadn't mentioned him by name, but Ton Lee had mentioned him and Ton Lee had tried to kill me, and I wasn't that bad at putting the ketchup on the catfish.

The waterfront was an eerie place at night, covered in grit, fog, and the stench of the Hudson River. Black silhouettes of giant cranes stretched toward the sky, and ships floated in shadowy docks like ghostly whales. I parked my chopper across from the warehouse, near an abandoned hotdog stand that reeked with the presence of long dead sauerkraut.

Mags was on top of the warehouse. It was midnight, and the wind started howling, and light rain began falling through the spooky mist. I saw a silver van and a black Mercedes pull up.

Magnolia's voice crackled in my earpiece. "Ron, I think Melvin is in the van, and a guy who I'm guessing is Wong Tong Song is in the car. I also see your friend Ton Lee."

I clenched my teeth. *"Ton Lee?"* I had a score to settle with that guy. Then a clunky-looking blob come warbling through the air and crashed down near the Mercedes. There was no mistaking that style of uncoordinated flight. It was Small Harry.

We watched as he lit up a cigarette and started coughing. Obviously, the evil guys were all sharing a steam room. The door to the warehouse opened like a drooling pie-hole, and the van drove inside. Ton Lee stayed outside.

Mags said, "I'm going to go inside and check things out." I watched her sleek outline fly into the warehouse, near the top of the open door. I put away my phone and started sneaking closer. Of course, I'd studied the art of sneaking. It mostly involved being quiet. It also involved staying low to the ground and avoiding that big pile of hubcaps.

Bong! Crash! Clank! What a crazy place for those hubcaps to be. I was across the road from the warehouse, though, and no one inside heard it. But Ton Lee heard it. He had razor sharp ears, and it was hard to sneak a clanging hubcap past him.

I froze and got my bearings—and then I whirled fast. *Clong! Splash! Crash!* Damn—more hubcaps. I was caught in a hubcap hullabaloo, that was for sure. I hadn't seen such a clever hubcap trap in years, but I was prepared. I ran like a Lamborghini, hitting a few more hubcaps along the way. They kept on crashing and clanking.

I stopped running and crouched behind the hotdog stand.

It was a small building with a boarded-up façade. On the roof was a big plastic likeness of a hotdog, hanging from two chains like a swinging sack of meat. I watched a hubcap roll all the way across the street and vibrate to a stop at Ton Lee's feet. He motioned to somebody back in the fog, telling him to wait while he went patrolling. Then Ton started walking across the road, heading right toward me.

I gritted my teeth as Ton approached the scattered hubcaps. Somehow, he managed to avoid walking into them—oh, he was a sneaky one, quiet as a box of bubblegum. I gritted my teeth and shouted as I jumped out from behind the building.

"Ton Lee, prepare to die!"

His eyes popped open, and I reached for my daggers. And that's when I realized I'd left my daggers at home—damn. I knew

I should have tacked a note on the refrigerator to remind myself about the daggers. Ton stared at my empty hands and smirked.

"So we meet again, *Sensei Ron,* on a day you cannot stop walking into hubcaps, and you cannot remember your daggers." Then he pulled out a pair of daggers.

Ah, so that's how it's done. I appreciated his particular fighting stance. But as I looked more closely, I noticed he wasn't holding daggers at all—no, Ton Lee was holding bananas. I grinned.

"Ton, it looks like some bad magic has cursed your daggers. You should've stayed home and put those things in your cereal."

I reached into my pants, and I pulled out my daggers. Yeah, I'd been reaching into the wrong pockets before. But then Ton Lee smirked again and flipped his wrists, and there underneath the banana peels were daggers.

I gaped and grimaced—this could only mean one thing. I flipped my wrists and watched with horror as my daggers vanished and were replaced by bananas. So now I was the one with the fucking bananas. I pondered the reality of life, and how fast a great victory can turn into a fruity pile of shit.

Ton Lee laughed and slashed with his stinging blades. Instantly, my bananas were cut to pieces. I searched desperately for a weapon, and then I remembered my samurai sword.

I screamed as I yanked the blade from the sheath across my back, slashing and missing and punching a crevice into the plywood that covered the front of the hotdog mausoleum. I jerked the weapon free, screamed again, and swung hard. Ton Lee took a big step back and walked right into the hubcaps.

Clang! Bong! He tripped and fell down into a pile of scattered steel. I lunged and almost stabbed him, but he rolled away and I only punctured a hubcap. I tried to shake it loose, but it wouldn't budge. Ton grinned and started flailing away with his daggers while the hubcap clung to my blade.

Ton grinned. "So my hubcap magic has made you helpless!"

I laughed and clobbered him on the head with the hub-cap-tipped blade. He tumbled to the ground. I smirked as he lunged at my foot with one of his daggers. I laughed again and deftly avoided his stabbing hand. Then I looked through the fog and saw a black lump hurtling toward me. Damn!

The lump crashed into my chest and knocked me down as my sword went flying. I staggered to my feet—and there was Small Harry. He was perched on the roof of the abandoned hotdog stand, right underneath the hanging dog. He was lighting a cigarette and laughing. He had no fear whatsoever of carcinogens.

"So, we meet again," he said. He gagged a bit and coughed like he was about to spit up a few burnt tobacco plants.

I was calm as I got to my feet. "Yeah, and you haven't grown one bit since your last thousand cigarettes."

He took a long drag on his butt. "Listen, you can keep heckling me about my size, or we can fight to the death. Which is it gonna be?" I saw Ton Lee sneaking toward me, and I reached for my thesaurus.

"Harry, you're small," I said. "You're tiny, little, inadequate, diminutive, meager, undersized, and paltry—and the only way we'll see eye to eye is if you stand on top of a lunch counter." Then I assumed fighting stance number forty-one, *the ass of the aardvark*. It's a simple position to assume but difficult to hold without getting arrested.

Ton burst out laughing. Harry scowled and said, "What are you laughing at, Chong?"

Ton frowned. "My name is *Ton*. Do not worry about my laughing; it is over your head."

"Yeah," I said. "Just like my kneecaps."

Harry snarled and smoked. "Okay, first I'm gonna turn you into chopped meat, and then I'm gonna wrap Chong into an egg roll and *shoot him back to Moo Goo Gai Pan!*"

Harry shouted and flung himself from the roof.

I reached to the ground and grabbed my sword, but he sailed right past me and crashed head first into the hard asphalt beyond. Ton stared at the pile of errant midget meat while I grinned and slashed a gash into his leather jacket.

Ton's eyes blazed. "My sweet mother gave me this clothing, and you will pay!"

I laughed and cut another slice into Ton's maternal-given leather. "Call your mom and tell her you'll need some new clothes for the funeral."

"I would not speak with my mother."

"Why not?"

"I never do enough good for her. In third grade, I win third place in Bicycle Safety Contest, and she say I bring shame to whole family."

I suddenly felt a wave of empathy for Ton Lee, even as I lashed out at one of his major arteries. After all, I'd finished second in the Bicycle Safety Contest. I'd ridden that motherfucker through the cones, parallel parked it, and used it to save an old woman from drowning. My mother had taken one look at the ribbon they'd given me and said, "Ronald, I'm glad that old fart will live another day, but your father and I are getting divorced."

I swore as I tripped backwards over Harry's body and fell to the ground.

"Oof!" I said.

Harry said, "Dammit!"

Ton said, "I would be first but I run over orange cone!"

As I lay flat on my back, staring at the warm, inky sky, I realized how tired I was of his whining. Not running over the god damned orange cones is the whole point. My empathy was gone, and I was looking forward to cutting his throat.

Meanwhile, Harry staggered to his feet and grinned. He raised his hand and gathered up a plasma energy blob. This wasn't paint; obviously, he'd been practicing. From the corner of my eye, I also saw Ton Lee walking toward me with his daggers held high. Things were looking grim, and I wondered where the cavalry could be.

"I'm over here," said a voice. She was really getting to know me. We all turned and looked up on the roof of the hotdog stand. There was Magno Girl.

"Magno Girl!" we said.

She looked a little embarrassed. "Right."

Harry threw the plasma blob, and it struck Mags in the chest. Like I said, he'd been practicing—complete humiliation will make a guy do that. There was a poof of smoke but nothing much happened. I don't even think he burned her T-shirt.

Harry snarled. "So, you're a little tougher than I thought, or maybe I'm just a big loser."

Mags laughed. "You've never been big, Harry." Then she turned her eyes on Ton Lee and blasted him with the Gaze of the Guilt.

Ton gasped as he dropped his daggers and fell to his knees. He started to stammer and shake.

"I never want to be gangster and bring shame to my sweet mother! I never want to hurt people! I never want to be involved with grocery store scheme to polish dull fruits with vegetable wax!"

Harry listened to Ton's confession and looked at him with disgust. "I ask for a fearsome samurai, and what do I get? Some guy who's monkeying around with the bok choy—how pathetic. *Magno Girl, here I come!*" He hurled himself at Mags.

Mags didn't budge from her position near the big wiener. I guess at this point we all knew Harry was destined to miss and slam into the giant hotdog. And he did—with a loud thud.

The hotdog was ripped from its chains with Harry's legs and ass sticking out of it. Harry swore as he and the frankfurter crashed to the ground.

Across the street, the van and the car started pulling away from the warehouse. Ton Lee seemed to regain his composure. He staggered to his feet and ran toward the vehicles. Mags hopped off the roof and dropped to the ground as Harry struggled to escape from the fat Germanic sausage. As he yanked himself free, she hit him with the Gaze of the Guilt.

"No! Not again!"

I almost felt sorry for the little half-man. After all, he'd been *gazed* the other day, and it can take a lot out of a guy. But this time, his guilt was of a different nature. He stammered and groaned, and said, "I could cause the death of a million kids!"

Magnolia's eyes got wide. "What? Why, Harry? What are you involved in?"

"I'm a smoker."

"And?"

"And I smoke cigarettes—unfiltered."

"And?"

"And I'm a huge role model for millions of kids! They all want to be like me. They all idolize me, and yet I'm filled with anger and emphysema!"

Mags gave me a sideways glance and relaxed. "Oh. Well, that could be true. I mean, do you have a fan club or something we don't know about?"

"Arrg! I despise you, Magno Girl. You were born so beautiful, and so smart—and so immune to peer pressure."

She paused and shook her head. "You don't really know me, Harry. Now what is Thaddeus doing with the fooki?"

"I don't know."

"Who else is working with him?"

"I don't know!"

"Why don't you quit smoking?"

"I'll quit when I die! I'll die when I quit! *I love, love, love to smoke!*"

He gagged a few more times and passed out.

I looked at his potato sack body, unconscious and breathing hard.

"He really hates you," I said.

"Yeah, I know."

"I almost feel sorry for him."

"Yeah, me too."

"I could stab him while he's unconscious."

"No."

"Let's get out of here."

"Right."

16 — NO GIANT ROBOT OCTOPUS?

It was a great night to ride a bike in New York City. I gunned my machine all the way down 42nd Street, past the blazing Theater District and through the canyon of groping skyscrapers surrounding Times Square. I was thinking about nothing but the roar of my motor and the wind in my face, and I knew it was the greatest thing a guy could feel. But then I thought about Magnolia—and it felt just as good. I grinned and twisted the throttle hard.

I strode into Magnolia's sweaty kitchen. "It's late, I'm tired, and I have no real memory of what we were doing down at the waterfront."

Mags bit into an apple. "We were investigating. We were secretly gathering information."

"How did it go?"

"The secret part didn't work out. You walked into those hubcaps."

"Right. But we found out some important stuff anyway, huh?"

"Yeah." She gave me a serious look. "We know that Ton Lee and Small Harry are definitely working with Wong Tong Song and Melvin Shrick. We also know that Wong Tong Song is supplying Melvin with fooki, because that's what was in the warehouse. I didn't see any microwave ovens."

"Okay, so I guess there's no giant, robot octopus."

"It doesn't look that way."

Damn. I had a fantasy about battling a mechanized sea-fiend.

"Mags, do you think we should probably try to find out what's in Thad's basement?"

"Yeah," she said again while tossing her apple core into the trash. "I think Subterranean Bob is using the fooki for some evil purpose. I think Wong Tong Song is supplying fooki and some 'thug support.' I think Song and Shrick hired Harry to help fight off any superheroes. We need to find out what the fooki does. We need to establish a solid connection between Thad's fooki scheme and the death of Joey. When are you supposed to cook dinner over there?"

"Tomorrow night."

"Okay, let's worry about it tomorrow."

Her green eyes softened like a melted snow cone, and she gave me a kiss, and I was suddenly overcome with desire. So I tore off my shirt, and then my pants. I was naked as an unpeeled orange— but twice as sweet.

Mags looked at me. She seemed to admire the results of my muscle-crushing workouts. She grabbed the collar of her T-shirt and ripped it down the middle. She also unsnapped her bra from the front. Her breasts burst into the moonlight like fleshy fireworks, and I groped for some romantic words.

Finally, I said, "Are you going to take off the pants, or what?"

She reached out and stroked my heavy prick. I'll admit that I'm extremely well endowed. Of course, if it weren't true I'd lie.

"You seem anxious," she said.

"I'm ready for love, baby. How about you?"

She touched my ribs and kissed my neck. "I don't know about love, but I'd like it if you fucked me."

Once again, we failed to make it to the bedroom. At least we got to the living room where there was a rug on the floor. And I fucked her hard. I know women love tenderness and sensitivity and all that good stuff—but really, as long as a guy's not a complete asshole, most girls love a hard fuck from a tool the size of a tyrannosaurus. So I pounded into her, and she pounded back, and she moaned and scratched, and she kissed me wild and sloppy, and if it wasn't love it was something better—but I knew it was love, and I was sure she'd know it too, someday.

For a long time we were lying together in the darkness. Then I had a thought.

"Hey, Mags, did you have a reaction to the Gaze tonight?"

"Yeah. But I was alone here, so no one heard me."

"Oh. What did you say?"

She gave a soft laugh. "Nothing I want to repeat. Why? Do you like it when I say embarrassing things?"

"No. I'm curious about you, that's all. Of course, I understand why you don't want anyone to hear embarrassing stuff. I'm sure glad I don't make those kinds of confessions."

"Oh? What would you say?"

I laughed. "Lots of things."

"I hope I never hear any of it."

"That's nice of you. Aren't you curious?"

"I am. But you can tell me when you're ready."

I reached out and touched her. "You're a sweet girl, Magnolia. Next time you start confessing, I'll try not to listen."

"Thanks. I'll appreciate that."

We were silent again for a bit. Finally, I said, "Do you want to get some Thai food?"

"No."

"How about Indian?"

"No. What I want isn't in a restaurant."

"What do you want?"

"I want to stop Thad's plot, and I want to break the curse that's been put on Karina."

I sat up. "That's what you want? You really think she's cursed?"

"I do."

"Why? Because a guy didn't call her after sex? Mags, there are a *billion* girls who've felt that curse."

"Yeah, yeah," she said. "I know lots of guys lack empathy and decency—I'm not that naive. I'm also not completely innocent; I've lacked it myself a few times. But I think she's cursed, and I want to help her. The world doesn't need any more blank people."

I studied her outline in the moonlight, or maybe just a streetlight.

"Do you think I lack empathy, Mags?"

"No. I didn't mean you."

"How about decency?"

She sighed. "Ron, if I thought you were no good, I wouldn't be here. "

I lay down again beside her and listened to her breathing in the dark. Eventually, I fell asleep.

17 — A BAD DREAM

She came to me in a dream. She was thin like a whip, friendly like a razor, and blond like a bottle of peroxide. I could hardly see her; she was also blurry. But I could hear her voice, and it was cold like ice cream, sugar free.

"Do you love her? Then keep away from the fooki. Do you love her? Keep away or you'll both suffer like fools."

The message was repeated over and over with the cadence of a narcotic nursery rhyme—and then I jerked myself awake.

18 — THE ELVIS ROCK

It was a bright Saturday morning, and Magnolia was gone. I wandered across town toward Greenwich Village, through the circus-maze of humanity. The nightmare had pumped feelings of doubt and anxiety into my head—a head already crowded with thoughts of love and sex and chaos.

I passed a newsstand where a headline said, "ELVIS ROCK ARRIVES TODAY."

The Elvis Rock was a diamond that resembled the head of Elvis Presley. It looked like the young Elvis, before all the bacon and fried bananas. As I walked past a shop selling televisions, I saw Holly Honey on the screen, interviewing SuperStan. I went in and watched.

Holly looked great, and her hair was filled with a chemical afterglow. SuperStan's head was equally professional and featured a lush coating of gelled ultra-turf.

Holly smiled. "SuperStan, do you think someone will try to steal the Elvis Diamond? Smashboy says his radar smells trouble."

SuperStan snorted. He adjusted his face a bit and squinted into the camera. "Holly, Smashboy has done a fine job helping me clean up crime in this city, and I appreciate his assistance. But if anyone tries to snatch that stone, they'll end up dancing to some jailhouse rock." Then he preened a bit and flexed a chin muscle.

"What about Magno Girl, SuperStan? Did you happen to see her defeat Beef Man the other day? Do you think she might be able to help you in the future?"

SuperStan forced out a constipated-looking grin. "Who? Oh—right, right, the girl. What's her name? Mango Woman? She looked okay, Holly. I was wondering what brand of shampoo she used. Her hair has a lot of luster."

"You don't think she's a legitimate superhero? She looked good to a lot of people. After all, it took you quite an effort last year to defeat the Beef."

"Well, the Beef isn't what he used to be," SuperStan said with a smirk. "After the pounding I gave him, why, he's never been the same."

"So you're saying you softened him up? You tenderized him a bit, SuperStan?"

He laughed. "Yeah, I guess you could say that. Just call me 'the tenderizer'—that would make a good little slogan for a commercial, don't you think? I'm 'the tenderizer,' yeah, 'the tenderizer.' Any steak sauce companies listening?"

"And there you have it," Holly said, "a commercial in the making. This is Holly Honey with SuperStan, the Man of Steak, for Channel Six News."

I walked along and eventually came to the Museum of Overrated Objects, located on West 4th Street near the entrance to Washington Square Park. I saw a line of people waiting to get inside. They were armed with cameras and credit cards, and they were gulping down hotdogs, fries, and other nutritional atrocities. One guy even had a rack of ribs slung over his shoulder like an ammo belt.

There were lots of cops jack-booting around the place. I also noticed a truck out front with a crew of guys working on the sewer. They all wore white jumpsuits and a type of breathing apparatus. I had a hunch, an eerie premonition—something sure did stink. I was glad the impending incident involved a museum and not a library. At least the integrity of the Dewey Decimal System would not be violated.

I made a call to Magnolia.

"Hi, Mags. I'm over at the Museum Of Overrated Objects. I think someone is gonna grab the Elvis Rock. Where are you?"

"I just finished teaching a class. I'm at Gristedes, buying tofu."

"You might want to get over here. Something is going to happen. Soon."

She said she'd come by. As I hung up, I noticed the sewer guys setting up a big, snaky pipe. It was attached to the back of the truck, and I guessed it was headed for a nearby manhole—until they swung it around fast and aimed it into the flabby heart of the chomping rabble. A geyser of blue smoke exploded from the pipe's opening, and everyone stopped eating as shrieks filled the air.

The cops were the main targets, and they went down like heaps of dead donuts. A lot of other people went down, too. Most folks barely finished their hotdogs before tasting the pavement. I didn't go down, because in my pocket was a gas mask. I snapped it onto my face just as one of the sewer guys removed his outfit. Underneath, he was wearing a lime green, double-breasted suit with patent leather shoes. He also carried a briefcase. It was Legalman.

He threw back his head and laughed long and hard. "It's time to pay, *pari passu!*" he said. "That's Latin, people, and it means you're all a bunch of chumps, except for the guy in the mask—hey, who is that guy? Well, whatever, Legalman is back, so write your depositions and scribble on your briefs. Where the hell is that stone?"

Legalman was a well-known supervillain who created a bunch of problems for the cops. Were they using regulation bullets? Were they endangering a criminal? Were they endangering a crime? Legalman had squirmed through the net of justice lots of times, always on technicalities.

Now he dashed into the museum, leaving a bunch of his boys out front with gas guns. Then I looked up into the sky and saw SuperStan. Meanwhile, Smashboy was also roaring onto the scene in his red rocket-mobile, which he slammed to a stop on the side-walk. His ass-strangling bodysuit glistened in the morning sun as he leaped from the car.

The gas guys fired away at Smashboy, but he was wearing a protective mask. They started to fight, and Legalman came out of the building with the Elvis Rock. He laughed and said, "Save it, boys—I knew these clowns would show up. In addition to the fact that Smashboy is illegally parked and SuperStan has not filed a flight permit, neither one of these jokers is a *de facto* police officer. I will sue, sue, sue, just as soon as my monster, Brian the Brickyard, is done *tearing them limb from limb!*"

Right on cue, the top of the truck peeled open. The crowd gasped as a creature stood up. It was about five meters tall and looked like a guy made out of bricks. It wore a scowl, and the type of ragged denim cutoffs often favored by a slumming, rough-and-tumble monster. I figured it had serious marketing potential if it could hang in there with SuperStan for a few rounds—an action figure at the very least, or maybe a movie deal.

Of course, Legalman knew all this. He motioned toward the creature and shouted, "I have an exclusive deal with Brian, so if anyone out there is interested, contact me and we'll talk." He flung a bunch of business cards into the air.

Brian said, "Raaaarr! Destroy you me!"

Smashboy said, "The most exclusive thing in your future, Legalman, is a spot at the city jail!"

Smashboy threw a *smash-a-rang* at Brian. A smash-a-rang is a neon yellow boomerang fashioned from the letters of his logo; it was part of his awful shtick. It had a rope attached to it that was supposed to encircle Brian's neck, but Brian caught the smash-a-rang in his rocky fist as it whizzed through the air. He gave it a jerk and Smashboy went flying through the window of a laundromat.

Broken glass splintered in all directions as Smashboy's face slammed into a washing machine, interrupting the spin cycle.

Legalman roared with laughter. "Hey, Smashboy, do a load for me, and watch out for static cling!"

A crowd gathered across the street in front of the park. They bought hotdogs and cheered as SuperStan landed in front of Brian. Then a flock of news trucks arrived. SuperStan watched and waited as the camera guys scrambled into position. He flashed a smug look and said, "So, Legalman, do you think this monstrous stone thug can trample on the good people of my city?"

Legalman rolled his eyes. "I don't know about the *good people*, but he's certainly gonna trample on you!"

SuperStan jumped in the air with his fist cocked. He held the pose for a few seconds while the cameras clicked, and then he belted the mobile brickyard right in the head. Brian moved backward one step but seemed unimpressed. With a mighty roar he buried his stone fist in SuperStan's chest, and SuperStan went flying right into the laundromat, where he crashed into the machine next to Smashboy. He broke the door and the water spilled out, along with some lingerie. It was looking like his hair gel wouldn't survive.

Legalman roared with approval, and then he screamed, "Hey, if the owner of that laundromat wants a lawyer, I'm right here! We'll sue these soggy clowns right down to their jockey shorts. We'll slap the tortfeasors with undue assault of a major appliance!"

Legalman signed a few autographs while his Paralegal Gas Guys kept the cops down. Then he lifted the Elvis Rock above his head and waved to everyone. He let the news people zoom in for a few close-ups and started to enter a waiting Cadillac. But he stopped walking as a dramatic ripple sloshed through the crowd. SuperStan was stomping out of the laundromat. He'd dried off the suds and rejuvenated his hair.

SuperStan paused for a second, and then said, "It's time to clean up the dirt, Legalman, and I've got a wonderful brand of soap for you that I call 'justice!' "

SuperStan seized a police car, hoisted it into the air, and flung it at the monster. There was a loud crunching sound as Brian was squashed beneath the vehicle. A cheer erupted from the crowd, and Legalman scowled. SuperStan mugged for the camera and flexed his pecs—but the celebration was quick as the car was tossed aside and the monster rose to its feet. The creature let out a roar, and Smashboy walked out of the laundromat.

SuperStan frowned. "Stay out of this, Smashboy. You obviously need medical attention."

"No, I don't, SuperStan. I'm here to save the city."

"Go to the hospital, Smashboy! This is too big for you."

"Didn't I just see a pair of panties on your head, SuperStan?"

SuperStan was about to reply when Brian the Brickyard grabbed a taco cart. A unified gasp came from the crowd, since they'd been ordering Taco Supremes at a frantic pace. Brian said, "Raaar! Destroy you me!" and hurled the cart at Smashboy.

Smashboy saw it coming and dived out of the way—but he jumped right into the path of a wailing police car that was skidding to a stop. He bounced off the bumper, caromed across the sidewalk, and slid right back into the laundromat.

Legalman laughed again as his crew gassed the car and watched Lt. Rod Saint Royd tumble out of the driver's seat like a bag of barbells. Legalman said, "Would you like to borrow some change for the dryer, Smashboy? I hear the day job isn't going so well!"

The whole crowd was roaring now, including SuperStan. But they stopped laughing as Brian grabbed the humongous bronze sculpture of a Neolithic nutcracker that was standing in front of the museum. The crowd gulped—few works of art pay such homage to an optional ingredient in a chocolate chip cookie. Brian took a swat at SuperStan.

SuperStan was quick and dodged the blow. Brian was slow—a common problem for a guy made out of rocks. SuperStan stood on the sidewalk and laughed. "Legalman, your monster moves like a statue, but he'll stand for evil no more!"

While SuperStan was spitting out corny sound bites, Brian leaped forward with surprising speed and swung the fat club. With a loud *whump!*, he smacked SuperStan in the chest and sent him flying right back into the laundromat. The crowd went wild. They also tried to fish tacos out of the destroyed food cart.

Legalman jumped up and down. "Hey, maybe you guys can get a job in there! You'll always have clean jock straps."

I got on the phone and called Mags again.

"Mags, where are you? This thing made out of bricks has just knocked the cowboy pants off of SuperStan and Smashboy. You have to save them."

"I do?"

"Sure! These guys have high-paying sponsors, and this could be your chance to steal them away."

I heard cold silence coming through the line, and I fumbled fast for more words. "Mags, these guys also insinuated you couldn't fight, remember? You need to get over here and show them some fucking girl power!"

There was a long pause. "I'm on my way."

I grinned and hung up the phone. Meanwhile, Legalman and his gang were packing up. They walked over and around the passed out cops. Quite a few people in the crowd had been gassed, too. They didn't seem to mind. Most of them were just killing time until their favorite television show. And then SuperStan marched out of the laundromat.

I'll give him credit—he didn't quit, especially when the cameras were rolling. He looked like a beat-up banana peel, but he still had the kind of heroic grimace that impresses high-paying ad execs. He pointed at Brian and said, "Okay, you crooked pile of stone—I'm through fooling around. Prepare to meet that rock quarry in the sky!"

SuperStan flew right at Brian. He was a blur of muscle and sports clichés as he zoomed through the air and smashed into the monster—and then bounced right off his stone body.

SuperStan said, "Oooof!"

Brian said "Raaaaar! Me stronger you!" And then he grabbed SuperStan in a bear hug.

I knew it wasn't hard to escape from a bear hug; the trick is to have an automatic weapon in your hand. But SuperStan just said, "Ugh! Oooooh! Oooof!"

Brian walked over to the open sewer hole in the street. He flipped SuperStan upside down and chucked him into the hole, head first. SuperStan howled a bit, and then we heard a loud *sploosh* and he was in there with the poop. It was a humbling experience. I always hate getting thrown into the poop water.

Legalman was laughing so hard he was holding his stomach. "Hey, SuperStan, I know the address of a good laundromat! Maybe Smashboy can wash the crap from your ass. I'm sure he's done it before!"

He grinned at the cameras and started getting into his baby blue Cadillac. And that's when Magno Girl came flying down from the sky.

She was wearing her black yoga pants and a pink T-shirt. It was another shirt that featured a picture of a fist wrapped in a flower. On her feet were sneakers. She looked fantastic, though I knew the media craved something fleshier and assier and breastier.

The crowd roared. I heard people say, "Who is that? Oh, it's Magno Girl. Is that her? Yeah, that's the girl on TV."

She landed right in front of Brian. She looked tiny beside his bulk, but she radiated a quiet confidence that washed over the crowd and made my heart swell with pride.

She stared up at him. "Hi. I'm guessing you're the monster."

"Raaar! Me destroy pretty you!"

"Me think not likely."

She fired the Gaze of the Guilt at his head.

I held my breath, wondering if her magic stare would work on a shouting pile of boulders—but the big guy immediately threw up his arms in an attempt to block the guilt-forcing pink light. He also roared and staggered backward, and then started groaning—and in between groans he said, "Me sorry! Me very sorry!"

Mags grimaced and poured on the charm. Brian swayed and stumbled and crashed down onto the roof of the demolished police car. He put his head in his hands and said, "Me so sorry! Me unhappy!" And then to everyone's amazement, he started to cry.

It was a surreal vision, as an avalanche of golf ball-sized tears started tumbling down his head. He lifted his rocky face from his hands and said, "Me tired of this. Me not destroy. Me not be slave to contract written by sleazy man in ugly green suit!"

Mags took a step back and stopped her assault. Brian blubbered and lamented a bit more while the crowd of onlookers sat mesmerized and hungry. Then the creature wiped his face and pulled himself to his feet. Immediately, the crowd began to scream their slogans of sportsmanship.

"Get him, Magno Girl! Crush him! Kill him! Stomp him into the fucking street!"

Mags made no moves, though she glanced at the rowdy hoi polloi with a look of disgust. She looked back at the creature. He towered over Magnolia, and he said, "Thank you, pretty girl. Me go home to family. Have nice day!" And Brian the Brickyard stomped off in the general direction of New Jersey.

The crowd was stunned. For several seconds, not a single hotdog was consumed. Legalman looked grim from behind the wheel of his car. Finally, he said, "Honey, you've got an interesting style—wanna go out sometime? I've got a big diamond, you know."

Mags gave him a curt smile. "Thank you, but you're not my type."

And then SuperStan came crawling out of his hole. He ran his fingers through his gel-and-feces hair combination, and he leaped in front of Mags. He yanked the door from Legalman's vehicle and said, "In the name of justice, I arrest you!" SuperStan snatched the diamond from the front seat. Legalman's gang started to run from the back of the truck, but the cops had revived and were chasing them down.

Legalman looked at Mags. "Honey, you seem pretty nice. Don't let this cheese-fried super dud take all the credit for apprehending me. I can get you some great endorsement deals—have you trademarked that T-shirt?" He turned to SuperStan. "Hey, stud, you smell like shit."

SuperStan pulled Legalman from the car, even as he rattled

off a bunch of potential lawsuits involving the cruel and unusual punishment of his olfactory nerves. Rod Saint Royd was on his feet. His boys put the cuffs on Legalman and most of his crew. Saint Royd said, "Thanks, SuperStan. We don't know what we'd do without you. We'd probably have to work a lot harder."

Mags turned and looked at the crowd. She was silent in the midst of their frenzied adulation. They were screaming stuff like, "Magno Girl, you rule! Magno Girl, you're number one!" I wondered what she was thinking—and I was hoping she'd get out of here before she made some sort of guilt-ridden confession. But she leaped into the air, and she was gone.

Legalman screamed, "You're the best, Magno Girl! And you're gonna need a good lawyer. I can sue for you! *I can suuuuuuuuuuuuuue!*"

SuperStan was adjusting his hair and preparing to recite one of his proclamations from the top of Mount Olympus when Holly Honey shoved a microphone under his mouth. "SuperStan, that was quite a battle. Do you appreciate the way Magno Girl flew in here and saved you without a single blow?"

SuperStan turned the color of an angry radish.

"What? Are you kidding?" he sputtered. "She didn't save me! It was my inspired punching that softened up that hideous mountain of rocks!"

"Was that before or after he dumped you into the sewer, SuperStan?"

I'm glad Holly was on our side. SuperStan huffed and puffed. "I have other crimes to fight, Holly. I'd love to talk, but see you later!"

He jumped up into the sky. The crowd was laughing as his sewer-stained cape faded from sight.

19 — YOUR BROTHER HAS NO EGGS

Things were looking up as I started walking home through the wreckage of people, cars, and publicity—but then I stopped.

Once again, I saw the mysterious blond stalker.

She was about ten meters away. I started moving toward her, but the crowd was thick and filled with obesity and I lost sight of her. By the time I'd elbowed my way through the shuffling pork-herd, she was gone. I cursed to myself and then heard a voice echo in my brain. It was a woman's voice, and it had a certain midnight-at-the-graveyard flavor.

"I know her weakness, and you'd be surprised to know who's on our side. Stay away from the fooki."

I grimaced and then felt a tug at my arm. I leaped—but it was only a reporter named Jim Riteangle from Channel 5. He flashed me a ringmaster's smile.

"Hello, are you Ron?"

"Yeah."

"So you're Magno Girl's manager?"

"Maybe."

"I'm Jim Rightangle. Can we arrange an interview with her?"

"I don't know. She's kind of busy saving the world."

"Great. Has she dated any celebrities? Any actors or athletes?"

"She's a smart girl. Very sharp."

"Did she have an affair with any of her teachers? Do you remember their names?"

I brushed past Jim, but then someone else leaped into my path. It was Holly Honey, and she gave Jim a serious stiff-arm. As he hit the ground, Holly said, "Hi, Ron. I'd like to do a special piece on Magno Girl. Can you please tell her I'm going to call?"

My natural instinct was to put on face number seventeen, *the rot of the kumquat,* but Holly had been okay so far and I decided to just smile. After all, I wanted Mags to be famous.

"Sure, Holly, she'd love to do it. But I have to warn you, she's not always talkative."

Holly smiled. "The world could use a quiet superhero."

"Okay, but sometimes she's more uncooperative than quiet."

Holly laughed. "I like her."

It took me about thirty minutes to get to Magnolia's apartment. I wanted to talk about fame, fortune, and the plastic dolls that would carry a distorted likeness of her image. I wanted to discuss the magazine covers, the interviews, and maybe the Magno Girl breakfast cereal that would be advertised during the Magno Girl Saturday morning cartoon hour.

I also wanted to have sex. She'd just been in a fight and her hormones would be bubbling. She opened the door to her apartment, and I walked in—and all I could do was lunge forward and give her a hug.

"Mags, that was amazing! I'm glad you weren't hurt."

She rolled her eyes and pulled away from me. "Thanks for your concern. I guess if I'd been crushed I wouldn't have impressed any sponsors."

"I don't care about the sponsors, Mags! Really, I don't."

She glared at me. "Good. I don't care, either."

"Right. Neither of us cares. I mean about the sponsors."

She gave me a sideways glance. I surveyed the shabby surroundings of her kitchen and said, "Still, you could have hit him a few times. It would've been more photogenic."

She groaned and turned away.

"Mags, don't you watch movies? In America, violence is hip, it's cool, and it's edgy. It gets you the big bucks."

"I hurt him enough. Besides, I think mental pain is stronger than physical pain."

I laughed. "You've obviously never had your foot caught in a carpet-cleaning machine. By the way, I saw your stalker again— that blond woman. She was there again today."

Now I had her attention. I told her about the woman and about hearing the voice.

"Ron, are you sure this woman isn't stalking *you?*"

"I doubt it. Her message is about *you.*"

Mags started to say something—but then she stopped and put her fingers on her temples. It was a delayed reaction to the Gaze of the Guilt, following her fight with Brian. It was more delayed than usual but still as strong as ever.

She gasped and dropped to her knees.

"I should stop ignoring my brother! And I never should have hurt Stacy the way I did! And I really need to tell Martina I'm not interested in a relationship!"

As quick as it came, it was over. Mags stopped talking and caught her breath. Then she rose to her feet and shook her head.

She gave me a sober look. "Ron, I don't know what to say. Anyway, next time you see that woman, snap a picture."

"Right," I said in my most nonchalant voice. "That's a great idea. Hey, do you want to have dinner tonight?"

I thought I did a nice job of ignoring her confession, and I could tell she appreciated it. I then proposed that she sneak into Thad's mansion tonight. We'd eat there, and after Thad was done cuddling with his dinner pile, we'd check out the basement. She liked the idea.

Her phone rang. It was Karina on the line, along with some spirited shouting in the background.

"Magnolia? Magnolia, this is Karina. Are you busy?"

"Karina, what's wrong?"

Karina gave a teary laugh. "Just about everything. I was wondering if I could come over and hang out."

Magnolia's eyes flashed. "You can always come over here, honey. Come over now, and we'll go to the dojo a little later. But maybe you should tell your mother where you'll be."

"Yeah, sure, I'll mention it to her—like she really cares."

"Or maybe just send her a text message. Tell her you're with a friend."

"Okay, thanks. I'll be over soon."

Mags hung up and scowled. "That poor girl. It's so sad. Why do so many morons have kids?"

I shrugged. It doesn't take a lot of smarts for a guy to have an orgasm.

Mags said nothing while I did some calculating. Karina wasn't that far away, so she'd be arriving soon. This meant my "sex window" was closing like a clamshell, and I needed a strategy. I prepared to rip off my pants. But the damn phone rang again.

This time I heard the voice of Magnolia's mom. I cringed as my sex plan disintegrated in a libido death-bomb of motherly love. The voice said, "Hello, Magnolia. I was just watching you on television. You looked pretty."

"Thanks, Mom."

"Do you think you'll look that way forever?"

Mags sighed. "Are you calling to make me miserable?"

"Of course not. But I used to be pretty, and look at me now. I'm a wreck."

"You're not a wreck. Far from it."

"Yes, I am, and you'll be a wreck, too. One day you'll wake up and see the wreckage."

"Thanks for the positive message. Thanks a lot."

"I'm only trying to help. One day I'll be joining your father in the graveyard. I'd like to see your wedding before I'm gone."

Mags shook her head and laughed. "You might have to hang in there for a while."

"Are you kidding? The way I drink every night?"

"Maybe you should quit."

"Magnolia, I don't care how tough a girl thinks she is—she still needs a husband and a family. Otherwise, her life will be empty."

"I'm a teacher, Mom. I'm around kids all the time."

"They're not your kids! Without kids of your own, your life will be missing something."

"Mom, we've been through this a hundred times." Mags paused and took a deep breath. "All the things I enjoy would be impossible if I had a family."

"Who ever told you life was about *enjoyment?* Being a mother is about sacrifice! It's about pain, and heartbreak, and regret."

"Oh, really? I was kind of hoping to avoid those things."

"You want to avoid being a real woman?"

"I'm already a real woman. Why should I make a huge commitment to something I don't want to do?"

"Because that's what you're supposed to do."

"But why?"

"Why do you ask so many questions all the time?"

"I don't know. Maybe I want an answer that makes sense."

"There's no sense to this! You just shut up and do what everyone else does!"

"Oh, so you want me to be an idiot?"

"Yes! You'll be happier that way!"

"Will I be happy? Like you were happy with Dad? Like Grandma was happy with Grandpa? *Will I be so happy that I'll be miserable—and want to die?*"

There was a long moment of silence. Finally, Mags said, "I'm sorry, Mom. I shouldn't have said that."

"You never listen to me, Magnolia."

"You never listen to me, Mom. The whole time I was growing up, you never listened, and you're still not listening. How come you don't give Tommy all this advice? He needs it more than I do."

"Your brother doesn't have any eggs. And he's doing fine."

"Fine? He's a degenerate gambler and a criminal. Other than that, I guess things are great."

"He's a lot like your father. Your father's death was very hard for him."

"And it was so easy for me?"

"Why don't you give him a call? He'd like to talk to you. Just don't show him any of the evil things you know."

"I don't know any evil things! And besides, you know them, too. And those things wouldn't work for him, anyway. Look, I have to go. Take your medication. You need it."

Mags hung up the phone and rubbed her forehead.

"Why do you talk to her?" I said.

"I don't know. Maybe I love to suffer."

"I better get over to Thad's place. Don't worry about it, Magnolia. You're a nice girl. You can beat up anybody."

She sort of smiled. "Right. I'll see you later."

20 — A LITTLE SUGAR

I rarely give much thought to my relationships with girls. Here today, gone tomorrow—or maybe later today. But so what? Two people can have a lot of good times in one day. In fact, it's possible to wake up dehydrated and not know how many days were involved.

But now things were different. I wanted to give Mags a little more planning and consideration. Of course, I didn't have to plan anything yet. She didn't seem interested in the whole "family thing," and that was fine. We were both camping on the same side of the cradle with that one. It also sounded like her past involved a pile of regrettable encounters, and I could relate. For now, my goal was to make sure any future regrets involved no one but her. I guess that was one definition of love.

I clenched my fist and told myself to stay cool. I had bigger fish to fillet, like that voice in my head. Who was "on their side?" I decided to stop at my brother's pizzeria to clear my mind.

I grinned as I walked into Al's place and found a day of tomato-pie pandemonium. A horde of people waited on line to buy his pies, and there was a new picture hanging on the wall—a picture of Magno Girl.

Al walked out of the back room and saw me looking at the photo. He dusted some flour from his fat fingers and started chopping a few red peppers. "Hey, Ronnie," he said. "When are you gonna get your girl's pretty little butt down here to sign a few shots for me?"

"She's kind of busy right now."

"Oh, yeah? Well, I've got some ideas. I was wondering if she'd put on a bikini and pose on top of a giant stromboli."

I paused and tried to imagine the day I'd ask Magnolia to pose half-naked on top of a giant phallus made of pizza dough.

"Al, she's trying to save the world."

"Okay, maybe she could just hold the boli in her hand and say some sexy stuff."

"Look, when she comes in here for a slice you can discuss the exploitation of her vagina."

"Hey, who's exploiting? I just want her to show some skin and help me out. Hot girls are like cold beer—always in style. I'm figuring a bit of boob is worth ten new toppings... So, are you pounding her good, or what?" He leered and made a pumping motion with his hand.

I gave him a tight smile. "She's happy, at least with me. Just make your pizza, okay, fat man?"

Al laughed and motioned with his head. "Let's go in the back." I walked behind the counter, through the kitchen, and into a sweaty little office. Al glanced around and opened a closet. He brought out a box that advertised something called "The Atomic Can Cleaver."

"I got four thousand of these electric can openers," he said. "They work great. Slicing a can feels better than cutting off your ex-wife's alimony."

I grabbed a few samples. "I don't have an ex-wife, but I'll see what I can do with my guy in Staten Island. Anything else?"

"Yeah, what about the five thousand teapots?"

"Still no takers on the tea stuff."

"They're real silver!"

"Silver tarnishes. Do *you* wanna blow out an elbow shining a teapot? Now what else have you got?"

Al shifted his eyes. "Hey, Ron, I got expenses. Listen, what do you know about Melvin Shrick? I'm sayin' what do you *really* know?"

I considered the question. His tone was strange, but my brother had always been strange. As a kid, he'd spent hours helping Dad in the bakery, building little bread men who were supposedly destined to occupy Brooklyn and resist an impending tax on pumpernickel. Unfortunately, the army got moldy and only ended up occupying a dumpster.

I shrugged. "I know what everyone else knows. His crusts are pre-fab and his cheeses are low class. His sauce is sweeter than a kid's breakfast cereal."

"I put a little sugar in my sauce, too. It gives it a distinct flavor."

"Some people would say that's cheating."

"Cheating sells more pizzas, and sugar ain't against the law."

"No, but how about an attack on the fabric of our society?"

"You're talking about cotton, right? Scrub it with dish detergent and it'll come right out."

We wandered back into the pizzeria, where there was now even more drool and anarchy. "Al, what's the story here? I've never seen so many people jammed into this place. Gimme a slice." I reached for one.

"No!" he said, jerking my hand away. "I got a better one."

"Okay, sure." He gave me a slice from a different pie. "Thanks. See you later."

I left the pizzeria with a bad feeling.

I knew one day the giant robot octopus would rear its metallic head. Sooner or later, everyone has a giant robot octopus show up at the door. For some people, it sneaks in quietly, but soon enough they're swigging whiskey every night and trying to untangle the tentacles. For others, it's a noisy situation involving a messy divorce and lots of screaming about "that sucker-armed floozy." I decided to stay alert.

21 — FISH TANK DISASTER

I turned on the television when I got home and saw Magnolia talking to Holly Honey. I was surprised, but I opened a beer and sat down.

Holly smiled. "Magno Girl, you really saved SuperStan. Do you think he resented your help over at the Waffle Empire?"

"I hope not," Mags said. "I'm sure he has a certain amount of pride, but I'm not trying to muscle in on his thing. In fact, I use a lot less muscle."

"Yes, you can crush opponents with guilt—and it's so impressive to see! Is it easy for your magic gaze to bring all this guilt out of someone?"

Mags shook her head. "I'm not necessarily 'bringing it out.' If it's not there, the Gaze creates it. I like to think it creates guilt where it should be."

"That's interesting, and very powerful. How do you respond to people who claim it's a sinister form of magic?"

"It's not," Mags said. She tossed back her hair and gave Holly a little smile.

"Well, that's good to know," Holly said with a laugh. "That monster tossed SuperStan around like a rag doll, yet your Gaze handled him easily—so maybe the Gaze is only a problem if you're a bad guy, right? Are you afraid of anything?"

"Ha, lots of things. You should see me try to kill a cockroach."

Holly laughed again. "That's a girly attitude."

"I'm a girl. But just because I hate bugs doesn't mean I let people push me around."

"So you can wear high heels and still kick butt, is that what you're saying?"

"It's very hard to fight in heels, Holly. But yeah, I can take care of myself."

I smiled. Mags never wore heels—ever. But I was glad she hadn't mentioned it, because maybe we could get a deal with a shoe company. Women love, love, love to buy shoes.

Holly continued. "You seem to be in great shape. Do you eat anything special?"

"Hm, I like apples."

"Apples?"

"Yeah, or peaches. I love fruit."

I cursed and slammed my fist down on the kitchen table. How many athletes endorse *fruit*, Magnolia? Fruit hangs on trees until some shit-kicker in overalls sends it down to civilization where it's dried and fried and rolled into pastry. Name a breakfast cereal, dammit!

"Magno Girl, are you finding any acceptance from the city's male dominated police force?"

"Ha, I haven't been invited to any parties yet."

"Do you think the fact that you're a woman is a problem?"

Mags laughed. "Maybe, but if that's how it is, it's a problem that will continue, because I intend to stay a woman."

"Do you think a female superhero is less appealing to certain segments of the population—or maybe to certain advertisers?"

"I don't know," Mags said. "But I do know there are things more important than selling beer and pickup trucks. Or whatever."

I grimaced. She'd just sacked a zillion dollars worth of NFL commercials. Then I gazed around the apocalypse of my apartment, and I wondered if it mattered. The average guy's a beer swigging slob who'd be living in a cave if he didn't need to keep a woman happy. As I stared at Mags and Holly, I realized there *were* things more important than beer and pickup trucks—there were entire retail chains dedicated to women's clothing.

Right on cue, Holly smiled and said, "Do you have a message for the girls of America?"

"Not really. Maybe 'Don't be afraid.' "

"That's a good message."

"Yeah, and I guess it sounds more sophisticated than 'Take no crap.' "

Holly laughed. "'Take no crap'—I love it! This is Holly Honey for Channel Six with Magno Girl, the coolest superhero in the world."

I grinned and turned off the television. I also wondered how many commercials she could do for an empowering form of brassier. I drank another beer and dozed off on the couch.

When I woke up, Mags was standing over me.

"Ron, don't you have to get over to Thad's place? Aren't we going to check out the basement?"

I leaped to my feet. "Mags! I saw you on television."

"Yeah, it wasn't bad. I like Holly."

"You were great, honey."

She smiled. "Thanks. What are you cooking tonight?"

I gave her a blank stare while my brain groped for the least irresponsible answer.

"I'll bring Thai food," she said. "Now what about the listening devices?"

With a triumphant grin, I pulled a tiny electronic sensor from my pocket. I held it up to the light. "I've got two of these, and we'll stick them right under Thad's big nose. If he coughs up one fleck of phlegm we're gonna know about it."

"That's great," she said. "It's also a little more than we need to know, but let's do it."

I remembered something and pointed to a carton stashed against the wall. It was stuffed full of clothes and a few other more expensive items. "Mags, I almost forgot that I went shopping. I got you some things."

She glanced at me and then went over to the box. I knew they were things she'd be happy to have, especially the pink T-shirts and the new laptop computer. Mags looked through everything and even examined the Atomic Can Cleaver.

"Thanks, Ron. That's nice of you. Look, don't go spending a lot of money on me. I don't need anything."

"Don't worry about it, Mags. I got a lot of good deals."

She stared at me, and I knew that look. I had a flashback, and I was a kid, and I'd just swiped a bunch of unguarded crayons. But what could I do? I was all out of "Jazzberry Jam."

"I don't want you going broke over me," she said.

I tried not to shift my eyes around. "I did some extra work. I unloaded a few trucks." Then I looked at the clock. "I gotta go, baby—here's money for the Thai food!" I crammed a fat roll of cash into her hand and kissed her goodbye. She started to speak but I was already half way to my chopper. I had a job to do and a conversation to avoid.

I hopped on 3rd Avenue and did some circus-style driving all the way to the Upper East Side but made it to Thad's house on time. I found Jonathan in the kitchen sweeping the floor. He seemed nervous to see me, especially when I grabbed a cleaver and started slicing some fruit.

"Hey, John, is there a room in this place where the big guy likes to do business?"

Jonathan sighed and smoothed a wrinkle in his shirt. "There is a large study on the second floor. It's the first door on your right. He has meetings and makes calls from there."

"Any chance I can slip up there and not be noticed?"

"I assume he won't be occupying that room during dinner. It could be done if you were quiet."

"Are you trying to say I might walk into a pile of hubcaps?"

"Why, no—not at all."

"Is Thaddeus having company tonight?"

"As a matter of fact, yes. He's invited a lady friend. I tend to think they'll be expecting a decent entree."

He was right, of course, but I figured Magnolia would save my ass from a culinary Little Big Horn. Soon enough she came jumping through the window, wearing a blond wig and fake eyeglasses. I smiled and noticed she was wearing one of the T-shirts I'd given her. She also had a bag filled with top quality Thai stuff.

I gave her a quick kiss. "Hi, Mags. Hey, Johnny, can you serve the food? I'll be busy planting my bugs."

"Why, certainly," Jonathan said. Then he turned toward Mags. "So nice to see you again. May I ask you a question? Are you Magno Girl?"

"Yeah," she said, squirming a bit. "That's what everyone calls me—except for my mother."

"And what does your mother call you?"

"Unmarried, with no children."

I peeked into the dining room and saw Thaddeus waddling in with a female dinner guest. She was a trite little truffle, bursting with giddy enthusiasm and the lust for a fat bankbook. I heard Thaddeus say, "Aruba will be nice in the winter. The ocean looks like a bowl of crystal brine."

The girl giggled. "That's so funny, Thad. You're so funny. You tell such funny stories."

"Did I ever tell you about the time I fell asleep while eating brownies?"

"No," she said with another giggle. "I'll bet it's hilarious. Tell me, Thad, tell me."

I told Mags it was time to slip upstairs.

Jonathan peered over his bifocals. "Do be careful. Thaddeus has a large dog up there."

"A dog?"

"Yes, but he's old, blind, and stupid."

I grinned. Nothing's easier than fighting with a crippled idiot.

We slipped out of the kitchen and up the stairs. At the top of the landing we saw a hallway and a few closed doors. Mags was about to open the first door when I had an impulse. I leaped in front of her, yanked the door open, and lunged into the room. Immediately, a big dog started barking, *"Rooo! Rooo! Ruff! Ruff!"*

"Damn!" I said.

I started contemplating a good method of dog murder, but Mags gave me a dirty look—and I don't mean dirty in a good, let's-have-monkey-sex-on-the-balcony kind of way. She said, "Quiet, doggy," and threw him a piece of boloney. The dog stopped barking and started eating. I smiled at her clever use of cold cuts and then surveyed the room.

There were some bookcases against one wall, along with a mahogany desk that overlooked Central Park, and a nice little view of trees and winking towers. I slid into a high-backed chair behind the desk and grabbed an old-style telephone that was sitting there. Then I noticed a coffin-sized fish tank in the corner, filled with greenish water and bad omens.

Mags said, "Don't worry about the fish tank; just start putting the listening devices in place. And hurry up. I'm almost out of boloney."

I hated boloney. As a kid, my dad had ridiculed me for eating it. It wasn't a 'man's sandwich.' As a nine-year-old, I didn't realize how eating the wrong meat could undermine my masculinity. My dad ate hunks of roast beef. My dad drove himself to the hospital in a state of coronary arrest where he watched football and played with power tools right up until the moment of his triple bypass.

I put one bug inside the phone and attached another one to the underside of the desk. "Okay, Mags, we're done. Let's go downstairs and get some Thai food."

"Ron, look!"

Standing by the fish tank was the ghost. His hair hung down in greasy spaghetti strands, and his eyes glistened like bong water. Quick as a flash, I sprang into action.

I shouted and leaped from the chair. I faked a punch, whirled to my left, and fired off *the kick of the Cajun*. This advanced martial arts move usually involves cayenne pepper, but in this case it involved my foot completely missing its target and smashing a hole through the evil fish tank—*kasplish!*

The tank shattered and burst, spilling its contents onto the floor. I cursed and tried to yank my foot from the broken fish prison, causing the glass tank to jerk from its perch, crash to the floor, and break again.

My awful destiny was complete. Meanwhile, the ghost smiled and faded away. And the dog started barking again, *"Rooo! Rooo! Rooof!"*

Mags tried to quiet the beast while I tried to pull my foot from the wreckage. Quite a few fish were wriggling on the floor, trying to regain their water. I hopped around, dragging the broken fish-casket. Mags hissed, *"Quiet, doggy! Quiet!"* The dog said, *"Rooo! Rooof!"* and started charging around the room. He was blind, of course, so he bumped into a few things.

He collided with a couple of golf clubs. He caromed off a metal wastebasket. He smashed into a suit of armor, and it came crashing down on top of a huge pile of dishes—and then he hit the hubcaps. They'd been sitting there innocently, but now they were clanging, and the dog was barking, and it sounded like this:

"Rooo!"

Clang!

"Rooo!"

Crash!

I'm just glad I wasn't the one who ran into the hubcaps.

Mags cursed and rolled her eyes. "Let's get out of here," she said. I finally shook my foot free, and we bolted for the door. We were heading down the hall, back toward the stairs, but someone was coming up. We ran the other way and ended up in a bedroom. It must have been a guest room because it was pretty bare, and there were little mints on the pillows.

Mags looked out the window while I yanked open a closet door. We were about to make a stupid decision when the ghost reappeared in the center of the room. I reached for my daggers.

The ghost grinned. "I'm unarmed, dude, and your daggers are

in the saddlebag of your chopper. Anyway, in the closet there's a secret passage. It goes to the basement." He grinned again and vanished.

Mags and I looked at each other, and then we bolted into the closet and discovered a door. It led to a cramped passageway and we shoved ourselves into it. We felt along the walls and discovered a light switch, and then we saw a stairway. Down the stairs we stumbled, until we came to a door. When we opened it, we were in the basement.

"What do you see?" I said.

"Nothing, it's dark."

That's right. I kept forgetting she didn't have x-ray vision.

"Okay, let's find a light switch."

I started doing an *advanced light switch sweep*, which was a tactic I'd learned in Get Out Of The Dark School. The course had been a good metaphor for life, as we were taught to grope methodically through the blackness until a special friend shows up and helps illuminate the way. With a pinging sound, Mags snapped on the lights.

I took a quick look around. I'd been expecting a sinister laboratory packed with beakers, Bunsen burners, and man-sized glass receptacles imprisoning creatures in various states of undead animation. Instead, I saw a fireplace, a wet bar, and some sofas and chairs. At the far end of the room there was a door set into the stone wall. We headed toward it.

It looked like a door that would lead to an evil lab. It was white with a frosted window, and it had that doctor's office vibe. I could almost hear a receptionist ask for the name of my health insurer. Attached to the door was an electronic lock that sported a small keyboard.

Mags shook her head. "What do we do now?"

"We have to guess the password."

"That's impossible. It could be anything."

I typed it out—A-N-Y-T-H-I-N-G. A message appeared telling me that my dry cleaning was done.

"No, that's not right," I said. "I don't have anything at the dry cleaners."

She gave a snort. "Ron, we're not going to guess it. We need another way."

I pulled out a credit card and slipped it into the space between the door and the door frame. Mags shook her head, but then her eyes got wide as I cajoled the plastic with outlaw expertise and pushed the door open.

She stared at me. "That's amazing. I've never seen that trick actually work."

I grinned. Easy credit and shoddy construction will often win the day. It was good to be an American.

We strolled into the lab. The whole room was a shade of hospital-white, and it held a counter, some tables, and a bunch of rats in cages. We also saw a lot of pizza. There was pizza on the counter and pizza in the toaster oven and pizza in pizza boxes. Most of the pizza boxes were painted with the logo of Melvin Shrick's pizza chain, Pie Hole Pizza, Inc.—but there was one box that had the logo of The People's Pizzeria.

Mags grabbed the box. "Ron, look—this a tangible piece of evidence that connects Shrick and Thaddeus to the death of Joey the Round Man! And obviously the pizza is central to the plot."

"Right!" I said. Then I used my finger to sample the tomato on one of the Pie Hole slices. Mags watched me lick my digit with keen interest; she was aware of my affinity for tomato sauce.

"Hm."

"What?"

"It's sweet, but not as sweet as usual. He's cut down on the sugar a bit."

"And this is significant?"

I shrugged. I also wondered why my parents had made my brother the favorite son. They'd given Al a bicycle and a pair of congas, while I'd gotten stuck with some dirty Play-Doh and a broken ukulele. Then I noticed the piles of dried fooki.

"Ha! Someone's been playing with the fooki, Mags."

Her eyes got wide, and she grabbed a handful of the stuff. "More evidence that these are the guys who whacked Joey."

"Yeah! Let's bust them."

She shook her head. "It's good evidence, but it's still circumstantial. And fooki isn't illegal."

"Okay, then let's roll it up and smoke it."

She ignored my remark and sifted through more fooki.

"Ron, I think Bob has tested pizza to see how it interacts with fooki. For some reason, they're using pizza to secretly distribute fooki to the population. Obviously, Joey must have been involved."

"Of course," I said with a snarl. "Joey was the point man for the pizza, but he wanted a bigger slice of the pie—so they wrapped him in a stromboli body bag."

"Hm, I suppose that's one scenario. And look over here... What do you think about this?" She pointed to a pricey Rickenbacker bass guitar that was sitting in a stand near the rat cages. It was plugged into a shiny Eden amp head and a 4 x 12 speaker cabinet.

I gave a low whistle. "This is high-end gear. It's better than the average rat is used to hearing, that's for sure."

On a countertop we both noticed a sparkling glass bubble. Under the glass was a human brain.

"Okay," Mags said. "This must be significant."

"Right. It means there's one more brainless idiot walking around New York."

As she spoke, a figure materialized in the room, shrouded in a nonchalant haze of smoke. It was the ghost again.

He smiled. "Hey, man, remember me?"

I was ready to leap, but Mags motioned for me to keep cool. "Yeah, you're the ghost," she said. "Thanks for the information about the secret passage. By the way, who are you?"

The ghost took a long drag on a short pipe. "My name is Hal. I'd rather be called a 'spirit,' though—it sounds more festive. Want a hit?"

"No thanks," Mags said. "I kinda gave that up."

"Yeah," I said. "She doesn't even eat meat, really."

"Meat and weed are different," Hal said. "Weed grows outta the ground, man. Meat, it comes from a hotdog cart."

"So why are you haunting this house?" Mags said.

"I've got issues. It all has to do with my mother. You wouldn't understand."

She laughed. "Try me. I have a mother, too. In fact, we've recently had discussions about my ovaries."

"Oh, yeah?" Hal took another hit from his pipe. "I never had any ovaries. I'll bet they're a real nuisance, huh?"

Mags shrugged. "Not really. I just wish my mom would stop telling me how to use them."

Hal grinned. "They make pills to prevent accidents, I think. I've taken a few pills in my day."

"You had a drug habit?" Mags said. "Is that how you died?"

"I suppose. I smoked some pot. I did a little coke. Also meth, X, acid, H—whatever. Yeah, that's what killed me." He blew some smoke.

"That's a sad story," Mags said.

"Yeah, it's sad. I never got to learn taekwondo."

Mags cocked her head. "Taekwondo is okay. Did you ever consider jeet kune do?"

"Nah, that's a lot of hand blows. I needed my hands to play guitar."

"Oh, did you play a lot of guitar?"

"When I wasn't too high. I was loud and funky."

"I see. And how long have you been haunting this place?"

"A couple of years. No one really noticed me until the last few months, though. I was kinda taking it easy. I didn't want to sprain my quadriceps or anything."

"I didn't know quad sprains were common in the spirit world."

"They're a lot more common than necrotic enteritis. You'd have to be a chicken to get that one."

"Right. And why did you help us?"

"I figured it would annoy my parents."

"You mean they're wandering around in here, too?"

"Yeah. My mom, she only comes by once in a while. If I were you, I'd avoid her. She's nobody you want to tangle with, that's for sure."

Mags leaned forward. "You didn't like your mother?"

Hal looked away. "She wasn't much of a mom, really, and she knows it." Then he stared at Mags. "If you ever get into a scrap with her, just remember—she's not so strong when she's not so sure."

And then Hal vanished.

Mags seemed to make a mental note of his words. "We better get back upstairs," she said. "Someone's probably figured out that you were in the study, and you've got some dead fish to explain."

We ran back through the secret passage and backtracked until we arrived in the kitchen. Remarkably, Thaddeus and his babe were still eating. I heard her say, "Oh, you're so funny, Thad. Tell me more."

Thaddeus preened a bit. "There was the time as a child that I sprayed my spaghetti with the garden hose. And then I ate a cupcake!" His date roared with laughter.

Jonathan looked at me. "Are you done obliterating the study? I knew you'd walk into the hubcaps."

"It was the dog in the hubcaps, old man!"

Mags said, *"Shhhhhh! Will you be quiet?"*

I smiled. "Hey, what are you worried about? I work here."

Mags turned to Jonathan. "Who came upstairs to investigate the noise?"

"I did. I explained that the dog was a little rabid, and the cook was a little dumb."

"Okay, thanks. And what do you know about this house? How long has Thaddeus been here?"

"From what I've been told, he has owned this home for approximately fifteen years. I've only worked here for the last two." Then he narrowed his eyes. "Unfortunately, some of the recent guests seem determined to destroy the place."

"She's not a guest," I said, pointing at Mags. "She's more of a spy. And I'm an employee. All my destruction is on company time."

Jonathan sighed and poured himself a glass of brandy. "Will you be staying much longer? Your time on the clock is giving me a headache."

Mags shook her head. "No. But Jonathan, can you do me a favor? Can you call me if Thaddeus has a meeting with anyone in his study? Or maybe if you hear him on the phone?"

"Why, certainly. I'll be happy to assist the famous Magno Girl."

"I'm not that famous. Is there any Thai food left?"

"You're somewhat famous. There is no more Thai food."

I was furious. The idiotic blind dog and the stoned hippie ghost were trivial compared to my ferocious hunger. There had been a lot of food there. I would have my gore-filled revenge on that fat ball of suet.

Mags said, "Forget about your gory revenge, Ron. I think we need to pay a visit to Melvin's pizza factory. Can you meet me there tomorrow morning? We'll figure out what's going on."

I smiled and wrapped my arms around her waist. She felt good against me.

"Of course I'll meet you there, Mags. I'll meet you anywhere. I'd swim rivers of blood for you, honey."

She gave me a little laugh and pulled away.

"Okay," she said. "So meet me there."

She gave me a quick kiss, turned fast, and jumped out the window.

I stared at the empty spot where she'd just been standing.

"Is it my imagination, Johnny, or did she just run off before I was done sweet talking her?"

He shrugged. "Perhaps she's not ready for a man who comes home soaked in other people's plasma. I suggest patience, young sir. The best things in life sometimes require a bit of a wait—and a lack of stupidity. Now if you'll excuse me, I must attend to Thaddeus."

He gave me a little smile and left the room.

I stood there thinking for a long couple of long seconds. Then I slipped out the door and headed home.

22 — UNDERGROUND GIRL REVENGE FORCE

I woke up to the sound of the phone ringing. It was Martina, who owned the employment agency that had placed me at Thad's house.

"Hi, Ron. I have some bad news—*tengo malas noticias*. You've been fired."

"What? Why? Was it the fish tank?"

"No, it was the way you served takeout Thai food. Tell me the truth, honey, were the Chiang Mai Noodles too spicy?"

I cursed myself for not asking Mags to order the Pad Ga Pow.

"Okay, Martina, thanks. It's been fun."

"That's okay, honey, any time. By the way, listen, is Magnolia okay? I haven't heard from her in a while."

"She's fine. I'll tell her you're looking for her."

"I'd appreciate that. Tell her I'd like to see her, okay? *Gracias*."

I hung up and reflected for a bit. Then I shrugged off my unemployment and headed down the street. I also shrugged off Martina's request. Mags was busy enough not fully responding to me; there was no need to get anyone else involved. As I walked along, my eyes got wide. Everywhere I looked, I saw Magno Girl.

The Daily News proclaimed "MAGNO GIRL SAVES THE DAY— RESCUES SUPERSTAN FROM CERTAIN DEATH."

The New York Post's headline read, "DON'T BE AFRAID, IT'S MAGNO GIRL. REALLY, SUPERSTAN, SHE'S OK." I bought all the papers and laughed at the thought of SuperStan's thermo-mousse meltdown.

I wondered what Magnolia's mother was thinking. She was probably hoping the fame would help her daughter attract a good man. I was hoping against it. Then I wondered what my own mom was thinking, since my name had been sloshed around in connection with Mags. My mom probably thought Mags would dump me, but I didn't care—after all, I knew I was the product of ten beers and a night of forgotten birth control. I hopped on my chopper and rode to the pizza factory where I was meeting Magnolia.

The factory was on Mulberry Street, near the Canal Street intersection, packed in among the tourists and the parking violations. The old building had been beautified to fit the slick style of modern Manhattan, and it looked like a stone-covered spaceship sitting between a Chinese grocery and a cold cut emporium.

Mags was standing in front of the place, looking great. Her skirt was black and clingy, and her shirt was a professional shade of va-va-voom vanilla. She was also wearing an auburn wig that hid her red and black hair.

I'd decided to take Johnny's advice and play it cool. After all, Mags and I were having great sex. I'd never needed to be patient before because I'd never been waiting for anything else. But this was different, and I didn't want to blow it. I found myself in a cold sweat, and I heard my dad's voice, telling me something about the way I'd burned a few dozen loaves of his ridiculous rye bread. I parked my bike and walked over to Magnolia.

She gave me a little smile. "Hi, Ron. I've got a plan. We're posing as job applicants."

I laughed and gave her a quick kiss. "Who's posing? I just got axed from the chef gig. If there's no fish tank in this place, I'm in."

She was about to make a remark when her phone rang. She looked at the display and shook her head. "Damn. It's my brother.

Ron, I'm going to take this and get it over with—just give me a minute." She turned away and put the phone to her ear.

The street was noisy with the squealing and honking sounds of traffic, so I could only hear one side of the conversation. But it was obvious her brother was one more thorny scrap of DNA in her life. I'll admit, I absolutely tried to hear as much as possible.

"Tommy, I told you to stop calling me... Yeah, thanks, I'm doing fine... I know you've helped me in the past, but things have changed... Yeah, I'm sure you'd still throw a meatball at Anton Karvosky, but I don't really eat lunch with him anymore... Grandma showed me those things because I was born with the power—and just because you weren't is no excuse for you to act like a jackass... Look, I have to go... No, don't come over... No, I don't want any bananas... Yes, I still like them but I'll get my own... I hope you work things out—goodbye."

She hung up, shaking her head like a dog shakes off a few fleas. Then she looked at me with a steely spark in her eyes.

"Let's get some fooki pies, Ron."

"Right."

We opened the door to the factory and walked into a silvery reception area occupied by a fat guard behind a blank white desk. He wore a badge that said "Jose." He held a box that said, "McDonalds." He shoved a chicken McNugget into his mouth and said, "Can I help you?"

Mags smiled. "Hi. We'd like to apply for a job."

"They're not hiring. They just got done with all that."

She started to say something else, but I jumped in and saved the day. "Jose, our car broke down! Someone robbed us at gunpoint! I've got the measles! My girlfriend is *pregnant!*"

Jose crinkled his forehead. "What?"

Mags gave me a sideways glance and looked away.

"Look, we're here from Ireland," I said. "We really need to check your vending machines. You might be all out of Twizzlers."

Jose swallowed another blob of crusty grease and handed me a clipboard. "All right, sign in. I hate running out of those things."

Mags glanced at me, then shrugged and signed a couple of phony names.

"Jose, can you tell us who we need to see?"

"Yeah, Mr. Nathan."

The inside of the factory looked more typical than the outside. Pipes and ducts were suspended from the high ceiling, while assembly lines filled the main floor. The newborn blobs of dough would come out of a machine at one end of the line before a short guy from another country would roll it and twirl it around. Then it would head on down the line, where people were slapping on the sauce and the seasoning and presumably the fooki.

Mags narrowed her eyes. "Okay, all we need to do is grab a few pies and get out of here."

Just then a guy saw us. He wore a white short sleeve shirt with a pocket protector, and a crew cut. He looked like a guy who spent lots of time removing dandruff from his glasses.

He pointed at us. "Hello, excuse me. Where do you think you're going?"

Mags gave him a tight smile. "Hello. We're here to…make pizza."

"Oh, you must be the new people—right, right. Well, please don't wander around. You should have reported to me right away. It's very important to report, do you hear me? Everyone must report. Did you punch in?"

"Yes."

"Okay, then come this way and I'll show you what to do. Did they tell you what to do? By the way, my name is Mr. Nathan. I'm the supervisor of the pizza line." He paused to wipe a flaky coating of dandruff from his glasses. "Follow me," he said, and we walked over to one of the assembly lines. "Okay, so which one of you is the sauce distributor?"

"I am," Mags said.

Nathan snorted and wiped a little spittle from his lips. For the first time he really looked her over. "Hey, you're not a foreigner. You're a very sexy girl. Why do you want to make pizza?"

"It seemed more interesting than my job at the atomic weapons factory."

He laughed with a hee-haw kind of sound. "Oh, it is, it really is. Atomic weapons, they've got no panties—I mean pizzazz— they've got no pizzazz. So, what's your name, honey?"

"Alice."

"Alice, why don't you step into my office? We need to go over a few things." Then he glared at me. "Stay here for a minute. Don't wander around. No one is supposed to wander around."

Mags followed him into a room behind the line. As soon as they closed the door, I ran over and opened it a crack.

Nathan said, "Why do you want to make pizza, honey?"

"I need the money. My mother is sick."

"Oh, yeah? You must be pretty desperate."

"Maybe I am. Is that a bad thing?"

He snickered a bit. "We just met, but I see some potential here. I could move you up the line. Get you a better rate."

"That would be nice. Why would you do that for me?"

He chortled like a chicken. "How sick is your mom? If you're willing to do a few extra things for me, I can do a few things for you. Right off, I could get you on the *vegetable detail*, which is better than being a sauce distributor. And then maybe I could fill up your nasty little produce bin with something special, huh? What are you doing tonight? Do you need some *extra training? Auuugh!*"

I opened the door, figuring Nathan had done something stupid—and there he was, on his knees, basking in the pink light from Magnolia's eyes. He wasn't enjoying it.

"Okay, I'm sorry!" he wailed. "I know I've behaved badly. I know it's wrong for me to force myself on all the hot, young employees. But I was so tired of women made from plastic, and styrofoam, and cheesecake!"

Obviously, this guy had issues.

Mags shook her head. "Did you know that approximately fifty-five percent of women and fifteen percent of men will experience some form of sexual harassment in the work place?"

"No! I didn't know!"

"And did you know that fifteen thousand cases of sexual harassment are brought before the Equal Employment Opportunity Commission each year?"

"Ugh! Wait a second! I didn't harass you yet. I never even touched you!"

"You were harassing me. And you would have done worse."

Mags stopped her gaze. She glared down at Mr. Nathan, who was breathing hard and shaking. When he finally regained his Attila-the-Geek composure, he looked up with hateful eyes.

He said, "Alice, you're fired!"

Mags laughed. "Mister Nathan, do I look like a pizza maker? I'm a special agent from, uh, the Underground Girl...Revenge Force. I was sent here because of repeated complaints against you. I've recorded this whole incident, and you're in serious trouble. Tell him, Ron."

I knew my cue, and I burst into the room, holding my cell phone high. I waved it in his face and said, "Nathan, it's all right here. I've also got a video, some color slides, and a pop-up book. You're in big trouble, pal."

Nathan looked like he'd been sodomized by a fire hydrant. He was in a sweat, and he gritted his teeth and clenched his bony fists.

"But I didn't do anything! I'm gonna get a lawyer."

"Yeah, why don't you do that?" Mags said. "I'm pretty sure the recording will show you're a criminal. Especially when we're done editing it."

"Are you saying you're gonna frame me?"

"In the name of justice, we'll do whatever is necessary."

"But that isn't fair!"

"I don't like you, so I don't need to be fair. Let's go, Ron."

"Wait, wait! Is there anything I can do?" He was whimpering now. "I don't want any trouble."

Mags and I looked at each other. "Okay, there are a few things," she said.

"Name them."

"First, you can apologize to all the women here."

"But I haven't harassed them all!"

"Yeah, but apologize to them all, anyway—just for being such an all around asshole."

"Okay, I'll do it."

"Do it in writing," Mags said. "I want you to pin a letter on the bulletin board out there telling them what a lowlife you've been. And tell them you're sorry."

"Okay."

"And then," I said, "get a sex change operation."

"*What?*"

Mags gave me a sideways glance. "That's a bit extreme, Ron—though it wouldn't be a bad idea for you to wear a Wonder Bra for a few weeks. Look, just write the letter and you'll be okay."

"I'll do it right now."

"Good. And hey, do you think we could have a few frozen pizzas?"

"Well, sure," he said. He removed his glasses and started wiping them on his shirt. "What kind would you like? We have seven different toppings, you know."

"Peppers and onions. With fooki."

"No problem."

We left Nathan to ponder his narrow escape, then grabbed the pies and waltzed out the door. I had to admit, I was hungry.

Out on the busy street, I smiled at Mags. "The Underground Girl Revenge Force? You never told me."

"I've never told you a lot of things—*ugh!*"

She dropped to her knees, holding her head in her hands. The Gaze was hitting her hard, and she started to stammer.

"I shouldn't have played with magic! I should stop hiding what I really am! I'm sorry, Grandma. I'm sorry!"

Several people on the sidewalk stared at her as they walked by, but no one even slowed down. After all, this was New York.

I knelt down and put my arm around her as she took deep breaths.

"Mags, are you okay?"

"Yeah, I'm fine. Thanks."

I coughed a few times. "So, what were we talking about?"

She stood up and sighed. "I don't remember, but let's forget about what I just said, okay?"

"Mags, I didn't hear a word."

She looked me over, like she was deciding what else to tell me. Then she pulled off her wig, releasing her black and red hair.

"Ron, I was about to say we should take the pizza to a lab and see what's going on."

"Good plan. Do you know someone who owns a lab?"

"No."

"I thought the good guys always know someone with a lab."

"I don't know anyone. Why don't you have a lab?"

"I once had a Great Dane."

"You owned a dog?"

"I didn't. I had a girlfriend from Denmark, and she could really fry the *frikadellers*."

Magnolia laughed. "Ron, you're a funny guy." Then she sighed and looked at me with her dazzling green eyes. "You're also a good guy. I'm sorry if I seem evasive sometimes. That's just the way I am. Give me some time."

My heart got light like a balloon. Obviously, I was on the right course, and I grinned big. "Don't worry about it, Mags. You're good, too."

"Thanks."

We stared at each other for a few seconds—but I stayed cool, restraining my urge to grab her right there on the street and suck her face like it was a sweet can of beer.

Finally, she said, "So, do you have any ideas concerning the fooki pie?"

I shrugged. "Yeah. I think I'll just eat the thing and see what happens."

"That's not very scientific. In fact, it's probably stupid."

"We can discuss it all day, but we both know I'm going to do it."

"I suppose it's inevitable."

"Let's get back to my place and fire up the oven."

23 — IT'S ALL ABOUT THE SHOPPING

I remembered telling Mags I'd ignore her forced confessions, so I tried to do that. But there was a lot of confessing going on, and it sounded like her past was filled with some spectacular shenanigans. I forced myself to grin. I was still the guy sleeping next to her, and I needed to let it go.

Mags flew back to her apartment. She said she'd come to my place in a half hour, so I threw one pizza in the oven. The other one went into the freezer, just in case we located a guy with a laboratory. I decided to take a shower, so I ripped off my clothes and headed for the bathroom. I was just getting into the shower when I heard a noise—someone else was in the apartment.

I clenched my fist. I'd left my clothes on the kitchen floor, and like most warriors, I didn't like fighting naked with my nuts hanging out. Luckily, I had a skin diving suit in the bathroom closet, so I pulled it on. I also grabbed a nearby harpoon gun and sneaked into the living room.

I peered around the corner and saw no one, but I heard a guy rummaging around in the kitchen. Instinctively, I knew he was after the fooki pie. I crept toward the doorway and saw a shadowy figure staring into my freezer. He was dressed in ninja-black and wore a ski mask. I looked at him, and he looked at me. Then he gave a shout and tossed a frozen fish at my head.

I dodged the flying tuna steak, then snarled and fired the harpoon gun. I missed and watched the harpoon sail into the fridge and puncture a half gallon of organic orange juice—damn! I hate running out of that stuff. The burglar cursed as the gushing liquid covered his feet, and then he reached into the fridge and pulled out a javelin. So that's where I'd left it! I didn't even think a javelin could fit in there.

He threw the ancient spear at me, and it struck me in the chest. It would have killed me, except the point was safely buried in the heart of a potato, creating an ineffective, tuber-tipped spear. That's the problem with pulling a javelin from a strange refrigerator. I laughed and reached for my daggers.

Damn—no daggers. All I had in my wetsuit was a can of shark repellent. The guy was charging at me, so I blasted him in the face.

He screamed as the goop splattered into his eyes. He tried to wipe it away, but I was too quick for him. I snatched a handful of arrows from the counter and stabbed him in the head. Unfortunately, the arrows were stuck inside a toaster, so he only got clobbered with my clunky kitchen appliance. Crumbs flew everywhere as he went down.

I hammered him a few more times as he screamed. Then I said, *"Who are you? Why are you after my fooki pie?"*

He snorted and snarled and tried to jam his thumbs into my eyes. He grimaced as I turned the toaster upside down, spilling a thousand burnt crumbs into his mouth and nose. He sputtered as I reached up and grabbed the microwave oven from the counter, slamming it down on his head and knocking him unconscious.

I gave a triumphant shout and then jumped up and grabbed some duct tape from the bathroom medicine cabinet. I put him in a chair and started taping him up just as Mags came flying through the window.

"Hey, what's going on?" she said. "Are you okay?"

"I'm fine. Some guy was burgling my freezer."

She stared with wide eyes at the taped, masked man. "Wow. Who do you think it is?"

I reached down and pulled off the ski mask—and saw another mask. It was Smashboy.

"Mmmmmf!" he said. Mags reached out and yanked the tape from his lips.

I scowled. "Smashboy, why were you in my freezer?"

Smashboy was fuming. "Let me out of here, you lunatic! I was just trying to help you. I know all about the fooki, and I think, um, you might be in over your head."

"How do you know about the fooki?" Mags said.

I snarled. "Let's cut him into pieces. Let's stuff his body into the garbage compactor."

"Don't be ridiculous," Mags said. "If we do that, he won't tell us anything. Besides, you don't have a garbage compactor. You don't even have a microwave any more."

She had a point. My microwave was seriously damaged from the effect of hitting Smashboy's brain. I noticed he was also trying to move his hands and reach his tool belt.

"Looking for this?" I held the belt in front of his eyes. Of course, I'd removed it. I wanted that fancy nose hair trimmer.

Smashboy frowned. "Okay, I'll admit I was trespassing, and I'm sorry. Can't we just forget the whole thing? From now on, I'll leave you alone. I'll even replace your microwave."

Mags shook her head. "I'm afraid it's not that simple."

"Right," I said. I wanted a toaster, too.

Magnolia crossed her arms and smiled. "Smashboy, you came in here looking for fooki, and you're going to get some fooki. Ron, I think the pizza is about done. Let's watch him eat it and see what happens."

Smashboy's eyes opened wide. "Hey, I'm not gonna be anyone's laboratory rat! That's cruel and unusual punishment!"

I grinned. "He's got a point, Mags. Forcing someone to eat pizza is not the usual thing. I say we just cut him up."

"No!" Smashboy slumped a bit. "I'll eat it."

Mags shrugged. "They wouldn't be selling something that instantly kills people. Most fast food doesn't cause death for quite a few years."

"So I've got to keep him here for years?"

"Ron, we're not trying to kill him."

"Oh."

"Just get the pizza."

"Right."

I took the pie out of the oven. I had to admit, it smelled pretty good.

Smashboy said, "Can you untie me so I can eat?"

Mags laughed. "No, Ron will just shove it down your throat, and you'll chew it or die."

He snarled like an angry cannon. "I can't believe you're doing this to a fellow superhero."

"I'm not a 'fellow'—I'm a woman. Now open wide."

I jammed a slice into his mouth. He started squealing as I gripped his forehead with my left hand and used the fork in my right to jackhammer it in there. When he started choking, I moved his jaw up and down and forced him to chew while still pushing the pie into his food pipe. He cursed and thrashed around, but I was merciless.

Finally, he was done. He stared at us with eyes like burning ovens.

"You two will pay for this!"

"Bill me," I said.

Mags said, "Give him another piece."

"*What?*" he said, and his eyes were wild. "Are you insane? I just ate before I came over here!"

I laughed, knowing it's a bad idea to burgle on a full stomach. Then I repeated the procedure with another slice, and this time he really struggled. In fact, I had to use a big wooden spoon to pound that wad of dough into his squirming throat. When he started to resist, I crushed his nostrils shut and threatened him with cheesy suffocation. I grinned as he swallowed it all.

"Okay," Mags said, "I'm thinking that two pieces should be enough. Now, we wait."

Smashboy glared at Mags with white-hot hatred. "I'm gonna

ruin you, honey! You're dead meat! I'm gonna destroy your pretty little ass!"

Mags ignored him. I snarled and said, "Keep your eyes away from her ass—let's give him the rest of the pie. Let's stuff him until he bursts."

"No, let's see what happens. So, Smashboy, how do you feel?"

Right on cue, Smashboy's eyes started to develop a greenish tint. He took a few deep breaths and said, "I want to go to the sporting goods store."

Mags looked surprised. "What?"

"I need new golf clubs. A set of irons!"

Mags raised an eyebrow and looked at me. "Ron, what do you think?"

"I think he'll get more power and accuracy with better irons."

Smashboy smirked. "I'm gonna break these bonds. I'm going to humiliate you, Magno Girl. Then I'll buy a dining room set made from cherry oak!"

"This is weird," Mags said.

I nodded. "Yeah. I don't think there's any such thing as cherry oak."

Mags eyed him with curiosity. "Smashboy, do you feel sick?"

"No. I can't wait to get to the mall. Gimme another slice—just cram it into my face."

I would have been happy to oblige, but Mags stopped me. She said, "The fooki makes people want to shop."

Smashboy grimaced. Then he shouted, "I'm a hero of law enforcement and I deserve a new credenza!"

He started struggling to break free—grunting and howling and heaving. He said, *"Auuuuuugh! I will...break...free!"* And then his effort collapsed. My duct tape artistry was the stuff of legends.

He whispered, "It's only a matter of time. No chains can hold me. I'll break free and head over to Macy's."

Mags looked thoughtful. "We should get the other pie analyzed."

"What do we do with Smashboy? Hey, let's rip off his mask."

Smashboy's eyes exploded with panic. But Mags said, "No."

"Why not?" I asked.

"It's not honorable to unmask a superhero," she said. "Besides, why should we be so mean? It's not necessary."

"But I almost choked him to death."

"Yeah, but that was necessary."

"Mags, he tried to steal my pizza. He ruined a half gallon of organic orange juice."

"Forget it. I think I'll just dump him off in front of the police station. They'll probably cut the tape and invite him in for coffee."

Smashboy's plastic eyebrows shot upward. *"Wait! You can't do that!* Someone will see me all tied up and I could lose my endorsement deals."

Mags laughed. "Okay, you can keep your shameless commercials, Smashboy—but there's one more thing I have to do." Her eyes turned a withering shade of pink as she blasted Smashboy with the Gaze of the Guilt.

Smashboy screamed, "Auuugh!" and rolled off his chair. He hit the ground hard and tried to turn away from the brain-crawling light—but it was no use, and he started to smash-babble.

"I kicked a ball out of the rough! I didn't pay for my hotdog on the 8th hole. I groped my caddy's hot girlfriend!"

Mags took a few steps forward and kept the pink rays shining on his face. "How do you know about the fooki? Why were you stealing the fooki pies?"

"I owed a favor! I didn't kill anyone! Those microwave ovens are crap!"

I grinned. "Hey, Mags, that reminds me, I need a new microwave. Let's go to Americamart."

She looked at me for an instant—and that's when Smashboy broke loose. I don't know how he escaped, but he was suddenly leaping to his feet. He shouted and raised his arms high, displaying the broken shards of his former bondage. He also snatched a chair and hurled it at Mags.

She dodged it, and it crashed against the stove. He did better with the coffee maker—it hit her in the head and she went down.

Smashboy screamed, "You fucking bitch! I'll get you! Believe me, you will regret what you've done here today!"

He snarled and looked at me with raised hands. I snarled back at him and prepared to attack—but in one graceful movement he leaped out the window. I jumped forward and stuck my head outside, watching his descent to the street below. He had some sort of special wings that popped from his suit and allowed him to float to the ground rather than fall. He glared up at me and shook his fist. He shouted, "That evil bitch will pay! And so will you!"

I watched him run off, figuring he was headed to the nearest department store. I considered pursuit but then turned back toward Magnolia.

She was standing again, and I ran to her.

"Are you okay, Mags?"

"Yeah, I'm fine. I guess my head is harder than the average coffee maker."

"I can't believe he escaped those bonds."

"Hey, he is a superhero—did he call me 'evil'?"

"Yeah, 'evil bitch.' "

"I was just doing my job."

"That's right. And it happened to include torturing him with a potentially dangerous narcotic and then interrogating him with a powerful mind-groping technique. Don't worry, honey—it was beautiful."

She frowned. "Hm, maybe I was a little cruel."

"Sometimes justice needs to be cruel."

"Ha, I'm not so sure. But you know what? The 'fooki effect' makes perfect sense." She smiled. "Thaddeus Stone owns Americamart, one of the biggest chains of discount stores in the country. If he creates an addictive drug that makes people want to shop, he stands to benefit in a huge way. So Melvin Shrick gets people addicted to his pizza, and Thaddeus gets people running to his stores. It's quite a scheme."

"Yeah, but how does Thaddeus get people running to *his*

stores? I mean, look at Smashboy—Americamart doesn't even sell credenzas."

"That's a good point." She scratched her head. "And who did Smashboy 'not kill'? Joey the Round Man? Or someone else? And who does he owe a favor to? And what's the story with the microwave ovens? There's a lot we don't know. Anyway, I called a guy over at Columbia University who said he can analyze the pie. He needs a little time, though, to perform complete tests. I'll drop a pie off tomorrow and—"

She stopped talking and suddenly looked pale. I knew the delayed effect of the Gaze was about to hit her.

"Mags, are you okay?"

Her eyes flashed like fire as she grabbed my shirt and pulled me close.

"Don't listen!" she hissed. She ran into the bathroom, locked the door, and turned on the water.

I wanted to know what she was confessing in there, but I didn't listen. My heart went out to her, and I wished I could help. When she emerged from the bathroom, looking a little beat-up, I just smiled.

"What are you doing tonight, Mags? I need a new microwave."

She gave a short laugh. "Let's go shopping."

24 — AMERICAMART

That night Mags and I went to Americamart.

Pepe and Jenni met us in front of the chain's glowing new superstore in Greenwich Village. The place was right on Broadway, sitting like a fat aneurysm on a major artery of the city. Pepe grinned and let his ponytail writhe in the hot summer breeze. Jenni stroked his snaky tail and smiled while the cars and people roared past.

The kids nodded their heads at me. Mags put her arm around Jenni, and we walked into a crowded labyrinth of overflowing aisles. Merchandise hung from the ceiling, the walls, and sprouted from the floor. Everywhere I looked, big-assed people jousted for junk on a grabby battlefield where they snatched up the stuff on sale—and it was all on sale. Dishes, towels, cereal, lawn chairs, school supplies, candy, motor oil—everything but exercise equipment. No, wait! They had that, too.

Jenni's jaw dropped. "Is there anything this place doesn't sell?"

Mags gave a short laugh. "Dignity, self-respect—wow! What a deal on paper towels!" She grabbed a few rolls.

Jenni laughed. "Magnolia is an idealist."

"Yeah," Mags said. "Unless I need to clean the kitchen counter."

"Look!" I said. "We found it!"

We'd reached the Great Wall of Microwaves. We stopped and stared.

It was high, and it was wide. Each machine was like an oven-shaped brick in a mammoth, microwave fortress. There was also a Pakistani guy unloading boxes. His nametag said, "Asad," and he wore the apron all Americamart employees wore. It was a greedy shade of green and had blue letters stamped across the back that said, "WE HAVE MORE! JUST ASK!"

I pointed at one cheap model. "Hey, Asad, is this a good one?"

"No. That one I would not buy."

"Oh, yeah? Why not?"

"That model will be on sale soon."

"Really?"

"Yes. The hugest of microwave sales is coming. It will be the biggest sale ever."

"Hey, maybe I'll wait. Thanks for telling me."

"You are welcome. They give me no commissions here."

I pulled Mags aside. "Maybe this is the one Smashboy mentioned. No wonder he sounded so guilty. These are the microwaves we keep hearing about."

"Yeah, you're right," she said in a low voice. "And I keep wondering, has Smashboy learned more about the plot than us, or is he part of it?"

We walked out of the store without incident. As we burst into the warm wave of evening air, I felt like an escapee from some glittering temple of ass-crack consumerism. We ended up in a nearby place called Hope's House of Coffee.

25 — BLACK COFFEE

Mags didn't drink coffee. She preferred green tea, and I wondered if she knew anyone in need of 5,000 teapots. At the front counter, I got some coffee that was blacker than engine grease. I made my way through the gulping crowd to a tiny red table near a window that viewed the neon street. As I put down the steaming cups, I heard them all talking about Karina.

Pepe shook his head. "All she does is worry about her lips, and talk about how she's got no boyfriend."

"Yeah, she used to be smart," Jenni said. "Now she's just an idiot searching for cosmetic surgery."

Mags swore softly. "It's the Curse of the Modern Blank Girl. She's starting to think it's cool to be stupid. We've got to break it somehow."

"We better hurry," Pepe said. "Her brain is turning into a pile of designer horseshit... Hey, Ron, this coffee looks like mud."

"It's strong. It'll make a warrior out of you."

Mags winced. "It'll keep you awake for three straight days."

"That's good," I said. "It's easier to fight when you're awake. I learned that the hard way."

"My whole family loves coffee," Jenni said. "Even my mom. She used to drink tons of it when I was little."

"How's your mom doing?" Mags asked.

"She came by last week, looking for money. Same old shit. There was a big fight and it was pretty typical."

"Did they fight about you?"

"Not really. She doesn't give a crap about me. My uncle threatened to call the cops."

The cops had dealt with Jenni's family before. From what I understood, Daddy had a six-by-nine suite on Riker's Island. Of course, he'd be back in five years or so to resume being a complete asshole.

"It's not your fault, honey," Mags said. "It's hard to help someone who doesn't want help."

"Yeah, I know. I don't really care what they do, because I'm not going back there. Hey, they have good cake here."

I knew Jenni didn't care about the cake. I also realized my own parental complaints were trivial—after all, continuous ridicule and a lack of faith in one's son is small stuff compared to a complete lack of love and a heroin habit. I made a mental note to visit my dad's grave and remove my spit.

I got myself another cup of coffee and a piece of chocolate raspberry cake for Jenni.

Pepe looked into his cup with far away eyes. "I kinda like this stuff. I never had coffee when I was little. My mom didn't drink it. I'll bet my dad did, though. In movies, army guys are always drinking coffee."

Pepe had been born while his dad was in the army getting himself killed. I forget which war, but it had been a popular one at the time. Pepe shrugged and took another sip.

I thought about my own father's death and gritted my teeth. There was no point in letting my memory coddle that deranged bastard of a baker. Unlike Pepe's dad, my father had deserved every bullet. I cancelled my trip to the cemetery.

Mags said, "If you need anything, just say so."

Pepe and Jenni gave Mags a warm look. "You're great, Magnolia. If *you* need anything, just say so."

They both nodded and we headed out.

26 — INSIDE THE DEATHMOBILE

I woke up a happy man, thanks to a buyer for a national book chain who'd jumped at a truckload of cheap thesauruses. Few people question a good deal, even when it's too good. Plus, when I told Al the great news, he told me about 40,000 bags of chopped walnuts he'd scored—high in vitamin E and a quick sell. Every restaurant needs a few more nuts.

So I was grinning and walking north up 1st Avenue—and that's when a long, black limousine drove past me, lumbering like a funeral procession. As it pulled over to the curb, I jumped into a state of alert, waiting for the evil to start. Right on cue, a guy stepped from behind some trash and graffiti.

I blinked. It was Subterranean Bob.

He squinted his eyes in my direction. "Hello there. Do you remember me?"

He was trying to look tough, but he mostly looked like a geek in need of stronger eyeglasses.

"Yeah, sure, Bob. What do you want?"

"I have a proposition. Will you please step into the car? We'd like to have a conversation with you—yes, yes."

I glanced at the hearse-mobile and laughed. Did they really think I'd be dumb enough to fall for the ominous "car by the curb" routine? As the door of the car opened, I saw the fleshy mound of Thaddeus Stone sitting inside.

I started to think fast. Thaddeus was fat and slow, and Bob was puny and ridiculous, and I might be able to collect some great information for Mags. Also, a car like this probably contained a fully stocked bar. I smiled and recalled the many "car escapes" I'd learned in a class titled *After You're Dumb Enough To Enter The Deathmobile*. I slid into the back seat.

The car was cavernous and the leather was cushy. Thaddeus was sitting opposite me, behind a table. Then my eyes popped like a couple of pistols—sitting next to him was the blond woman I'd seen three times before.

Thaddeus was drinking scotch and eating a steak, and his pile of chins jiggled with every bite.

"Hello, Ronald," he said, and then nodded in the direction of the woman. "Please don't be distracted by my associate. We're just giving her a ride."

I finally took a good look at her. She was slim, blond, and pretty in a way that radiated no warmth. When she looked at me with her ice-pick eyes, I had the brief sensation of a bug crawling around inside my head. I shuddered and snarled at her.

"You were there the night Joey died," I said. "Something tells me you weren't just picking up a calzone."

"You're probably right," she said. "I would've had it delivered."

"What were you doing there? And what were you doing at the Waffle Empire the day Magno Girl battled with The Beef?"

She smiled like a thin blade. "You must have seen someone else. I was at home with my children."

Meanwhile, Bob slithered into the car and the door closed. I noticed the driver of the car was Terrence, the friendly guy I'd met the first day I'd visited Thad's mansion. The limo started to move.

"Where are we going?" I said.

"That's not important," Thaddeus replied. "All that matters is that we keep moving—after all, most of New York is a tow away zone."

I knew he was right. "Okay, then what do you want?"

Thaddeus put down his fork and pulled a pad from his jacket. "I've been doing some research on your meddlesome girlfriend.

According to my notes she's a reckless, impulsive person who often carries ridiculous weapons, leading to absurd antics and embarrassing incidents."

I paused. "Are we talking about Magnolia? Because I only have one girlfriend."

Thaddeus glanced again at his scribble. "Ha, wait… I'm sorry—these notes are about *you!* Let me see what I have about her. Oh, yes, here are the correct notes. She tries to act like an idealist who won't sell out. She believes that as a superhero she must remain true to her beliefs and help humanity." He laughed and slapped his hand on his knee. "Forgive me—too funny. Anyway, I understand you're her manager, or at least someone she will listen to."

I smiled. Mags listen? I figured he didn't need to know the truth. "Sure, sure—of course," I said. Then I reached across the table to the bar and grinned at blondie as I poured myself a nice-sized jigger of Jack.

Thaddeus smiled. "Very good. I would like her to do some advertisements for me. The ads will be tasteful. They'll feature her curvaceous silhouette, dressed in skin-tight clothing, transposed above a montage of stylish images. She will not need to speak, but she'll have to smile and bite into a piece of pizza. She'll be required to chew it with enthusiasm and show a touch of cleavage—exactly how much will be specified in the contract, but it won't be more than a few inches. For this small effort I'll pay her a fee of one million dollars."

I almost dropped my whiskey.

He continued, "Of course, if she's doing advertisements for my pizza, she'll also need to stop interfering in my affairs. In other words, *leave Pie Hole Pizza and Americamart alone* and forget about all investigations and crimes pertaining to them."

I swallowed my booze and imagined all the stuff that could be bought with that cash. I also figured that Mags wouldn't do it.

"Okay, I'll talk to her."

Thaddeus nodded, and I watched his chins flap around. "Good. See if you can force a little sense into that pretty little head of hers. As an added incentive, if she agrees to do it, I will pay you a 'personal service bonus' of two hundred thousand dollars. And she doesn't need to know about it—noncommissioned cash for you."

"What?" I said with a scowl. "You mean take a bribe behind her back? We don't work that way, fat man. She trusts me, and I trust her."

He laughed. "Of course—trust. And what will that trust be worth when she's bored with you? She is serious, and she is intelligent. And you? I've been in your place, young man— believe me, 'trust' will disappear like so much cheesecake, but a good investment portfolio will last forever."

The blond woman smirked at this remark and nodded her head.

I laughed. "Yeah, well, I think the cheesecake lasts a little longer in my house than it does in yours."

"No matter!" he roared and pointed a tubby finger at me. "We will be in touch with you, and if you're wise you'll get her to accept. Keep in mind this is not my only option to alter the situation in my favor." Then he looked at the blonde, and she looked at me. Once again I had a sickening feeling inside my head—like a set of fingers was groping through my medulla oblongata. She smiled and said nothing.

I leaned forward and stared into the icebox of her eyes. "Who are you?"

She stared back at me. "I can be a friend. I can help Magnolia be the best woman she can be. Or I can make her suffer and regret her bad choices. Take the money, fool."

I growled and almost reached for her throat—but Thaddeus held up his hand.

"Don't be an idiot your whole life, Ronald. There's a time to fight, and there's a time to get paid. And getting paid is always better."

The car slammed to a stop, and the door swung open. I looked at the woman one last time and stepped out.

27 — CASH

A little later I walked through the muggy night air to Magnolia's apartment. My head was filled with a hurricane of thoughts. As I got near her building, my eyes zeroed in on more trouble.

Sitting out front was a Harley Softail Slim. It was illegally parked, but that's the best way to park that kind of bike. I gritted my teeth as my *softail savvy* kicked in—a special sense I'd developed over the years to tell me when a fellow biker was messing with my babe. My temper sparked fast.

I burst into a sweat and raced up the steps to the third floor. My fist was poised to pound on the door, but then I froze; I heard a guy talking inside. I moved my ear close to the door but couldn't make out any words. The voice didn't sound threatening, but I was still ready to bust in and make a few threats. Suddenly, the door swung open, and Mags was standing there, looking like a cool, beautiful flower in the slick summer heat.

"Hi, Ron. My brother Tommy is here, but he was just leaving."

I walked into her cramped kitchen and saw a sturdy-looking guy who obviously didn't own a hairbrush. So this was Magnolia's brother. He looked like a derelict. He looked a lot like me.

He seemed vaguely familiar, but I couldn't place the face. I guess all of us derelicts look alike. He gave me a once over and nodded his head, and we shook hands. I suppose I wanted to make a good impression, and I guess I did. I wasn't sure if that was such a great thing.

Tommy turned back toward his sister. "If *you* needed help, Maggie, I would help you."

"If I ever need help betting on the wrong team, I'll call you."

"Hey, not all my bets are bad. I'm just going through a rough stretch. I've had some tough breaks, a couple of bad bounces, a few guys busted for steroids and domestic violence... It's not like I'm not trying. Anyway, I'm looking for a new gig."

"Yeah, you're looking for more things you can steal. I'm done enabling you, Tommy."

"What are you talking about? I just need to make a couple of payments, that's all. Maggie, if you don't help me out, I'm gonna have to go to Mexico!"

"*Adios, mi hermano.*"

"What? I have no idea what that means—and that's exactly why I can't go down there, see? I don't know how to say shit."

"I think *mierda* is the word you're looking for, but I could be wrong. *Yo no hablo espanol muy bien.*"

"Stop talking to me in Mexican! I've been trying to help you more than you know. And didn't I just bring you bananas?"

He pointed to a bunch of bananas on the kitchen counter. They did look fresh.

Magnolia's green eyes flashed with anger. "This isn't about fruit, Tommy—and it's not about money, either. It's about how you never change and you never learn. You're a criminal and I'm a crime fighter and it's just not working."

Tommy's eyebrows shot upward. "We can make it work! Just give me a little cash and I'll figure something out."

"There's nothing to figure out. Quit gambling and stealing."

"Okay—done."

"Congratulations. I have no money."

He glanced at me and then leaned toward Mags, lowering his voice. "Can we talk in the other room?"

"No."

"Okay—fine," he said, shaking his head. "Why can't you teach me some of that stuff Grandma taught you?"

Mags rolled her eyes. "How many times do I have to say this? It won't work for you. And I don't use that stuff."

"Come on, we both know that's bullshit. I've seen you use it lots of times. Remember what you did to Stacy Scunata?"

"I was a kid. We were kids. I made it up to her later."

"Yeah, but you still did it. It took months for her hair to grow back. You still know it and you still use it. You've always used it."

"*Tommy, I don't!* Look, call me if you want help getting *real* help. Otherwise, get out!"

They glowered at each other, and I didn't say a thing. I knew better than to get involved in a family quarrel. Tommy gave her a final glare and snatched the bananas from the counter. He stormed out the door and Mags watched him clomp down the stairs. When he got to the bottom, he turned back around.

"Call me if you need anything, Maggie. Because I'd be there for YOU!"

She just shook her head as the door slammed behind him. Then the door swung open, and he was there again. He puffed out his chest and laid the bananas on the bottom step.

"Guess what? I'm such a great guy I'm still giving you the fucking bananas!"

He slammed the door for a final time and disappeared.

There was silence.

"Are you okay?" I said.

She shrugged. "I'm fine, Ron. Don't pay attention to anything he was saying. I'm glad you're here."

"Do you want me to go down there and get the fucking bananas?"

"Sure. I love fucking bananas. I mean—you know what I mean."

I knew, so I ran down and snatched the fruit. Then I came back into the kitchen and gave her a kiss.

"So, that's your brother."

"Yeah. I didn't pick him out."

"I can see he's giving you some trouble."

She blinked back a few tears. "We were close when we were young. He always stuck up for me, before I started doing it myself. In fact, he's the one who got me into martial arts, and it was a great thing for me at the time. That stuff he was saying about my grandmother—he's just mad because he doesn't have super-powers, that's all. I'd rather not go into it."

"Hey, I understand. I have a brother, too."

"Yeah, I know. Let's not talk about either of them."

I nodded my head. "Good idea." I decided to follow the general principle of not asking too many questions, and thereby avoid having to answer any in return.

I smiled. "So, Mags, what's new?"

I watched her chest heave under her tight pink T-shirt. She walked over to the fridge and pulled out a frosty bottle of Guinness. She handed it to me, along with a bottle opener, and gave me a little shrug. "I signed up a few new students. Maybe you're right about all this publicity. Maybe I'll make some extra payments on my credit card balances."

I was thrilled. I felt the atmosphere in the room lift a bit, so I took a swig of beer and said what was really on my mind.

"Mags, that's great news. Now tell me, *do you think you'll ever get bored with me?*"

"What?"

"You're serious. You're intelligent. You've probably never broken a fish tank in your life, and Thaddeus wants to give you a million dollars."

She cocked her head and stared.

"Ron, is there something I should know about?"

I proceeded to tell her about my meeting with Thaddeus. I told her everything, including the appearance of the evil blonde, and Thad's idea of a "bonus fee" for me.

"So, what do you think?" I said.

"About what? You know I won't take any money from him."

"I'm not talking about the money." I was practically jumping up and down. "Are you too smart for me? Will you get sick of my ridiculous antics and embarrassing incidents?"

"Ron, why do we need to discuss this?" She threw up her hands. "I'm never bored with you. We have a lot in common."

"Oh, yeah? Like what?"

"Lots of things."

"Name one."

"I don't know! We both like Thai food."

"So it's all about Pad Wan Sen?"

"No! We both like to work out."

"Pad Wan Sen and a few sets of heavy squats?"

"Look, we both love martial arts."

"Advanced eye gouges? The mutual ability to decimate an eyeball?"

"No!" She sighed. "The sex is good."

"I knew it!"

"What?"

"It's all about the sex."

"It's not."

"So the sex is no good!"

"I just told you it was good."

"But not great?"

She paused, staring at the ceiling with exasperation. "The sex is great, Ron. It's the best ever. My head explodes in an atomic fireball every time we do it, okay?"

"A *big* atomic fireball?"

"Ron, it's not about the sex!"

"Okay, I hear you. Then what is it?"

She looked at me with soft eyes. "Maybe I'm just attracted to a ruggedly handsome biker warrior with a good heart. I mean, it's possible."

That seemed to make sense. "All right."

"Okay. I'm glad that's settled."

"So am I."

"Right."

"Good."

"So what about the money?"

She rolled her eyes and laughed. "I told you—no way."

"Mags, I know how you feel, but think for a second. Think about a new dojo, a nice apartment, no more worries about your mother's bills. You can still fight crime—just not *this* crime."

"Ron, not only would I be accepting a bribe, but I would actually be *endorsing* his crime. Now what kind of superhero would I be if I did that?"

"Typical, honey—typical."

"I'm not typical. And neither are you."

I laughed and shook my head. "I'm not so sure about me—but okay, let's forget about it for now. I'm still worried about this blond woman. There's something seriously bad about her."

"Yeah, we definitely need more information about our mysterious blond nemesis. Now that we know she works with Thaddeus, it should be a lot easier. Maybe Jonathan can give us some information about her."

"Hey, good thinking. But maybe we shouldn't mess with her. You know, maybe we should just take the money until we figure out a better plan."

"I see. And then maybe we should keep it, right?"

"Yes."

She shook her head. "No."

I made a decision and reached into my back pocket, pulling out an envelope.

"Mags, since you're too damned principled to take money from our sworn enemies, I want you to have this—for your expenses, for the school, for your mom, whatever."

She looked at me, and she looked at the envelope.

"Where did you get this money?"

"I've had it stashed for a while," I said, looking away. "I used to work as a mechanic, remember? I've changed a lot of brake pads."

Mags narrowed her eyes. "I appreciate your offer, and I'm glad a few less people will be skidding around out there—but I can't take it."

"Why not? Are you accusing me of selling hijacked thesauruses or something?"

"What? Of course not. I don't want any money from you, that's all. I can take care of myself."

I shook my head. "I know you can, but I want to help you. It's something friends do for each other. It doesn't mean you owe me anything."

She leaned in close and touched the side of my neck. Then she took the envelope from my hand—and shoved it into the waistband in the front of my Levis.

"I appreciate your friendship," she said. "If I need help, you'll be the first one I come to, okay? But in the meantime, don't do anything stupid."

I shrugged and looked away in defeat. I knew my limitations in this area and didn't feel like arguing.

Her cell phone rang and she glanced at it. "Hey, it's from Jonathan! Hi, Jonathan, I was just talking about you. I wanted to ask you about something—right. Okay. I'll talk to you later. Thanks."

She hung up. "Guess what? Melvin Shrick is at Thad's house, and they went upstairs to the study. Turn on the listening device and maybe we'll hear something valuable."

She was excited and that excited me, so we turned to the kitchen counter, where I'd set up the radio set. I switched it on and we heard the calculated voice of Melvin Shrick and the slobbering rumble of Thaddeus Stone.

28 — TWENTY MILLION MICROWAVES

"We're going to start earlier than expected," Melvin said. "We'll try and head off all this unwanted interference. The ad campaign starts tomorrow. Are you sure the formula is working?"

"Yes, it's been thoroughly tested," Thaddeus said. "The narcotic effect is strong. As soon as we've distributed enough fooki, we'll start the second phase. I don't anticipate a lot of lag time."

"Let's not get ahead of ourselves. The Distribution Phase has to be right before we go to Phase II. I understand the music is perfect. Is the test item still the same?"

"Yes. I've just received twenty million microwave ovens from China."

"Great. America will be drowning in microwaves, and we'll be drowning in cash."

They laughed long and hard.

"And then we'll assume complete control."

More evil laughter—longer and harder.

"What about the situation with our last pizza maker? Are the cops getting any closer?"

"No, they're inept—a great wad of tax money squandered on blue suits."

"And how about Magno Girl? She's been to my factory. She interrogated a pervert there, and she knows about the fooki."

"All true, but I've made her an offer. Maybe she will accept."

"And if she doesn't?"

"If she doesn't, she is finished. I've learned some useful secrets about her. If she refuses to cooperate, she will be destroyed by her *ultimate fear.*"

The suggestion was ominous, and the evil laughter was deafening. I recalled a day in grammar school, during physical education class, when for some inexplicable reason our teacher, Mr. Kadowski, had insisted we learn square dancing. I was a clueless kid who could not *do-si-do*. When it was my turn to *promenade* I would cause the whole line to crash into the corn pone.

Mags said, "Ron, what do you think?"

"Everyone laughed at me. I was in the corn pone."

"Look, forget about the corn and adjust the signal. We're losing it."

I turned a few knobs, and we heard Thaddeus say, "...but Sandra is far stronger and far more sinister than Harry. I should know—I'm the one paying her alimony. I almost feel sorry for Magno Girl. If she's smart, she'll take my offer. If not, she will meet a painful and humiliating fate."

They had a few more evil laughs and ended the meeting.

Mags looked at me. "They're going to try and use the fooki to sell microwave ovens. They must be developing a way to target specific products. I'll bet that's 'Phase II.' The big sale at Americamart is part of the plot."

I snarled. "Mags, these guys want to hurt you."

She shrugged. "I'm a crime fighter. It goes with the territory."

"That might be so," I said with a sneer, "but if that pompous pile of plutocracy touches you, he's dead. No frying pans, no giant hotdogs, and no techniques involving tropical fruit. I'll scoop out his eyes with a spoon and stuff them down his throat."

Magnolia's eyebrows jumped. "Ron, I've never heard you sound so serious about graphic violence."

"There's a time to be serious, Mags—and I'd carve out a guy's liver for you any day. With my teeth."

She glanced away. "Thank you. That's, uh, very sweet."

"Would you do the same for me?"

"Ron, you know I don't eat liver." Then she stared into my eyes. "I would do it. I really would."

I was overcome with emotion. I leaped on top of her like a man bungee jumping from a bridge, and I started tearing off articles of clothing.

"*Ron, wait!* Hang on a second—what are you doing? We have a lot to do."

"Yeah, but before we start all that stuff I want to do this."

"Ron, we have to think about the things we've just heard!"

"We can do it later," I said as I pulled off her jeans and buried myself between her thighs.

She rolled back her head and looked at the ceiling. "Okay, okay—but when we're done with all the smoking hot sex, one of us has to find out about 'Sandra' and Thad's ex-wife."

"Right. That will probably be you."

"I suppose so."

29 — IN THE MIDDLE OF THE NIGHT

"We had a good moment, Ron. Don't ruin it with more of your insecurities."

"I'm insecure, Mags? You're the one who's afraid of commitment."

"I'm not afraid. I just don't like it."

"You don't like it because it scares you."

"It doesn't scare me. That's a bullshit cliché, and I told you I might not be relationship material."

"No, you didn't. You said you weren't good at relationships."

"Isn't that the same thing?"

"No. You can suck at something and still want it."

"Look, maybe I suck *and* I don't want it."

"Maybe you don't know what you want."

"Maybe you're not paying very close attention! Or maybe I don't want exactly what you want *right now!* Maybe you should be more patient and not screw everything up."

"Are you kidding me? I thought I was being patient."

"No. Not really."

"Damn! So you think we have a good thing?"

"Ron, go to sleep. Please."

30 — MORE FOR ME DOT COM

I woke up early, before the morning sun started shoving its sunshine into the night sky. I noticed Mags was gone, and I guessed she was over at her dojo, so I did 700 squats and puked until it felt good. I ate a fat scrambled egg sandwich and turned on the television.

The first thing I saw was a commercial for Melvin Shrick's Pie Hole Pizza chain. Melvin was advertising something called the "More For Me" pizza.

The commercial started with a throbbing bass riff. A smash-mouth guitar joined in as images flickered across the screen—sporty cars, city skylines, and airbrushed young models sucking down gooey hot pizza. There was no dialogue, only the pounding rhythm and that single riff. And then words flashed onto a black screen: MORE FOR ME, followed by more blackness, followed by more words: AT PIE HOLE. Finally, there was another black screen before the final text flashed: MORE-FOR-ME-PIZZA.COM.

I ran down to the street, where exhaust fumes were already starting to circulate and the stink of garbage hung in the air. I jumped into the honking blitzkrieg of cars and busses and then trotted over to the dojo with a big box in my arms. I found Mags there along with Karina.

"What's happening, girls?" I said with a grin. "Karina, shouldn't you be in school?"

Karina smiled at me. "I am in school. This is a school, right?"

"Yeah, but Mags only teaches you how to survive in a world of violence. Those other schools teach useful stuff, like multivariable calculus."

Mags cocked her head and looked at me. "Hi, Ron. Karina stopped here on her way to school. A better question would be why are you here so early?"

I puffed out my chest. "I saw a commercial for Pie Hole's new pizza. I also brought you 25 bags of chopped walnuts."

Mags gave a grim nod of her head. "I know about the pizza. They started selling it last night, and I'm guessing the shopping malls will be packed by noon."

I smiled. "Can you imagine? A pizza that makes people want to buy stuff. It's even better than a religious holiday. By the way, is this pizza even illegal?"

"I don't know. It's probably less dangerous than tobacco."

"What's wrong with Pie Hole Pizza?" Karina asked. "I was thinking about applying for a job there."

Mags narrowed her eyes. "Pie Hole is a bad place. Don't do it."

"But I need to make some money," Karina said with a shrug. "Because, you know, I really need to get breast implants."

Mags almost leaped from her chair. "Karina, don't be ridiculous! You do not need breast implants."

"Ha! That's easy for you to say—you have a boyfriend. But me, I'm a loser. I'm all alone with my tiny lips, and my 'A' cups."

"You need to think about what you're saying."

"Please don't tell me about what I'm saying! How could you understand? You're totally gorgeous and every guy wants you. Be honest—when you were in school, every guy thought you were hot."

Mags rolled her eyes but said nothing.

"So it's true, right?" Karina said.

Mags sighed. "Sure, there were guys interested in me, but there were others who felt intimidated—because I could fly, and I could beat the crap out of them. It was complicated."

"But you had a lot of boyfriends, right?"

"I had a lot of issues, Karina, and I had other things to think about. My dad left my mom, and then he died, and then my grandmother committed suicide—and it just seemed like everyone I cared about was disappearing. So, yeah, I got involved with some guys, but I never got too close to anyone, at least not in an *emotional* sense. I made a lot of mistakes, okay? But you do not need surgery. You're very pretty, and even if you weren't, there's more to life than that, believe me. A lot more."

Karina was quiet. "Okay, maybe you're right. After all, I am cursed."

"Exactly, Karina! And you've got to think your way out of it. I only wish I'd learned more from my grandmother before she died. Damn."

"Learned more about what?"

Mags just shook her head. "You don't need to look like the cover of a men's magazine to be attractive—or a women's magazine, either."

Karina gritted her teeth. "Okay, I'll try to think. But I still might need liposuction on my inner thighs. Maybe someday I'll meet somebody cool like Ron."

I laughed. "You hear that, Mags? Someone likes me."

"Did I say anything bad about you?"

"No, and you better not. I have a Harley, and I have all these walnuts."

Karina laughed. "I better go to school now."

"Come back later. I'll be around."

"Thanks, I'll come back. So long, Ron."

Karina left, and I just stared at Magnolia. I wanted to wrap my arms around her, and hold her tight against my pounding heart, but I didn't. Finally, I said, "Mags, what are we going to do about the pizza?"

"What?"

She was looking off into space.

"The pizza, remember? The pizza, Thaddeus, the giant robot octopus that's gonna hoist its slimy head?"

"Oh—right. I don't think a robot octopus would be slimy. Slime tends to come from organic stuff."

"A really evil robot might be more authentic."

She gave me a little smile. "We have to move fast, Ron, before the fooki guys start contributing money to elected officials. We need to pin Joey's murder on Thaddeus. We need to find out how he plans to make people specifically purchase *his* merchandise. And we need to learn more about Sandra—that's the name of your blond stalker, and she's Thad's ex-wife. Jonathan told me last night. He says she's very secretive."

The phone rang. As she picked it up, I heard the voice of Magnolia's mother.

Mrs. Mags said, "What is this box of stuff?"

"Hello, Mom. I'm glad you got the package. I ordered your medication on the internet."

"You what? You don't have the prescription."

"I ordered it for you. Keep it in a safe place."

"You pretended to be me? You want all my problems, Magnolia? I'm the walking dead. And do you come visit me? No. You send me pills—*in the mail*. What did I do to get such a daughter?"

"You performed a basic biological function, Mom."

"Don't be disgusting. You think I don't know how much this damned medicine costs? It costs a fortune. Where did you get the money?"

"I have a business," Mags said with some pride.

"Flying around with your funny-looking hair? That's a business? The man you're with is a crook! I can tell."

"You don't even know him!" Mags shot back.

"I know that my unmarried daughter is sleeping with a criminal! Why can't you ever sleep with a nice guy? Why are they always punks and gangsters?"

Mags rolled her eyes. "He's not a gangster, mom. He's just a guy who…buries dead bodies for a living. Now take your medication. Please."

She hung up. I thought she'd be upset, but she seemed okay. She looked at me and said, "Mom sends her love."

31 — BOB AGAIN

Later that afternoon I decided to visit my brother, so I headed toward that rollicking part of the Village. I'd made a deal for his 40,000 bags of walnuts with a guy from Crown Heights who owned a bunch of kosher ice cream shops— it seemed that vanilla, larceny, and the Five Books Of Moses were a winning combination. I took about twenty steps, and there was Subterranean Bob.

He was standing on the sidewalk with a smirk on his face

"Hello, Bob. Are you looking for someone special?"

"Ooooh, no, no. I'm only looking for you, heh-heh."

I laughed and unleashed face number forty—*the stare of the superior sex life.*

This was a bonus face I'd earned for my extra effort at The School Of Thirty-Nine Faces. This condescending expression is accompanied by a telepathic transmission that rips into an opponent's brain and asks, "Have you seen my girlfriend? Are you getting anything that good?" Obviously, this face is only useful if your girlfriend is attractive.

Bob staggered backward as he was hit by my extrasensory envy bomb.

He grimaced. "Ooh, you bastard! I'm not doing so badly. Why, just the other night I had a date… Okay, I suppose it was more of a meeting… Oh, all right, she sold me some Tupperware! *Argh!*"

I just looked at him and smiled.

He adjusted his glasses and frowned. "Let's get down to business. Oooh, I hate you. Anyway, I need to know if your girlfriend, who I'll admit is very sexy—ooooooh—has she considered Thaddeus's kind offer to make her devastatingly wealthy?"

"No, Bob," I said in a smug voice. "She doesn't want the money. In fact, all she wants is me—all the time, every night, and in the morning, too, you loser."

Then I blew by him and headed toward my brother's pizzeria. In the distance, I heard him howl with rage.

32 — THAT IS NOT SALAD FORK

Did I expect to see what I saw? Of course not. That's why it was such a surprise.

I was standing on Bleeker Street, across from Al's pizzeria. I saw a dense, squirming crowd inside—and I saw Ton Lee coming through the front door.

I rubbed my eyes in disbelief. Did Ton love my brother's pizza? Or was my brother a traitor and part of the plot? I didn't have time to start a debate, so with the anvil of shock still vibrating in my head, I started trailing the evil assassin.

I'd studied the art of following someone. Naturally, I had to conceal my scent, and I was hoping that third garlic and Limburger cheese sandwich wouldn't do me in. I stayed on Ton's tail as he weaved through the crowds crossing Broadway and finally descended into the noisy Lafayette Street subway station where we both squeezed onto the 6 Train. He rode it two stops to Canal Street in Chinatown and eventually entered a seedy little pawnshop on Baxter.

I stood on the bustling street for a minute and then snuck a look through the shop's greasy window. I saw lots of grungy junk, and an old Chinese guy behind a counter. I walked inside.

I didn't see Ton anywhere, but when a customer came in and started talking to the old guy about a pair of rusty rickshaws, I slipped through a curtain of hanging beads and found myself in the dark underworld of people's trash.

I walked through a cluttered room that led to another cluttered room. I wandered through a twisted maze of dresses, chairs, and player pianos. I slinked past birdcages, aquariums, and a slippery-looking salad bar. Pretty soon, I was surrounded by ominous toys and oily old fishing gear—and I heard a sound. I turned on my heels, and there—with his back to a splashy mural of Moby Dick, the Great White Whale—was Ton Lee.

I puffed out my chest and glowered. "Ton Lee, we meet again. Prepare for a whale of a fight!"

He glared back at me with a smirk. "The fight in your fish is small, I think—and you will die, ha-ha."

I reached for my daggers. Ton also pulled out his blades, and we headed into a clearing among the junk where we started circling each other.

I grinned and said, "Call me Ishmael."

Ton snarled. "From hell's heart I stab at thee!"

"Queequeg probably had some serious issues involving the sea and his spear."

"The whale population decline for centuries as asshole Japanese hunt great beasts to extinction."

"What were you doing in that pizza place, Ton?"

"I look for job. Killing you does not pay so well."

"What do you know about Joey the Round Man?"

"Joey enjoy dressing up like chicken."

I scowled because I knew about the chicken thing. "Yeah, but what about his death? Are you the guy who killed him?"

Ton laughed and slashed at me—but like a ballerina of the blade, I danced away unharmed. As he lunged again I stepped aside and counterattacked. Unfortunately, I missed, and my daggers struck a naked mannequin. I growled and pulled the knives from her filthy plastic navel and then lashed out. This time my daggers punctured a flabby, water-filled mattress. It burst and sent scummy mattress-water cascading across the grimy floor.

Ton cursed. "You destroy much personal property."

I smiled, knowing he'd just stepped under a hanging bag of coconuts.

"Let he who is without sin cast the final coconut, Ton!"

With a flamboyant slash of my weapon I cut the nearby supporting rope. Ton glanced up and barely had time to gasp as a bag of hairy boulders crashed down from the sky.

"Augh!" he said as the coconuts fell, clobbering him like bombs before bouncing and ricocheting across the floor.

I roared with laughter, finally vindicated for my past blunders involving pineapples, hubcaps, and wayward bananas. After all, anyone can get suckered by a depraved piece of fruit, but only a real dumb fucker gets clocked by the falling bag of coconuts.

I got down close to Ton's unconscious form and gripped his chin in my hand. I decided to attempt the ancient *art of the sleeping truth,* in which a semi-conscious person can be coerced into answering unwanted questions.

I touched his forehead and whispered, "Ton Lee, do you hear me?"

"Errrrr, hmmf."

"Ton, why were you in the pizzeria?"

"Rrrr...to...discuss...fooki."

"Is my brother involved in the plot?"

"Yes."

"Who killed Joey the Round Man?"

"Beware...the...sure...one."

He was fading fast. But then his eyes snapped open and he said, "What you do? Do not touch my magic tool!" Then he reached into his pants—and pulled out a telescope.

He said, "Damn! Where my daggers go?"

I sucked in my breath and winced at the thought of being examined at such close range. I also laughed at his inability to control his daggers—but then he brained me with the damned spyglass.

I fell backwards as Ton leaped to his feet. I also whirled to my left and spotted a giant crayon. It was at least five feet tall. It was "flesh" colored, which of course was a relic from another time when flesh was exclusively considered to be the color of a Caucasian. I wasn't surprised it was rotting in the bowels of an evil pawnshop, right next to Indian Red.

I seized the crayon and charged at Ton. His puny stargazing tool was no match for my mighty keg of white man's wax. He screamed, "You better not ruin jacket again!" But it was too late. I laughed as I rubbed a cruel, Caucasian-colored mark across the right sleeve.

Ton was furious. He tossed down the telescope and grabbed a huge soupspoon. It was bigger than my crayon and made me feel inadequate. But then I spotted an equally large fork that was obviously part of the same silverware set. I grinned at Ton's stupidity—when fighting with oversized eating utensils, it's always best to grab the fork. So I did.

Ton laughed. "Do you think to twirl me like pasta? Or toss me like salad?"

I grinned. "Maybe."

He laughed again. "That is not salad fork, you fool."

Well, he was right. I'd never been too good at identifying my silverware. While I was pondering the idiotic rules of etiquette, Ton charged with his spoon.

I easily stepped aside and lunged with my fork. I missed and instead stabbed a red beach ball that resembled a huge cherry tomato. I turned and parried Ton's next blow, which sent him spinning into a bin filled with pumice. With a crunching sound, he crashed down into the heap of volcanic rock.

Ton looked up at me with glazed eyes. "Ow, I much prefer to land in soft sand." Well, geology is funny that way. Sometimes you get the sand and other times you get the pumice.

I snarled. "Tell me about phase two of the fooki plot!"

"No, I can not tell. They would fire me, or take away vacation days."

"And where would you go?"

"Gettysburg would be nice."

Ah, Gettysburg. I'd been there as a teenager. My dad had lugged us there to see the historic battlefield where piles of young men had endured death and amputation—but my mom had picked out the worst motel. The bathroom had no sink; the sink was in the living room. At night I'd been forced to examine my acne in front of the whole family, and it had been embarrassing.

"Gettysburg is nice," I said. "But you've got to pick the right motel."

"Yes, I know—as child, my mother pick motel with no bathroom sink."

I suddenly felt great empathy for Ton. We were struggling and fighting, yet we had so much in common. I yearned for Abraham Lincoln to say a few words and heal the wounds. And that's when Ton hit me with the pumice.

"Ouch!" I said and tumbled backwards, landing in a beanbag chair. This was great luck, but Ton was charging at me with the spoon. I groped for a new weapon, and right there beside the beanbag I found a Viking shield. This was more great luck. Also, there was a helmet with horns. I held the shield up high and put on the helmet. Ton shouted and struck with his spoon as I leaped to my feet. The spoon did no damage to my ancient warrior gear, and I now reached for a nearby broadsword.

Ton cursed and stepped back. "So, you have found matching combat gear—luck is with you today. I only discover spoon."

I grinned and advanced toward him. He kept retreating until he reached a window. He jerked it open and smirked. "We will meet again, Sensei Ron, on a day when you reach down and find only bag of marshmallows."

I cringed at his prediction. I'd grabbed the marshmallow bag before, and it was a humbling experience. He jumped through the window and fled, while I roared with laughter.

33 — AL TALKS

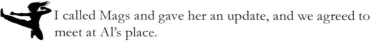I called Mags and gave her an update, and we agreed to meet at Al's place.

I ran all the way back to the restaurant. The sidewalks were crowded, and I muscled past the hundreds of little jewelry-donut-pizza-clothing-sandwich shops while trying to ignore the raw screech of treachery in my head.

I reached the pizzeria and called Mags again, and soon enough she dropped down from the sky. Al was there, twirling his dough, when we walked in and got right to the point.

"Hi, Al. Does Mom know you're working for Melvin Shrick and Thaddeus Stone?"

His mouth hung open with fake surprise. "Hi, Ron. Hey, what do you mean? I don't know what you're talking about, and Mom doesn't know much. She still thinks you broke that fish tank."

I frowned at the memory—another fish tank disaster. We'd been young, and we'd both been responsible. But I'd been blamed because it was my socket wrench that had ended up in the water with the dead Angelfish.

"Al, you could go to prison."

"Nah, I think there's a statute of limitations for killing a fish."

"I'm talking about Thaddeus, and his evil scheme to poison the world."

"I don't know about any scheme, okay?" he said, waving his floury hands. "Melvin talked to me. He asked for some advice about pizza. They're looking for a little help to handle a big deal they've got going—and I'm the king of pizza, right? So I charged them a consulting fee, and that's it."

I shook my head with disgust. "Ton Lee made it seem like you were in this thing up to your yap."

"Ton Lee is a liar! Who are you gonna believe, the rice or the risotto? I'm just a consultant, that's all—and hey, I guess this is your super-duper girlfriend. Hi, honey, it's good to finally meet you. I've got your picture on the wall."

Mags gave a little smile and fired the Gaze of the Guilt.

Al gasped and staggered backward. He crashed against an oven and started rattling off his sordid confessions.

"I've been cheating on Sheila! I lied to Jane! Those battery powered Mold-A-Matic hair dryers I was selling are a fire hazard!"

I smirked. "Better fine tune it, Mags. He's full of guilt, but it's all about girls and people he's set on fire."

She narrowed her eyes a bit, and Al kept talking. "Augh! I gave Greta a fake ring. I gave Dorothy a disease. I gave Marcia a pair of pot holders for her birthday!"

Mags glared at my brother. "Look, stop talking about what an asshole boyfriend you are and start telling us about the pizza. What about Melvin Shrick? Did he kill Joey the Round Man?"

"I don't know! He paid for some info, and I told him the sauce was too sweet. I told him where he could find your brother!"

Al collapsed onto the floor. Mags stopped the Gaze as her jaw dropped.

"These guys asked you about my brother?"

"Yeah," Al said while trying to catch his breath. "After Joey got clipped, they came around and said, 'Watch out for Magno Girl.' Well, I know Tommy, and he talks about you. So I told Melvin I knew him, and he said, 'Great, where can I find him?' Then later he said Tommy helped him out, but I don't know for sure. I ain't seen Tommy lately."

An alarm was ringing in my head—crap! I guessed Tommy was one of the guys supplying Al with the stolen stuff I was selling. Plus, he was a traitor! I felt like a pair of punches had just knocked me out.

Mags looked like she'd been equally hammered. "Is that how they learned about my weakness for tobacco smoke? From Tommy?" She gave Al a hard stare. "It can't be. How do you know my brother?"

"I don't know him that good," Al said, shifting his eyes. "We both hang out at the DB Bar, just now and then. And he talks about you sometimes. He talks to a lot of guys."

"Al knows everybody," I blurted. "He's a friendly guy. Now what about the fooki?" I snatched a pizza slice from the counter. "Is there fooki in this pie?"

Al hesitated. "Some of the pies have fooki. That was the deal—they wanted to test it out, and it works great. People love fooki. It's the best thing since beer."

I couldn't believe my ears. Was he really comparing beer to some stinky Asian weed?

"And what about Joey The Round Man, Al? Were you there when he was *strombolied*?"

Al threw up his hands. "I had nothing to do with that! I don't know anything about it!" He looked at Mags with wide eyes. "I didn't know they were gonna try and kill you, honey. I'm sorry. Pick out any item on the menu—any topping, it's yours."

I snarled. "How about your fingers?"

"Forget it," Mags said. "They're too fatty."

I was livid, and I considered making a special boli that would feature most of my brother's pancreas. I reached for my daggers, but Mags stopped me.

"Forget it, Ron. Let's go."

Mags walked out the door, and I followed with my head spinning. Of course, I'd come back later and get my walnut money. I still couldn't find anyone who wanted those damn five thousand silver teapots.

34 — NO ITCHING, NO FLAKING, NO DANDRUFF

We left the restaurant and started walking down Bleeker Street in the direction of Washington Square Village. As we maneuvered through the crowd, Mags said, "So, my brother knows your brother. That's interesting."

"Yeah, it's a small world," I blurted. "Maybe it's a sign that we're supposed to get together, huh?"

She gave a little snort. "Maybe it's a sign that they're both up to no good."

"Right," I said, feeling a little warm and sweaty. "But Al's okay sometimes."

"You mean when he's not helping the guys who want to kill us?"

"Yeah, exactly." I glanced at her, looking for a sign of rage or sadness—but there was none. "Mags, are you okay? I mean with the 'Tommy thing?'"

"My brother didn't sell me out," she said.

I didn't answer too soon. This had to be a touchy subject.

"Mags, we just heard that he did."

"Yeah, but he didn't. Tommy's no saint, but we've been through a lot together, and he would never do that to me."

"But Mags, he's obviously mad at you—and he's desperate for money. He's also a criminal."

Her eyes flashed like steel. "Tommy's more of an idiot than a crook. He would *never* deliberately hurt me, just like I would never hurt him. Besides, the story makes no sense. If he sold me out and got paid, why would he be asking me for money? I'll call him when I get home."

I put my arm around her shoulder and gave her a quick hug. But inside, I was cursing my bad luck. Why did Al have to be working with the one crook in the whole damned city related to my girl? I was in no hurry for her to talk to him, since he might mention how he was stealing and fencing the stuff through Al—and me. I also didn't understand why she believed he was innocent. A degenerate gambler always needs more money. Her faith in Tommy was inspiring, even if it was delusional. I wondered if she could ever have such faith in me.

I was about to make another comment when Mags got pale and dropped to her knees. It was the Gaze of the Guilt, hitting her back. She was shaking and stammering.

"Oh! I should've watched over Tommy more often! I should've kept him away from that punk, Julio! And I never should've had sex with Julio in his dad's garage!"

Her body kept heaving for a bit—and then she stopped. She was silent, catching her breath. She looked up at me. I was just standing there, being quiet and visualizing things.

I shrugged. "Are you okay, honey?"

She stood up and sighed. "Can we just pretend that never happened?"

"Hey, no problem. I just wish I had a garage."

She almost laughed. We started walking again, and I once again put my arm around her. Despite the summer heat, she seemed to like it. But then she pulled away and lowered her voice.

"Ron, I think we're being followed. A little ways back."

He was a tall guy in a trench coat. He wore a hat, dark glasses, and a phony beard that looked like it had once been the back end of a hyena.

"Who is it?" I said.

"I'm pretty sure it's SuperStan."

"Whoah! How can you tell?"

"An educated guess. I'm good at spotting pomposity."

Mags started moving toward SuperStan, and SuperStan started walking fast the other way. He made a right on Thompson Street and then ducked into a place called Toni's Toys. We were right behind him, but he was looking to lose us inside a maze of marketable junk.

We raced by the sci-fi action figures. We trailed him past the stuffed animals, games, and toy army vehicles waiting to feel their first splash of imaginary blood. Finally, Mags turned around and stormed up the next aisle, where she found SuperStan— pretending to be interested in Japanese coloring books. He glanced at us and buried his head deeper in the Manga scribble.

Mags walked up to him. "Are you planning to take up art, SuperStan? I think they have a sale on crayons."

He sputtered and then hissed, *"I'm undercover, and I'm not SuperStan!"*

"Oh, I'm sorry. Underneath that hat, I thought I saw some genuine superhero hair."

"I don't know what you're talking about," he said with a smirk. "Though my hair does have strength and body."

I laughed. "That's all well and good, but is it soft and shiny?"

"It's shiny and healthy."

"But is it full and bouncy?"

"It's full and bouncy, not too dry, and very soft."

"All that gel can't be good."

"I use a special formula with polymers and humidifying agents. It doesn't weigh my hair down or leave an oily residue."

"It seems unlikely."

SuperStan whipped the hat from his head. "The conditioner *softens* and *moisturizes*. The gel *molds* and *styles perfectly* when the hair is dry."

I had to admit, he had a lovely crop of head-turf. All he needed was a golf ball and a little flag.

I whistled. "Very impressive. And you never have any problems with your scalp?"

"None. No itching, no flaking, no dandruff."

"Pretty good system."

"Thank you."

Mags shook her head in disgust. "So, SuperStan, why were you spying on me? Were you looking for hair care tips?"

SuperStan snarled and tossed his coloring book to the floor.

"Hell, no! Though I'll admit, your hair does have an amazing degree of luster." He poked a sinewy finger in Magnolia's face. "Look here, little lady, I know about the new pizza from Pie Hole, and I watched you go into that pizza place. So tell me, are you trying to muscle in on my endorsement deals?"

"What?"

"Don't play the innocent little girl with me! I know that fat pizza maker is testing Melvin Shrick's new pie, and I was contacted about an endorsement deal—but then he wouldn't meet my price. *And now you're underselling me, right?*"

Mags gave a sardonic laugh. "Excuse me, SuperStan, but the price of my dignity is apparently higher than yours."

"Ha! You lie! No one sells their dignity for more than I do! It's something I've earned. Do you know how many criminals I've brought to justice by the sweat of my brow and the flex of my biceps? And now you come along with your sexy little strut and your bag of cheap carnival tricks, and you want to snatch it all away from me!"

"SuperStan, I'm not interested in the money."

He laughed and threw up his hands in disbelief. "Then why be a superhero? Why be anything, for that matter?" He grimaced and crossed his sizable arms. "There have been other female superheroes, Magnolia. People like Kitten Girl and Warrior Queen—but they were predictable bimbos who played by the rules. They wore skin tight latex jumpsuits, and they carried phallic edged weapons while wearing skimpy leather thongs. But you! You are sneaky and devious—cultivating an air of sexual mystery by not flaunting your physique—like you really don't care about the money and fame! Like you're really not as hollow and superficial as the rest of us! I'll have you know that in commercials shown in Japan I proudly wear a chicken suit!"

He puffed out his chest and glared. "The graveyard is full of losers who've challenged me. Do you remember the Magnificent Bulk? *Killed* trying to bench press a trailer full of vitamin supplements! And how about *The Poet?* He was looking smart for a while, until that cute little haiku shot a hole through his iambic pentameter. Look me up in a year, sweet cheeks! Maybe I'll need a new shampoo girl."

With one final growl, SuperStan shoved Mags backward and charged out of the store.

I cursed and started to go after him—but Mags grabbed my wrist and stopped me.

"Forget it, Ron."

"He tried to intimidate you, Mags. I'm going to cut out his eyeball and put it in the jar."

"I'm not intimidated. Forget about your eyeball jar." She picked up the coloring book SuperStan had thrown on the floor and started leafing through it.

I was quiet for a minute. Finally, I said, "Hey, maybe your apparent lack of interest in advertising is a clever strategy. As your adviser, I might be smart."

She smiled. "Yeah, but my lack of interest is genuine."

"Damn. So I'm still stupid?"

"No. I'm just not cooperating."

"Right. Why do you never cooperate?"

"I do cooperate, when I think it feels right." Mags closed the coloring book. "This Japanese animation has such a mass-produced look."

"Sure, but it's popular. It makes big money. Michelangelo never had his own line of coloring books, honey."

"That's true, Ron. He was too busy painting masterpieces."

35 — MY FRIENDS ALL HAVE AUGUSTO

That night I sat with Mags, Pepe, Jenni, and Karina in Genarro's Pizzeria on East Houston Street near Avenue B. We sat in a booth with a view of the street. It was raining outside, and the speeding headlights were spraying blurry gold light across the wide, shimmering highway.

Hanging over the main counter was a television screen that showed the news, along with the ads that paid for it. I bought everyone slices. I was thinking about the cash I'd collected from Al for the chopped walnuts, and about the 20,000 "PermaPower Cold Packs" he'd just acquired. I was also thinking Mags shouldn't be getting her hands dirty with a swag-selling grease monkey like me.

Still, I felt good when I managed to sneak a fat roll of cash into her tiny purse. I took my pizza to a counter across the room where they had condiment shakers. Right before I started scattering the seasoning, I looked down at my slice—and I lost my appetite. Swimming in the gooey sheen of melted cheese was the image of Sandra's head.

She smiled up at me. "Hello, Ron. We meet again."

I froze, staring at her face all mixed in with the mozzarella. I glanced around quick. No one nearby seemed to notice her—but I didn't want to get the kids involved in this, so I turned my back to the table where they were sitting and leaned close to the pizza.

I whispered, "What are you doing in my slice?"

"Would you prefer I appear in your goose liver paté?"

"Sure, why not? I'd never put that shit in my mouth. So what do you want?"

"I know Magno Girl's greatest fear, and she will suffer soon—far worse than Joey did. Unless she takes the money."

"*What? Did you whack Joey? If you touch Mags I'll kill you! I'll—*"

My threats were cut short by a booming voice that said, "Hey, c'mon! What's the holdup?" I turned and saw a line of people waiting to use the condiment counter. Luckily, no one seemed concerned that I was screaming at a slice of pizza. That's what I love about living in New York.

"Sorry," I said, and moved over a bit. I looked back down at the face in my pizza.

"She doesn't want your money."

The face kept smiling. "Good! I guess her greatest fear will come true, ha-ha—and she'll love it. By the way, did you know that she's a witch? That little fact won't get her any good publicity—and neither will all that stuff you've been stealing."

With a flash of light Sandra vanished, and I stood there in a stunned rage. Then I snarled and chucked my slice into the trash.

I stomped back to the table and sat down. I was filled with anger and guilt, because I suspected this was all my fault—even the stuff that wasn't.

Mags cocked her head. "Where's your pizza?"

I frowned. "Mags, what's your greatest fear?"

Mags and the kids looked at me, and she laughed. "Is something wrong, Ron?"

"*What's your greatest fear?* I mean, I was just wondering."

Now the kids laughed but looked at Mags, who shrugged. "I've always been scared of getting stuck in a life I didn't want, and I guess that's still true. But it hasn't happened yet—so that's good."

The kids seemed happy with that answer, but I was still grim, and I sat in silence—for a few seconds. Then I blurted, "What do you know about witches?"

I saw a spark of surprise in her eyes. She ignored the looks of curiosity from the kids and leaned toward me a bit.

"Why would you ask me that, Ron? I don't know a thing about witches."

I felt a wave of relief—not because I cared on a personal level, but because witches weren't popular like superheroes. Even the good ones were viewed with suspicion by the media—and advertisers hated them.

Suddenly a new commercial for Pie Hole's "More For Me" pizza came on the screen.

Pepe pointed at the television. "Look, Pie Hole Pizza."

The commercial was similar to the first one, except that this version featured occasional images of Smashboy's silhouette doing basic martial arts moves while the bass line boomed and the blazing images popped like firecrackers across the screen.

Mags gave me a sideways glance and shook her head. "Can you believe Smashboy? I guess Thaddeus didn't want to pay for SuperStan, so he reached a few rungs down the ladder, and then he reached down a few more."

Karina pouted a bit. "Magnolia, why don't you have a cool outfit like that? You'd look hot in black leather. And maybe an Augusto Expensile handbag."

Pepe and Jenni looked at each other with bleak expressions. They were trying to ignore all signs of Karina's decent into blankness.

Mags said, "Maybe I'd look hot, and maybe I'd look cool—but I wouldn't be able to throw it in the washing machine."

"A better outfit could make you a lot of money," I mumbled.

Karina said, "Will you ever do a commercial, Magnolia?"

"Maybe for a good cause," Mags said.

I gave a sarcastic laugh. "Making money is a good cause."

"Making money is not a cause at all."

I crushed a can of Coke in my fist. "Mags, why are you so stubborn? There's nothing wrong with a more comfortable lifestyle."

She smiled. "That's true, but I'm not that uncomfortable. I don't need to sit in a heated swimming pool and watch three-hundred channels of bullshit on satellite TV."

Jenni said, "Magnolia will never sell out."

Pepe nodded. "Yeah, she's hardcore, Ron."

I smirked. "Yeah, and she's broke, Pepe."

Jenni said, "Have you heard the term 'morally bankrupt'?"

"Yeah," I said. "It's usually about some bastard who's no worse than anyone else—he's just richer."

Everyone laughed, except Magnolia. Karina said, "Hey, what's the story with fooki? Is it like pot? Are any movie stars using it?"

"It's not as popular as pot," Mags said. "At least not yet. But it's catching on. The American Association Of Mainstream Mega Marts is already donating money to politicians. They've commissioned a study, too, that will probably show fooki is harmless."

Pepe grinned. "Maybe I should give it a try."

"Don't do it!" Mags said. "It's a dangerous drug. It's being sold by an evil guy, and for only one purpose—to make money."

I banged my fist on the table. "Look, the guy who owns Pie Hole has tried to kill Magnolia, and he'll probably try again! So I don't want to hear any more talk about eating fooki, or eating that fucking pizza!"

Everyone looked surprised at my five-alarm outburst.

Pepe said, "Hey, sorry. I didn't know. I won't touch it." Then his voice got sharp like a spear. "Anyone who's against you, Magnolia, is against me, too."

The other kids strongly agreed. Meanwhile, Mags quietly studied me like she knew something was out of whack. Then the screen above showed Jim Riteangle, newsman.

Jim was in front of a Pie Hole Pizza store in Brooklyn, surrounded by ravenous members of the Bensonhurst hoi polloi. Jim smiled and said, "There's a new kind of pizza in town, and it's charming the cheese out of everyone. I'm talking about Pie Hole's "More For Me" pizza. I'm here with a few satisfied customers."

He shoved the microphone under the nose ring of a pretty teenage girl who was chomping on a fooki slice. "What's your name, and where are you from?"

"Dawn, from Rockaway Beach."

"And how do you like that pizza, Dawn?"

"I like it. They sell it at the mall, too. I'm going to buy a new pair of shoes and a pair of Augusto Expensile sunglasses."

"Oh, those are pricey. Do you go out in the sun a lot?"

"No, but my friends all have them."

Jim stared into the camera. "I'm Jim Riteangle for Channel Five—standing in front of Pie Hole Pizza." The camera backed up to highlight Jim and his pizza groupies holding their slices high.

The news anchors smiled and shook their heads. The laminated woman said, "People sure do love that pizza." The polyurethane man replied, "They certainly do. I'll have to try it myself. Len is up next with sports."

We all turned away from the screen. Len was made from especially lightweight styrofoam.

36 — A FISHY INVITATION

The next morning I stood in Magnolia's office, arguing with her about the image in last night's pizza slice.

"Mags, she practically admitted to killing Joey!"

"Maybe. But I don't think a talking slice of pizza is admissible in court. What else did Sandra say?"

"Just the stuff about your greatest fear. Fear and suffering and best wishes for everyone. Oh, yeah—and she said you were a witch."

Mags kept her face blank. "Anything else?"

"Anything else? Isn't that enough?"

I decided to leave out the reference to stolen merchandise.

She sighed. "Ron, there's something you should know about me."

"Wait—let me guess. You're a witch."

She gave a short laugh. "No, I'm not a witch. But my grandmother was a witch, and I was born with some of that ability."

"So you're a witch."

"No! Being a witch is a lifestyle. My grandmother used magic to expose my superpowers, but I'm not a witch because I've never followed the lifestyle."

"But you have the blood of a witch. So you *could* be a witch."

"Yeah, I guess. But I don't practice witchcraft, so I'm *not* a witch."

"Never?"

"Never."

"Not even a little bit?"

She hesitated. "Well, okay, there is one little thing."

I rolled my eyes. "Great! Do you know what the media is going to do with this?"

"I use it on my hair, okay?"

"What?"

"The red streaks and highlights. Do you know what they would cost in a salon? And do you know how often they'd mess it up?"

"So you use witchcraft as a form of cosmetology."

"Yeah. And that's the truth."

I pondered her words and realized I didn't really care. I loved her.

"Okay," I said. "Maybe you can get away with that. Or maybe you can open a salon of your own."

Mags laughed. "No salon for me. But I'm glad you approve." She gave me a sideways glance. "Does it bother you that I'm part witch?"

"Hell, no. I think it's sexy."

She laughed again. "Good. As for Sandra—who I suspect is a *real* witch—I don't know what she has planned. I'm guessing we'll find out soon."

"What about your brother? Have you talked to him?"

"No, not yet. I called and left a message. I went to his apartment and he wasn't there."

"You went over there without me?"

"Yeah, I did, Ron. He's my brother, and I'll deal with him. And like I said, he wasn't there."

I was quiet, but annoyed. I thought we were in this thing together, and I thought this thing made her problems my problems. I also thought her confidence in Tommy was going to end in some flaming, twisted wreckage.

"Maybe he's hiding out somewhere," I finally said.

"Yeah, I suppose he could be another person gone from my life. But I don't think so."

She glanced into the big training room, where Biff Taylor was finishing his workout in front of the mirrored wall. She moved closer to me. "Look, let's forget about Tommy right now. We need to think about this." She pulled an envelope from a drawer and handed me an embossed invitation addressed to Biff.

Thaddeus Stone III, CEO of Americamart, Inc., and Melvin Schrick, CEO of Pie Hole Pizza, Inc., cordially invite you and one guest to attend an evening of dinner and dancing at the Milstein Hall of Ocean Life located in the American Museum of Natural History. Come and celebrate the food of the future.

Mags said, "It's Biff's invitation to tonight's big pizza bash. I'm going to go as his date."

A mushroom-cloud alarm exploded before my eyes.

Mags put her hand on my arm. "Don't start freaking out, okay? I have a plan. I'll meet Thaddeus and Melvin at the party, and then I'll hit them with the Gaze. I'll get full confessions in front of a few hundred witnesses. We'll cover Joey the Round Man, the fooki plot—and any other topics they might care to discuss. In one master stroke we'll end this thing."

My heart was pounding like a pachyderm. "Mags, it's a set-up."

She smiled. "Maybe."

"And Biff is in on it!"

Her eyes narrowed. "You don't know that. True, Biff knows Thaddeus, but Thad might be using him without his knowledge—if he's using him at all. Anyway, Biff knows how much I love museums."

"So he thinks it's a real date?"

"No, I don't think so. I mean, not really."

I threw my hands up. "Mags, you don't understand the male mind."

"Of course I do. You think about food, and you think about sex."

"Exactly. Now how much food is going to be at this party?"

"Ron, it's a pizza party."

"We both know Biff isn't there to eat pizza—so that means it's all about sex!"

"*Will you shut up?* He'll hear you."

I dropped my tone to a fierce whisper. "You need to hit him with the Gaze, and find out what he's hiding."

"I will not!"

"Then I'm going to hit him with my fist." I started walking toward Biff.

Mags reached out fast, grabbing my shoulder and yanking me against the wall. "Biff is a friend! I don't go blasting my friends with mind-groping techniques."

"*Oh, really? But you go shoving them against a wall?*"

We stared at each other, our eyes barely a nose apart. Then she let go.

"I'm sorry, Ron."

I took a deep breath. "It's okay. I'm sorry, too."

I glanced away and watched Biff practice his sword thrusts. When he looked in my direction, he started slicing with more hatred than usual. He finally stopped his assault and walked toward us. I stopped talking to Mags but kept frowning.

Meanwhile, Biff smiled like a buzz saw. "Hello, Sensei Ron. I'm ready to fight. Lead me to the bad guys, and it'll be *my time to shine!*" Then he assumed a fighting stance that seemed to suggest fellatio.

I sneered at his pre-orgasmic posture. "Biff, I hear you're a real master of the hairbrush and a guru of the *nunchaku* combs."

Biff shot me a look of rage. "Sensei Ron, I'm a little tired of your insults."

"Biff, I'm a little tired of all the tuna I eat."

"What?"

"You heard me. Now go fetch me a turkey sandwich."

Biff shouted and lunged at me. I lunged back. We locked our hands around each other's throats and screamed in the strangled vocabulary of mortal combat.

"Arg! Mmmf! Rrrrrr! Motherfucker!"

Mags jumped in and ripped us apart, and we both went flying backward.

"Will you guys stop it?"

I laughed, and Biff looked away. We were still thinking bad thoughts.

Mags stared at Biff. "I'd like Ron to come with us tonight."

His face fell even as my smirk exploded. "What?" he said. "I can't do that. The invitation says 'one guest.' "

"I'm sure you can use your influence to get Ron into the party. I'd really appreciate it."

Biff scowled but then tossed a smile-grenade in my direction. "Okay, I suppose I can help. I'm sure he'll try not to damage any of the ocean's most priceless artifacts."

He gave Mags a cheese-stinking grin and then packed up his gear and left.

I watched him head down the stairs. "Mags, I'm a little worried. Tell me, how priceless are we talking?"

"Seafood can be expensive, but few fish are priceless."

"We're walking into a trap."

"It's not a trap if we're prepared. It's a fight, and we'll be fine."

"That guy is a snake! What do you see in him? I mean besides the money and the good looks?"

"Nothing! I'm trying to solve a crime, remember? And he can help us. Why do you have to be such a jealous idiot?"

I shrugged. "Does it turn you on?"

"No."

"Not even sometimes?"

She sighed. "Maybe sometimes. But stop doing it anyway."

"Okay. But one of these days I'm going to flatten that guy."

"Biff's a good fighter."

"Yeah, but when he does that high side kick he always leaves his testicles open."

"His opponent doesn't know he's going to throw a side kick."

"Mags, he always does the same little fake to his left, then his right, and then he throws the side kick. He does it *every* time."

"Well then I should probably tell him—after all, I am his teacher."

"My *future sense* tells me you should wait."

"Until when?"

"Until you need to kick him in the balls."

"I hope that isn't any time soon. He's my only private student, and he's probably not going to pay if I obliterate his testicles."

"Mags, I keep telling you—endorsement deals."

"Ron, you never quit, do you? I'm *not* going to be a corporate puppet who jerks her way through ads for feminine hygiene products."

"Puppets live well, honey. They own big mansions. They stay fresh all day."

She gave me a sober look. "Ron, I've been thinking. We need to talk."

I froze like a tree in front of a lumberjack. "You're sick of me, right? *I knew it!*"

"No! I'm not sick of you." She reached into her nearby purse and pulled out the chunky roll of cash I'd slipped her the night before. "This money…"

I wasn't listening. Instead, I was gazing down the length of her body, and I was suddenly seized by a moment of passion. I leaped forward and embraced her, kissing her hard. She was surprised and almost kissed me back, but then pulled away.

"Mags, don't you like kissing me?"

Her eyes were stormy. "You know I do. I just like to know when it's coming. And I want to talk to you."

I took a step back and spread my arms. *"Magnolia, I'm going to kiss you now.* Look, we don't need to talk. I care about you, okay? Take the money."

She rolled her eyes and then let them rove over me. She tossed the cash onto the desk and said, "Okay, kiss away."

I wrapped her in my arms, and I kissed her again. She behaved better this time, and after a few more kisses she starting getting passionate. Naturally, I kept on kissing, and then I whispered in her ear, "Stop being concerned about a world that doesn't care."

She whispered back, "The world is important. It's right to be concerned."

"Being concerned is overrated. Just stay hot and sexy."

"Hot and sexy is way, way overrated."

"You're probably right, but I'm still going to drop my pants."

My jeans hit the floor, and Mags stared at my inflated organ. "I didn't know you were so philosophical, Ron."

"Yeah, but you knew I had a big prick."

She ripped off her shorts and panties. She left her T-shirt on, though, and stared at me with her snazzy vagina.

"I think we better fuck now."

"Right."

37 — ON THE FLOOR AGAIN

The raging sex was over, and we were lying on the floor in the training room. I was wondering if we were ever going to do it in a bed, but I wasn't complaining. After all, the training room had all those cool mirrors on the walls.

Mags sat up and crossed her arms on top of her knees. She seemed calm, like a deserted beach after a typhoon. I stayed flat on my back, looking into her eyes. I could tell she was about to say something significant.

"Ron, I'm sorry I snapped at you over the situation with my brother. I want to deal with him alone, okay? Sometimes I like to do things by myself, and I don't want to involve you in a family problem."

I sat up. "Is that how you look at it? Like I'm some kind of stranger?"

"No! It's not like that. I'm not sure what it's like—but I appreciate the fact that you're concerned about me. I really do."

There were a lot of things I could've said. I could've accused her of trying to send a message, a declaration of independence launched by a fear of emotional commitment. I could've mentioned how we'd been through a lot together, and she should have a little more trust in me. I also could have told her she'd ripped a few holes in one of the training mats with her fingernails—but I decided to let everything slide.

"Mags, I'll call my brother and ask him about Tommy. Maybe he knows something else. Now let's get ready for this party tonight." She gave me that little Magnolia smile. "Sounds good, Ron." She leaned over and gave me a quick kiss. "Thanks."

38 — THE MILSTEIN HALL OF OCEAN LIFE

Magnolia wore a black kung fu outfit to the museum, because no one does a spinning back kick wearing a strapless gown and five-inch pumps. As for me, I was well prepared for a fight. I had some typical edged weapons, as well as a boomerang, and a life-sized, rocket-propelled cardboard podiatrist named Dr. Franklin Foot.

Mags gave me a suspicious look. "What is that thing?"

"I found him on a website. Trust me, no one can shake a shoe like Dr. Foot."

I was happy Mags hadn't mentioned the "money incident" since yesterday's moment of passion. I knew it would pop up again—but for now, I wanted to think I'd sexed it right out of her system. I put Foot on the back of my chopper and raced all the way down 57th Street on my way to the Upper West Side. Mags flew over and met Biff. They were waiting for me in front of the museum when I roared up on my bike.

The American Museum of Natural History looks like the love child of a nerdy professor and a medieval fortress. I spotted Biff near the entrance on Central Park West, standing on the sidewalk in front of the wide stairs and towering columns. The place was officially closed for the evening, but there was a guard admitting people there.

Biff was wearing some sharply creased pants, Italian loafers, and a libido-colored sport blazer. It was the kind of outfit that really rubbed your face in its price tag.

I said, "Hi, Mags. You look great."

I barely grunted at Biff, who moved close to Mags—just as a photographer jumped from behind a column and snapped a picture. Biff shoved his smile into the flash and then the photographer ran away.

"Publicity!" I said. "Hey, maybe next time one of us should show some cleavage."

Mags shook her head. "Maybe next time I'll loan you a push-up bra. Let's go inside."

We approached the guard at the door. He examined our invitation and then looked at the extra guests. Biff explained that I was with him, and I explained that Dr. Foot was a podiatric legend. I also slipped the guy a hundred bucks.

The guard motioned for us to enter. We walked through a bunch of passages and then entered the Milstein Hall of Ocean Life.

The hall is a spectacular place. Visitors descend a sparkling staircase and walk into a cavernous room bathed in ocean-blue light, complete with a glass roof that shimmers high above a polished oak dance floor. The entire hall is ringed by a walkway, as well as a series of huge video screen panels and dioramas that glitter with splashy images from the bottom of the sea. There's also a life-sized replica of a blue whale dangling from the ceiling.

The room holds about a thousand people, and it can be hired by anyone with enough dead presidents to pay for the dance. Tonight there was a string quartet playing in the corner of the room, and the room was filled with guests. Schools of butlers were swarming around with platters of shrimp, and people were scooping them up and shoving them down. I spotted Thaddeus standing next to Sandra. As always, she reminded me of a golden-haired hypodermic needle.

Biff waved. "Hey, it's Thaddeus!"

Thaddeus and his ex-wife approached us. Thad said, "Magno Girl! What a surprise." He turned to Sandra and said, "Sandra the Sure, meet the famous Magno Girl." Sandra held out her hand, but Mags just nodded. Thad smiled. "I hope we won't be needing your services this evening. Magno Girl is the city's greatest crime fighter."

Biff seemed to bristle at Thad's introduction, but then he grinned. "I've been studying martial arts with her, Thaddeus. She's great."

Sandra nodded at me. "How nice to see you again. And Magno Girl, we meet at last. Thaddeus has told me quite a bit about you. I find your special gaze fascinating. How long have you had this power?"

"A long time," Mags said. "Since I was young."

"You're young now."

"Can you call my mother and tell her that?"

"I'm sure she knows. A mother has a way of knowing everything."

Mags smiled in a special way, like she was trying not to puke. Sandra said, "By the way, that's an interesting outfit. I'm glad my children were never interested in martial arts—too much violence. My daughter plays soccer at the University of Hawaii. The coaches say she's the best one on the team."

"Hawaii is nice," Mags said. "Has your daughter tried poi?"

"Certainly not! She's completely heterosexual."

Mags gave me a sideways glance. "Right."

Sandra grinned. "My other daughter plays soccer in high school. She's probably going to get a scholarship. She has a boyfriend."

"Oh, do they give scholarships for that? I hope he can keep her away from the evil root of the taro plant."

Sandra grimaced and her eyes sizzled. "My daughters don't do that stuff! They don't! Still, you're right to mention it; it's everywhere today. A mother has to be so careful. Do you have any children, Magnolia?"

"No."

"Someday you'll understand."

"I already understand. That's why I use birth control."

Sandra frowned and then stretched a bayonet-smirk across her face. "It was nice meeting you, Magno Girl. We'll talk again sometime."

Thaddeus said, "Yes, perhaps we will." Then Thad and Sandra walked off to greet other guests.

Biff said, "Thaddeus might want to put you in a commercial— hey, there's Fig Rider!"

Fig Rider was a professional golfer, and he was attracting an audience. Biff ran to fête the Fig, and I turned to Mags.

"Why didn't you blast Thaddeus?" I said.

"Relax, I'm waiting for Melvin. I want to get them both at once. We've got all night."

Her words caused a knot to form in the pit of my stomach. I knew that patience was a virtue—but I still liked to shoot first, ask no questions, and then shoot again, because that's what usually works.

"What do you think of Sandra?" I said.

Mags glanced around and lowered her voice. "I did some more research on her this morning, and in addition to being Thad's ex-wife, she's definitely a witch."

"Right," I said, catching my breath. "You looked this up somewhere?"

"Yes, in the International Witch Registry."

"Are you kidding?"

"Of course I'm kidding. But I suspected it after your pizza incident, and now that I've met her, I know."

I smiled. "Takes one to know one, huh?"

She gave me a short laugh. "Actually, yeah."

"Well, she reminds me of a nasty sorority sister. What else do you know?"

"Thad and Sandra were divorced ten years ago, back when Americamart was a much smaller chain. So the press didn't report much. Do you follow me?"

"I'd follow you anywhere, Mags. How about a vacation in the tropics?"

A booming voice behind me said, "Hey, try Aruba! Just watch what you do on the beach, brother—all that sand can really get into a girl's sandbox, if you know what I mean."

I turned to see Al, dressed in a tuxedo.

He had a girl on his arm and a glass of wine in each fist. Despite the fancy clothes, he still looked out of place in the room, like a half chewed hunk of sausage in a bin of truffles.

"Al, what's up?" I said. "Are you cooking tonight?"

"Nah, I'm a guest." He yanked at the girl on his sleeve. "Trish, this is my brother and his famous girlfriend, Magnolia the Magno Girl."

Mags ignored Al, but gave Trish a polite nod. Trish said, "Oh, I've seen you on television. I love your hair! What kind of conditioner do you use? And where did you get that outfit? Is that a designer thing?"

Al said, "Yeah, what's with the karate suit? Are you gonna do some party tricks tonight?"

Mags smiled. "Yeah, I'm going to pull a sloppy fat pizza maker out of a hat." She turned and walked off.

Al gave Trish a little squeeze. "I told you she was sassy, but she doesn't mean it. She loves me. We're gonna mingle a bit, Ron." He started to saunter off in the general direction of the bar but after ten steps he motioned for Trish to wait, and he walked back over to me.

He pulled me aside. "Hey, brother, what about the teapots?"

I gave a snort. "Let's just say we can still hold a tea party for five thousand." I glanced around and lowered my voice. "Al, do you know anything about Magnolia's brother? Where is he?"

Al shrugged. "I haven't talked to him, but I heard he might be in Mexico." Then he slipped me a piece of paper and whispered, "Here's something else. It might help you out."

I glanced down and saw a scribbled address somewhere in Chinatown.

"What's there?"

He shifted his eyes and kept his voice low. "It's where your friend Ton Lee hangs out. If they knew I told you—"

"My mouth is sealed, brother." I stared at him and he stared back.

"Thanks," I said and walked away.

Meanwhile, the room was starting to fill up, and I saw a bunch of celebrities wandering around. There was Dudley Doostein, the mayor of New York. There was Ray McCallahan, the Chief of Police. There were lots of political types, guys I didn't know, who reeked of money and fundraising. And then the butlers brought out the pizza.

Everyone smiled and started gobbling up the food while Thaddeus walked toward the front of the room. Melvin Shrick had arrived, and he was standing by Thad's side. Thaddeus was about to speak in his mouthy rumble. I spotted Mags moving closer to him, and I started moving closer to her.

Thaddeus said, "Hello, everyone. I'd like to thank you all for coming. We're here tonight to celebrate the success of a new product—the 'More For Me' pizza. Yes, Americamart has partnered with Pie Hole Pizza Incorporated to bring the world a new and better version of this traditional Italian-American fare. Please eat multiple slices and enjoy yourselves."

Mags was right near him. I knew she was about to fire the Gaze—and then out of nowhere jumped Biff Taylor. Actually, he stumbled right into her and spilled two drinks all over her kung fu outfit.

"Oh, damn! I'm so sorry, Magnolia!"

"That's all right, Biff. I'll clean it later." She tried to go around him. I tried to push Biff out of the way. But three waiters were right there. They were the biggest waiters I'd ever seen—these guys had been lifting some serious silverware.

One of the waiter-goons said, "No! We'll get something to clean that up!" His friends were blocking our path. A waitress jumped forward and started to wipe Mags off.

Mags said, "I'm sorry, but I need to talk with these guys." She was ready to leap over them—but Thaddeus was moving fast for a guy of his tonnage and was already quite a few hoagie lengths away from Melvin, who was dashing off in the opposite direction.

Biff smiled. "Thaddeus has some business that just came up—trust me, it's not a good time to talk. He's coming back in thirty minutes to take a few questions and then pose for some photos with Shrick."

Mags hesitated. Thaddeus was almost out of the room, and Melvin was lost in the crowd. They were just too far apart. She looked annoyed but said, "Okay, I'll talk to him later."

Biff smiled. "Magnolia, would you like to visit The Hall of Northwest Coast Indians with me?"

"Thanks for the invitation, Biff, but I'd rather stay here and keep an eye on things."

"Can't Ron do that? I mean, if he doesn't get too drunk?"

"Hey," I said, "I can keep an eye on things when I'm plenty drunk."

Biff said, "Did you know the Indian exhibit is the oldest one in the museum? I'd love to give you a tour. It'll only take a few minutes." He leaned close to Mags and whispered something in her ear.

Mags glanced at me. "You know what, Ron? Maybe I'll check it out. I'll be right back—don't worry."

Then she walked off with Biff.

I was incensed, but only for a second—because I realized she wanted me to follow. Or maybe not. Either way, I tossed my drink, checked out my concealed weaponry, and left the room.

39 — THE HALL OF NORTHWEST COAST INDIANS

The Hall of Northwest Coast Indians is a funky room full of ancient artifacts. The lighting is soft like a glowing moon. The atmosphere is primitive and looks like a garden of totem poles.

Mags and Biff came walking toward me. Biff spotted me and made a sour face, like he'd just found a bug pissing in his caviar.

Mags said, "Hi, Ron. Biff was just giving me a tour."

I stared at Biff. He smiled at me. I tried to maintain control—but I failed and seized him by the throat.

"Keep away from her, you bastard!"

"Gaaag! Grrr! Motherfucker!"

Mags cursed and leaped between us, flinging us apart. *Will you guys knock it off?* She was about to say something else, but she froze and narrowed her eyes. "Someone's coming."

I peered out from behind a totem and saw a bunch of ninjas slipping fast into the room. Right behind them was Subterranean Bob, carrying what looked like an oversized peace pipe.

Bob said, "Ooooh, hello there, Magno Girl. I've come to make you another offer. Well, not really, heh-heh." Then he put the pipe against his shoulder and pulled a tiny trigger and a flood of smoke filled the room. Mags took a step back—it was tobacco smoke.

Bob roared with laughter. "The Surgeon General can kiss my cancer cluster! *And Magno Girl, you will die!*"

More ninjas followed Bob, fanning out in all directions, and I knew we were in trouble. I heard Mags cough and step farther back into the collection of primitive doodads. I reached for my samurai sword.

I could've waited for the right moment to strike, but I've learned over the years there's never a right fucking moment. So I shouted and leaped out from behind my totem, unleashing a mighty blow that missed its mark and stuck in the totem's wooden face—*kerchunk!* With another shout, I yanked my blade free and watched the totem pole crash down onto a glass case filled with Indian birth control devices or maybe just arrowheads. Either way, the destruction of priceless artifacts had begun.

I cursed and shouted, "Look out for those two!" There were a couple of guys charging right at us. Mags leaped into the air and hovered near the ceiling. I dueled with two of the masked men, and sparks flew from the clash of our blades. I kicked another totem pole into the path of two more charging ninjas and then tossed a Chilkat blanket at them. I also flung a ceremonial headdress, and a wooden duck, and an argillite bowl.

One ninja sneered at me. "It's bad luck to fling a wooden duck."

"Really?" I said as our swords locked. "And what about the argillite bowl?"

"No, I think argillite is okay."

I smiled. "Argillite is fragile—a lot like your testicles."

I kicked him in the balls. As he gasped and hit the floor, I noticed Biff in the corner of my eye. Biff punched a guy and then was struck by the hilt of a weapon. He tottered for a second and went down. Meanwhile, the smoke was really starting to fill the room. Mags dropped from the ceiling and clobbered two guys running toward me.

They tried to get up, but she was too quick and stomped on them hard. A good face-stomping is worth a hundred spinning back fists. I whirled and headed for an open area of the room, near a humongous Haida canoe that featured a replica crew. I figured if I hurried maybe I could sail that baby right into the Hayden Planetarium.

A pack of guys with scimitars was racing after me. I jumped onto the deck of the boat, and I reached for my boomerang. Quick as a kangaroo, I hurled it into the air and shouted an ancient battle cry.

The flying Australian cudgel warbled through the smoke and then ricocheted off a totem pole—right before it whizzed harmlessly out of the room. I grimaced and cursed my misspent time at Arunta's Online Boomerang Academy. In the distance, I heard Bob laughing and shouting, "Breathe the sweet fire of your destruction, Magno Girl! *Die! Die!*"

The smoke was thick like a billowy curtain of death. A pack of ninjas was converging around the sides of my ship. I shouted and started striking and spinning like a razor-blade tornado. I hadn't seen this many swords since that night in Tokyo where I'd won the daughter of a radical Buddhist cult leader in a ping pong match. One weapon sliced my arm and another slashed my leg. I cursed and shouted and swore to have my revenge—and then I saw Mags in the distance, down on the floor.

She was crawling and gagging and in lots of trouble. I saw another pack of bad guys racing toward her with their murderous blades held high. I recalled the words of my old teacher, "It's always darkest before the donut." He was a little plump for a kung fu master, but I made a quick decision—it was time for the Leap of Unfathomable Faith.

A warrior who learns the Leap can only perform the spectacular maneuver three times in his life, and this would be my second leap—the first leap having been used during an ill-fated job interview where I'd totally botched the question about "where do you see yourself in five years." I grinned and shouted, *"Woohoo!"* as my thighs exploded.

I was propelled high into the air and far across the room while simultaneously executing a series of backward somersaults.

It's been said that certain warriors have seen god during this maneuver, while others have seen only the contents of their stomachs. I landed on my feet a few steps from Magnolia with my sword up and ready. The shocked ninjas stared from a distance, and then they shouted and charged toward us.

"Mags, are you okay?"

She coughed and tried to stand. "Yeah, I'm fine." Then she fell back to the ground. I set my jaw and gripped my sword and prepared for a bloody fight to the finish—and then I remembered I still had one great stunt left in my sock drawer. I snarled and hit the remote control button for Dr. Franklin Foot, the rocket-propelled podiatrist I'd stashed near the bar in the other room.

Foot's location might have been a problem for a lesser piece of cardboard, but I guess Dr. Foot had graduated near the top of his class. He had no trouble blasting off from his spot near the whiskey and navigating a few simple turns until he reached the Hall of Northwest Coast Indians.

A thundering roar filled the air. Everyone stopped and stared as Franklin Foot came whooshing into the room. His eyes were electric, and the rockets blazed from his igneous feet. The ninjas froze in terror as Foot targeted them. And then the cardboard podiatrist crashed among them and detonated in an awesome fireball.

The cotton clad warriors screamed in horror. They were all on fire as they ran from the room. Bob was blown to the floor, and his peace pipe conked out. He reached for it and pulled the trigger and saw only an incidental puff of tar.

Bob snarled. "I curse you to cardboard hell! Ugh!"

I ran toward Mags as she staggered to her feet. The tobacco smoke had made her weak, but she'd recover soon enough. And that's when Thaddeus appeared.

He came drifting through the smoke like an overloaded garbage scow, and beside him was Sandra the Sure. Thaddeus stopped and coughed a few times. He said, "Magno Girl, I'm here to make you an offer. Wait, no—that's not true. I'm here to put an end to your meddling—yes, that's right." He laughed long and hard.

I reached for a hand grenade. Sandra smiled and unleashed a thunderbolt from the fingertips of her right hand that struck me in the chest.

"Damn!" I flew across the room and crashed into a glass case full of wooden masks. The case shattered and a dozen wooden grimaces tumbled to the ground.

I tried to move, but I was paralyzed. I started to panic—how would I twist the throttle of my Harley? Sandra said, "Don't worry, your paralysis is temporary."

Mags snarled and fired the Gaze of the Guilt at Sandra. The pink rays stormed from her eyes—but some type of barrier prevented them from reaching their target. Sandra kept smiling as Mags turned up the intensity, but either the tobacco smoke had weakened her too much, or Sandra was too strong.

Sandra stood there and laughed. "I am protected by the Shield of Sureness, Magnolia. I know my way is the best way, and I feel no guilt. And you, Magnolia—you are protected by *nothing*."

She raised her right hand again and fired multiple thunderbolts. Mags dodged the first two but was hit by a third. She was flung across the room and crashed hard into a totem pole. The pole toppled over and Mags fell to the ground.

Sandra laughed again. "You really should get married and have a few children, Magnolia. It's hard work, but you'll stay on your feet more often."

Mags slowly got up from the floor and glared. She said, "You really should stop giving me advice. I already have a mother." And then Mags flew at her.

Sandra fired a fast bolt that struck Mags in the torso, but this time Mags gritted her teeth and kept coming until she crashed into Sandra's shield. There was a loud bang and Sandra tumbled backward. Mags went head over heels and smashed into the floor. Thaddeus sort of skipped out of the way. Sandra was knocked to the ground, but she got up and raised her left hand, which featured extra long fingernails painted in complex acrylic designs.

She aimed her nails at Mags. "You're too weak to fight with me, Magnolia."

With a *whoosh*, all five of her fingernails flew through the air—and they hit Magno Girl. Mags sucked in her breath and staggered backward and then fell down. I could tell she was in real pain.

I was incensed. I'd never wanted to do anything more than I wanted to protect Magnolia. And here I was frozen like an engine without oil.

Sandra chuckled. "Don't worry, the poison in my nails won't kill you. It will just render you helpless while I cast my spell."

Mags writhed on the floor. She struggled to speak and finally said, "Why are you involved in this evil plot?"

Sandra smiled. "You ask too many questions." Then she pointed her hand at Mags and fired a thunderbolt into her head. Magnolia screamed and collapsed into unconsciousness. Her shout went through me like a car crash. I struggled to move but I couldn't budge.

Sandra stood over Mags and waved her hand. Then she chanted a few words no smarter than the lyrics to an average pop song:

"You have no worth
Until you give birth
And you'll lose your power
Until that hour
Search yourself
Know it's true
I've made a woman
Out of you
And for this spell
There is no cure
As long as I am
Sandra Sure"

The lights in the room flickered a bit. Sandra said, "Now it is done, Magnolia. Every minute you're alive your powers will weaken, until you are a completely normal woman living an ordinary life—which is the best thing a girl can do. The only way to break the spell is to get married and give birth to a child—or defeat me completely. Of course, when you have a child, you'll be too busy caring for it to be meddling in other people's affairs—a joyously ironic punishment that you will appreciate one day."

And then Sandra turned toward me and said, "Now what can I do with you?"

I growled. "I was kind of hoping you'd let me go so I could introduce you to my pet chainsaw."

She laughed. "I think every useless derelict needs a wife. Maybe you should become the lucky groom."

She zapped me with a thunderbolt, and I grimaced.

She smirked. "What have you got to say for yourself now?"

I was engulfed by waves of agony; I felt like the batter inside a waffle iron. When the pain finally stopped, I had a great revelation.

"Hey, I need to get married," I said. "I need to buy a ring. Let me out of here so I can get Mags down to the courthouse."

Sandra laughed. "Yes! You are obsessed with marrying Magnolia and getting her pregnant. It is your greatest ambition."

Meanwhile, Mags rolled over, barely cognizant, and fired the Gaze of the Guilt once again—at Thaddeus. Thaddeus shouted and staggered backward as a wave of pink light struck him. His reaction was unexpected.

"Augh!" he wailed. "It was all our fault! We should have known what he was doing! We should have saved him from those drugs! I killed my son—we both did, Sandra. He's gone and we can never get him back."

Sandra cringed as her face turned a tortured shade of crimson.

"Shut up, Thad! It's not true. It wasn't our fault!"

"It's true Sandra. You know it's true!"

"No, it's not true! Shut up now!"

While they were fighting, I realized something—I could move

again. With a sneer and a shout, I ran toward the witch. Thaddeus stopped talking and stared at me with his pie plate eyes. Sandra whirled and fired off a bolt—but I dodged it, and managed to hit her in the throat with my fist. We both fell to the ground.

She coughed and gagged. "Get off of me!"

I tried to get a good hold on her—but she was slippery like a sewer pipe and jabbed a finger into my eye. As she rolled away I grabbed a chain that was dangling from her neck. She screamed as I started to choke her with it—but then it broke. Sandra was free and jumped to her feet.

But Mags was also up on her feet. She shouted as she leaped into the air and slammed her foot into Sandra's head. Sandra went down again.

The victory was short. As I leaped toward Sandra, she reached up from the floor and fired a multitude of new thunderbolts. I screamed as I felt my body freeze. Meanwhile, Mags was a magic wand's length away from stomping on Sandra's face when she also got hit. She let out a shout and fell to the ground.

I had to admit, Sandra was tough. She staggered to her feet, and she was furious.

"A momentary distraction, you fools! Now feel my power again!"

She unleashed a flurry of thunderbolts, and Mags screamed as they hit her. I watched in horror as her body jerked around on the floor, flooded with spastic orgasms of pain. Sandra tortured her for the longest minute of my life, and then finally stopped.

It was quiet. Sandra said, "That's the end of your magic gaze, Magno Girl. I've destroyed it—consider it the first of your powers to be eliminated. You should have learned a little more from your grandmother. Now if you'll excuse me, I have to go call my daughter. She's playing in a tournament tomorrow. Did I tell you she's the best player on the team? I also have to walk the dog and make some tuna salad."

She spun on her heels and left the room.

Thaddeus surveyed the wreckage throughout the hall, and he looked at Mags and me.

He sighed. "I wish I'd been a better parent. If you have children, Magnolia, make sure you watch over them." He turned and left.

I struggled to my feet and shook my head. This was the worst defeat I'd suffered since that drunken night in Atlantic City where I'd lost $4,000 playing the parking meters. I knelt beside Mags and put my arm around her as she sat up.

"Mags, are you okay?"

She massaged her temples. "I'm going to destroy that bitch."

She seemed okay.

"Look, we need to get married."

"What?"

"I want to marry you. Let's do it now."

Mags groaned. "Ron, let's go home. Hey, where the hell is Biff?"

I looked around, but Biff was gone. "He must have left. He's probably on the fifth hole by now."

40 — MAGS HAS A HEADACHE

I put Mags on the back of my bike, and we slipped out of there before the reporters and police showed up. By the time we got back to my place, Mags was feeling sick. On the bright side, I think her body was too exhausted to have a bad reaction to the Gaze. I put her in bed and covered her with PermaPower Cold Packs. I eventually fell asleep.

I woke up early the next morning and saw Magnolia standing in front of me. I leaped to my feet.

"How do you feel, Mags?"

She dumped a pile of PermaPower onto the floor. "I think I have frostbite. But thank you for your effort." She slumped onto the sofa. "I feel like I've been run over by a truck."

I sat down next to her. Outside, we heard the *kathump* of a fresh car accident and people cursing at each other in two different languages. Inside, neither of us spoke. Finally, I said, "Magnolia, will you marry me?"

She sighed. "No, of course not."

"Why not?"

"Ron, you're under a spell. And I don't want to get married."

"You don't love me?"

She looked at me with sober eyes. "Let's forget about it until after the spell is broken, okay?"

"Okay, but I'm going to rent a tux."

She rolled her head back against the sofa. "I never really thought a tux would be your style."

"Oh, you've thought about our big day?"

"No! Forget it."

"The tux is out. I'll get new boots. Hey, what did Biff whisper into your ear before you went into the Indian room?"

She hesitated. "He told me that Thaddeus wanted to meet with me in private and offer me a deal."

"*What?*" Now I was incensed. "You must have known it was a set-up! Why did you go without me?"

She gave me a weary smile. "I knew you'd follow. I thought we could handle it and make something happen."

"But that wasn't the plan."

"Yeah, I know. They were obviously on to us, so I made a decision. It seemed like a good idea at the time."

"We need to find that fucker, Biff. We need to make him blab like a barber."

"Yeah, I'd like to find him, too. Do barbers blab?"

"Sure, when you pound nails into their kneecaps."

She groaned. "Don't worry, we'll find him soon enough. You know, for a minute there I felt Sandra's spell disappearing."

"Yeah, she was distracted by Thaddeus."

"Was it just a distraction? They were having quite a discussion."

"I didn't catch all the details. I was too busy getting my ass kicked."

"It was a humbling experience."

"Even the best get beat sometimes."

"I know, but it still hurts."

"Mags, you're not a true warrior until you get clobbered—and then get back on your feet."

She stared at me, and she stood up. "I'm going to destroy that woman."

"Marriage and one kid will eliminate the spell. You'll be powerful again."

She started pacing around the room. Not too fast, though.

"That's really not an option, Ron. It's a clever spell. If I'm married with a child, I won't be able to *do* anything with my power. I'll be too busy changing diapers and telling everyone how my gifted little kid can burp up his dinner better than anyone his age. Or her age."

"Hey, I'll change a few diapers. If they don't smell too bad."

"Great. I'll leave you the ones that smell like honeysuckle. Like I said, it's not an option. And besides, we don't even know if her spell worked. Let's see how I feel later. I have to teach a class this afternoon."

"Are you crazy? You're injured."

"I'm all right. I just have a headache."

"Ha. Would you like a PermaPower Cold Pack? I have lots of them."

She gave me a cool look. "Okay," she said. And then her phone rang. She glanced at the number and rolled her exasperated eyes—but she still answered it. It was her mother.

"You're sending me cash, Magnolia?"

"Hello, Mom. Yeah, so you can go out and buy what you need."

"Go out? You know I don't like to leave the house. It's part of my condition."

"It would be good for you to go out."

"Oh, and would it be good for me to have a panic attack and end up dead in the gutter? Get rid of that loser, Magnolia, and marry someone with potential."

"Sure, right. Hey, do you know where Tommy is?"

"Your brother is in Mexico."

"What?"

"He said he was going there for vacation. Maybe he'll meet a nice girl. Mexican girls are good cooks."

"Can you contact him?"

"His phone doesn't work there, and I don't have the number where he's staying. I'm waiting for him to call."

"Mom, can you please contact Tommy and tell him to call me? It's important."

"I just told you I can't."

"Look, I don't have time for this crap. We both know you can reach him without a phone."

"Excuse me? What are you saying, Magnolia?"

"You know what I'm saying so please do it!"

"All of a sudden you want to talk to Tommy, but you never want to talk to me. You hate me!"

"I'm not getting upset," Mags said, mostly to herself. "I'm not going to let you upset me right now."

"Well, you're going to be upset! Because that's what I do, right? I upset you with all my good advice. Poor Magnolia, she has a mother who actually cares about her. Poor Magnolia, she has a mother who wants her to do something with her life—before her boobs are saggy and her uterus is dead!"

Mags covered the phone with her hand and swore with gusto.

"Mom, I'm having a bad day and I *really* have to go. Please, contact Tommy. And then buy yourself a dinner *that doesn't come in a bottle!*"

She hit the 'disconnect' icon on her phone—and then swung her fist at a nearby lamp, smashing it into a thousand pieces.

I started to make a joke, but didn't.

She looked at me and said nothing.

41— CORN MUFFINS AND BOY SCOUTS

That afternoon I went with Mags to her martial arts school. There were some people outside the place, standing around like a bunch of fat fire hydrants. I noticed someone had stolen the sign from the front door. I also saw Pepe and Jenni, who had keys to the place.

The kids ran toward us, and Pepe said, "These people came to see Magnolia. They want autographs and stuff. They ripped off the sign and the welcome mat. Some dude was even trying to take the magazine rack but I kicked him out."

So the adoring public had come. And they were leaving with the furniture.

Jenni took a good look at Mags. "What happened, Magnolia? Are you okay? You look tired."

Mags rubbed her eyes a bit. "I am tired. I was in a fight, honey. No one needs to know about it." She leaped into the air ahead of the advancing rabble and flew into an upstairs window. Meanwhile, I turned to face the grubby, drooling public.

A kid ran up to me. He was about nine years old. He wiped his grimy glasses on his T-shirt and said, "Can you get me some Magno Girl autographs?"

"Sure, no problem."

"Can you get me a lot of them?"

"Why do you need a lot?"

"My dad wants to sell them on the internet."

Some other people arrived. "Do you know Magno Girl? Do you know her?" Part of me didn't want to get involved, while another part of me was proud I'd seen her naked.

I noticed everyone was eating, and the deli guy looked happy. There were also several reporters hanging around, taking pictures of the place. One of them approached me. It was that joker from Channel 5, Jim Riteangle.

"Hello," Jim said, grinning like a game show host. "Can I interview Magno Girl?"

"No. She's teaching a class."

"Is it true that she's lost all her superpowers?"

"No, of course not. She's as super as always."

"How about the rumor that she's pregnant?"

"What?"

"Is the father someone famous? An actor? A rap star?"

"She's not pregnant."

"She had an abortion?"

"She didn't have an abortion."

"What about Biff Taylor? Does that name sound familiar?"

"No."

"So Biff is the father of her child?"

I resisted an urge to smash Jim's jaw through the back of his skull. Then I left Pepe on guard and went up to the second floor. Mags was busy stretching in the main room when some guy came slithering in. Pepe was right behind him and said, "Sorry, this guy got past me. I'll go down and lock the door." The guy wore a suit and tie, and his hair was plastered with a chemical compound that was probably contributing to atmospheric destruction.

The guy grinned. "Hello. I'm sorry for my aggressive style, but I just had to talk to you. My name is Edward Gowin, and I'm an agent. I represent some top talent, and I can make Magno Girl a star."

I reached for my daggers. Mags put her hand on my arm to restrain me.

"Edward, I'm not having a good day," she said. "You can talk to Ron."

Edward looked at me. "Of course, of course. It's great to meet you."

"Right," I said as I put on face number two, *the grimace of the onion.*

Edward's eyes watered a bit, but he continued. "I'm not trying to infringe; I'm trying to work with you. If you knew I could make you both very rich, would you be interested?"

Mags looked away, but I was still listening. "How, Edward?"

Eddie's eyes got wide. "Comic books, movies, dolls, T-shirts, ads for cheese."

"Ads for cheese?"

"I'm well connected with the dairy industry. With a little luck, you could be Miss Havarti."

"Havarti? That's not one of my favorites. What about Gouda?"

"Sure, sure, of course," he said without missing a beat. "Maybe even Swiss, or Kraft Single Slices—*an all American cheese for an all American girl.* The hee-haws in the Midwest will eat it up."

Mags said, "I have nothing against the Midwest."

"Oh, me neither," Edward said with a smirk. "They represent a viable market for all kinds of crap. We'll shove you under a cowboy hat and sell a ton of cheddar. We'll tweak your look a bit and you'll be the Princess of the Plains."

Mags suddenly seemed interested. "What's wrong with my look?"

Edward laughed. "Nothing, nothing—you're a very sexy girl. You just need to smile more. You need to—"

"I smile."

"Ha-ha, of course. But I've seen you on television, and you don't smile enough. A woman needs to smile *a lot* to be attractive. That's what studies show—big smile all the time, even while you're talking, with lots of bright teeth and maybe some blond hair."

"Excuse me. Do you see blond hair on my head?"

"No, and that's another issue. It's also the reason some brilliant guy invented hair dye. Studies show that blond hair will increase your marketability by a significant percentage. You could go with just a few highlights, of course, but the numbers aren't as good. I'll have to run a report concerning any kind of tint, but I'm sure it would be an improvement over dark brunette with red streaks."

"Get out," Mags said.

"Hey, I'm just giving you the facts."

"I said 'get out.' "

"How many Playboy centerfolds are blond?"

"I don't know. All of them?"

"Yes! All of them!"

"Great! I'll call you when I want to spread my legs for Playboy! *Now get out!*"

Mags eyes lit up, and she fired the Gaze of the Guilt at Edward. He staggered back as the rays hit him, and I waited for a stammering confession—but it didn't come.

Instead he paused and flashed a sugary smile. He seemed pretty pleased with himself. "I have two kids," he said. "Here's a photo... Billy is nine and Cindy is seven. Billy's teacher can't believe how fast he's learning the alphabet. And Cindy is in the school play. She's a carrot."

Mags stared. She grimaced and fired the Gaze again—only brighter.

Edward just grinned like a camera flash. "Do you have any kids? I think my son Billy is going to become an altar boy. I hope no one molests him."

Magnolia turned away. "Ron, get this guy out of here."

I grabbed Edward by the back of the neck and shoved him toward the window—another body was about to rain down on the deli below. Also, I was hoping to kill a few of Magno Girl's fans. Mags stopped me and pointed Edward toward the door.

Edward threw a bunch of business cards as Pepe and I tossed him down the stairs. He crashed to the bottom, shook off a few contusions, and then started talking again. He looked up at us and shouted, "My daughter is on the honor roll! My son collects string! My wife cooks one heck of a corn muffin!"

I stomped down the stairs and shoved him outside and then slammed the door. Then I bolted back up to the office, where I found Mags sitting in a chair, staring into space.

"Okay, Mags, so the Gaze is broken, and now it brings out the soccer mom in everyone. Big deal."

Magnolia said nothing. Pepe and Jenni looked into the office.

Pepe said, "Are you okay, Magnolia?"

"She'll be fine," I said. "Just give her a minute. And give me a beer." I reached into the icebox and pulled out a frosty one.

Mags rubbed her eyes. "Pepe, can you open the door down there, and tell anyone who comes for the class that I'll be right there? Get everyone stretching, and tell them to ignore the fact that Ron is getting loaded."

Pepe nodded. "Okay."

I grinned. "One beer is not loaded. If they're still here after fourteen, then we'll talk."

Pepe walked into the other room. "Jenni, can you go with him?" I said. "We'll be right out."

"Is Magnolia okay?"

"She'll be fine."

"What's wrong? Is she sick?"

"No—yeah. Maybe."

"Is she pregnant?"

"No!" Mags said. "This is a small problem, honey. I won't be buying a crib any time soon."

Jenni kept staring with concern, but then she went to join Pepe.

I put my beer-free hand on Magnolia's shoulder and caressed her a bit. "Honey, I'm sure this is all temporary. By the way, still no news about Biff?"

"No."

"We're going to find him and hit him with the Gaze—"

A pained look stabbed into her eyes. "Sorry," I said. "Mags, let's get married. I'm serious."

Mags rose from her chair. I'd never seen her look so tired. She reached out and touched my face, and she traced a line with her fingers. She said, "I'm really not the marrying kind, Ron. It's something I thought we had in common. I thought you were married to your motorcycle."

I waved my hand. "Yeah, but I've been thinking about that— see, my motorcycle doesn't have any breasts. Let's go to the courthouse."

"Oh, that's very romantic. Ron, you're under a spell. Think about it; we're not married now, and you see my breasts all the time."

"Hey, that's true. But it will be different when we're married."

"I don't think so. It's going to be the same old boobs, buddy. Unless there's more to that ceremony than I realize."

"Honey, forget about the fooki. Let's get you healthy again and have a kid."

Mags ignored me, and then said, "Thaddeus mentioned a dead son, and it caused Sandra to become weak. We need to get more information. And you need to stop annoying me."

"Okay. I'll try and stop the marriage talk, but I don't think it's the spell. I really like you."

She sighed. "I like you, too. After this class I've got an appointment with Professor Pooka at Columbia University. He's the guy who's been analyzing the pizza. We'll see what he's learned."

42 — PROFESSOR POOKA

I rode my chopper to Columbia University, located in Morningside Heights, between the hubbub of Harlem and the dirty Hudson River. It's pretty up there, with a big city blend of colleges and taxicabs and gray Gothic towers.

Professor Pooka laughed and looked out the window of his 3rd floor office high above the noisy traffic on Broadway. Pooka was a fat little guy, and let's face it, I wouldn't trust a thin guy to analyze a pizza. He also had a European accent.

Mags got right to the point. "So, Professor, what have you discovered?"

The professor rubbed his hands together. "I've done quite a bit of research, and I've made a fabulous discovery—very few people have ever studied fooki's effects on humans. So I will be the first to publish a major article."

"Yes, but what have you learned?"

"Oh, I've learned that I have a chance to be famous. It's very exciting."

"But what about your research?"

"Well, I fed it to a monkey, and he tried to buy an espresso machine."

"That must have been tricky."

"Yes, especially with his credit. I also ran it through some advanced chemical analysis and fed it to a bunch of student volunteers. Then I dissected a couple of the kids' brains—well, not yet, ha-ha—wishful thinking."

The professor looked back down into the bustling cityscape and chuckled. "The few studies done about fooki suggest it produces strong emotional feelings when mixed with certain substances at the proper temperature. The pizzas being sold by Pie Hole are obviously intended as delivery systems for the fooki. The fooki mixes with the tomato sauce at a high temperature and produces the effect you've already seen, causing humans to seek gratification through materialistic means."

Mags gave a sardonic laugh. "You mean they want to buy all kinds of crap?"

"Exactly," the professor replied. "However, there's more to the reaction. As the concentration of fooki builds up in the brain, the victim's brain becomes very susceptible to suggestion. Especially while hearing certain types of sound."

Mags raised an eyebrow. "Such as?"

"Low frequency sound works best—and the louder the sound, the more the effect is accentuated."

"Low frequency? You mean like a bass guitar?"

"Oh, that would do the trick. Something low and dark and evil."

Magnolia's eyes got wide with excitement. "Something like the song on the Pie Hole Pizza commercial!"

I grinned. "Ha, and I always thought the Antichrist would be singing a country song."

Pooka said, "This is monumental news. I will get a big award."

Mags walked over to the professor's computer and typed in a web address. "That makes perfect sense with this," she said. As the website appeared, the pounding riff blared through the room. The site was filled with ads for pizza. The site was also filled with ads for microwave ovens currently on sale at Americamart. And red text scrolled across the screen: "EAT MORE PIZZA! COME BACK SOON! EAT MORE PIZZA! COME BACK SOON!"

Mags said, "So a victim eats the pizza, and then sees a commercial ordering him or her to the website. The website tells the victim what to buy, and then tells him to eat more pizza and 'come back soon.' It's a mind control drug—and it will control a never-ending cycle of mass consumerism. It's a 'one-day sale' that happens every day. Professor, what are the long-term effects?"

Pooka looked thoughtful. "The fooki works very fast to break down the brain. Too much fooki and too much bass might produce a 'fooki overload effect' that will cause some other, more terrible reaction. I'll have to keep studying my volunteers."

"Do these kids know their brains are being destroyed?"

"Oh, don't worry about it. They are all failing."

"Can the effect be reversed?"

"It might wear off in time. Or maybe not."

Mags said, "We need to warn the world."

I said, "We need to book a restaurant."

"A restaurant?" Pooka said.

Mags glared. "We're not getting married, and I wouldn't want a restaurant, anyway."

"You wouldn't?" I said. "You're going to get married and not serve dinner?"

"I would elope. I mean if we were doing it, which we're not."

"If we were doing it, would you want to go to Vegas? Because I can theoretically book a flight."

"Vegas? I suppose it's the right place for such a big gamble—*but we're not getting married!*"

The professor said, "Weddings are very beautiful. You would make a stunning bride."

Mags sighed. "We need to warn the world about the fooki."

Pooka grinned. "Yes, I was thinking you should call up some reporters and have them interview me on television. I could straighten up the lab and take a shower. We will get on the cover of major magazines, maybe."

"I can call Holly Honey," Mags said.

Pooka's eyes got wide like a pair of pancakes. "Oh yes, call her for sure. She is very pretty. I will cook her a dinner rich in lycopene and antioxidants."

I laughed. "If you want to score, you should throw in a couple of steaks."

We said goodbye to the professor and walked outside.

"What about Biff?" I said.

"I did some checking," Mags said with a nod. "According to his maid, he went to Europe for a month."

"Do you believe that?"

"Of course not. I'm going over to his apartment."

"You're not going alone."

"Ron, I can take care of myself. Don't tell me what to do."

I stopped walking. "Mags, I'm not telling you what to do. I just want you to be safe, okay?"

She gave me a hard stare. "Look, right now I feel tired and I'm going home." Then she paused and softened her eyes. "Maybe later we'll go over there."

"Okay."

Mags turned and leaped into the air—and fell right back down to the ground. She hit the pavement hard and I ran to her.

"Mags, are you okay?"

"I'm fine! I'm fine."

"It's the spell! You're losing your ability to fly."

She looked furious. She didn't say a word as I helped her to her feet. She jumped up again, and this time she got airborne. She hovered above me but seemed to be struggling, like a guy in a circus trying to balance five flaming bombs on his nose.

"Mags, are you sure you should be up there? What if you fall? Get back down here."

"No! I can do it. Stop worrying about me. I'm going to go home and call Holly. Maybe tomorrow we'll warn everyone."

She wobbled off through the air. I watched her disappear above the buildings.

43 — TON LEE'S LAST STAND

My heart was heavy as I watched her fly away. I found myself wandering the streets of New York, riding fast trains to nowhere. Eventually, nowhere turned into Chinatown, where I had a job to do.

With a clenched jaw, I rambled through the swarming mobs on Canal Street and plowed past the shops filled with exotic cuisine— vegetables that looked like hairy hand grenades, and racks filled with dried tongues, and cartoonish pressed ducks smashed flat by steamrollers. I smelled noodles cooking and dumplings frying, and I saw bent old guys with wispy cotton beards selling piles of stinky herbs.

I checked the address on the slip of paper Al had handed me, and then I walked into a bar sandwiched between a grocery and a Chinese restaurant. It was a seedy little dive. A few faces peered through the sour-smelling darkness, and one of them belonged to Ton Lee.

Ton was sitting at the bar, drinking his rice wine. He glanced at me with two drunken eyes.

"So, Sensei Ron has found me at last," he said with a belch. "It is unlucky day for you. A plague of snakes and baboons will enter your world."

I grinned. "Is your whole family coming, Ton?"

He put down his drink and glared. "Do you call my mother a baboon or a snake?"

"Take your pick."

He gave it some thought, and then said, *"How dare you call my mother a baboon!"*

Ton leaped from his chair. He reached for a weapon, but I held up my hand.

"Do you even like your mother, Ton?"

Ton paused. "She is okay. I suppose she did best she could."

"Right. That's all a guy can ask for, I guess."

"I was no saint of a son. I should have done more good for her."

"Yeah, I know what you mean."

"It is not easy being mother. It is much responsibility. I do not know if I could handle it well myself."

"True, Ton, true."

He relaxed his fighting posture a bit. "So, what you want?"

"Can I buy you a drink?"

"No. I will buy you drink. Then we fight."

"Okay."

We sat at the bar. Ton ordered me a shot of whiskey and a beer. I downed the shot and said, "I think I know who whacked Joey the Round Man. I just want to know—was my brother involved in the hit?"

Ton laughed and sipped his drink. "And why I tell you?"

"I don't know. Maybe you have doubts about your job. Maybe you feel unappreciated by your boss. Or maybe you're just shit-faced drunk."

Ton laughed again and gulped more booze. "With all three, you are right. Anyway, we did not whack dough boy. That was not us. We only supply fooki and try to whack you and girl. I should have finished you off after pineapple blow. I make mistake with that fruit many times."

"Don't feel bad, Ton. I've had some fruit problems over the years, too. So what about my brother and Joey?"

He leaned closer to me. "A witch kill Joey."

"A tall blonde? Talks about her kids a lot?"

"Yes. Daughter plays soccer. Other girl has boyfriend and scholarship. Family dog go to Harvard soon. Very big fucking deal."

"And my brother wasn't involved?"

"No. It was witch. She visit girl's family, too."

I put down my drink. "What? When?"

"After your girl see dead dough boy. I drive witch and science guy to Brooklyn. They had scam—pretend to be movie producers. They meet brother, and witch look into brain and learn things."

"Damn! So Mags was right, and Tommy's a dumb-ass but not a traitor. That witch is causing big problems for me and my girl."

Ton shrugged. "Your girlfriend is pretty, and hard to kill. I wish I could meet girl like that. Does she have sister who might go for Chinese guy?"

"She has no sisters."

"Too bad. I need girlfriend to wash socks."

"Did you try the laundromat?"

"Yes, and supermarket. I met girl in frozen fish section."

"Did you get her phone number?"

"No. I want girl who cooks fresh fish. Frozen stuff not so good."

"Maybe you're being too picky. My girl eats tuna right out of the can."

"Really? Maybe I must be more realistic."

"That's right," I said, waving my beer. "You can't always expect a girl to do the wash and fillet your flounder. Sometimes you have to compromise."

"Ha, I could maybe eat tuna in can. But frozen bok choy is not so tasty."

"Well, you've still got a right to your vegetables. I didn't say you'd have to give up everything. But you also need to think about what you have to offer. It's a two-way street."

"I have job!" he said, banging his fist on the bar. "I am not so bad looking. I am funny."

"You don't seem funny."

"I am *very* funny. She will laugh or I will kill her."

"I'm sure she'll find that hilarious."

"Yes! And I also have nice apartment."

I paused and raised an eyebrow. "What about your mother? Is she the kind who interferes?"

"Only with sister—girl has eggs."

"So I've heard."

"Plus, I start my own business one day soon."

"What are you going to do?"

"I will be Chinese grocer or martial arts instructor."

"You better work on the fruit stuff. It's got to be fresh. And never let a guy get up after you've hit him with a pineapple."

"Ha, true. Maybe we fight now."

He flashed me a vicious look as we both leaped from our stools. Then he grabbed a nearby spear, and with a grunt he hurled his weapon through the air. He shouted, *"My giant pole to penetrate your ass like one thousand raging dragons!"*

I was starting to see why Ton couldn't find a girl. I ducked under the sailing missile and quickly tossed a handful of nutritional yeast into his eyes.

"Ugh! You hurl active cultures into my irises!"

I laughed at the quick success of my old baker-warrior trick. Ton was completely blinded by my favorite kind of bread mold, and he promptly crashed into a coat rack and started staggering around the room with outstretched arms.

I sipped my beer and watched him stumble. After a few more accidents, he stopped.

He turned his head in my general direction and said, "I will call upon my inner eye to guide me." He took a few deep breaths and assumed a fighting stance—and then he leaped like a leopard, smashing right into a brick wall.

That inner eye thing never works. Ton swore and fell to the floor. He whispered, "Damn you, inner eye!" and passed out.

I laughed and whipped out my battery powered Mold-A-Matic hair dryer. If Ton wanted a girlfriend he'd need more style, and I felt a sudden surge of generosity toward the guy. I worked fast, blowing his hair from a few obtuse angles, but then the hair dryer caught on fire. A tongue of flame shot from the muzzle and burned off Ton's eyebrows.

"Damn!" I said and tossed the machine to the floor where it fizzled out. I turned to the bartender. "What do you think?"

"Not bad. Where are eyebrows?"

I shrugged as Ton started coming around. Thinking fast, I grabbed him in the *Hug Of The Harlot*, an ancient hold I'd learned from a high priestess of Zen prostitution. I squeezed him a couple of times and a few coins fell from his pockets.

"Ton, do you hear me?"

"I… hear… you."

"What do you know about the fooki pie website?"

"I am just simple assassin. I know little details, only that they use private FreeBSD Unix servers with Apache software to host."

"Good. Now what the hell does that mean?"

"It means website computers are in fat man's house, stupid."

"And what plans do your people have for Magno Girl?"

"Melvin wants girl eliminated when powers fade."

My head began to whirl like a washing machine. "What? Eliminate the girl I plan to marry?"

"Better have wedding quick. By the way, I do DJ work."

"It's bad luck to hire people who want to kill the bride."

"I give good rate. Play best tunes."

"She doesn't want to marry me, anyway."

"She wants to marry."

"How do you know?"

"I know this thing. My dear mother tell me—all girls want to marry."

I shook my head. "Magnolia's different, Ton. She's got her own way of doing things."

"She can fly. She can fight. She still wants to marry one day. I know for sure."

At this point, the bartender said, "When you guys done cuddling, I need pay for drinks."

Suddenly, my hold was broken. Ton's face lit up and he yanked himself free.

He said, "I will play only funeral song at your wedding!"

I jumped to my feet. *"What about Small Harry?"*

Ton spat on the floor, and his saliva bubbled with contempt. "He is no friend. Melvin hire him to help fight girl. Now he guards fooki factory, but he cannot fight, only cough and smoke. *I will fight!"*

Ton whirled and plunged his hand into a nearby fish tank, yanking out a fat carp. It was heavy and wet, and he prepared to strike—but as he pulled back his fist full of fish, he noticed his reflection in a nearby mirror.

He gasped. "My hair is changed."

"Do you like it?"

"Where are eyebrows? *How will I get girl if I have no brows?"*

I flashed a sheepish grin. "Maybe they'll grow back while you're asleep." Then I reached into a tank of my own, grabbed a live lobster, and slugged Ton across the side of the head with it—*sphlat!* It was the sort of beautiful crunching thud that only fresh seafood can produce.

Ton tumbled against the wall and tried to recover, but I was quick with my crustacean and gave him an upward chop into the groin. It was a nice meaty blow that used the full, rounded area behind the gills. Ton gasped as his eyes rolled upward, and once again he went down. This time I knew he'd be there for a while. I followed the ancient custom of respect and threw my lobster onto his face, along with some lemon and a head of garlic.

"May you find a good woman to cook this food for you, Ton—and may you remember that a lobster has an exoskeleton, making it a better weapon than a fish."

I paid the bartender and walked out into the street.

44 — CALL TO MAGS

It was dangerous to stand still in this part of town; the tidal wave of people would pummel anyone who stopped moving. I ducked into the doorway of a beat-up brick apartment building and pulled out my phone.

I called Mags and gave her a quick update on my latest brawl. I also told her about Sandra and "science guy" visiting Tommy. I was guessing the science geek was Subterranean Bob.

She was quiet for a second. "I knew Tommy would never hurt me," she said. "He probably talked to those clowns thinking he was helping me—and he was, right off a cliff."

I laughed. "Hey, I'm glad I was wrong about him double-crossing you. I guess we can get more details when he gets back from Mexico. Now what about Biff?"

"I'll get to him later. Right now I have to get ready for a live interview with Holly Honey."

"Okay, that sounds great. I'll be watching."

I tried to smile as I put away my phone, but there was a bad feeling in my gut, like I'd swallowed ten pounds of rigatoni. My *future sense* told me something awful was going to happen. It also told me not to eat Italian food for lunch.

I clenched my fists and headed for home.

45 — SELL OUT

The fooki effect was everywhere. It was in the malls, on the streets, at the banks, and in the ATM machines. All across America, people were piling on the pizza and jacking up their debt. I decided to watch Magnolia's evening interview at a little pub on 8th Avenue, near the towering slabs of the CCB building that loomed over Columbus Circle.

I took a seat and swigged my beer while the bartender snapped on the television. I was annoyed at Mags; we'd just had a fight. Apparently, when she'd mentioned getting to Biff "later," she'd meant as soon as she got off the phone with me. So she'd gone over to Biff's apartment alone, and I was pondering the irony of my feelings. I loved her rebel heart, but I hated how she wouldn't listen. At any rate, there was no sign of Biff, and even less sign of our wedding invitations.

Pam the bartender said, "You're Magno Girl's boyfriend, right? She's pretty famous now. What's she doing on the news tonight?"

"She's going to tell you not to eat Pie Hole's pizza."

"Oh, yeah? I hear their new pizza is great."

"Don't eat it, Pam. If you want to forget your problems, stick with alcohol."

She gave me another brew just as Holly Honey came on the screen.

Holly said, "Hello, I'm here with Magno Girl, the superhero who's been in the news so much lately. Magno Girl has had extensive testing done on the new 'More For Me' pizza from Pie Hole Pizza, Incorporated. Magno Girl, you say this pizza is laced with a drug that makes people want to shop."

Magnolia looked great. She was wearing a pink T-Shirt I'd given her that featured a cute picture of a dinosaur, something from the Cretaceous Period. She smiled and said, "That's right, Holly, but it doesn't just make a person shop. It also makes a person very susceptible to advertisements and suggestion—especially when used in conjunction with low frequency music."

"And what kind of music would that be?"

"Anything with lots of bass. Anything like the music on the Pie Hole Pizza commercial."

"And you're saying this pizza, and this music, is responsible for the recent increase in consumer spending?"

"Yes. Look at the sale of microwave ovens at Americamart. People are being directed by the fooki to purchase this product."

Holly looked into her lens with a dramatic face. "Also here with us is James Pooka, who is a Professor of Chemistry at Columbia University. The professor was good enough to come in today and be interviewed about this impending crisis."

The camera showed the professor, who looked like a globe-headed goblin.

He smiled. "Are we on television?"

"Yes."

"You mean people can see me?"

"Yes, if they're watching."

Pooka mugged a bit for the camera. "The fooki pie is dangerous. It represents a grave threat to humanity. Read all about it in my new book, *The Fooki Factor.*"

Holly looked at Mags, who looked surprised. Holly hesitated and said, "You've written a book, professor?"

"Yes."

"And how long have you been working on this book?"

"Years and years. I am the world's leading expert on fooki."

"And what can you tell us about Pie Hole's pizza, professor? Is it laced with this dangerous substance? Does the substance cause the effect that Magno Girl claims?"

"Oh, yes!" he said with a grin. "I tested it extensively. When mixed with tomato sauce at a temperature above 100 degrees Celsius, it will produce something I call the *Pooka Effect.*"

"The *Pooka Effect?* Can you explain this effect?"

"I don't think we have time for that, Miss Holly. Maybe everyone should read my book, or better yet—see the movie. It would make a great movie, with lots of action, as one daring scientist races against time, fights the forces of evil, and then wins a Nobel Prize."

"Can you tell us what happens when a person eats the pizza?"

"It is a very dangerous thing, Holly. I have dedicated an entire chapter to pizza in my book. You can buy the book online at 'the Pooka effect dot-com.' That's p-o-o-k-a-e-f-f-e-c-t dot com. Hurry, while supplies last."

"Professor, is it true the fooki pie will make a person shop until they drop?"

"Yes, this is serious stuff. Visit 'the Pooka effect dot-com' immediately."

"And does the drug render people more susceptible to advertisements?"

"I'll be raising the price soon, Holly, so people should act now."

"How many people did you use in your test, professor?"

"I'm available for speaking engagements and awards."

Holly grimaced and turned to Mags. "Magno Girl, do you have anything you'd like to add?"

Magnolia paused and flashed two stormy eyes. "Don't eat the pizza—please."

"There you have it, people. This is Holly Honey with Magno Girl. Don't eat the pizza."

The anchor people came back on and said stuff like, "Wow, poisoned pizza. I guess *that* will generate some controversy. Stay tuned for Len with all the sports."

I swigged another shot and considered how humans are unpredictable—except when there's a chance to make a lot of money, and they turn into complete assholes. Pam switched the channel and there was Jim Riteangle, interviewing Smashboy.

"Smashboy, how do you respond to allegations that the new pizza you're helping to promote is dangerous? I understand that Magno Girl is saying it's a poison."

Smashboy scoffed. "Jim, there's always someone out there making unfounded accusations. Now someone is attacking pizza, an American tradition. I hope that traitor is booted out of the country."

"So you think it's unpatriotic to oppose Pie Hole Pizza?"

"Pie Hole is a good American company," Smashboy said, puffing out his chest a bit. "The United States of America was built upon the principles of capitalism and free enterprise that Pie Hole represents. Obviously, Magno Girl is a socialist. I've also heard rumors that she's a witch, and she associates with communists and organized crime figures. Anyway, she's got no staying power. I hear her superpowers are fading already."

"Now that's very interesting. Can you tell us more about this?"

Smashboy lowered his voice a bit and looked sly. "I don't want to start any gossip, Jim, but I hear she's getting weaker every minute—and no, I don't know anything about this idea that she's pregnant with Biff Taylor's child. I also can't validate the whispers about her boyfriend's mob-related activity, or the fact that she comes from a long line of witches that practice human sacrifice. There are lots of pretty faces out there, but only a few real superheroes. I just hope nothing bad happens to Magno Girl now that she's been labeled a traitor by so many people."

I laughed and wondered where I should bury Smashboy's body. Maybe next to Pooka's. I paid my tab and walked out.

46 — THE MEDIA GLARES

Mags was just leaving the skyscraper citadel of the American media. A ravaging pack of reporters swarmed around her, and camera flashes fired as microphones were shoved into her face.

"Magno Girl, is it true that you've lost your superpowers?"

"Please don't eat the pizza."

"Magno Girl, how about the rumor that you're pregnant with Biff Taylor's child?"

"I'm not pregnant."

"Magno Girl, are you secretly married to a mob guy?"

"I'm not married."

"What about the accusations that you're a traitor to the American way of life?"

"I have a tattoo of the American flag on my inner thigh."

A roar erupted from the crowd. They teemed around her like a pack of piranhas—screaming and shoving to get their cameras closer. One guy shouted, *"Can you give us a picture of that, Magnolia?"*

Mags smiled. "Sorry, I'm just kidding. Please tell people not to eat the pizza."

Then she leaped into the air—and fell down hard on her stomach.

"Ooof!"

People shouted and camera flashes exploded like a hundred smiling suns. Mags didn't look up, but she jumped to her feet and tried again.

This time she fell even harder.

"Ugh!"

Reporters shoved each other and surrounded her. They started screaming questions.

"*Magno Girl, what about the claim that your magic gaze is broken?*"

"*Magno Girl, are you a mafia princess?*"

"*Magno Girl, will this loss of power affect your pregnancy? Or will your baby be a witch like you?*"

Mags was still on the ground, and she looked hurt. She was also completely encircled by the drooling gossip-sharks, along with the empty grinning eyes of their digital equipment. I could feel them wishing with all their hearts that she'd fall again, or burst into tears, or do something worthy of immortal humiliation. And I felt myself boiling with rage.

With a shout, I started punching my way through the crowd. My fists were like a heavy pair of hammers. The gang of news-hacks responded with the typical prose of a thousand failed poets.

"*Hey! What the fuck? Fuck you, you fucking fuck-headed fuckity fuck!*"

A lot of guys punched me back, but they hadn't trained in thirty-two different martial arts, and they weren't wearing brass knuckles. I busted my way through the cluster of salivating rumor-maggots, and I scooped Magnolia into my arms. As I helped her to stand, a few guys pushed and shoved me, and a few more stuck camera snouts in my face. I growled like a meat grinder and they backed off.

I leaned close to Mags and whispered, "Honey, don't worry about it. We can ride home on my bike."

She looked at me, and I saw the pain and anger in her eyes. But then it faded and was replaced by an odd serenity. "Thanks for helping me, Ron—thank you. I'll meet you back at your place."

She gritted her teeth and leaped into the air again—and this time she got airborne. She hovered above the rush of cars on Columbus Circle, wobbling for a few shaky seconds above the statue of Christopher Columbus and his sloshing ring of fountains. She looked at me again, and I waved to her as she faded into the dark forest of skyscrapers.

The crowd tried to run after her but she was gone. I sprinted to my bike and headed home fast.

47 — SANDRA UNCHAINED

All the way down Broadway I looked for her. The street was filled with swerving cars, and I was distracted, and I probably caused a few fiery accidents—but I didn't care. Most of those assholes deserved worse.

I ran up the stairs to my apartment and threw open the door. There was Magnolia, sitting on my couch.

"Mags, are you all right?"

She stared with eyes like empty coffee cups. "I could be better," she said in a soft voice.

"What are you doing?"

"Thinking."

"That's a bad habit."

She sighed. "Yeah, I know. But I'm going to keep doing it anyway."

"Honey, don't worry about the reporters. They'll find someone new to eat next week."

"I don't care about the reporters," she said, shaking her head. "But you know something? I really loved flying. I hate the idea of taking the subway."

Then she looked out the window, into the grimy brick wall of the adjacent apartment building a shoe-size away, and said nothing.

"Mags, about all those accusations. I've done some bad things."

I waited for a reaction. It was a long few seconds.

She gave me a weary glance. "Ron, forget it. I suspected you were involved with your brother. I should've mentioned it, but I kept putting it off. I spent that roll of cash you gave me on my mother's medication, and my school—but I guess I don't deserve to be a superhero. I'm a sellout like everyone else, and it's not your fault."

My heart pounded and my chest heaved. "Mags, that's not true! You're not like everyone else. You're a great girl! What kind of saint would waste hard-earned hijacking money on a monster like your mom? I'm the rotten bastard. I really let you down, and I feel like blowing my brains out. Have you seen my revolver?"

She half smiled. "Yeah, it's in the kitchen, next to the coffee maker." She laughed, before looking serious again. "I'm kidding, Ron. You've done a lot to help me. I appreciate everything you've done, and I don't even feel like it was so terrible."

I saw a glimmer of hope. "Yeah, that's true. I mean, what are a few stolen teapots compared to a world filled with poverty and war and injustice? Am I right?"

She sort of smiled again.

"And what about the kids?" I said. "Jenni, Karina, and Pepe. You've done more good for them than anyone was gonna do with all those bags of chopped walnuts. You're a great person, Mags— you're the best. You just made the mistake of associating with me. Hey, it happens."

She was silent for a bit. Finally, she said, "You're rationalizing your bad behavior, but you know, I think I can go along with it. I mean, nobody's perfect—and nobody seems to be trying too hard, either. Just don't sell any more stolen stuff, okay? No more crime."

"Okay. But what about the bad press?"

"Forget it. If it weren't true, they'd make it up anyway. It'll die down as soon as some actor files for divorce. By the way, did you ever unload those silver teapots? Ha."

"No! We've still got five thousand of them. Does your mother like tea?"

"Sure, if it's full of whiskey."

I grinned. "Hey, can you get Pooka to autograph a copy of his new book for me?"

Mags laughed. "He'll probably want an honorarium. Can you believe that guy?"

I sat down next to her. She moved a little closer to me, and I put my arm around her shoulders.

"So, Mags, tell me again, why the hell do you want to be a superhero?"

She gave me a little smile. "I'm starting to wonder. My father was a cop, and his father was a cop, so I could say that law enforcement is in my blood. But that's only part of the reason. Believe it or not, it was the books."

"Books? You mean those things in a library?"

"Yeah. I did some crazy stuff as a kid, but I didn't have many real friends, and I spent a lot of time alone, and I used to read. Sometimes, I'd read literary stuff—but mostly, I read science fiction and fantasy. I loved stories where there was a hero, someone with noble ideas who saved the world. And I wanted to be like those people, and then I got these superpowers, so that's what happened. I guess it was a stupid plan."

"Mags, it wasn't stupid. You've done some great things, and this story's not over."

"Good point."

"I'm glad you agree. So, what do we do now?"

She sat back on the couch and looked thoughtful. "Well, I figure the fooki pie is going to keep selling. Pretty soon people will notice it's a bad thing. It'll take time, though, before anyone takes action."

"Yeah," I said with a grin. "But maybe after years of damage a law will be passed, and a warning will be slapped on the side of the pizza box. I hope it mentions the Surgeon General."

"Exactly."

"Mags, I feel compelled to ask you to marry me."

"I know you feel compelled. I've been thinking about it."

"You're thinking about getting married?"

"No! I've been thinking about the spell, and all the information we've collected."

"Oh. So, how do you feel?"

"You mean now that I'm going to be a 'normal' girl?"

"Yeah."

A steely look flashed in her eyes. "I can take care of myself. I'm not an invalid, you know. Besides, we're going to beat this thing."

For some reason, I shoved my hand into the back pocket of my jeans—and found a gold chain with a locket. I took it out and looked at it. Mags said, "Is that for our wedding? How did you know I hate diamonds?"

"Mags, this belongs to Sandra. I pulled it from her neck."

Mags examined the heart-shaped piece of jewelry. She opened it, and her jaw dropped.

"Ron, look at this!"

I took a look. I saw a tiny photo of Sandra, Thaddeus, and three children—two girls, and a boy. I looked a little more and realized the boy seemed familiar, but I couldn't place the face.

Mags pointed at the tiny photo. "This is a picture of Hal—the ghost in Thad's house. It's so obvious now! Remember how he said his parents were around? He must be the son of Sandra and Thaddeus! He also must have died in that house, apparently from a drug overdose."

"Ha!" I said, feeling her excitement. "Sandra forgot to mention the dead kid thing. I wonder if he played soccer?"

She closed the locket with satisfaction. "I suspect he was more into eight balls than soccer balls. And his mom is in denial about the whole thing."

"I suppose a dead junkie in the closet screws up her perfect vision of parenting. Is this significant?"

"Yes—maybe."

"Okay, but if it isn't, I still have a bunch of weapons available. In fact, some of them are under the sofa you're sitting on, so be careful."

She looked at me, and she kissed the side of my face. "Ron, thanks for being here. I just want you to know...you're the best friend I've ever had."

At some point we were lying together in the dark, and then I fell asleep.

48 — TOTAL FREE FALL

When I woke up the next morning, Magnolia was gone and the phone was ringing. It was the first of a few calls. "Hello?"

"Hi, this is Jeremy Flash with Channel Nine, and I'd like to interview Magno Girl. Is she distraught about the loss of her superpowers? Is it true she's a gangster's girlfriend? Will she be checking into rehab soon to cure her cocaine habit?"

Jeremy wanted to ask her about the fooki, too. He wanted to talk about Smashboy and his accusations, and he wanted her to wear something sheer and short. I stopped answering the calls. I went downstairs to the coffee shop and bought a newspaper. The headline shouted: "THE FALL OF MAGNO GIRL."

There was a picture of her hitting the ground. She had a pained expression on her face, and there was nothing flattering about the photo. I read the article.

As quickly as she arrived on the scene, Magno Girl seems headed for an early exit. After appearing on CCB news with reporter Holly Honey, she appeared unable to fly. This loss of her superpowers comes amid rumors of broken love affairs, witchcraft, links to organized crime, and possibly an unwanted pregnancy.

There was also a picture of Mags and Biff together. It was the shot that had been snapped in front of the Museum of Natural History, and I noticed I'd been cut out of the picture—a bit of my left arm was all that remained. Then farther down the page I saw a better headline, "NEW PIZZA FEELS THE HEAT."

The new "More For Me" pizza from Pie Hole is sweeping the nation, but some people are claiming there's more to this pie than meets the eye. Is the pizza's overwhelming success the result of a powerful narcotic produced by a mysterious South Pacific plant called "fooki"? Several people, including defunct superhero Magno Girl, are claiming that fooki is the answer.

I called Mags but she didn't pick up, so I headed down the street.

I went to The Three Eyes See Martial Arts Academy, where I found a crowd hanging around outside. The group was a blend of adoring fans showing support and media people hoping to capture the perfect morsel of misery. The crowd surrounded me as I reached the front door.

"Ron, is it true Magno Girl has gained ten pounds since Biff Taylor left her?"

"Ron, how do you respond to rumors that Magno Girl is broke and addicted to diet pills?"

"Has Magno Girl's license to practice witchcraft been revoked?"

"Is it true that both you and Magno Girl have associated with members of the mob? And has she changed her brand of deodorant?"

I'd never expected to become a celebrity. In first grade, I'd been the kid who'd eaten the most plastic dinosaurs—but my fame had been short-lived, and my stomach had been pumped. So I unlocked the front door and slipped through without saying a word. I did manage to slam the door shut on a few groping fingers.

I went upstairs and found Mags alone in her office, staring at the computer screen. She was studying Pie Hole's "More For Me" website. She looked up as I walked in.

"Hi, Ron."

"Mags, are you all right?"

"I'm okay," she said. And she did sound pretty good. "I'm reading about a big rally tonight in Times Square."

I scanned the web page.

The organization "Freedom To Feed" has just announced a rally tonight in Times Square in support of Pie Hole's new "More For Me" pizza. A spokesman for the group said, "It's not about pizza. It's about the right of

Americans to be free to choose what they eat. We will not yield to smear tactics from the enemies of freedom."

"Fooki people are everywhere," I said. "It's hard to find a microwave at Americamart."

"Yeah, I think the fooki is wearing away a lot of brains. I have a feeling something even worse is going to happen."

Right on cue, the phone rang. Mags looked at the incoming number and answered it. I cringed as she said, "Hello, Mom." Not what Mags needed right now.

Momma Mags said, "I saw you on television, Magnolia."

"Yeah, I was there."

"Why are you causing trouble? That pizza tastes good, and I just bought a new microwave at Americamart."

"You bought a microwave?" Mags said, incredulous. "What about your pills? I sent you money for your pills."

"I'm sick of taking pills. Those pills are supposed to help my depression, but they just make me more depressed. Besides, they cost so much—and I'm not supposed to take them with alcohol, so I don't take them. At least when I'm dead you can sell the microwave, if you bother to come over and get it. Why do you send me money in an envelope? You can't bring it over? Are you afraid your mother's going to bite you like a rabid dog?"

"Mom, I'm busy right now. Don't eat that pizza! Don't go to that website!"

"I was a good mother! I tried, but you wouldn't listen to me."

"Stop eating that pizza, Mom. And stop drinking."

"We sent you to a shrink because you needed help. You were getting into bad stuff, and you wouldn't play with the other girls."

"What other girls?"

"The girls on the street. Mrs. Scunata's daughter, Stacy."

"I played with Stacy, Mom—more than you know. It didn't work out."

"I know all about Stacy! She had dolls, and eventually she had *boyfriends!* And now she's married to a *man,* and she just had her third baby. You don't even have one!"

"Mom, I keep telling you, I'm different."

"That's right, and it's my mother's fault! I never should've let you hang around with her. Why can't you be normal?"

Mags rolled her eyes, exasperated. *"You're not normal, Mom! None of us were ever normal! And just because you're unhappy about who you are doesn't mean that I am."*

"What are you talking about, Magnolia? That's not true! And why are you still causing trouble? Everyone thinks my daughter is a traitor!"

"I don't care what people think."

"Are you pregnant with an illegitimate baby?"

"There's no such thing as an 'illegitimate' baby! Anyway, I thought you wanted me to be pregnant."

"I want you to be respectable. And now you're doing all kinds of stupid things and running around with a criminal. Your poor father is turning over in his grave!"

Mags paused and took a deep breath. "I'm not pregnant, and I don't know any criminals. And dad was cremated. Look, I have to go."

"My friend's daughters are all married. Some of them are already divorced! You're way behind."

"Mom, don't eat the pizza."

"I'm sick, and I'm broke, and my daughter is a traitor. I never should have said all those nice things about you to the movie people."

Mags stopped herself from hitting the "disconnect" icon.

"What 'movie people?' "

"Two people from a Hollywood studio, Magnolia. They sent a man and a woman over here right after the pizza maker got killed. Your brother was here with me, and we talked to them. They said they were going to make a TV special about you and maybe a movie, so they wanted to know some things. So we said lots of nice things… The woman was very friendly. She has daughters, too, and understood my pain. They said they'd call with an offer, and we should wait and let it be a surprise."

Mags struggled to keep her voice level. "So you were there with Tommy? Did you tell them anything about tobacco smoke?"

"No. We said nice things. But I had a headache after they left."

Magnolia gritted her teeth as her eyes flashed with rage.

"Mom, those people aren't making a movie—*those people are trying to kill me!*"

"What?"

"You of all people should have known she was picking your brain! This is what you get for ignoring Grandma and all the stuff she taught you. Dammit!"

Mags hung up the phone. I could tell she was upset. I stood behind her and put my hands on her shoulders.

"Look on the bright side, honey. Your family didn't betray you. They're just stupid."

Magnolia shook her head. "Can you believe that? Both of them! Unbelievable!"

"Mags, they thought they were helping you make a lot of money. How could they know? At least you told your mom, and next time she'll know what's going on."

Mags gave a snort. "My mom knows that Stacy Scunati has three babies, and I have no babies."

"When a raccoon has babies, they give it euthanasia."

She almost laughed. "That's rabies, Ron. Stacy has babies."

"Right, whatever. I know that a raccoon has an opposable thumb."

"And why is that significant?"

"Well, it means that a raccoon can open a can of beer—though I prefer bottles." And with these words of wisdom I cracked open a cold one.

Mags was still for about a minute, but then she stood up.

I grinned. "Would you like a beer?"

"No."

"Oh. Can I get you something else? Just name it—anything."

She shrugged. "I could use a ride to Times Square."

"No problem."

49 — TIMES SQUARE

That night we rode my chopper to Times Square, wading into a rollicking sea of heads and eyes. I parked near 42nd Street, and we started walking toward the Pie Hole Pizza store just as the crowd started to build. Mags wore black jeans and a pink T-shirt decorated with a picture of Lisa Simpson. Despite her recent bad luck, she still looked good.

People surrounded us. A woman who looked like she held the deed to a silo of hairspray said, "Magno Girl, I just love you! Congratulations on the baby thing."

"Magno Girl, can you autograph my iPad?"

"Magno Girl, do you think you could come to my daughter's birthday party? She's got cancer. We're having cheesecake."

I took a step back and absorbed the urban energy—the horde of screaming people, the wheezing herds of buses, and the cars swarming like insects across the floor of a canyon made from skyscrapers. Everywhere we looked there were digital billboards, and most of the mammoth screens were broadcasting crackling images of pizza slices. There was pushing, shoving and shouting, and a rippling wall of police officers standing near mobile barricades. There were throngs of reporters running around setting up cameras. I saw Holly Honey and her film crew. She spotted us and bulldozed her way through the crowd.

"Hello, Magnolia, did you get my message? How are you doing?"

She gave Mags a hug. "Would you like to say a few words to the public about the accusations against you?"

"I'm okay, Holly," Mags said with a half smile. "And thanks for the call. But I'd rather not talk right now."

"I understand. If I can do anything, let me know. I'm tougher than I look, honey."

We maneuvered closer to the center of the action, which was a platform in front of the restaurant. On either side of the platform were tower-sized speakers, while high above there was a flickering banner advertising the message, "FREEDOM TO FEED." Then the low frequency battle-riff of Pie Hole Pizza exploded through the air like a thousand angry bombs, and the crowd roared.

Big guys started yelling and pounding their chests. Girls were dancing to the throbbing beat. One big goon in a Jets jacket shouted, "We want Pie Hole! We want to eat!" His girl was wearing a Jersey shade of hair dye and some equally trashy makeup, along with a pair of jeans that strangled her ass and hurt my eyes. Meanwhile, some guy with a megaphone kept shouting, "Down with the food police! Up, up yours!" It had a certain catchy cadence, and a violent, juvenile appeal. It was only a matter of time before it would be turned into a pop song and maybe a trendy line of athletic wear.

Mags pointed. "Look! There's Thaddeus."

I was surprised he'd come. He was in a roped off section near the platform, and the crowd gave him a certain respect. He was rich, he was ruthless, and he was overweight—he was the big, fat American dream. Standing right next to him was Melvin Shrick. They were smiling and laughing. The mayor made his way toward them, and I saw everyone shaking hands.

Thaddeus had a woman with him. She was young and pretty, and eyed her man the way a bank robber eyes a vault. Melvin seemed to be solo. Smashboy stood on the platform above them, basking in the flash-bulb media glare. I searched for Sandra but didn't see her anywhere. Then a guy grabbed the microphone. He looked like a classic servant of evil, dressed in a suit and tie.

He said, "Hello, thank you for coming."

The crowd erupted with shouts and applause. He continued, "It's good to see so much support for free enterprise and the American way." The crowd whooped and hollered and let their stomachs billow in the warm evening breeze.

"And now, let me introduce a man we know so well, a great patriot who has put his life on the line countless times in the name of justice, here he is—*Smashboy!*"

Smashboy appeared on the side of the platform, and the crowd went crazy. They cheered and shouted as he walked toward the microphone with his fist held high.

He was smart; he didn't move too fast. He took his sweet time and let the noise build as he swaggered along. By the time he reached the microphone, the air was filled with a cacophony of praise and party sounds. He paused while the cheers caressed his rubber ears for another full minute. Finally, the music stopped.

Everyone was quiet.

Everyone stared hard as Smashboy leaned toward the microphone and gazed into the ocean of vacuous eyeballs. He scanned the mob for another thirty seconds—and then he threw back his head and screamed, *"Are we gonna let them stop us?"*

The crowd roared in the night. Smashboy preened like a pop star, raising a slice to his mouth and chomping off a hunk. Then he held the slice of pie above his head like a trophy, and the crowd went into a frenzy as he spoke again.

"There are some bad people out there. There are people against our pie. These people are a threat to the American way of life!"

Someone shouted, "Kill'em all!" and the crowd erupted with support.

"I'm talking about the scientists and intellectuals. They sit around thinking all day, while we have to go out and get dinner!"

The crowd hooted and hollered. "Tell'em, Smashboy!"

"Good American folks like us—we don't have time to think. We're too busy eating pizza and waving the flag!"

The crowd screamed, "Yeah! Yeah! Woo! Woo!"

"Are we gonna let the brainiacs win?"

"No! No!"

"Are we gonna be slaves to the weaklings who think?"

"No! No!"

"You bet we won't! We're gonna keep right on eating, and shopping, and loving ourselves—and loving our country!"

"Yeah! Woo! Woo! God bless America! Smashboy for president!"

The sea of heads and stomachs bobbed and swayed. They were ecstatic to be members of a great, chomping herd. And then Smashboy leaned very close to the microphone.

Silence swallowed up the racket.

Smashboy lowered his voice. "The other day I was watching television, and what did I see? I saw Magno Girl talking about our pizza."

Angry grunts came from the crowd. Someone said, "Magno Girl is a traitor!" A few others honked in agreement. One guy even screamed, "Kill her! She's a fucking witch!" and then vomited a special pizza and beer combination all over the pavement.

Mags stood with her arms crossed and laughed. She was obvious enough, with her multi-colored hair and awesome sexiness, but no one in the immediate area had sucked down enough liquid courage to antagonize her—not yet, anyway.

Smashboy said, "Magno Girl, if you're out there, I have a message for you—start eating some pizza. End your association with criminals and witches. And stop spitting on this country's flag!"

Smashboy crammed the rest of the slice into his mouth, and the crowd entered a state of hysteria. The music started blaring and the people started bobbing.

Mags leaned close to me. "Remember what Pooka said? The 'fooki effect' is accentuated as the volume increases. These people are really going to start feeling it."

I looked around and saw the green eyes getting greener. Even from a distance, I could see Smashboy's eyeballs shining like a pair of pea-green pearls. He started laughing. He started roaring. He started shouting, *"I want everything I don't have—how about you?"*

The crowd responded, "Yeah! Yeah!"

"It's my right as an American to have more!"

"Yeah! Woo-hoo!"

"And I'm going to get it!"

"That's right!"

"Are you ready to take what you want?"

"Yes!"

"Are you willing to take what you need?"

"Yes!"

"Then do it! Do it now!"

People screamed. They shouted. And then they started rioting.

Windows along the street exploded in showers of broken glass. Flurries of punches began to fly as people started robbing and stealing from each other.

"Hey! Ow! Gimme that!"

The screams and shouts erupted around us, and I realized the fooki-filled brains no longer wanted to buy the merchandise they craved—they wanted to take it. An army of green-eyed monsters was running amok.

I said, "Let's get out of here."

Mags said, "Look out!"

Someone hit me in the face with a hotdog. And then a fist.

Magnolia kicked a few people. I reached for my daggers—and I had them. I shouted and started slashing, and people backed off the way they do when they see a couple of sharp knives. But before one of the cops could shoot me, I was clobbered from behind by somebody's pointy elbow. I hit the ground hard.

I looked up and saw a bunch of guys attacking Mags. She was surrounded. I jumped to my feet and found myself in a real brawl.

I bashed a few heads, and gouged a few eyes, and then I was overwhelmed. I was on the ground, getting stomped and kicked. I saw Mags get punched in the face and then get clobbered again from three different angles.

Mags is a very tough girl, but it was obvious her superpowers were almost gone. And there was Jim Riteangle, along with two camera guys. A few more reporters surrounded the fight, while a riot mushroomed around us. They were trying to get close-ups. A big guy grabbed Mags from behind and held her while another guy punched her in the stomach, and then again in the face.

That's when Holly Honey appeared. She came running with her camera crew, but as she got near the action she shouted and flung herself at one of Magnolia's attackers. A couple of the guys turned on her. One of her camera guys clobbered one of Jim's camera guys. I struggled to my feet.

Green-eyed people were rampaging in every direction. They were beating each other senseless and stealing from their fellow fooki-eaters. I shouted and jumped back into the fray, and then Smashboy arrived.

He came bounding from the podium. He leaped like a leopard and slammed one of Magnolia's attackers in the head with his boot. He punched. He kicked. He made it look easy—too easy.

Our attackers bolted as a bunch of cops came running. Rod Saint Royd was one of them. Meanwhile, Mags was on the ground, and she did not look good. Smashboy tried to help her up, but I leaped forward and grabbed him around the throat.

I said, "Get away from her, you plastic-faced phony!"

He said, "Grrrr! Motherfucker!"

He tried to poke my eyes. A bunch of cops wrestled me to the ground while a few others helped Magnolia to her feet. Her face was swollen and battered. She was obviously hurt. Camera crews swallowed it up like starving garbage trucks.

Holly was trying to compose herself. She was yelling and cursing at Jim Riteangle, who was yelling and cursing back at her. They both joined a crowd of reporters who were surrounding Smashboy, who waved them off.

Royd said to me, "I should have you arrested for various crimes—but I won't, because there appears to be a riot going on. Take your girlfriend to the hospital."

I snarled. "Royd, it's so nice to see you working tonight. Is the gym closed?"

He sneered. "I'm here to serve the public. I can bench press three-ninety."

I put my arm around Magnolia. "Mags, how do you feel?"

"Great, except for the pain. I'll be okay."

I shoved a few cameras out of her face, but we were surrounded by an army of paparazzi and reporters. Rioters were everywhere. A lot of them hadn't even eaten the fooki pie—they were just jumping at the chance to grab free stuff.

I reached for my blow-up battering ram.

The blow-up battering ram is a kick-ass contraption I'd purchased from my favorite psycho website, *Take No Shit*. I yanked the ripcord, and with a hearty whoosh my battering ram inflated.

I gave Mags a kiss. "Hang on, baby!"

I gripped the two handles, put my head down, and with a scream we plunged ahead. Police, reporters, and fooki-people were tossed aside like heaps of filthy city snow. They shouted, "Augh! Ow! Watch out!"

Piles of idiots bounced off the front of my huge inflated tool, but I kept going, thankful for my near death-inducing thigh workouts. We crashed through the mayhem and arrived at my motorcycle. I triggered the ram's self-destruct sequence and put Mags on the back of my Harley.

Just as we were leaving the scene, I saw SuperStan flying down from the sky. I laughed at the sight of him in his fluorescent pajamas. I knew he wasn't interested in chasing after every window-breaking, shoe-swiping criminal. He'd probably just grab a few well positioned looters and wait for the cameras to click. I laughed again at the pathetic thought.

We roared off in the direction of home.

50 — TWO CARATS OF LOVE

I helped Mags up the stairs of her apartment. She was groggy and discombobulated as I got her into the bedroom and onto the bed. I turned on the light and took a good look at her.

Her one eye was smashed shut, and her face was puffy and swollen. She also had a few bloody cuts. There was no doubt she'd been hammered like a hockey puck.

I blinked back a few tears. "Mags, I never should've brought you here. I've got to get you to a hospital."

Instantly, her one good eye flickered with life. "No! Ron, I'm not going."

I cradled her head in my hands. "You're really hurt, honey. You need medical attention."

"I'm not going to a hospital. I'm not as bad as I look."

"Mags, your health is more important than bad publicity."

"It's not about the publicity," she said in a fierce tone. "I'm not going to a hospital."

"Do you want to die here?"

"I'm not going to die!" She reached out and grabbed my arm. "Ron, please. I don't want to go."

I stared at her for a long few seconds—and then I gently kissed her on the forehead. I wasn't going to argue, because I understood irrationality as well as anyone. Also, my *future sense* told me she would be okay. I got her some ice, and I got myself a beer. I watched her for a while until she fell asleep. Eventually, I went into the living room and dozed off.

I woke up to see Mags standing in the doorway.

I blinked at the sight. She looked like a tomato that had been arguing with a tire iron. I said, "Hey, how do you feel?"

Okay, dumb question. She groaned and said, "Not my best," and slumped into a chair. "Put on the TV. Let's see what's going on."

I hesitated, but then I turned on the television. Holly Honey was still standing in Times Square. She'd primped up her hair and re-simonized her head. The cameras showed police, smashed windows, and the general remnants of disaster. Anchorman Eddie Foam, who was back in the studio, asked Holly questions.

"So what's happening now, Holly?"

Holly said, "The police have this area under control, but the rioters have spread throughout the city. Apparently, too much fooki causes people to become violently obsessed with having more of everything. It's gone from being a drug that makes people shop to a drug that makes people steal, rob, and loot."

Ed smiled. "Green-eyed people who always want more—what's the country coming to? How many of these people are out there, Holly? We have reports coming in from all over the city about green-eyed people committing violent crimes."

"There were thousands of people at this rally, Ed, and it looks like we could be in for a long night."

"Holly, we have reports coming in from other parts of the country. It appears that a similar effect is happening to individuals who've consumed too much of the fooki pie—but does anyone know why the entire New York crowd ran amuck?"

"No one knows for sure, Ed, but it may have been the effect of the huge speakers blasting out that bass-heavy music. If that's the case, Magno Girl was right about everything, and the fooki pie is part of a larger plot that must be stopped."

"And where is Magno Girl? I understand she was at the rally."

"She was here, and she was injured during the rioting. I'm not sure where she is now—but wait, here comes Smashboy."

Smashboy was walking toward his glittering red rocket car. He was flanked by an honor guard of suits from Pie Hole Pizza. Reporters yelled questions.

"Smashboy, how do you respond to charges that you incited a riot?"

"Smashboy, what about the effect of the fooki pie?"

"Smashboy, do you still think Magno Girl is a traitor?"

Smashboy paused from his walk and looked at the cameras. "I did nothing to incite a riot. People are angry, and a few of them have overreacted. There's no conclusive evidence that any of this was caused by the pizza. As for Magno Girl, I'm glad I was able to save her from certain death. It's tough being a superhero. It's not for everyone."

Reporters continued to scream questions, but Smashboy waved them off and got into his vehicle. I switched the channel and was surprised to see my brother.

He was standing in front of his pizza place on Bleeker Street. The front window was destroyed, and the place was a shambles. It had been stomped on by a fracas with a very big foot. A reporter named Burt Brickman said, "Al, can you tell us why the rioters demolished your particular store?"

Al was wide-eyed and foaming. "I don't know anything! Don't look at me! Why do you ask?"

"And what will you do now, Al?"

"I guess I'll rebuild. I guess I'll stop making my child support payments."

"How do you respond to allegations that you're connected to organized crime?"

"That's all lies! If we were really organized, would we steal a bunch of fucking dictionaries?"

I laughed and turned off the television. "For once my brother has a point."

Mags said, "We need a plan."

"I have a plan. It involves a lot of violence, though."

"We need a plan that doesn't land you in prison."

"That's going to be tricky. Maybe you should retire."

"No. If I defeat the witch my powers will return."

I leaped to my feet. "Are you crazy, Mags? How are you going to do that? Don't take this the wrong way, honey—but you're a wreck."

"I know," she replied with a sober look. "But I have to try."

"Mags, forget about the fooki. Who cares? These idiots get what they deserve."

"I can't let Sandra beat me. Besides—this is all I have."

I stood next to her. "That's not true."

She shook her head. "Ron, don't start. Sandra knew that creating this marriage obsession would really annoy me. When I destroy her you'll be cured of this 'marriage disease.'"

"Mags, it's not the spell."

"It is the spell. And we need to break it, but it's obviously powerful."

"Let's get married," I said. "Then we'll have a kid and break the spell."

"I don't want to get married. And I don't want to be a mother."

"I'll give you a diamond."

She rolled her eyes. "I don't want a diamond. I don't need to impress anyone with the size of a shiny rock. I'll let you know if I change my mind."

"Honey, I don't think you understand. I'm supposed to let you know when I'm ready, and then you're supposed to be thrilled."

"Oh, is that how it works?"

"Of course. I'm supposed to keep you hoping, and you're supposed to wait in quiet desperation—and then one day I give you a ring and I'm a big hero."

She gave me a weary glance. "How about I let you know when I'm ready, and you'll be the one who's thrilled."

"But that's not the way the world works."

"That's the way *my* world works."

"Well your world is no place for a man."

She laughed. "You've been in my world lots of times, and you've liked it. Unless you were faking."

"What? I wasn't faking. What guy would do a thing like that?"

She shrugged. I said, "Hey, Mags…were you ever faking?"

"No."

I smiled. "Good."

"Don't be so smug. We're still not getting married."

"Right." Then I pulled out a 2-carat diamond and pushed it into her hand.

Mags stared at the ring with a blank expression.

I grinned. "My grandfather won this in a poker game fifty years before I was born. He handed it to me from his hospital bed with three slugs in his stomach. Someday, I'm supposed to give it to the right girl. And that's you."

She sighed. "It's very pretty, Ron. I appreciate the thought—I really do, but forget it, okay? Please."

"When we get married, I'll buy you a motorcycle."

I saw smoke in her eyes.

"Look, I don't want a motorcycle! We're not getting married! *And if we do, you're getting rid of that stupid machine!*"

Whoah! I staggered backward, my head spinning like a cyclone. "Get rid of my bike?"

"Yes! I'm tired of watching you drive around like an idiot!"

My mind was an empty space as I looked at her.

"Magnolia—*the wedding is off!*"

"What?"

"You heard me. *The wedding is off!*"

She stared. "You mean…you don't want to get married?"

"*No!*"

"Oh, are you sure?"

"*Yes!*"

She was stunned, and she sat up straight.

"Ron, do you know what this means?"

"Yeah. It means I'm going on a road trip."

"No! It means that the spell is broken."

"Hey—yeah. That's true. I don't want to marry you at all."

"That's great."

"Yeah, great."

"I mean, it's a good thing."

"Yeah, it's good."

"Sandra's spells can be broken. So, you're done with the marriage thing?"

"Yes."

"Still feel nothing?"

"Not a thing."

She handed me back the ring. I hesitated and returned it to my pocket.

She smiled. "Someday you'll give that to someone special."

"Someday I'll give it to you—and you'll take it."

She glanced at me. "Maybe I will. But not today."

I leaned forward. "Mags, do you really hate my motorcycle?"

"No, no—of course not," she said quickly. "I'm a little bitchy right now—the loss of my superpowers, the public humiliation, getting my face smashed in, etcetera. I'd never want you to get rid of the bike. It's part of who you are and I like it. I do."

"That's good to know."

"Um, I'm going to get some more rest."

"I'm right behind you."

"Good."

51 — VISIT FROM AL

I was jolted awake by someone banging on the door. With a brain full of sleep, I reached for my samurai sword and stumbled from the bedroom. Was this an assassin? A reporter? Or maybe the giant robot octopus of my nightmares? No—it was my brother.

"Ron, let me in! You gotta help me."

I smelled a trap. Or maybe just his sweat-oozing flesh.

I gripped my weapon. "Oh, you think I'm gonna just open the door for you and your half-baked squad of killers?"

"What squad? I brought a pizza and it's baked just right."

I realized I was hungry, and I yanked open the door.

He was a mess, a splattered wreck of a pizza maker. He shoved a pie into my hands and started raving. "Ron, you gotta let me in! Those weren't rioters who destroyed my store—those were a bunch of goons sent by Melvin Schrick. They were after me!"

"Shut up!" I said. "You'll wake up Mags."

I checked out the pie—peppers and onions, my favorite. "You know what they say, Al. If you sleep with big dogs, you get big fleas. Also, a bunch of goons stomping on your pizza store."

"They think I know too much!" he wailed. "They think I might try to sell my story."

"Oh, yeah? Who did you try to sell it to?"

His eyes got big. "Hey, I needed the money. I want to buy a boat."

I laughed. "Does a guy need a boat when he's buried in a landfill?"

He tried to take a step into the room, but I held up my weapon and stopped him.

"Ron, please," he said in a pleading voice. "I didn't know the pizza was gonna do all that bad shit, and I didn't know they were gonna try and kill you. Plus I gave you Ton's address, remember?"

"Yeah, that's true. Why did you do that?"

"Because you're my brother, and I knew they were after you and your girl. Also, those cheap motherfuckers never paid me what they said they would."

I snarled. "You were playing both sides of the piccolo, brother—and you sold us out a little too often. Every time I flip the covers, you're sleeping with the enemy."

"I didn't sleep with her!" he blurted. "Sure, she's got a nice body, but she looks a little expensive, you know, like she'd want real jewelry and stuff. Anyway, what about all the times we had growing up? Didn't I show you how to fight? Didn't I protect you from big kids trying to grab your lunch?"

"I did my own fighting. All you did was eat my Scooter Pies."

He looked at me. I looked at him.

"Al, there's really nothing I can do."

He frowned. "Ron, can you forgive me? How about that?"

I toyed with my weapon and considered his words.

"Is there fooki on this pie?" I said.

"No way, brother. That's a great pizza—the best in New York."

I put down my sword, and I put down the pizza. Then I embraced my brother.

"Al, good luck."

"Thanks, Ron. Hey, by the way, I got you some stuff."

He pulled out a bag of what appeared to be marbles. I picked one up and saw that it was a glass eye.

"You're giving me a bag of glass eyeballs?"

"Yeah. They were on a truck out of JFK. I guess they were headed for a hospital or something. Anyway, I got sixty thousand of them. Hey, did you find anyone for the PermaPacks?"

"I'm out of that business, Al. I promised Mags."

"Okay, I get it. I also got you a hundred bottles of Flamin' Fred's Hot Sauce."

"Thanks."

"What about the silver teapots?"

"Al, I'll see you around."

"Right."

I closed the door and listened to his feet clomping down the stairs. Then I went into the kitchen and threw the pie into the trash.

I checked on Mags. She was still asleep. I lay down next to her and closed my eyes.

52 — BIGGEST THING SINCE ROLLING PAPER

The next morning I turned on the television and saw a gang of fat sloths protesting outside the pizza factory. It looked like a serious case of morning-after indignation, and the start of many lawsuits. I also remembered Ton telling me that Small Harry was protecting the place, and I guessed that mixing one grumpy super-midget with a mob of testy plaintiffs was a recipe for trouble.

I left a note for Mags, who was still sleeping, and I hopped on my chopper. I rode through the alphabet streets, past Tompkins Square Park, and then down East Houston toward the Bowery. Everywhere I looked, I saw signs of last night's anarchy. I eventually stopped at a deli to check the newspaper headlines.

"GREEN-EYED PIZZA MONSTERS CAUSE RIOTS IN NEW YORK."

"PIZZA PERIL!"

"MORE FOR ME FIASCO!"

I shook my head and read the excerpts.

A rally for Pie Hole Pizza's "More For Me" pizza turned violent last night as the fooki-filled product caused its followers to loot, rob, and steal. The mayor has called for an immediate investigation.

There was a picture of Magnolia's bloody face. There was

another story that said: "SMASHBOY SAVES MAGNO GIRL FROM PIZZA PUNKS!"

Smashboy stated, *"I felt an obligation to save the poor girl from harm. I wish her luck in her next career."*

There was also this: "MAGNO GIRL WAS RIGHT!"

Several experts now agree with defunct superhero Magno Girl's claim that the fooki-filled pizza is actually a drug that causes a powerful urge to acquire more and more consumer goods. If taken in large quantities, it can cause an unstoppable urge to purchase retail merchandise.

I gunned my bike all the way down Mott Street, past lingerie boutiques filled with string clad mannequins and then through the Asian provinces of Little Italy. I eventually found myself at the bottom of Mulberry, by Columbus Park, heading toward the pizza factory just south of Canal, where the street was dense with crawling vans and cars, and where a crowd of people stood among the food and fire escapes, the banks and bakeries, and the awnings covered with Chinese writing. Everyone was holding signs and eating pastry. They were slurping coffee and puffing cigarettes. They seemed thrilled to be part of a mob planning to file a major class action lawsuit.

I parked my bike right near SuperStan, who was standing on the sidewalk like a hunk of chiseled protein. He was giving an interview to Holly Honey. Holly said, "SuperStan, wouldn't you say Pie Hole Pizza is in big trouble?"

SuperStan tensed his jaw and flexed his strapping nostrils. "We don't know all the facts yet, Holly. We don't know who is responsible for this crime against humanity."

From somewhere close behind him, a voice shouted, "Oh yes, we do!"

It was Legalman—he was free. Apparently, he'd plea-bargained an array of felony charges down to a misdemeanor involving toxic waste. He jumped into Holly's camera and said, "Pie Hole Pizza will pay! The city will pay. Everyone responsible was irresponsible!"

Holly Honey said, "What's going on here, Legalman?"

Legalman smirked. "The victims of fooki are here with a habeas

Hail Mary, etcetera. They've all been wronged by the greedy owners of this factory, though our suit isn't about money—it's about justice."

"I understand you've filed a gazillion dollar lawsuit."

"That's right. A gazillion dollars can buy a lot of justice. Check the website 'sue pie hole pizza dot com' for information about joining the struggle."

SuperStan snarled a bit. "Legalman, it wouldn't surprise me if you're behind this plot. But justice will be done."

"Are you accusing me, SuperStan? Are you tarnishing my character?"

"Ha, you were a tarnished snake on the day you were born."

"Are you slandering the snake guild?"

"No. The average snake is a better man than you."

"The average snake can't sue your sorry ass."

"My ass is tremendous, and your sense of fashion is suspect."

"Your spandex costume is a blatant attempt to expose your posterior."

"Your naked ass would expose only cellulite."

"I'll put my naked ass up against yours any time."

SuperStan considered this remark. He was about to respond when Holly said, "Gentlemen, the real issue is pizza—and let's not forget Smashboy."

Legalman scoffed. "Smashboy's ass is no better than mine."

SuperStan said, "Yes, I'll agree with you—his ass is getting soft. He doesn't have a superhero's ass."

"He shouldn't wear tights."

"No, he should go with a heavier material until he gets into better shape."

"I should sue him for *indecent ass exposure.*"

"Go ahead. I have lots of footage that shows his ass—I mean, while he's fighting crime."

Lieutenant Rod Saint Royd came barreling over. "Legalman, get the hell out of here! You have no business in this business. Be glad this isn't your business. I'll have you arrested for littering."

Legalman snarled. "I have business here, Royd; I'm here to assess the scene of the city's negligence. I'm here to represent these unfortunate victims of illegal food proliferation. And I never litter, you fat barbell turd."

Royd screamed, "Get him out of here!" The cops tried to move Legalman along, but he shouted, "My rights are being violated! I have a copy of the Constitution in my pocket! I have people filming every second!"

In fact, there were lots of people filming with their phones. The police immediately put away their truncheons and pushed Legalman out of the street and toward the sidewalk, but he returned and they did nothing. Then Legalman unfolded a big sign. It said: "$$$ATTORNEY RIGHT HERE. LIVE THE AMERICAN DREAM $$$."

People started fighting to line up. A guy with a battered face pushed his way to the front of the line, and I heard Legalman say, "Fractured retina? Great, I can get you a million. Do you know anyone else who's lost an eye?"

Holly turned to Rod Saint Royd. "Lieutenant, do you feel any drastic measures are necessary to maintain order? Don't these people have the freedom to demonstrate?"

"Holly, they've got their freedom and all that crap, but we are not going to allow another riot to occur. If anyone tries anything, we will respond with police brutality. I mean, we will be brutal. I mean, women shouldn't be reporters. I mean, oh shit—can I say 'shit' on television?"

Suddenly, the whole crowd gave a loud gasp; somebody was posing on the roof of the factory. He was silhouetted against the sun like a dramatic-looking tree stump. He was Small Harry.

The crowd roared as Harry's half-sized shape became visible against the morning light. SuperStan saw him and walked nearer to the building. He looked at Harry and said, "Harry, you will be brought to justice for your crimes."

Harry raised a megaphone to his mouth. "SuperStan, I promise you a slugfest battle to the death with your ultimate foe!" Then he lit up a cigarette.

SuperStan shouted back, "My ultimate foe is taller than a

wastebasket, Harry. Get ready to kiss the bottom of a trash can!"

Harry laughed. He turned to hear someone who was motioning from a doorway on the roof, and then he turned back toward the crowd. He spoke again into the megaphone. "Okay, the management wants me to tell you all that they don't authorize any kind of battle. They hired me to protect this dump, but apparently they didn't realize what a wild beast I really am—so don't hold them responsible for any incidental deaths that might occur."

Holly turned to Legalman. "How about that remark, counselor?"

"No way," Legalman replied. "In fact, his admission of employment by the factory is a great piece of evidence against them. We plan to sue for every death."

The crowd cheered at Legalman's words. Meanwhile, Harry put down the megaphone and pulled out a flaming pink energy ball. Someone screamed, "Look out!" as he hurled it at SuperStan.

The bomb whizzed through the air and hit a police car. The vehicle burst into flames. Then Harry tossed another heater into the mob. This time he hit a hotdog cart, and it also exploded.

I heard Jim Riteangle talking into the camera, "I'm here at the battle scene, Sue, and a major hotdog cart just went down. If we lose another vendor, I don't know how we're going to keep all these people fed."

SuperStan raised his hand and all eyes turned his way. "Harry, you have violated the laws of decency for the last time. Now feel the hand of justice!"

He leaped from the ground toward the micro-villain.

Harry flexed his muscles, and a red-tinted bubble appeared around his body. It was the Bubble of Redness—a villain-certified protective shield. A blustery ripple of noise rose from the mob as SuperStan grimaced and hurled himself against the bubble. There was a loud explosion, followed by a blast of smoke as SuperStan bounced off the bubble and crashed to the ground. SuperStan looked up and saw Harry still standing there, tall as a fire hydrant.

Harry was laughing hard. "Nice job, Super Stud. You're no match for the red bubble, and now your hair is a mess!"

SuperStan shook his head a few times. He was a bit bruised but recovered fast. He said, "Justice will prevail, you sawed-off little snot." Then he motioned to a pair of young girls standing in the crowd.

The girls were allowed though the police line. They raced to the downed hero and held a mirror for SuperStan while he fixed his hair. One of them even ran a comb through it. When the Man of Mousse was satisfied that his style was secure, he jumped toward a fire truck that was arriving on the scene.

Harry spoke into his megaphone. "The tall people of the world will suffer the way I have suffered!"

SuperStan said, "We didn't make you so short."

"Yeah, but you all laughed when I couldn't play basketball."

"Not everyone can be in the NBA."

"You all laughed when I couldn't get a date."

"Some people are meant to die alone."

"I still buy my clothes in the kids' section!"

"Yes, and maybe it's time for you to check out the swim wear!" Then SuperStan aimed a firehouse at Harry.

Harry scowled and flexed his muscles again, causing the red bubble to reappear. The jet stream of water splattered against the bubble, but seemed to have no effect. Harry laughed and shouted above the roar of the spray. "Did you really think my red bubble could be burst by a fire hose?"

SuperStan kept spraying. "Yes, because those bubbles are defective, Harry. They were recalled last month."

Harry sneered with contempt. Meanwhile, the red bubble was becoming a light shade of pink. The bubble's color began to run, and the water gushing into the street started to resemble thin tomato sauce. Harry flexed and grunted and squinted his eyes, but the bubble kept fading. The water started to punch through. Harry was getting wet while he grunted and strained. In fact, he was getting wetter than the bubble. Then the bubble burst.

"Auuuugh!" Harry screamed as the stream of icy water crashed into his face, hurling him backward and knocking him down.

SuperStan roared with laughter and flew into the air with the hose in his hands. He kept blasting away, drenching Harry and making it very difficult for him to light up a smoke. Harry shouted as he fumbled for his lighter, but the water was relentless.

Harry said, "That damn bubble company will hear from my attorney!"

Legalman jumped into action and grabbed a megaphone. "The red bubble guys are clearly liable for your wetness. Also, the roof you're standing on is unsafe. There should be orange cones around the perimeter."

SuperStan kept drenching Harry, who stumbled and fell off the roof. Then SuperStan flew a little too far and pulled the hose out of the truck. He said, "Oh, my hose has gone limp."

Legalman waved his hand. "That's out of my jurisdiction."

Harry said, "I fell off the roof. *Why were there no orange cones?*"

A guy ran from Legalman's booth and handed him some paperwork. SuperStan dropped the hose and landed near Harry. SuperStan said, "You're a soggy little midget now, Harry."

Harry scowled and lit up a cigarette. "Look, SuperStan, I might just know your weakness, and I've come prepared with a new weapon. I have a gun that shoots silver-coated Brussels sprouts."

He pulled a pistol from his shirt. SuperStan laughed. "Silver Brussels sprouts don't hurt me, Harry. You're thinking of some other superhero who is allergic to vegetables. Now watch carefully as I crush your face like an empty can of Spam."

Harry aimed the gun at SuperStan. With a sneer, he pulled the trigger, and a tiny silver cabbage blasted out and struck SuperStan in the chest. SuperStan said, "Ugh!" and staggered backward. He teetered for a second and then went down like a sack of steak.

The crowd gasped. SuperStan flailed his fingers and struggled to lift his chest from the pavement. He tried to pontificate, and he did manage to swipe a wayward tuft of hair back into place—but then much to everyone's amazement, he collapsed into unconsciousness.

The crowd said, "Ooooh!" as Harry roared with laughter.

Harry said, "Hey, SuperStan, you eat too much red meat. You can't handle a big burst of low-fat ammo." He exhaled a long stream of smoke and raised his hand in the air. The crowd was impressed and responded with a loud round of applause, while hoping he wouldn't destroy any more hotdog carts.

I heard Jim broadcasting again. "Well, Sue, it looks like SuperStan is down, apparently the victim of his diet. I wonder if this will cause changes in his lifestyle. There could be other criminals lurking out there, ready to blast him with fruit and fiber."

Harry lifted his megaphone. "As you can see, size doesn't always matter. I'm going back into the factory to smoke and watch television. If anyone tries to destroy the place, I will squash you like the full-sized people that you are."

Suddenly, there was a ruckus at the edge of the crowd. I heard lots of crackling and commotion—and then I saw a bunch of people crossing Canal Street. In front of the pack was Magno Girl.

She was dressed in a black kung fu outfit. Her face looked a lot better, though she was still bruised—maybe her super ability to heal hadn't completely faded. Either way, she was limping a bit, and I could tell her left knee was tender with pain. She also had the kids with her, and they were each carrying a Japanese bo; basically, they had a bunch of big sticks. The small herd behind them had apparently attached themselves along the way.

Her arrival caused screams and cheers. Magnolia looked annoyed as reporters swarmed around her and the kids. Jim Riteangle pushed a microphone into her face.

"Magno Girl, have you come to save SuperStan from another dirty vegetarian assault?"

She shot him a sardonic glance. "If he needs help, I'll try to help him. But I'm almost a vegetarian myself."

"Who are these people, Magno Girl? Are they your fans?"

"Some of them are my friends. Some of them I don't know."

"What do you plan to do here?"

"Hopefully, something smart."

One reporter stuck a microphone into Karina's face. "Are you a friend of Magno Girl's? Can you tell us about the secret diet that keeps her so sexy? And where does she buy her shoes?"

Karina laughed. "She usually wears sneakers, but I'm trying to get her to go shoe shopping with me. She needs about a hundred pairs. Lots of accessories, too."

Another mic was in front of Pepe. "Can you tell us about Magno Girl's wild parties and rumored drug use?"

Pepe waved his hand. "She's not like that. She keeps her body pure."

"Pure? Has she taken an oath of celibacy? Is it true she's found God?"

I barreled my way through the crowd. Mags smiled in my direction and said, "Hi, Ron." The kids all said, "Hey, Ron!"

I got close to her. "What are you doing here? You can't fight Harry now. He'll frazzle you with his energy balls."

"I can still fight."

"No, you can't. But I suppose you're going to do it anyway."

"Yeah, I am."

"I'm going with you, honey. I can help."

She gave me a fiery look. "Good," she said. And for one beautiful instant there was no clanging city, there was no writhing mob, there was no evil midget waiting inside an insidious pizza factory—there was only a moment of passion and understanding, and it felt so right.

"Let's go, Ron."

I clenched my fist. "I'm ready."

Pepe grabbed Mags by the arm. "Magnolia, we wanna come, too."

"No, Pepe. It's too dangerous. Just wait here. I'll be back soon."

"But we want to help."

"You've helped me already, just by being here—but you can't help me with this. Thanks for coming. I'll be back soon."

We turned away from the kids and walked toward the front door of the factory. I gave them a wave as they watched with looks of concern. Meanwhile, cameras were clicking and people were cheering. The crowd was aching for another fight, but Lt. Rod Saint Royd stopped us.

Royd smirked. "I can't let you through, Magno Girl. We don't want the situation to escalate. Besides, you're not that tough anymore, and we don't want you getting hurt. You're a mess, honey."

Mags stared at the cop and then turned to the crowd. "What? You had no problem letting SuperStan fight. Don't these good people have the right to gawk at the embarrassing spectacle of my death?"

Behind her and beyond people roared with agreement, and then Legalman once again jumped from the crowd. He was right in front of Holly's mic, and he said, "Clearly, this is a case of sexual discrimination. It is a violation of this young woman's rights as an American. He turned to the crowd and yelled, *"Are we gonna let this dumb cop spit across the glorious pages of the United States Constitution?"*

The crowd responded in force, "No, no, no!"

"What are we gonna do?"

"Sue, sue, sue! Sue, sue, sue!"

They had a good cadence going, with the accent on the third "sue" of each triplet. Legalman looked at Saint Royd and grinned. "We're gonna sue your dumb ass, cop—right down to your bulletproof jockstrap."

Holly spoke to her television audience. "The action is furious, and the litigation is flying. And everyone here is wondering—*can Magno Girl still fight?"*

Rod Saint Royd looked unsure of himself. He gnashed his teeth like a hungry trash compactor, but then did nothing as Mags and I walked through the door. The crowd roared with approval.

As the drone of the circus faded away, I said, "Hey, Mags, exactly what are we going to do?"

"Fight, I guess."

"Good, that always works. I mean, if we win."

We walked into the factory; the place was dark and empty. I figured all the workers had been told to stay home until they became citizens, or maybe until the fooki issues were resolved. The pieces of pizza-making machinery were quiet, but the smell of fooki hung in the air like a mix of sweet fruit and zombie breath. The stuff was everywhere, bails of it and piles of it. And then we saw our enemy—Small Harry.

He was standing in the corner, smoking a cigarette. He was surrounded by piles of what looked like dried fooki. He was wearing a leather jacket and a pair of biker boots.

I pointed at him and said, "Hey, I thought the Hells Angels had a height requirement."

Mags laughed. "Maybe he's the mascot. I'll bet he can't do as many tricks as a pit bull."

Harry kept smoking and then sneered. "I knew you'd come, Magno Girl, and I knew you'd bring this idiot *sensei* with you—prepare to die."

Mags looked at me and raised an eyebrow. "Harry has a little plan."

"A big plan would never fit in that jacket."

"You think he'll pull it off before he dies from cancer?"

"If he doesn't, the coroner will remove it."

"I mean his plan, not the jacket."

"Oh."

Harry frowned. "If you two are done with the bad comedy routine, I'll show you how I'm going to do it."

"You're going to do bad comedy?" Mags said.

"No, I'm going to kill you both."

I shrugged. "I don't think our comedy is that bad. It's certainly good enough for such a small audience. There's not a full-sized person in the room."

"It's not fair that you were born bigger than me!"

"Smarter, too," Mags said.

"And better looking," I added.

"With better breath."

"Your magic gaze is gonzo, honey! Stop laughing and start coughing!"

Harry grinned, and a plasma bomb appeared in his hand. Then he hurled the bomb—right down into the pile of dried leaves at his feet. The pile burst into flames. Mags suddenly looked pale and staggered backward.

Harry screamed, "This pile isn't fooki—it's tobacco!" He inhaled deeply. "Ah, sweet, sweet smoke. How I love your lung-killing stench."

I acted fast. I knew Mags had little power left to lose, but I also guessed the smoke would still make her sick. I spotted a nearby fire extinguisher, and I ripped it from the wall and started blasting. But as the flames withered, Harry grimaced and flew right at me. I lunged to my left and watched him sail by, plunging head first into a mountain of fooki. His tiny body made a thud as it disappeared into the heaping pile.

I continued my assault on the burning cancer leaves. The flames were smothered, and the smoke began to thin—but then Harry reared his head from under the fooki mound. He spit out a few dried strands of the evil plant and brushed it from his tiny eyebrows. He said, "You're no match for me today! My time has come, big people. Hear the marching of my size-five feet!"

He fired three quick bombs. They whizzed past Mags and struck a few bails of fooki behind her that burst into flames. Fire alarms started to wail, and all around things started igniting.

Mags jumped toward Harry, and I could see the action caused her to wince with pain. Still, she kicked him in the face and his tiny body flew across the room. But then he leaped through the air with the grace of a boulder and clobbered Mags in the stomach.

Mags tumbled into a pile of fooki. She tossed the weed aside and jumped to her feet. Harry whizzed around the room and dropped down on top of her. She gave a shout as they collided; she was flat on her back with Harry on top.

Harry laughed. "Soon, you'll be dead!"

"Maybe," she said. "But I'll never be short!"

She poked Harry in the eyes and smacked him in the groin. He shrieked as she rolled him onto the ground. I came running and clobbered him over the head with the fire extinguisher. I knocked his burning cigarette into his mouth, and he screeched as he swallowed the acrid, flaming butt.

He leaped into the air and hovered near the ceiling to regroup. Mags jumped to her feet. Harry unclipped a silver orb from his belt and flung it. The orb changed shape as it flew, unfolding into a spider web of light. The burning web came down around Magno Girl and trapped her inside some kind of fiery cage.

I ran toward her but Harry hurled a bomb that exploded at my feet and knocked me down. My fire extinguisher went flying, and while I was on the ground another cage popped up around me. I jumped to my feet and tried to break through—and was thrown back down by an electric jolt. From high above us Harry laughed.

He said, "Let me introduce you to the Net of the Nonviolent— the cage will exist as long as your mind has one violent thought. And since you're both pretty violent, you're both eternally trapped!"

Mags scowled and flung herself at the bars of her burning prison. There was a brief sizzling sound, and she was thrown back to the ground. Harry grinned and started lobbing energy bombs at her. They zipped through the air and exploded upon impact.

Mags tried to avoid them, but he was relentless. I watched in helpless desperation as she jumped and jived—but she was trapped, and then she was hit by a bomb.

She screamed as the energy ball hit her in the thigh. I shoved my arms through the bars of my jail and groped the air, as if I could somehow reach her. Then I watched Mags fall to her knees in great pain, and I felt a heaviness in my raging heart.

Harry grinned. "What? That's it? I kinda liked watching you jump around, honey. Hey, take off your top and maybe I won't fry you. Take everything off and I'll let you live."

Mags gave Harry a look that oozed venom. "Maybe you should get yourself a Barbie doll, Harry. She's closer to your size."

Harry snarled and hurled another bomb. Mags dodged it, but the little man was incensed, and he started flinging bomb after bomb. She let out a shout as a bomb exploded across her back. She hit the ground hard. She tried to get up, but he hit her again. She gasped and collapsed onto her stomach. Her kung fu outfit was burned and frazzled, and she was completely still. The cage around her flickered and vanished. I hung my head and clenched a tight fist.

Harry roared with laughter. "Too bad, bitch!" He landed on the opposite side of the room about 30 meters away and created another flaming blob in his hand. He set the blob on the floor, and he smirked. He waved his hands, and the ball of flame started to swell into a monster globe of death.

"I may be small, but my bombs are big. I've learned to make the biggest bombs in the world, and no one can stop me!"

The ball of fire kept growing. It grew to be six meters high. Harry flew over to me and stared through the bars of my cage. He lit up a cigarette and said, "So here's the plan… That ball of fire is going to roll right over both of you, and then detonate against the wall. It'll probably barbecue everything in this room pretty good. *And then I'll be the biggest thing since rolling paper!*"

He snapped his fingers, and the huge energy ball started to spin toward us. I gritted my teeth and reached for my Oxygen Pistol. I hadn't used it yet due to all the fire in the room; fire and oxygen tend to make more fire—something a few flaming catastrophes had taught me. But at this point I had nothing to lose.

From behind Harry, I saw Mags still lying there like a pretty piece of road kill. How badly was she hurt? Was she…worse than hurt? I shoved the thought out of my mind. But then Harry said, "Don't get your hopes up, chump. There's no more cage because she has no more thoughts—and that's because she's dead. Yeah, you heard me. *I killed Magno Girl!*"

Stars and white light flashed in my eyes. In a blind rage, I heard myself screaming, *"You evil fucking midget! Suck on this!"* I shoved the pistol under his nose and pulled the trigger.

With a loud pop, a ball of pure oxygen rocketed from the barrel and struck Harry in the face. He screamed and staggered backward and then fell on his ass.

With my chest heaving, I continued to fire. Harry rolled around and avoided a few shots. Then he flew up toward the ceiling, but he also dropped his pack of cigarettes. "Damn!" he said. He swooped down and tried to snatch them from the floor—and that's when he got nailed by another blast of oxygen. And another, and another.

Harry screamed and hit the ground, desperate for a breath of smoke. But it was useless—the fresh air was like poison to him. He heaved and stammered and turned a dead-penguin shade of blue. Then he gagged and collapsed onto his stomach, trying to crawl—but his little arms just flailed and went nowhere.

He stared up at me with bitter eyes, and he whispered, "I love to smoke, you hear me? I'll never quit. *Never!*"

He passed out. And that's when Mags staggered to her feet. My heart almost burst with happiness—she was alive! She was also burned and battered, and her clothing was full of charred, black-edged holes. The huge ball of fire was about ten meters away and heading straight for us.

"Mags, forget about me!" I screamed. "Run for it! Give my bike to Pepe!"

Her eyes were wide. "Ron, I think the cage gets its power from conscious violent thought—so if you're unconscious, it disappears."

"Oh," I said. "That's interesting."

"So knock yourself unconscious!"

"Right!"

I turned my Oxygen Pistol around and hammered my head with the butt.

When I woke up a few seconds later, the cage was gone. I saw Mags pulling an orb from Harry's belt just as he was waking up. She released the insidious thing, and a Net of Nonviolence unfolded around him.

She laughed. "Think sweet little thoughts, Harry. I'm sure the little part will be easy. *Let's go!*"

The fireball was close. Harry shook his head and evaluated the situation, and his eyes bulged like bowling balls. He screamed, "You bitch! I'll kill you! You hear me? *I'll smoke a cigarette on your fucking grave, you god damn bitch!*"

Harry started whipping around the cage like a rattlesnake caught in a clothes dryer. Meanwhile, we were running hard for the exit, and Mags was really limping—but she gritted her teeth and slogged through the pain. The fireball was rolling right at Harry. We burst through the door of the factory and bolted back into the New York sunshine. As the crowd of people on the street craned their heads to see us, Mags shouted, "Everybody run! The factory is going to explode!"

A few people chewed their donuts, and then there was an explosion.

It was an awesome blast. On a normal day it would have tossed minimum wage workers clear into the East River. The windows of the factory shattered, and mammoth fireballs unfurled through the gaping holes. The building didn't collapse, but it was instantly turned into a charbroiled carcass of ash and concrete. Pieces of the factory rained down on the screaming crowd.

Mags and I limped through the scene. I shoved a few reporters out of the way as they screamed questions.

"Magno Girl, what happened in there?"

"Magno Girl, how do you respond to rumors that Biff Taylor has left the country in order to avoid child support payments?"

"Magno Girl, would you say this ends your complete humiliation as a superhero?"

We kept moving toward my bike, determined to annoy the drones of the media with silence. Finally, we were surrounded by Karina, Jenni, and Pepe. They had pushed and shoved and slipped their way through the crowd. Pepe gave me a warm handshake, and a big hug. The girls both hugged Mags. They talked to us while we kept walking.

Pepe's eyes were wide. "Are you gonna fight that witch now?"

Mags nodded. "Yes. And you can't come."

Karina wiped away a tear. "You look terrible. You could use our help—and some new clothes. You'd look awesome in an Augusto Expensile skirt. There's a big sale downtown. Also—" She stopped talking and looked at Mags. "I know, I know," Karina said. "I'm trying to keep my girl power together, but it's not working. Can't we come fight with you?"

Mags smiled at Karina, and then looked at all the kids. "Thanks, everyone, but I'll be fine—besides, I have Ron."

I gave them a big grin. They looked nervous. It was easy to see why—Mags was in a lot of pain. I could see her trying to contain a grimace every time she took a step, but we were almost there. Then just before we reached my bike, Mags stopped walking. She stopped dead in her tracks.

Standing in front of us was her brother, Tommy, along with a woman. I instinctively guessed this was Magnolia's mother.

Momma Mags was wearing a white sundress that went well with her flowing blond hair. She was probably in her early forties—and she was very attractive. She was much more impressive in real life than on the phone. I guessed that would change if she started talking, but I was wrong.

She looked stunned. She stared at her daughter with two greenish eyes and said, "I saw you on television. Tommy got back in New York this morning, and here we are—and you're all beaten up. Magnolia, you're a mess."

Mags gave a weary sigh. "Hi, Mom. I feel like a mess."

They ran toward each other, and Mags collapsed into her mother's arms. They hugged each other hard.

Cameras clicked and people stared. The clip would be on the internet in two minutes.

"You think I was a bad mother?"

"No. You did the best you could."

"You were angry and weird, and I didn't handle it well."

"I know."

"I was drunk and stupid."

"That's true." Mags wiped away a tear.

"Do you think all these assholes care about you? If you get yourself killed, they'll tell everyone they saw it, and then they'll go back to eating their fucking hotdogs."

"I know that, Mom."

"I make you feel guilty? That's what you're famous for... Everything you have is because of me—and my mother."

"I've thought about that. Maybe you're right. You might be right."

"Of course I'm right. I'm your mother."

They hugged for another few seconds, and then Magnolia released herself from her mother's embrace.

"Mom, I'm sorry, but I have to go."

"You're going to go fight someone else, aren't you? You need to go home. You need to rest."

"I'll rest soon. I'll call you later. I promise."

Mrs. Mags gave her a kiss on the cheek. Then she looked at me.

"You must be Ron," she said. "I've seen you on television. Well, you're even more handsome in real life... My name is Connie. It's good to meet you."

I puffed out my chest and shook her hand. "It's nice to meet you, Connie. You've got an amazing daughter. She's a real warrior."

Mags looked at Tommy. "Hey, brother. Thanks for coming."

They embraced, and then Tommy frowned. "I was real stupid with the witch, Maggie. I should've known. But you can't fight anyone now—forget it! That's just crazy talk."

"I'm doing it, Tommy," Mags said. "I'll see you later."

"No way are you going to fight. No way!"

"Tommy, you know me better than anyone. And that means you know I'm going."

Tommy gave her a long stare, and I noticed he had his sister's green eyes. I also noticed he had his sister's general badass attitude.

He raised his fist. "Okay, then I'm coming with you. Didn't I teach you how to fight?"

Mags gave him a warm smile. "Yeah, you did—and thanks for that. But this isn't your kind of fight, so stay out of it. You really can't help with this. Take care of Mom—please."

Then Mags turned and embraced all the kids again.

I gave Connie a grin. We got on my bike, and I gunned the throttle as the machine jerked forward. I didn't tell Mags that while she'd been busy hugging Pepe, Karina, and Jenni, I'd slipped Tommy some cash for a taxi, and told him Thad's address.

I also told him to bring the kids. As far as I was concerned, a fight was a fight, and we were going to need all the help we could get.

53 — HEAD IN A BALL

After a fast ride out of the chaos, we stopped in a shop on Lafayette Street so Mags could pick up some new clothes. The ones she had were barbecued rags of cotton. Her skin was bruised and crispy, too.

I was also stalling for time. I knew Tommy and the kids needed to catch a cab.

"So, Mags, what are we going to do now?"

"Now I'm going to fight Sandra."

I knew she was going to say that, and I laughed. "Do you know how crazy this is? We should really just go home."

"No, I'm not going home. I have a plan, Ron—and look, I have new clothes." She'd picked out a pair of black yoga pants. "Now all I need is a shirt."

"Wait!" I said. "I have a shirt for you." There was no point in arguing about the ensuing battle. Mags will be Mags, and Mags will fight. But I would be there, too—and I wanted to get even with that witch. So I ran out to my bike and brought her a pink T-shirt with a custom design. It was a dynamic illustration of a girl leaping into the air and firing a flying kick as her hair billowed in the urban breeze. Beneath the drawing were the words "NOT AFRAID."

"I've been meaning to give it to you, Mags. I got some guy I know on Stanton Street to do it. I didn't steal the shirt, either."

She gave me a big smile. "Thanks, Ron. I really like it."

She put it on. The guy behind the counter was cool and gave her the pants for free. Then we walked out of the store—and saw a flash of light. There was a sphere hovering in front of us, right above the sidewalk. It was about the size of a beach ball. Inside was the face of Sandra the Sure.

"Hello, Magno Girl. Or should I call you Magnolia, now that you're a normal woman?"

Mags narrowed her eyes and said nothing.

Sandra cackled. "I'd love to talk a bit, but I just heard that my daughter is in a big tournament. The coaches say they really need her because she's the best player on the team. Anyway, I'm waiting for you, Magnolia. If you're smart, you won't come."

The bubble vanished.

Mags shook her head. "I'd hate to be her daughter."

We headed for Thad's house.

54 — MAGS MAKES A STATEMENT

I parked my snorting machine in the pristine cityscape along 5th Avenue, near sunny Central Park. Compared to where we'd just been, everything seemed quiet. Plants and flowers were nestled in their beds of soft dirt and stock options while people of wealth waltzed through their day. No one noticed two heroes leaping from a Harley and marching toward their destiny.

"Mags, this woman might hurt you."

"I know."

"She almost killed us last time."

"That's true."

"So what's the plan?"

"Remember Hal's words: 'She wasn't much of a mother and she knows it. She's not so strong when she's not so sure.' I think he was telling us her weaknesses."

"Okay, but how are we going to use this stuff against her?"

"I have an idea. It's an educated guess, really."

"So you could be wrong, and this could go badly?"

"Yes."

"Then why are you doing it?"

She gave me a look like iron. "Because I don't want to live someone else's version of my life. I have to do it my way, even if it kills me."

We reached Thad's house, and we stopped. Standing on the sidewalk was Smashboy, along with a few reporters. There was also a small crowd milling around.

Smashboy smirked. "Magno Girl, I can't let you into the house. Defunct superheroes are not allowed."

Mags laughed with disgust. "You call yourself a superhero? You're part of the evil plot. You're more defunct than I am, Smashboy."

"I'm not part of any plot. I was hired to do commercials, and I'm protecting a man who's seen his share of grief—and who is also innocent until proven guilty. That's the American way."

"Is stuffing your pockets full of every dirty dime also the American way?"

Smashboy rolled his eyes. "What country do you live in, honey? *Of course it is!* Anyway, look at yourself; you're a mess. Let me take you home and give you a nice massage. If you make me really happy, I'll let you do my laundry."

Then he grinned and flipped his wrist—and a dart flew through the air. It struck me right in the chest. In a second, I was down on the sidewalk, groaning and cursing myself for not paying more attention in "Dart Evasion" class.

I glared at Smashboy and swore again. "What's in the dart, you bastard?"

He grinned. "A simple paralysis drug. So now it's just me and the girl." He looked at Mags and smiled.

Mags scowled and hurled herself at Smashboy.

She threw three kicks at his face, but I could see the pain and exhaustion in her eyes, and Smashboy easily avoided the blows. Then he shouted and kicked Mags in the side of the head. He followed with a fast punch in the stomach, and then swept her off her feet. Mags said "Oof!" and hit the ground hard.

Smashboy roared with laughter. "Magnolia, you're really helpless without your magic gaze. You're just a girl! Get up so I can finish you off. *It's my time to shine, honey!*"

Mags blinked. Then she whispered, "What did you say?" She

cocked her head to one side and studied him for a few more seconds. She struggled to her feet and assumed a fighting stance.

Smashboy stood there looking smug. He faked left, and then right—and then fired a side kick. Mags timed it perfectly—and nailed him hard with a kick in the testicles.

"*Augh!*" Smashboy went down.

He rolled around on the pavement, and Mags stomped on his face—but he grabbed her foot, and she tumbled down on top of him. They grappled on the ground while cursing and snarling. They were a writhing ball of hands and feet and arms and legs; it was like watching two millipedes do the mamba. And then with a ripping sound, Mags tore off his mask.

And there was Biff Taylor.

A shout went up from the crowd. Cameras fired like rockets on the Fourth of July.

Mags said, "Biff! I knew it was you!"

Biff growled but said nothing. He was on his back with Mags sitting on his chest. I suddenly realized Smashboy hadn't broken into my apartment looking for fooki info—instead, he'd been trying to keep us from learning more about it. A lot of muttering filled the air.

Mags said, "Biff, did you write the Pie Hole Pizza song? Why are you helping Thaddeus? You have plenty of money."

Biff gritted his teeth. "It's a long story, Magnolia. Hal was my friend, and we liked to party. I should've stopped him, but I didn't. And after he died, I guess I felt like I owed his dad a favor." He rested his head back on the pavement and wiped a teary eye with his hand. "I guess I have a little guilt about the way things turned out."

Mags relaxed her posture. "Hal made his own choices," she said softly. "It wasn't your fault."

Biff frowned, and then he lowered his voice. "Magnolia, do you want to get out of here and come back to my place? I've always liked you."

Mags whispered, "I don't think it would work out, Biff."

"But I have a lot of money. I'd take better care of you than that biker idiot."

"Biff, I don't need anyone to take care of me—and besides, you're just a friend. Actually, you're not even a friend. You're an enemy."

Biff scowled and glanced around, staring at the gathering of press people. Then he smirked one last time and said, "Of course I'll pay the child support, Magnolia. I always honor my obligations like all good Americans. Now please don't make me hurt you!"

Mags winced with revulsion.

"Biff, I'm going to make a statement." And then she spoke, emphasizing each phrase with a punch in the face:

"I..."

BAM!

"am not pregnant..."

BAM!

"with your baby!"

BAM!

The people on the sidewalk cheered. Mags rose from Biff's pummeled body and suppressed a groan of pain.

She said, "Ron, are you okay?"

I struggled to my feet. The drug was weak, and I was strong.

A reporter said, "Magno Girl, do you have a message for the people?"

"Yeah," she said, brushing herself off. "A superhero should always wear a groin protector."

"What are you going to do now, Magno Girl?"

"I have an appointment. I'll see you later. Maybe."

She knocked on the door of Thaddeus's mansion. The door swung open, and we walked inside.

55 — SANDRA THE SURE

The entry area was dark and quiet like a crypt. We walked fast through the gloom and into the kitchen, where the appliances were shiny but the lights were low, and Jonathan was standing alone with a glass of brandy.

He looked at me. "Hello. How nice to see you again."

"Hey, Johnny," I said. "How did you recognize me without my disguise?"

"Your disguise was even more transparent than your failure to properly venerate an orange."

I shrugged. It's always something.

He looked at Mags, and he winced. "Hello, young lady. Would you care for some ice? Or perhaps a surgeon?"

"No, thank you."

"Hey, you have ice?" I said. "Can you put some in a glass for me, and surround it with whiskey?"

Mags said, "Can I assume that Sandra is here?"

Jonathan nodded. "Yes, Sandra and Thaddeus are expecting you, and I've been watching you in the news. Do you think it's wise to continue fighting? Sometimes it's best to just walk away. I'd hate to see you do something reckless."

"Hm, maybe you better stop watching."

"I wish I could help."

"No, that's okay. You should go into the eyeglass business."

Jonathan sipped his drink. "Yes, I will do that—good luck, Miss Magnolia." Then he looked at me. "And good luck to you, too."

"Thanks, Johnny. I'll call you when I'm blind."

Mags and I walked into the cavernous dining room, where the monstrous chandelier was hanging like a fiery octopus, spilling grim shadows across the walls. We heard Thaddeus say, "Welcome to my home, where you're not at all welcome." He was waddling into the room with Sandra by his side.

Thaddeus laughed. "Magno Girl, you have no more super-powers, and yet you have come. You've been beaten to a pulp, and yet you have come. I admire your determination and pity your stupidity."

Mags stood firm. "Your evil plot is over, and it's time to stop laughing."

Thaddeus sneered like a bitter bridesmaid. "Yes, the fooki plot has been derailed by a few miscalculations and some regrettable incompetence, but there will be other evil plots. Unfortunately for you, there will be no more Magno Girl. And so I will continue to laugh!"

He laughed a few more times.

Sandra smirked. "Magnolia, if you defeat me, my spell will be forever broken. If you are defeated, you will not die—because I'm merciful, and I know your mother would be saddened by your death. But you'll lose all your powers *permanently* and *forever.* Also, you'll experience a certain amount of excruciating pain and humiliation."

Mags gave a small shake of her head. "Has anyone ever told you how sweet you are, Sandra?"

"Yes, many people."

"Well, those people lied."

"Magnolia, why do you hate the idea of becoming a normal woman?"

"Why do you hate the idea that I don't want to be like you?"

"You resist nature."

"I was born this way. I'm part of nature."

"You were born to be a mother. You decided to be a freak."

"I decided to be the person I am. I decided to be happy."

"Is that so? And do you think you can be happy living the way you do? You will *never* be happy."

Mags considered Sandra's words. "I'll be happy soon, Sandra—when I'm done kicking your ass."

Mags leaped forward and punched Sandra in the jaw—and Sandra went flying.

I knew Sandra had a whole arsenal of thunderbolts, so I wasted no time pulling out my revolver. I'm not talking about an Oxygen Pistol or a Marmalade Cannon or any of that bullshit. There's a time for fun stuff, and there's a time for a weapon that creates bloody tunnels through the brains of your enemies. This was that time, and I started shooting.

I blasted away, and every shot was repelled by Sandra's Shield of Sureness. The shield surrounded her and reflected a few condescending bits of light.

Sandra rose to her feet. She looked at me and said:

"See the ceiling

Up so high

Watch the floor

Like a fly"

She snapped her fingers, and I felt myself whooshing through the air—and then *splat!* My back, arms, and head were stuck to the ceiling above the dining room table. What the fuck? I grunted and strained to move—no use. Damn!

Mags glanced up at me just as Sandra started unleashing her ferocious thunderbolts. Mags dodged the first one, but then got hit hard in the chest and crashed to the floor.

Sandra laughed. "How do you plan to defeat me, silly girl? You have no powers at all."

Sandra fired another blast. Mags rolled to her side. She was about to speak when she was hit by another bolt. She let out a shout as the energy stream pierced her head. Then three quick blasts hit her in the body. She screamed as the sinister beams flowed through her chest, making her twitch with waves of electric torture.

I struggled to pull myself free from the ceiling—no chance. "*Leave her alone!*" I shouted.

Sandra only laughed again. "There—your body is more or less paralyzed, Magnolia. That was almost too easy. Now feel a little more pain and remember who's in charge."

She started firing rays of various colors at Magnolia's helpless body. She said, "Here's a blue one! The red ones are so pretty! The green ones will make you beg for death! But you'll be happy soon."

I was boiling like a bratwurst, imagining Sandra's body in various stages of dismemberment—but I was still helpless, and it was infuriating.

Mags screamed and moaned as the paint-box of pain washed over her. Her face flashed with contorted pictures of agony. Sandra kept it up for a few minutes, happily smiling as she narrated the rainbow of suffering. Magnolia finally gave one last angry scream and passed out. Her body went limp, and my heart almost stopped.

Sandra smirked and ended her attack. "I'm sorry I had to do that, dear—but I need to set you on the right course. Now I'll begin casting one final spell that will end your chance to ever recover your superpowers."

Sandra started humming to herself while placing objects around Magnolia. I couldn't see everything, but they included a wedding veil and a pair of baby shoes.

"Soon you'll join the real world, Magnolia. You'll think about your children, your husband, your house, and the cuddly family pet. And you'll *love* it."

Mags opened her eyes. She was struggling to speak, and even breathing looked painful. She finally said, "Sandra...you killed... your son."

Sandra stopped humming, and her smile disappeared.

"What are you talking about?"

"You…killed…Hal."

"No, I didn't."

"Yes, you did. You…were a bad mother. And maybe that's why he became…a drug addict."

"No!"

"And now you're involved in a plot to poison other people's children."

"That's ridiculous! It's not true! Tell her, Thad."

Thad had been standing there like a blubbery mountain. He flexed his jowls a bit and said, "The fooki wasn't meant to poison children; it was meant to poison everyone. Of course, everyone is someone's child, so I guess maybe she has a point… Oh, hell, I don't know."

Sandra said, "Shut your fat mouth, you idiot! No wonder I divorced you."

Thaddeus frowned. "Magno Girl, it's not right for you to bring up our parental neglect."

Sandra said, "We didn't neglect anyone!"

I suddenly noticed that my arms and head were no longer stuck to the roof.

Mags said, "You *did* neglect your son. You didn't have any communication with him. You didn't *know him!* And so he turned to drugs, and he *died!*"

Now Sandra was incensed. "Shut up, you bitch! You don't know what you're talking about! *I'm going to shut you up forever!*"

Then a voice said, "No. Leave her alone, Mom."

It was Hal. He'd appeared next to Mags.

Hal said, "You never cared about me, Mom. You just wanted me to be like you and dad. You hated my hair, my music, my collection of classic traffic signs."

Sandra's eyes were wide open now. "Hal, it's not true. I didn't want you to make mistakes!"

"You didn't want me to be me. You wanted me to be you."

"I loved you!"

"Yeah, but you never talked to me."

"I talked all the time!"

"Yeah, but you never listened. And then you couldn't deal with my problems, and you dumped me into a prison."

"It wasn't a prison, it was a school! You were stealing from us and skipping classes. We sent you to a special school because you needed discipline!"

"That school was just an easy way to get rid of me! You just wanted to go shopping, and take your little girls to dancing lessons, and make your perfect recipe for chicken salad—and laugh and smile and tell all your friends about your corny, wonderful family—and ignore the kid you locked away who was crying himself to sleep every night!"

"You were constantly in trouble! I needed to get you away from your friends."

"My friends were all I had, and do you think forcing a guy to shine his shoes six times a day is gonna stop him from getting high? You were embarrassed by me! You just wanted me to be gone."

"They had activities there! They had kayaking!"

"Kayaking? Do I look like a fucking Eskimo? Do you know how hard it is to paddle a kayak while you're shooting heroin? Because that's all I did at that school, Mom!"

At this point, I fell from the ceiling and crashed onto the dining room table. It was twenty feet straight down, but I'd learned how to crash long ago.

Thaddeus grimaced. "Son, I'm sorry for the way we behaved. We were never there for you."

"I was there!" Sandra said. "Stop apologizing! *I was there!*"

Magnolia rose to her feet. She looked battered like a bowling pin and fried like a flounder and seriously beaten-up—but she was not beaten down. She looked at Sandra, and her eyes turned a fiery shade of pink as the Gaze of the Guilt came blasting forth.

Sandra's shield was gone, and she staggered backward as the resurrected beams of remorse struck her.

"Augh! No! No!"

Mags said, "Admit it, Sandra—you're not so sure."

"No! It's not true!"

"You feel guilty because you are guilty."

"No!"

Mags took two steps toward Sandra.

"Did you kill Joey the Round Man?"

"Yes! I did it!"

"And how does his mother feel now?"

"I...don't know!"

"And what about your own son?"

"It wasn't my fault!"

"It was your fault! You know what I'm talking about, Sandra—say it!"

"I won't!"

"Say it!"

"*No!*"

"You're guilty, so say it now!"

"*Ugh! All right—I admit it! I admit it! I failed my son, and I was a bad mother!*"

Sandra's whole body turned wavy and translucent. Then she screamed—"*Nooooooo!*" And with that final wail of agony she faded into oblivion.

For a breathless moment no one spoke. Hal sort of smiled and disappeared.

Finally, I looked at Mags. "Honey, you did it. You destroyed her with guilt."

"Yeah. That went pretty well."

"You really are your mother's daughter."

She smiled. "I suppose I am."

56 — ENTER THE OCTOPUS

We celebrated for a few seconds, and then Subterranean Bob walked into the room. He studied the situation through his beady eyes, and he smirked. "Oooh, I knew all that hocus pocus horse hockey would fail, but don't worry, Thaddeus; they'll never destroy the computers on the roof that are hosting your website."

Thaddeus cringed. "You imbecile, you've just told them where the computers are located."

Bob grimaced. "Oooh, that was unfortunate. I've always had a problem not revealing the location of the secret computers. But it changes nothing! My defense against Magno Girl is impervious—and completely immune to her magic gaze!"

He laughed and ran from the room.

Thaddeus said, "If you'll excuse me, Magno Girl, I'm going to take a break. And then perhaps I'll leave you at the mercy of Bob's evil creation—oh, god dammit."

He turned and left. Mags and I looked at each other.

"Let's go to the roof," she said.

"What do you think is up there?"

"Probably a piece of Bob's Junior High School science project."

We took the main stairs up to the roof and stepped outside.

The roof was long like a runway and flat like a parking lot. This was good, since fighting on a pointy roof is hard on the ankles.

At the far end of the roof was a red building made out of wood. It looked like a barn, standing 25 meters or so above the streets of Manhattan.

Then I saw the ninjas. There were lots of them, pouring out of the barn and storming across the blacktop in our direction.

I rolled my eyes in disgust. "What, more ninjas? Does Thaddeus grow these guys on a tree somewhere?"

Mags just gave a little smile and shook her head. Then she let out a battle cry and leaped into the air. Magno Girl could fly again! I was thrilled. I was also stuck on the roof with twenty screaming killers headed my way. I reached for my revolver.

I aimed at the first charging assassin and pulled the trigger. I heard a clicking sound. Damn—no bullets. I had a vague memory of emptying the thing into some bitch's magic shield. I cursed and hurled the useless weapon at my opponent's head. The barrel busted his nose, and I reached for my samurai sword.

Mags yelled, "Look out!"

They were coming in fast, and I parried two blows with my swinging blade. Then Mags dropped from the air, feet first, and clobbered a few of them. She snatched a guy's weapon and started to fight with it. For a second, we stood back-to-back, dueling like a couple of brawling buccaneers—but it was a useless position. They were everywhere.

I shouted and sprinted across the roof. I dashed and darted, swerved and slashed—carving a path through the ninja-necklace strung out around us. Meanwhile, Mags jumped into the air and floated above me.

I outdistanced the main bunch of bad guys, but I ran out of roof. I skidded to a stop an inch from the edge and spun on my heels. Two guys were charging at me. I parried one blow and ducked under another guy's overhead chop. He rolled across my back and went flying off the building, shouting as he fell to the concrete below. I growled and prepared for the next wave.

More guys were coming. A rain of sparks flew from the clashing blades. I ducked, I parried, I spun in a circle—I stepped right off the roof. I screamed as I plummeted toward the street, waving my arms like a bird made out of beer cans. And that's when Mags swooped from the sky and caught me in her arms.

We hovered above the street. I looked at her and said, "Thanks. I was really falling hard for you."

She laughed and zoomed over the building, dropping me back onto the sweet asphalt surface. She yanked out her weapon and said, "Get ready! Here they come again!"

I gritted my teeth, and I reached for my glass eyeballs. I grinned as I rolled a bag of Al's stolen prosthetic retinas across the roof in the direction of the oncoming assault. The ninjas plowed right into them.

"Whoah!"

"Yeeeeow!"

"God damn!"

They were slipping and falling and dropping like bowling pins. I smiled and grabbed my bottle of Flamin' Fred's Hot Sauce. I blasted the fiery juice into six sets of eyes. I roared at the sound of their screams.

"Auuugh! I can't see! Yaaaa!"

I laughed again, but then I saw another pack of ninjas racing from the barn and heading our way. I cursed in disbelief. No doubt Thaddeus had purchased these guys wholesale, and we were in trouble. And that's when the door to the rooftop opened—and Tommy, Pepe, Karina, Jenni, and Connie came walking out.

Mags looked at them and yelled, "*What are you doing here?*"

I flashed a huge grin. "*What took you so fucking long?*"

Each kid was still carrying a bo, and Pepe said, "Hey, you think it's easy for a bunch of people lookin' like us to get a cab? We had to take the train, and it was like twelve stops."

I should've known. Pepe gave a shout and the whole squad charged across the roof. The ninjas froze at the sight of our reinforcements while I smiled wide.

Pepe tossed an extra stick to Mags, who caught it as she dropped her sword. I wasn't surprised; she hates to cut flesh, which is why she continues to eat less shrimp and more avocados. She said, "All right, if we're going to fight, let's make it hurt!"

In an instant, our opponents were hurting.

A Japanese bo, also called a "long staff," has the tactical advantage of being much longer than a sword. In the right hands it's a wonderful weapon, and our hands were looking good. The ninjas were immediately exposed to some serious ass kicking.

Mags smashed a guy's face, followed by a thrust, a parry, and an upward chop into the groin. Jenni was a whirling typhoon of pain and contusions, while her boyfriend, Pepe, applied a sledgehammer's worth of hurt. And Tommy was one fierce stick fighter, quickly busting half a dozen heads. Karina didn't do much; apparently, the blankness was affecting her ability to mix things up, and she was worried about damaging her fingernail enhancement system. But all in all things were looking good—and then Connie fired a thunderbolt.

It wasn't that powerful, but it's amazing how a little shot of the supernatural will get someone's attention. She hit three ninjas with it, and they went down like broken tombstones. All the ninjas stopped fighting and looked at each other with wide eyes—and then they started running.

They bolted to the stairway and down into the house. They ran from the house and into the street below. I'd never seen so many ninjas spilling onto a sidewalk. They were a gang of masked idiots running back to their day jobs.

Everyone stopped and stared, while Mags looked at her mother.

"Mom, I thought you gave up witchcraft when Grandma died."

Connie sighed. "Well, a little now and then is useful, honey. I mostly use it to color my hair. Anyway, I don't have enough power to do another thunderbolt. I'm afraid that's all I've got, unless I really start practicing—and maybe I will. What the hell, I'm a witch, and maybe I should be proud of it."

Mags and Tommy smiled. Then Mags looked at the kids and said, "You shouldn't have come—but thanks. That was great. Thanks, Mom. Thanks, Tommy."

Tommy stepped forward and embraced his sister.

"No problem, Maggie," he said with a grin. "I told you I'd be there for you."

"I never doubted it," Mags said. "I was tired of watching you ruin your life—but if a bunch of ninjas come looking for you, I'll be there, too."

"I know you will."

Pepe smiled. "Thanks for teaching us, Magnolia. So where's the evil witch?"

"The evil witch is gone. You missed that part."

Jenni said, "So what happens now?"

I gritted my teeth. "Now we destroy whatever is in that barn."

"Right," Mags said. Everyone else nodded.

We walked across the roof until we reached the barn. Mags found a door, and she slipped inside with all of us close behind. I immediately sensed we were in an area of open space. I could feel something strange, evil, and foreboding. I groped for a light switch and found one—the room lit up, and then we saw it.

"Oh, wow," Mags said.

I said, "Wow."

Everyone else said, *"Wow!"*

It was not far from us. It was about twenty feet tall. It was a giant robot octopus.

The monster gleamed like a silvery shade of cutlery. It had two bubble eyes that started to glow red. I heard the pulsing hum of its cold metallic heart and realized I'd fought this thing a thousand times in my nightmares.

I surveyed the battleground. Above the mechanical monster, off to one side of the room, was a platform. Standing on the platform was Bob, along with a couple of control consoles, a few computers, and a small icebox. Standing in front of us was Thaddeus Stone. He had a smirk on his face longer than an oil slick.

He said, "Magno Girl, here I am again. I see you've brought along a little army of trespassers, and they've helped you to defeat my ninjas. Don't be too proud, people—the average ninja is a shopping mall security guard who collects low budget martial arts videos. But gaze upon the beast before you. It is Bob's greatest creation, and it is completely impervious to any kind of magic gaze. And so, Magno Girl, I think we should talk."

Mags crossed her arms and said nothing. Tommy, Connie, and the kids did the same. From somewhere outside, we heard the bleat of honking traffic. High above an airplane whooshed through the sky.

Thaddeus shifted his poundage and looked at Mags again.

"Ahem, well, as I was saying, I could allow the creature to obliterate you and your friends—but because I'm not vengeful, and because your tenacity could cause problems, and because I've signed a lucrative contract for the monster to star in an upcoming television series, and because you've abused my ex-wife in a way I've only dreamed about—I'm willing to offer you a deal. In fact, I'm willing to offer you a sum of *two million dollars*. All I ask in return is that you cease your actions against me, and you star in *one* commercial for Americamart that will only be shown in Japan."

Thaddeus rocked back on his heels like one smug pile of payola. The kids all looked at each other, and I looked at Mags.

Mags laughed in Thad's face. "I told you I don't want your money, and my self-respect doesn't end at the border. I'll never be owned or controlled by you."

Thaddeus smirked again and waved his hand. "Magnolia, if you won't do it for yourself, then think about your dear, sweet mother, who is standing right here. Yes, Connie, I know about your situation. Magnolia, if you take my offer, you can get her any medical attention she needs. As you know, the American healthcare system is very expensive and does not favor those who are sick. Will you deprive your own mother of the chance to live in comfort?"

Mags glanced at her mom. I could tell she wasn't sure what to say, but Connie made it easy.

Her eyes blazed. "You just tried to kill my daughter, you pile of shit! Do you really think I want your money? And does your mother know what you've been up to? You should be ashamed of yourself."

Mags smiled. "You heard the lady, Thad. My mother will be fine. She's a tough woman."

Thaddeus looked grim for a second, but then the cagiest grin yet slithered across his face. "Very well, Magnolia," he said. "But let me make one final addition to my offer—something for one of your friends. What would you say if I could break the Curse of the Modern Blank Girl?"

Everyone was stunned. Karina stared. Magnolia's mouth dropped like a box of rocks.

Mags spoke in a whisper. "How do you know about that?"

Thad's laugh echoed like the clang of a bank vault. "Have you forgotten that Sandra was a witch? She was an expert on the subject of evil curses, and she probed the brain of your cohort in my car. She didn't want me to offer you the cure because she was afraid you'd accept, and she wanted to fight you. She was always nasty that way. But now that she's met her unfortunate demise—so sad, so sad—I have inherited her complete Book of Spells, which I just happen to know contains the key to your little friend's problem."

I grabbed Mags by the arm and yanked her to one side.

"Mags, I know this guy is a rotten bastard—but think about it. The fooki plot is already smashed. You could get a new dojo, a new apartment, and Mom gets all the pills she can wash down— *and Karina is freed from the curse!* It's your dream! So what if you have to dress up like a chicken over in Japan? It's still a great deal!"

Magnolia turned to her mother. "Mom, do you know anything about the Curse of the Modern Blank Girl? Can you break it?"

Connie shook her head. "No. I'm way out of practice, Magnolia. If you can't do it, I definitely can't do it. I was lucky to get one thunderbolt working."

Mags frowned and stared at Thaddeus. Then she looked at

Karina. Then she looked at Thaddeus again, and she looked at the three kids.

Karina gritted her teeth. "Don't do it, Magnolia. I'll find another way to break the curse. I can put off my breast implants for a few more years. I'll be fine."

Mags was quiet for a long second—and then she sighed. "Karina, I don't care about the money, and I don't want to do a commercial. But I don't have to fight this guy any more. We've done a good job here. I'll get another chance to face him in the future."

"No! Sometimes I feel the curse start to fade. Maybe I just need to take more control of my life."

Mags shook her head. "You'd be taking a big risk. What if you can't do it? I don't want to see you reduced into total blankness."

My heart was pounding. The finish line was in sight! The whole enchilada wrapped in a blanket of smiling dead presidents! And that's when Thaddeus opened up his stupid, gaping mouth-cave and said, "Listen to your teacher, Karina. You are out-muscled. You are outgunned. It's nothing to be ashamed of—after all, your enemy is strong, and one small girl just doesn't have the power."

Karina blinked. Mags narrowed her eyes. And then Karina said, "It's not going to happen, Thad! Not a chance!"

In my head, I heard the sound of a planet-sized piggy bank being smashed to bits.

Karina gave Thaddeus a fiery look. "Sometimes 'one small girl' has to struggle to be who she wants to be—but I'll be tough, and I'll do it. That's what I've learned from Magnolia, and I'll never be blank as long as I can think for myself." Then she smiled. "Hey, you know what? I feel better already."

Mags turned back to Thaddeus with sparks in her eyes.

"Sorry, Thad," she said. "Your monster is going down."

I couldn't stand it. I looked at the other kids for a sign of hope, and I looked at Connie, and I looked at Tommy—a fellow biker and derelict—but they all nodded in agreement. So I said, *"Are you all crazy? Two million bucks! The end of the curse! And we* don't even know if this involves any kind of chickens. He might just want a commercial for patio furniture!"

Thaddeus raised his eyebrows. "The Japanese do love their patios."

Mags reached out and grabbed my hand, and she looked at me hard. "Ron, there are two kinds of people in this world. There are the ones who give up and sell out—and there are the ones who stand tall and fight the giant robot octopus."

Well, god dammit, I knew she was right.

I gritted my teeth, and I heard myself say, "Magnolia, I love you."

Mags smiled. "I love you too, Ron. Now are we going to fight this thing or what?"

Thaddeus erupted like a blubbery volcano. "You fools! Do you know how ridiculous you are? It is you who will be destroyed—and it is I who will eat a sandwich and watch it all happen!"

He roared off across the room and headed toward the control platform. Mags looked at me and smiled again; I'd never seen her so happy, and that made me happy. Then Bob spoke into the microphone, and his voice echoed throughout the barn.

"Oooh, you've really walked into some trouble now, Magno Girl. You should have taken the offer. You'll need it to pay for your funeral!" Thaddeus wheezed a bit in the background and snatched a sandwich from the icebox.

Mags said, "We're going to turn this thing into robot calamari."

"Hey, calamari is made from squid," I said. "This is an octopus."

"Yeah, but I couldn't think of anything made with octopus."

Bob said, "Feel the wrath of my avenger—right now!"

The creature let out a roar and lurched forward. The final battle had begun.

I whipped out my samurai sword as Pepe and I bolted to the monster's left—but the octopus was faster than it looked, and one of its tentacles shot out and grabbed me. Pepe said, "Ron!" as I whacked the log-sized limb with my sword—but it had no effect. I caught my breath as I was carried up high above the floor and bashed against the wall. The sword clattered from my hand.

Mags said, "Hang on, Ron!" She flew into the air and grabbed the fat appendage. Unfortunately, she couldn't force the arm to release me—it was one powerful piece of octo-machinery. The creature swung me toward the wall again while Mags hung on and tried to pry me loose. This time we hit the wall together and the whole building shuddered.

Mags grunted and kept struggling with the monster's arm. Bob laughed and said, *"Who says size doesn't matter?* It matters a lot, and no one has a bigger octopus than I do!"

Pepe dodged a sweeping arm and snatched my sword. He started bashing at random tentacles.

Mags said, "Damn, this thing is strong!"

Jenni turned to Karina and said, "Attack the eyes!" It's something Mags had always taught them.

Meanwhile, the creature slammed me against the wall a few more times. Things were getting blurry, but somehow I managed to slip a hand into my jacket. "Mags! Mags, try this!" I handed her the weapon I'd been lugging around for so many years.

She rolled her eyes. *"A can of 'octopus repellent'?* Ron, it's a robot."

"The label clearly says, 'repels all kinds of octopi.' "

The beast hammered me into the wall again.

Mags said, "All right! I'll try it!"

She left me in the creature's iron grip and flew down in front of its face. A couple of tentacles reached for her, and she evaded them—but right before she could fire a shot, one of the sewer-sized arms gave her a vicious swat and she went sailing across the room.

She hit the floor hard and skidded across the ground before slamming into the wall. The can of repellent flew from her hand.

Karina tried to reach the eyes with her bo, using the stick to deflect the giant, groping limbs—but the tentacles were too big. She was smacked across the floor and knocked into the wall. She went down in a heap.

Tommy used the bo to duel with two tentacles, but then a third arm swooped down and clobbered him across the skull. He was swept into a corner of the room, where he lay unconscious. Connie ran to help him.

Bob was ecstatic. "They laughed at Copernicus! They laughed at the guy who invented bottled water! But who's laughing at me?"

Pepe made a dash for the control platform—but a tentacle reached out and grabbed him. Pepe shouted, "Whoah! It's got me, man! *Shiiiiiit!*"

Mags sprang to her feet, and her eyes burned. She jumped into the air and flew right at the thing. She dodged one tentacle, weaved under another, and then with a mighty shout she kicked the creature right between its eyes.

The beast roared as its tonnage was tossed about five feet backward. Then Mags started whirling and firing a series of spinning kicks into the thing's metal face. The thing screamed. She kicked it two more times. The monster moaned again—and then Pepe and I were released.

We both plummeted to the ground. Pepe landed right on top of my can of octopus repellent. I grinned and raised my fist in the air as he stuffed it into his pocket. Then I scrambled across the floor away from the groping arms.

Bob screamed from his platform, "You pathetic metal sissy! You are made of impregnable steel. Stop being such a baby and make your daddy proud!"

The giant creature's eyes lit up in a blood-lust crackle of light. It roared and leaped toward Mags. She zoomed up toward the ceiling, but the thing shot up a tentacle and snatched her out of the sky.

"Mags!"

"Damn!"

It had her wrapped up tight. She tried to wriggle free but it was no use. Mags looked down at Jenni who was trying to dance her way through to the monster's eyes. Mags yelled, "Someone get the control center!"

The creature roared and then flipped Mags upside down and bashed her head against the floor—several times.

"Ugh! Ooh! Ahhh!"

Bob laughed hard. "You ruined the fooki plot, but now it's my turn to ruin your pretty head. And you will never reach the control center!"

But Jenni leaped and dodged and dived through the flailing appendages and raced up the stairs of the platform. Bob saw her coming with her bo, and he said, "Ugh! You bitch! You can't come up here without a security badge!"

Jenni said, "I'll make a badge out of your face!" She was swinging and smashing. She destroyed a bunch of stuff and even clobbered Thad's ice box.

Thaddeus was enraged. "How dare you destroy my refrigerator!" He hurled a ham, tomato, and mayonnaise sandwich into her face, covering her eyes with greasy mayo. She cursed and tried to wipe the fatty sludge away, and that's when a tentacle swung back and slapped her off the platform. She flipped over the wooden guard-rail and crashed to the floor.

Pepe was attending to Karina on the sidelines. He left her and tried to make his way toward Jenni. Mags was still in the monster's grip. And now my heart was like ice, and my rage was an inferno; I was really getting tired of this mechanical mother-fucker. I snarled, and I charged forward.

A tentacle swung right at me, and I hurdled it. Then I ducked under another swinging arm as yet another tentacle reached for my head. I dodged it, but it snagged my jacket and hoisted me into the air. Quick as a motorized monkey I wriggled out of my jacket, grabbed the tentacle, swung myself on top of it, and then slid down the arm.

I plopped onto the floor right in front of its big body. I reached for my octopus repellent—*damn!* Where was that octopus repellent? I turned my head—and saw the can flying at me, courtesy of a touchdown-terrific throw from Pepe. I caught it and turned toward the monster. I laughed and fired a blast into its face.

The thing screamed. Its eyes raged and flickered, and it staggered backward. And then it let go of Mags.

I let out a passionate battle cry and kept shooting the fishy stuff into its face. The thing moaned again. Its eyes continued to blink—and then the tentacles went limp.

Bob screamed, *"Arrg! Edgar, what have they done to you?"*

Mags rose to her feet. "Edgar? You named this thing 'Edgar'?"

"In memory of Edgar Allen Poe, my favorite master of the macabre."

Mags cocked her head. "I don't think Poe created anything like a giant, discombobulated sea monster."

Bob snarled. "What about *The Telltale Heart?*"

"The Telltale Heart is about a guy's guilt driving him to insanity. There's no mention of a silly-looking octopus."

"Oh, maybe I need to reread that one. How about *The Murders in the Rue Morgue?"*

"The killer is an orangutan."

"The Gold Bug?"

"No, I don't think so."

"Well how about *The Fall of the House of Usher?"*

"I didn't read that one. Really, I was more into sci-fi and fantasy—but I don't think there was an octopus in the house. Did you read much literature, Bob?"

"No," he said through clenched teeth. "I wanted to, but my father felt I should concentrate on becoming an engineer. It was his dream, really—to live vicariously through me, while he spent his day on a lunch truck, doling out pork roll sandwiches to lunch-bucket ass-cracks."

Meanwhile, the octopus was wallowing like a punctured pontoon. The tentacles were barely waving, though its body was still capable of moving around. Bob laughed and said, "We're not through yet, Magno Girl. Edgar, show them the gun!"

The thing let out a roar as a gun popped from the top of its head.

The gun was mounted on a flexible, serpent-like hose. It aimed its barrel our way and fired an arrow-sized dart. The missile sailed over our heads and hit the side of the barn. Instantly, a goopy blue splotch appeared on the wall.

Mags said, "What the hell is that?"

I squinted. "It's some kind of splotch. It looks like a gazelle."

"Or maybe a llama."

"Mags, I ate lots of animal crackers as a kid. I'm telling you, it's a gazelle."

The blue splotch exploded. Splinters of shattered wood rained down around us, and a hole appeared. Looking through it, we could see the blue New York sky.

Bob roared with laughter. "The entire area of each splotch detonates! I'm the first artist in history to use exploding paint."

Mags said, "I'll call the Louvre."

I said, "You're going to go through a lot of canvases."

Bob said, "I have hidden microphones down there, and I can hear every word you're saying! *Blast them, Edgar!*"

Edgar's eyes lit up again and the dart gun started firing. Darts started whizzing through the air. Wherever they struck, they splattered blue paint that exploded.

We heard Bob growl, and then we saw him adjust a few controls. We could also see Thaddeus opening the dented refrigerator and grabbing another sandwich. Then a beam of thin light shined from Edgar's left eye. It shined on a place directly behind Mags, and a dart quickly followed. The dart hit the wall and a blue splotch appeared—and exploded. A jagged rip in the wall also appeared as bits of wood scattered through the air. Another beam of light struck another wall. A dart hit the spot, and there was another splotch, another explosion, and another hole.

Mags said, "He's turned on some type of targeting system. Try aiming at the roof, Bob. This place could use a skylight."

Once again Bob roared with evil laughter, and I thought this was a mistake. I'd never been to a barn construction class, but I was guessing too many holes in the wall were bad. The building started to sway a bit.

Meanwhile, the kids had grouped near the farthest wall from the monster. Tommy was in another corner with Connie by his side. He was sitting up, but he looked woozy. Mags motioned for everyone to get down and stay out of the way. They followed her instructions; they could see she had a plan.

Mags flew into the air. A beam of light hit her. A dart screamed toward her chest, but she dodged it and the dart lodged in the wall. More blue gook, followed by an explosion.

Mags flew close to the creature's mass of injured tentacles. It fired another dart that stuck into one of its own silver arms, which began turning blue. Mags and I ducked as a big piece of robot octopus tentacle was blown off. Edgar waved his severed limb at us.

Mags laughed. "Okay, seven more darts and we can go home."

I said, "Bob, do you have a smaller, home version of this thing? Lots of kids would love to watch an octopus kill itself."

Bob said, "Ooooh, she's too fast, Edgar! Go after the guy!"

I resented this insult—and I knew it was time. I reached for my silver teapot. It was one of five thousand.

Bob screamed, "Get him, Edgar! Get the fucker before he makes tea!"

But Edgar was busy aiming at Mags, who was hovering in front of the control platform. I thought Bob was being silly—obviously, I couldn't make tea without a stove. Bob said, "Don't shoot, Edgar!" Edgar fired, Mags moved, and the dart struck a spot on the wall above Thad's icebox.

As the blue splotch spread Thaddeus quickly grabbed another sandwich from the fridge and then dived onto the floor of the platform. There was an explosion, and Bob and Thad both hit the floor hard. A bunch of control stuff was destroyed, but the platform was still there. Edgar then trained his beam on me.

I stood in a horse stance and held the teapot firmly in place. I placed my mind into the *Zone of the Antioxidant*, and I imagined a world free from cancer and heart disease. I also imagined a beam of light striking the teapot and being reflected back into the creature's other eye. My vision came true.

The gun spun around and tried to accommodate the strange angle. It had a hard time attempting to shoot itself, but somehow it managed. The dart stuck in the right eye bulb. It was interesting to watch the eye turn blue. Most monsters look better with red eyes, but the blue splotch, the red eye, and the white light created a rousing patriotic blend right before the dart exploded.

Pieces of monster eye flew through the air. Edgar let out a pained roar. Bob jumped up and down and said, "Edgar, you are such a jackass! I told you never shoot a teapot unless it's made of porcelain!"

Bob made adjustments to a few buttons. Edgar inched forward. Then he jerked a bit. His tentacles started to flail once again, and there were some raw noises. Then he let out a roar and went rocketing backward—smashing right through the rear wall of the barn and plummeting straight down to the street below. There was a loud smashing noise, like someone had just dumped a junkyard onto the street, and then bits of debris came raining down from the ceiling.

Bob screamed, *"Why couldn't I get into medical school?"*

Mags laughed. "Maybe you failed the question about the big metal octopus."

Bob yelled, "Edgar, destroy them! You must avenge these insults—you dumb, malfunctioning, mollusk-shaped piece of shit!"

Mags flew up to the platform. She grabbed the computers in her hands and then flew through the broken hole in the wall. She tossed the hardware down onto the street, where it smashed into a thousand pieces. I ran after her and watched the scene below.

Edgar had managed to right himself, but he was spinning out of control, spiraling closer and closer to the house with his mighty arms swinging like sickles. Magno Girl was flying above him. Edgar was whirling like a lawn sprinkler. He obliterated a parked BMW. Then he smashed into the side of Thad's mansion. He started crunching his way through the brick structure. He ruined the billiards room. He kept spinning and then decimated the kitchen. I felt a pang of sadness at the loss of all those beautiful appliances.

Edgar plowed through a few more rooms, and then the whole house started to shake. I ran through the broken wall of the barn and saw Tommy tossing a rope over the edge of the building. He waved to the kids. "Come on team—we're leaving!" The kids ran over and started climbing down. I knew the entire structure could collapse. Mags landed in front of me and said, "Do you need a lift out of here?"

"No, I'll use the rope."

Mags was about to respond when Hal appeared again. He was standing on the roof, looking a little sad.

Mags said, "Hal, thanks for your help."

"Sure, no problem," he replied. "You know, it wasn't really my mom and dad's fault. It was mostly my fault."

"Yeah, I figured that. But it can be our little secret."

Hal smiled. "Yeah, okay." Then he pulled a small black book from his pocket and flipped it at Mags. She caught it with one hand.

"What's this?"

"My mom's book of spells. The Curse of the Modern Blank Girl is on page three—easy to break. It mostly involves thinking for yourself and not being swayed by society's propaganda."

Mags shoved the book into a pocket of her yoga pants. "Thanks, Hal. I appreciate it. But I think we've already got it covered."

He smiled again. "See you around, Magno Girl. And good luck." He faded away.

Mags watched Jenni and Pepe reach the ground. Then she grabbed Karina in her arms and flew her down to the street. She did the same for her mom, and then watched as Tommy slithered down to safety. She came back up and said, "Ron, get off the roof."

"I'll be fine. I'll see you soon." She looked at me, then gave me a smile and took off into the air.

I stepped back into the barn and looked up at the control platform. I saw Bob and Thaddeus watching the destruction on a television screen. Thad had his hands around Bob's throat. He said, "This house cost fifty million dollars! Do you think my insurance is going to cover a mechanical octopus running amuck?"

Bob gagged, "Ooooooh, I did...my best...Thaddeus... But Magno Girl was too strong."

Thaddeus continued to throttle Bob. "You are the worst evil scientist ever! I should have left you there, working on the lunch truck with your sweat-sock father!"

Bob scratched at Thad's eyes and then kicked him in the groin. "Oooh, I should have poisoned your corned beef and pastrami!"

Thaddeus said, "Your sandwiches were shitty! Your potato salad tasted like vomit mixed with sawdust!"

I jumped on my rope and slid down fast to the street. I heard the barn on the roof collapse. The whole house sagged, but more or less remained standing in a ruined kind of way. The giant robot octopus burned itself out somewhere in the library and ended up buried under the rubble of several ceilings. Who knows, maybe he was even beneath a few books by Edgar Allen Poe.

I saw Jonathan standing in the street, watching the destruction. He gave me a little congratulatory salute with his hand, which I returned. I saw Mags and the kids surrounded by reporters as I ran to my chopper and gunned the engine. I flew right by Holly Honey, George Riteangle, and Lt. Rod Saint Royd, who were just pulling up to the house. I noticed SuperStan flying above the scene, looking to get a few photos of himself in front of the battle zone, but I knew it was useless. Everyone knew Magno Girl was responsible.

I thought about Magnolia as I screamed down 5th Avenue. I searched for her above the lofty rooftops lining both sides of Broadway. As I tore past 11th Street, I saw her on the sidewalk, across from the towering gray spires of Grace Church. And I was glad she hadn't signed any commercials or authorized any merchandise. I was glad there wasn't going to be any deal for a cheesy Hollywood sitcom. I was glad Magnolia was my girl.

I pulled up next to her on the sidewalk and watched her black and crimson hair blow free in the summer breeze. I twisted my throttle and let my motor roar.

"You look good, Mags."

"Ron, I look like a mess. And I don't care."

"Where are the kids?"

"I got them a taxi back to my place. I tried to get them away from the reporters. Tommy's taking my mom back to Brooklyn."

"Do you want to get something to eat?"

"No. I want to go home."

"What are you going to do there?"

"I'm going to thank the kids again for all their help. Then I'm going to call my mother and let her give me advice I won't follow—and maybe I'll thank her, too. I'll probably call my brother, and maybe even lend him some money. And then I'll see what happens."

I smiled at her. "Do you want to ride with me?" I leaned close and looked her in the eyes. "I mean—forever?"

She looked back at me, and I hardly heard the noisy song of the city, or the roar of my engine. She smiled and gave me a kiss.

"Maybe someday. But right now, I think I'd rather fly."

Then she leaped into the air, and she was gone.

THE END

ABOUT THE AUTHOR

Joe Canzano is a writer and musician from New Jersey, U.S.A. For more information, please visit his website at www.happyjoe.net.

Stories by Joe Canzano

MAGNO GIRL (novel)
SEX HELL (novel)
SUZY SPITFIRE KILLS EVERYBODY (novel)
MAGNO GIRL AND THE BEAST OF BROOKLYN
(novella)
GROUND AND POUND (short story)

For more information, please visit www.happyjoe.net.